OF SEA AND SEED

THE KERRIGAN CHRONICLES, BOOK I

OF SEA AND SEED

THE KERRIGAN CHRONICLES, BOOK I

A novel by

Annie Daylon

McRAC Books
British Columbia, Canada

Published by **McRAC** Books, British Columbia, Canada

Of Sea and Seed, The Kerrigan Chronicles, Book I
© 2015 by Angela A. Day (nom de plume: Annie Daylon)
All rights reserved.

For information, contact Annie Daylon: anniedaylon@shaw.ca or www.anniedaylon.com.

ISBN-13 9780986698040
ISBN-10 0986698040
McRAC Books Trade Paperback Edition
First Printing: November, 2015
Printed in the United States of America

Cover Photo copyright © Andrejs Pidjass www.nejronphoto.com
Map photo © @FilipBjorkman

Praise for
Of Sea and Seed

"With insight, wit, and great understanding of the all-too-human emotions of guilt and desire, Daylon draws the reader into a timeless story of yearning and loss." ~ Paul Butler, author of "The Good Doctor"

"With the skill of a poet, Daylon weaves the tale of a Newfoundland outport family in the early 20th century. Her mastery of the written word brings the reader into the lives of her characters as they deal with the truths and tragedies of everyday life…" ~ Ron Young, Founding Editor, "Downhome Magazine"

"A longing for the sea, and from the sea…lives out of control since birth, torn by land and by sea…souls steadily whipped by the rhetoric of religion. Pounding rhythms. Exciting narrative." ~ Darrell Duke, author of "Thursday's Storm"

"In Daylon's novel, you will draw in the scent of the land and the sea, your ear attuned to authentic Newfoundland voices. The old-world characters are compelling in their secretive lives and in acts of love gone wrong." ~ Nellie P. Strowbridge, author of "Ghost of the Southern Cross"

for love of Newfoundland...

Island of
Newfoundland

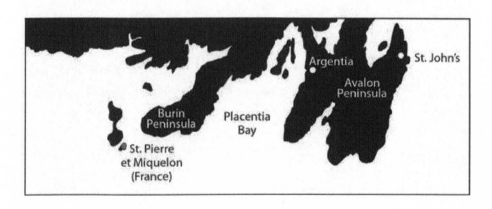

KATHLEEN

And I will take you back, Kathleen,
to where your heart will feel no pain,
And when the fields are fresh and green,
I will take you to your home, Kathleen.

~Traditional Irish Folk Song

CHAPTER 1

———◆———

IT BEGINS, AND ENDS, WITH the sea.

The North Atlantic surrounds this island, stretching to horizon, a living, limitless giant, a passage, a prison. It is generous, this sea, which birthed my island through glaciers, seeded it with life, and nurtured that life with its own bounty. It is treacherous, this sea, which mutilates my island, annihilates vessels, and reclaims the seeds it sowed. Nature's contradiction: the sea. Matriarch and murderer.

On this clear day, the sea is a jeweled reflection of sky. Rippled aquamarine. Unparalleled beauty.

A breeze whispers past, ushering me in. I am Kathleen Kerrigan: mother to Kevin, Clara and Jimmy; grandmother to Kate. Kathleen Kerrigan, who is long dead, yet still here. Am I the proverbial Newfoundlander who chose homeland over heaven? A trill of laughter—mine—floats on the zephyr. Heaven does not open its gates to women of my ilk.

The mystery of me reveals itself in time, every time. For now, I cast my eyes skyward, to the blinding white underbelly of a lone gull and soar with the gull as it keens and dips and alights atop the green gunwale of a yellow dory, its bow carving an easy trough through tomb of water. The oarsman, leaning in, stretching back, is my son, Kevin, just fourteen. With a wave of his oar, he banishes the avian scavenger, but me? I am ghost here, no more.

Kevin moves in cadence with creak of tholepin, whip of oar, slap of water against hull, all familiar rhythms to men whose lives depend upon their captor and benefactor, the sea. Any keen observer would say that this oarsman is boy, not man. True, but childhood is illusion if stomachs are growling. When men like my Alphonse braved the Great War, boys like our Kevin braved the sea.

The stench from the boat unmasks its cargo: hooks and twine and night crawlers and fish guts. In contrast, a hint of sweetness wafts from under the stern seat where a lunch pail crammed with bread and molasses sits—Kevin's favourite—tucked as far as possible from the slimy oilskins that are rolled up, and squirming, in the bow. Yes, squirming. Tiny fingers emerge around the edge of the slippery garments and push them aside. A giggle alerts Kevin and he turns to see a little girl start to weave her way toward him. He gasps when her foot skitters through fish slime and she grasps at the gunwale.

I brace myself for the splash.

There it is. No, not a fish breaching.

Kevin jumps and scrambles from centre to bow, oars clattering in his wake, dory weaving like a buoy in a gale. He screams and strains and clutches at ribbons of brown hair that slither through water's sheen. Face down in the sea, skirt ballooning, is Clara, his six-year-old sister.

The air churns as Kevin's terror surges around me, through me. The veins in his neck are blue and throbbing, sweat slides over his brow. Muscles straining, he locks one leg under the bow seat and stretches over the gunwale, all the while berating himself. The stupid boy had neglected to check for the stowaway. Kevin toils like the cod jigger he is, pulling hand over hand, sweating and grunting until his catch is alongside. He sucks in a deep breath and, arms burning, snatches Clara from the jaws of the sea. He hefts her over the gunwale and gravity does the rest, dumping them, safe, inside the dory, he panting, she spluttering, while the dory convulses, then calms to a gentle rocking. They lie there, trembling, his arms wrapping her tight, the sun smiling down. Kevin is wordless as he lifts her and tucks her back under the warmth of the oilskins. Before he reclaims his oars, he extracts a thick slice of lassy bread from his lunch pail and hands it to his little sister. Sighing, he heaves about and heads for shore.

The images fade and I cherish my relief this time, as every time. On this day, in the early summer of 1915, Kevin delivered his little sister safely home. Tragedy at sea avoided. But, at home, in their absence?

Sweating and grunting, pulsing and pounding of a different kind.

Maybe, had I insisted that Kevin swallow up his porridge that particular morning, maybe, had I taken the time to plait Clara's hair and tie it with scraps of blue ribbon like she wanted, they would have been with me longer, just a few minutes longer. That's what it would have taken to change the course of events in my life, and theirs. A few minutes. That's all Satan needed to stride from the sea and strip me, body and soul.

There was no help for it. What is a woman to do in face of brute, under threat of death?

But I am getting ahead of myself, and my purpose which is story, my story. It must be told in the proper order. This is not my first telling nor will it be my last. In my living years, I was a joyful teller of stories, but now? Even with all limitations of language banished, I am a reluctant narrator for the telling is atonement. I had hoped it temporary, this atonement, a purgatory of sorts, but the blackness of sin dictates that I am doomed, like some ancient mariner, to repeat my tale forever. Not purgatory then, but hell. My hell.

As for Satan? He's here somewhere. Not visible. *The greatest trick the devil ever pulled was convincing the world he doesn't exist.* One has to keep one's eyes peeled, one's wits sharp, else one could end up a victim of Satan or the cold or the damp or the sea which, when it's battling, can penetrate your flesh with the sting of a splitting knife.

I flit to shore and face a steep-roofed, wooden house—a salt box house— my home, the rear of which sits just fifty feet from the landwash. White clapboard. Forest green shutters. Nary ribbon of paint nor chink of putty gone astray. Three clothes lines loop the front yard, each with a Johnny pole propping up the middle, each pegged with sheets, beige flannel with faded pink horizontal stripes at one end. They hang without flutter, ready to billow at a poke from the wind. Boulders flank the path to the red front door: misshapen, painted cannon balls, alternating in green and white. A plume of smoke lifts from the chimney. Another straight line, awaiting its cue to drift. A study in still life, ruptured when the side door opens....

CLARA

CHAPTER 2

—————◆—————

1915

THE SIDE DOOR OPENED, NARY a whine from its well-oiled hinges. Six-year-old Clara emerged, prodded forward by her mother.

"Can I go out with Kevin in the dory, Mommy?"

Mommy sniffed.

"Can I go out with Kevin in the dory, Mommy?"

"'Tis me you'll be spending your time with today, Clara Kerrigan." Mommy pulled the door to and grabbed Clara's hand. Clara winced as Mommy dragged her and plopped her on a tree stump near the woodpile. "Can't be leaving you to your own devices, child."

Clara watched, silent, as Mommy picked up the axe with one hand, a small log with the other. What were devices anyway? All Clara knew was she wouldn't be chasing no more chickens. It was not her fault they tore into the kitchen. Kevin left the door open and he was supposed to be the responsible one. Some big brother. Tattletale. *'Guess what Clara did?'* he announced at supper just after the boiled dinner and just before the bakeapple pie. It worked out fine for him 'cause he got two pieces of pie and she got none. And this morning, she was parked on a tree stump, still as that dead mouse on the woodpile, while Mommy split and stacked. No devices here, that was for sure. Her whole body was bivvering something fierce; she burrowed into her itchy, wool sweater. Summertime was supposed to be warm. At least the sun showed up this morning; most days, all she saw was fog. Mommy said that Argentia gets two hundred days of fog a year. Two hundred was bigger than she could count. Too much grey.

Clara yawned and stared at the mouse. She had to poke that brown fur ball once to be sure it was really dead. She slid to the edge of the stump and planted her feet. Just then, the biggest, blackest bird she ever saw swooped out of nowhere, grabbed the mouse in its claws and took to the sky, its wings shushing the air. Her body tingled all over and she turned to Mommy. But Mommy was busy. Didn't even notice. Shrugging, Clara took a deep breath and blew it out. It formed a fog of its own so she did it again, trying to make a ring like Daddy always did with the smoke from his pipe. It was harder than it looked. She abandoned the effort, leaned back, and watched the glint of the sun on the blade of the axe.

She was a strong one, Clara's Mommy. She could swing that axe as good as Kevin and he was fourteen and nearly as big as Daddy. Clara rocked, forward, back, forward, back with the rhythm of the axe. It made a steady pounding noise, like the way the ocean smacked the landwash, only with a thump instead of a swish.

Kevin did all the chopping until Daddy went away to the Great War; now Kevin jigged for cod like Daddy used to do. Clara tried to go with Kevin many times; once, she sneaked into the dory and curled up like a snail in its shell in the bow of the boat. She didn't know why they called it a bow; it wasn't like when she bowed her head at Mass. When Kevin fished her out of the sea that day and took her home, he said she had to stay away from the dory. Yesterday, she tried to go with him again, but Kevin had a keener eye. She was mad, so mad that she took after the chickens and look where that got her.

Clara stilled herself and eyed the ocean. She could see the yellow dory bumping up against the wharf. But where was Kevin? Maybe he was gone to the shed to claim the oars. Nice day in the dory. No wind. Barely any waves. She focused on the ripples and followed them to shore. There were lots of smooth stones down there on the landwash, just waiting to be picked up. White ones were her favourite. She collected them all the time and plopped them into a jam jar that Mommy put on the kitchen window sill just for her, right beside her St. Joseph's Cloak plant. But there would be no collecting today. She could be picking berries or feeding dead flies to pitcher plants, but nooooo! Clara stamped her feet, making dirt and pebbles dance. She sighed, loud and whiny, like the world was over. Mommy cleared her throat. Clara let her body slump because she knew she was going to get a talking to. Darn chickens.

Sure enough, without missing a beat in her chopping, Mommy started in. "Her name was Clara, just like you."

A story? Clara straightened her back. She tucked her feet up under her skirt and hugged her knees. Goosebumps slid down her spine. Good ones, not scary ones.

"She was your great grandmother and you were born on the anniversary of her birthday."

Clara opened her mouth to ask about that anniversary thing, but didn't want the story to go away, so she clamped her lips tight.

"Your great grandmother had nine children and the lot of them lived in a mud hut that had only one room. The chickens and their pig lived with them, too, if you can imagine the likes of that."

Clara lowered her chin to her knees and curled her toes inside her boots. Chickens in their house? Maybe she was in for a talking-to after all. Maybe not. *She* never chased the pig. She stayed away from the pig. Last year they had one that she named Tom. Then, when she was munching away on her pork chop and Kevin told her she was eating Tom, she bawled. No, first she threw up—a slimy, pea soup mixture of mashed potatoes and carrots—and Tom. Then she bawled. Her eyes were stinging now so she shook her head to get the memory out and looked up at Mommy.

"They had one straw bed for the lot of them, on the floor in the corner. No shoes, no socks. Hardly a bit of clothing."

No clothes? Clara put one hand over her mouth to stop a snigger, but a tiny one slid out. Mommy raised her eyebrows. Clara switched her scoff to a cough and lowered her hand. "Didn't they miss having clothes and beds?"

"Can't miss what you never had, child. They were a happy bunch, living on faith, love, and potatoes. Just potatoes. Nothing but. Boiled them up in the fireplace; no chimney mind you, so the place was black with the smoke."

The squeal of gulls and swoosh of sea got loud now because Mommy stopped the talking and the chopping. She set the axe down and stretched to one side and then the other. Just like the song—*Ha, ha this-a-way, ha, ha, that-a-way.* Mommy stacked the splits, grabbed another log and, soon enough, was swinging the axe again. "Now, where was I?"

"...black with the smoke."

"Indeed. They sat around a huge basket full of boiled potatoes and ate the skins and all, using their hands. Too poor for any dishes."

Clara widened her eyes. "No forks or spoons?"

"Nary a one. Not in them times. Not in Ireland. The only people who had forks and spoons were the lords who came from England."

Clara folded her hands, the way she did every night when Mommy led the Lord's Prayer. "Did they pray to the lords?"

Mommy smiled big. The sun got brighter.

"The Irish only rented the land, me darlin'," she said. "The lords were men who lived in big houses on hills and told the Irish to raise cattle and grain and potatoes. All the cattle and grain went to England. The only thing the Irish ate was potatoes, because there were so many potatoes. Until the blight."

"What's a blight?"

"It's a sickness, a disease, but not for people. Only for potatoes. Caused by a tiny germ that hid in the ships that travelled to England from America." She paused, leaned on the axe, and wiped her forehead with the sleeve of her old, blue sweater, the one with the hole in the elbow. "Remember the time you couldn't find your kitten but, as soon as you opened the root cellar door, she popped right out?"

Memory gushed. Clara grinned.

"Well, ships have cellars called holds. As soon as the sailors opened the holds, the blight jumped out, just a tiny seed it was, that grabbed on to the first bit of breeze and danced right across the Irish Sea. When the wind got sick of doing the jig, it dropped the blight into a field outside Dublin. From there, disease slid like night time across Ireland. Just a brown patch on the leaves at first, but it slithered down the stem into the roots. One third of the potato crop died that year—1845. A sad time."

Clara scrunched up her face. "What's so sad about potatoes dying?"

"They couldn't grow them again."

"But what did the people eat?"

"Nothing. There was a huge famine—the great hunger, they called it."

"Why didn't they just make bread like you? Or go fishing, like Daddy and Kevin?"

Mommy turned her head toward the ocean. The wind was picking up now. It played with Mommy's hair and she brushed away the stringy bits that blew into her face. When she spoke again, her voice was soft, hard to hear. Clara slipped off the tree stump and sidled close.

"The grain all went to England, remember? As for the ocean, it's big and powerful and can feed the world, if it's got a mind to. But the shoreline in Ireland was mostly cliffs, too dangerous to fish and they had no boats. The people had no potatoes to eat or sell so they couldn't pay their taxes."

"What's 'taxes'?"

"Money that people must pay to the lords."

"But the people had no money. What did they do?"

"Nothing they could do. Starving in the streets, they were. The whole countryside went quiet. No children playing. No dogs barking."

"What happened to the dogs?"

Mommy shrugged, and in a tiny whisper, said, "The people were hungry."

Clara's whole body shuddered. She pushed the meaning of Mommy's words down hard. "What happened to the people?" she asked, her voice sounding so strange that she looked around to see who squeaked out the words.

"Many people died. But some sailed away."

"Like my great grandmother? She sailed away, didn't she?" Clara gripped Mommy's heavy skirt.

"Yes." Mommy placed an arm around Clara's shoulders.

"Did she go in a dory?"

"No, she went with hundreds of others in big ships." She sniffed. "Coffin ships."

Clara's mind raced. "What…"

Mommy drew her close. "They called them coffin ships because people got sick with the fever and died when they were crossing the Atlantic. Your great grandmother said that they threw so many bodies overboard that the sharks followed the ships, waiting for their next meal."

Clara raised a hand to her brow and scanned the ocean. The water glistened. Tiny waves, no triangles. Sharks had triangles on their backs. Big triangles and big mouths and many teeth. Daddy brought a shark home once. Caught in the net, he said. Clara trembled. Maybe Kevin was right. Maybe she shouldn't be in the dory. She hated it when Kevin was right. She turned back to Mommy.

"But my great grandmother didn't die."

"No, she didn't. But her baby did."

"But she had lots of babies, didn't she?"

"Yes." Mommy dropped the axe, slipped down to her haunches and their faces were so close that her breath slid into Clara's. "It doesn't matter how many children a woman has," she whispered. "It left a hole in her the size of the ocean when little Jimmy died. A hole even bigger than the ocean." She cupped Clara's face with her hands. "It's the saddest thing in the world to lose your child."

The tears in Mommy's eyes were so big that Clara was sure they were going to spill over. But they didn't. And Mommy did not turn away for a second. Thin lines, like knitting, formed on Mommy's forehead. Clara stood very still.

"I don't care about the chickens, Clara," Mommy said. "But you? That's another thing entirely."

"But I likes it," Clara whispered, "being in the dory, with Kevin."

Mommy tightened her hands around Clara's face. "You're too small for the dory. All it would take is a squall of wind or a spit of sea and you'd be gone." She let out a long sigh. "You got to ponder these things for yourself, child; Kevin won't always be there to protect you." Her voice was shaky now. "My grandmother told my mother and my mother told me and now I'm telling you: it's the saddest thing in the world to lose your child. It's more than a woman can bear." Mommy took a deep breath. "You have to stop this dory business, Clara. Do you understand?"

"Yes." Clara blinked.

"You'll never try to hide in the dory again? Never, ever again?"

"Cross my heart." Clara traced a line of promise across her chest.

"Good." Mommy searched Clara's face and pushed off Clara's shoulders to stand. She picked up the axe but she didn't chop, just leaned on the handle and stared at the water. "The saddest thing in the world," she said again, like she was talking to no one, or maybe to Clara's great grandmother in heaven.

Clara watched Mommy who was rocking from side to side and resting a free hand on her round belly; the fat teardrops in Mommy's eyes finally spilled over and kept coming, streaming down her face like a string of glass rosary beads.

Clara wanted to ask more about great grandmother's little Jimmy, but she knew that breaking Mommy's stillness right now would be the same as breaking her heart. Maybe Mommy's heart was breaking anyway. Clara's chest felt heavy and she looked at the wood pile.

A sudden flurry of movement drew her attention. The yellow dory was slipping away from the wharf, its bow cutting the water. Kevin paused from his rowing, raised his hand, and waved. Heart leaping, Clara waved back. Kevin adjusted an oar and started up again. Soon, he rounded the point and was gone. She stared at the water until it closed up behind him, like he was never there. Was that the way of things when babies died? Did life just close up behind them, like water, and keep on going? She returned to her spot on the tree stump where she sat quietly, waiting for Mommy.

It was the next spring, just after Clara's seventh birthday, that Mommy had a little Jimmy of her own. The angels brought him from heaven and took him back three months later. Daddy was home from the war then and him and Kevin cut down a spruce tree and used all of Daddy's tools to slash the branches, strip the bark, and shape the trunk into a tiny white coffin.

Clara tiptoed into the shed to watch Kevin build; she flattened her back against a wall and saw him put a sharp blade into Daddy's plane. He pushed the tool across the wood over and over again, making a whoosh-ing sound. The shavings that fell to the floor were thin and curly and blond, just like little Jimmy's hair.

There was a funeral Mass where Father Mahony walked round and round the coffin, waving a silver vase on a chain, making more smoke than a wood fire. The smoke smelled different though, kind of sweet. Maybe they put molasses in it. Father Mahony talked the whole time. Clara didn't understand a word but she knew it was Latin because Kevin said so. Besides, she had heard the priest talking like that every Sunday for her whole life. After the funeral Mass, they put Jimmy in the ground and everybody went home.

Mommy cried. She lay face down on the kitchen floor, her arms spread wider than angels' wings, and wailed so loud that the windows rattled like there was a heavy gale. Clara hid under the daybed in the corner with her hands over her ears. She wanted to run, but she was stuck, couldn't move, couldn't take her eyes off Mommy. The world is turned upside-down when it's the mommy that's doing the crying. And the angels brought no more babies to Mommy. It was the saddest thing in the world. And the sadness never left.

But, after a while, Mommy did.

———

1915 - 1917

IN THE DAYS AFTER THEY buried Jimmy, Clara tiptoed through the darkness of the house, fingering the rosary in her apron pocket, hoping her prayers would make Mommy better. She took to watching Mommy out of the corner of her eye, waiting for a glimpse of light to return to Mommy's face or a thread of story to fall from Mommy's mouth. When Mommy caught on to the spying, Clara started hiding, scurrying behind doors where she felt invisible or into the out-of-doors where she felt soothed by the pulse of the sea. All Clara wanted was Mommy. All Mommy did was cry.

Daddy never cried, but his face was hard, not like it used to be before the war. His dark eyes were hard now, too, hard and glittery, like flakes of coal. Clara pined for the days when his eyes were rich and soft, like the bit of black velvet ribbon in Mommy's sewing basket. He didn't say anything to Mommy about Jimmy dying. He never talked to Mommy much anymore, other than telling her to get the supper on the table.

Daddy and Kevin kept working at fishing through the fall and mending nets and sawing wood in the winter. Words rarely passed between them when Clara was around, but Clara heard curse words and fighting noises when they were out of sight, in the barn or the shed. Sometimes Kevin's face was purple, his eyes swollen. Sometimes Daddy's knuckles were bulging, his fingers bloody.

One time, Clara was collecting pebbles from under the bushes near the shed. When a busy spider caught her eye, she crouched to watch it spin and spin. Its web looked like lace, trembling in the breeze. All shiny and dewy and--

"You knows it was her what killed him!" Kevin's voice. Loud. Inside the shed. Clara didn't move. At the sound of a blow, she dropped her pebbles. Silence fell. She hugged her knees tight. Feet shuffled about. The shed door slammed. As Kevin stormed his way toward the house, Daddy's voice stabbed the air behind him. "Little Jimmy is better off dead." Clara rocked back and forth, back and forth. Was Kevin talking about Mommy? It made no sense, none of it. She raised an arm and, with a single swipe, dislodged the spider web, leaving the spider dangling.

After that, Clara did her chores and kept her distance, but she couldn't stop the nervous fluttering in her chest. Would the world ever right itself? The answer came after a year, a whole dark year, when Kevin announced he was going away to St. John's, then to someplace called Boston. The world would never be right again.

The day he was leaving, he tried to talk to Clara, but she would hear of none of it. She stomped out of the house, slamming the door. Straight down the path she went, past the brown meadow to the wharf, and eased herself into the dory. Sitting in the bow, her back to the house, she watched the ocean roll its shoulders and hurl itself to shore, breaking to smithereens on the rocks. The shatter of waves, repeating, repeating.

"You're not supposed to be in the dory by yourself." Kevin's voice.

Clara swung around and stared up at Kevin who was hovering on the wharf above her. "I'm eight now and I does what I pleases."

The boat pitched as Kevin hopped in. He dropped onto the thwart and stared her straight in the face. "Sorry, Clara," he said, his dark eyes clouding over.

Clara balled her fingers into fists and rubbed her eyes. "Why do you have to leave?"

He shrugged. "You're too young for reasons."

"I heard you and Daddy fighting in the shed."

"That's not the reason."

"So, how'd you get that black eye then?"

Another shrug. "That's nothing. It's time for me to go, that's all. I'm sixteen years old and I can get by on me own hooks."

"Remember what Daddy was like before the war?"

Kevin nodded. "War can leave scars on a man."

"You mean that ugly mark on his neck?"

"Not that kind of scar. I mean inside scars." Kevin tapped his chest.

"What happened to him in the war?"

"Lots. He dug trenches, and slept in mud and used a kit bag for a pillow and rats tried to eat all his food. Once, he talked about the machine guns, moving from one side to another, bullets flying, knocking down men like a scythe mowing hay. One of them bullets hit Daddy and he put a shell dressing over his neck and ran until he got past the barbed wire. He blacked out and woke up in a hospital where he stayed for a long time. Then he came home, bringing that ugly scar."

"And that hard face," said Clara.

Kevin placed a hand over hers and leaned in. "You have to take care of them. Dad'll be needing your help with Mom."

"Mrs. Dulcie Mullins is teaching me cooking and cleaning."

"You'll do your best to help then? Promise?"

"Cross my heart." Clara wrapped her fingers around Kevin's hand which was calloused, rough as pine bark, and held tight, making a memory. "Are you coming back?" she whispered.

"It would take some big sea to heave me home again." He pulled his hand from hers and ruffled her hair. "Bye, Clara." He hopped onto the wharf and kept on going.

Clara felt something well up inside her, a growing wave of words that had to get out. She lifted her head and dropped her jaw. "I heard you tell Daddy that Mommy killed Jimmy." She instantly clapped her hand over her mouth. Kevin didn't pause, didn't break stride. Had he heard? She shook her head hard. It didn't matter. She should not have said it, must have heard wrong in the first place; only a terrible daughter would even think such a thing. She would never say it again.

Clara shivered and turned back to watch the waves crashing. Eventually, she scrambled out of the dory and made her way back to the house.

Kevin was already gone.

CHAPTER 4

———◆———

1917 - 1920

THE NEXT DAY, CLARA AWOKE to the sound of the grandfather clock and the memory of her promise to her brother. She sprang from bed into the darkness of her room. The instant her feet slapped the floorboards, icy nettles shot through her and mouse-like squeaks flew from her. Fearful that she would disturb her mother, Clara clamped her lips into a thin line and flitted on butterfly toes to her chest of drawers. She tugged at the top drawer which gave way without complaint.

Shivering, she rummaged in the dark for her clothes. What had she been thinking? It was not like it was the first time an autumn chill had sneaked in overnight. From now on, she would stuff her stockings under the covers at night, right beside that big, grey beach rock she used to heat the bed.

Clara scrambled into her clothes and slid her hands along the top of the chest of drawers until she located a candlestick and matches. She struck a match and offered light to the stump of a candle but the wick was too short to catch the flame. She grabbed the scissor-like candle clippers sitting beside the candle and then puffed out the match. Back in the dark, blinded by the dark, she remembered the painful nick she had once given herself with the candle clippers. She abandoned them and used her fingernails to claw at the wax until the wick had grown an inch. Another strike of a match, another meeting of wick and flame. Success. Pleased with herself, Clara looked around, aching to share her accomplishment. But there was no one but herself, so she moved on, letting the candle come into its own while she scrambled to make up the bed. Holding the candle in a Jack-Be-Nimble way, she tiptoed into the hallway, her shadow claiming the wall like a ghost. Clara took a deep breath and held it as she padded her way downstairs and into the kitchen.

It was in the kitchen that the absence of Kevin clipped her like a winter wind. The Waterloo stove, which he had always tended, was ice cold to the touch. Clara blinked back tears. What had Kevin gone and done? She took a deep breath and exhaled. Her candle flickered. She swallowed and nodded. There were no back doors about Kevin; whatever he did, he did because he had to. No point in being miserable beyond hope. She set her candle on the kitchen table. With care, she reached to the center of the table and pulled the oil lamp toward her. She removed its soot-coated chimney and grabbed a rag from the back of a chair. After giving the chimney a good going over, she used her candle to light the lamp wick. She twisted the stubborn knob on the lamp, turning up the flame until the kitchen glowed. It was with a sigh of relief that she blew out the candle.

Next, Clara raided the kindling box and, with short, jerky movements, stuffed a bunch of paper and twigs into the stove. When the kindling jumped into flame at the first strike of a match, she clasped her hands in front of her chest and let out a sigh. She stoked and lifted the kindling with the poker to let the air get under it, just as she had seen Kevin do. When she figured the fire could get by on its own, she headed to the pantry, intent on filling the kettle with barrel water. Tears choked her a second time when she found the water crusted with ice more than an inch thick. Her father wasn't around to help; he was always off in the dory before first light. What would she do now? She shrugged. Nothing to do but get the hatchet from the kindling box.

Clara chopped until she met water. She grabbed a dipper and scooped water into the kettle. She fed and stoked the fire. She put the kettle on and dragged the broom across the kitchen floor while she waited for the kettle to sing.

Then, Clara did something familiar, something she had been doing since shortly after Jimmy died last year; she steeped tea and made toast for her mother. She crept to her mother's room, the parlour, where the door was always open a crack to allow the heat from the kitchen to seep in. Her mother must be half-frozen on this particular morning. But if the cold bothered Kathleen Kerrigan, Clara would never know. Today, as usual, Mommy didn't speak. Clara pulled the chamber pot with the blue and white flowers from under the bed and helped Mommy get up. She waited while her mother relieved herself, after which Clara helped her back into bed. She carried the chamber pot outside and emptied it and cleaned it. Then she returned it to its place. All the while, Clara filled the silence by nattering.

"Mrs. Mullins is teaching me to knit. I can make a scarf already, but she says it will be a while before I can have at a sock." One subject covered, Clara moved on to another. "The teacher told us a story the other day. The one about the prodigal son. I like her stories. Not as good as the ones you tell me..." Clara stopped. Mommy didn't tell stories anymore. "I know my five times tables now," she said. "Five times one is five. Five times two is ten..." On it went. Never a response. Clara just washed Mommy and fed her, holding the teacup so Mommy could sip, breaking the toast into crumb-sized pieces so Mommy could bite. When breakfast was over, Clara helped her mother up again and brought her across the hall to the kitchen. There, she eased Mommy into the rocking chair and placed knitting needles into her hands. She didn't dress Mommy. She tried once, but Mommy slapped her and then froze in position with one hand on her chest and the other straight out, like a statue of Jesus blessing the people. The slap stung Clara's face, but she didn't let on; she just reached out and lowered Mommy's hand.

"Mrs. Mullins will be over later to help you get dressed," Clara said this morning as she leaned in, planted a kiss on Mommy's cheek, and tucked her in with a quilt. "I have to go to school now." She inhaled, a hitching breath, and turned away.

After Clara had fed herself and cleaned up, she gathered her things for school. By the time she was ready to go, daylight had crept in. She checked the stove and cast one last longing glance at Mommy. As if on cue, Mommy started rocking and knitting. Clara dipped her chin to her chest and slumped through the door. She didn't raise her head again until she approached the two-room schoolhouse.

She arrived just as the teacher came to the door to ring the bell, a welcoming clang, one that pulled Clara from her sadness. She hurried to the steps, and smiled her best as she passed by Miss Hunter. Teachers were pretty strict, but Miss Hunter always returned Clara's smile. Clara straightened her back as she walked inside.

The classroom had bare walls except for a black chalkboard with a dusty ledge and a map of Europe. There were tall windows with no curtains; on sunny days, when buttercups splashed the meadows, planks of light spread across bowed floorboards and the children removed their sweaters. On windy days, when horses' tails danced across the bay, draughts of icy air sneaked through warped frames and the children burrowed into their coats.

The desks were long and bench-like, made to hold six students, side by side. It worked well as long as your neighbours kept their elbows to themselves. The students were learning handwriting now, working in copybooks with real pens and ink. It was the finest kind in the fall and spring, but sometimes in winter, the ink froze overnight. The boys were responsible for heating the school and had to bring kindling from home. Sometimes they didn't show up or forgot the kindling. On those days, the children just had to suffer the cold.

Clara squirmed now as she caught sight of the strap on the teacher's desk. There was no shortage of strappings; not knowing your poems from your Royal Reader by heart or not acting right always brought out that strip of leather. Clara had never felt the sting of the strap; that wasn't meant for her at all. She had no problems with her lessons, except for Arithmetic. Even that was more of a puzzle than a problem: if Newfoundland money was in dollars and cents, why were all the Arithmetic questions about pounds and shillings? Something to do with being a part of Britain, she supposed. She didn't ask. No one asked questions in school. It just wasn't allowed and Clara followed the rules. All the rules. Clara had never even been commanded to stand in the corner. No, Clara had no worries about school. In addition to loving her lessons, she loved helping the teacher. Sometimes, when it was her turn to sweep the floors after school, Clara delayed the process, just so she could stay longer. She even took turns for the other girls when the chance was offered.

Clara had friends at school, but sometimes the boys were mean. The girls, too. She heard them whisper and point. One day when she was walking by a group on her way home, one of the boys yelled "I hears your mudder's thoughts are too far aft." Clara stopped for a second, feeling the heat rise in her cheeks. A scream was roaring up inside her like spit from an angry sea, but she calmed herself and kept on walking. She was mad alright. At him? Maybe. But he was a truth teller. How could she fight truth?

But that was a while ago. On this day, with a new hole in her life created by Kevin taking wing, Clara was grateful that no mean whispers slid her way.

When Clara left school, the mauzy weather she had started with had been replaced by a needle-like glitter storm. She scurried home, drenched and shivering by the time she got there. As soon as she opened the door, she was greeted by Mrs. Dulcie Mullins, their middle-aged neighbour, who helped Clara out of her coat and dried her wet hair with vigorous strokes of a towel.

"You're soaked, child. I suppose somewhere on God's green earth the sun is shining today but it's not here. You just stand yourself by that stove and dry yourself off. Undo them plaits." She tugged at Clara's hair, three tugs, always three. "I'll fix 'em up for you later." Clara grinned into the full-moon face of this little teapot woman with wisps of hair sticking out from under her woven black scarf. Father Mahony once said Mrs. Mullins would give self and soul to help others. Clara figured God must have a feather bed waiting for Mrs. Mullins in heaven.

Every day, by the time Clara got home, Mommy was tucked back into bed wearing a fresh nightdress and smelling sweet and clean, thanks to Mrs. Mullins. Every day, Clara checked the rocking chair for the evidence of Mommy's activity: one completely knitted sock, end threads dangling. Today, as usual, it was there. This evening, as every evening, after Clara finished her lessons, she would take the darning needle, sew in all the threads, and set the sock in the growing pile at the end of the daybed.

Daily, Clara worked with Mrs. Mullins to make the supper. It was usually leftovers from dinner. Clara didn't know how, but Mrs. Mullins managed to cook a full dinner for both her own family and Clara's.

With Mrs. Mullins helping, Clara was making out fine. Mommy wasn't getting better, but life was going on. Sometimes every minute seemed as long as a wet Sunday, but the seasons kept sliding one into the other: autumn glitter, winter floes, spring thaw, summer breeze. Before Clara knew it, the circle of seasons passed, twice. She was ten years old.

CHAPTER 5

1920

AFTERNOON LIGHT CREPT OVER THE tops of wild rose bushes and through the kitchen window of the salt box house. Clara sat at the wooden table beneath the window, darning. She leaned into the light, needle in one hand, Daddy's grey woolen sock over the other one. She paused in her attempts to mend the heel and looked at her daddy who was tending the Waterloo stove. He lifted the stove lid, dropped in a log, and shuffled it about with the poker. Flames jumped; sparks danced. When Daddy muffled the fire by replacing the lid, all was silent save for the rattling of rosary beads in the parlour across the hall from the kitchen. Mommy must be praying again; she never uttered any words, just moved her fingers round and round the wooden rosary. Maybe she was thinking hard on one of the Joyful or Sorrowful or Glorious mysteries; Clara didn't know.

Daddy perked up an ear, then slipped a silver flask from his back pocket. He stared into nothingness as he unscrewed the lid and brought the flask to his lips. Clara watched his Adam's apple dance as he swallowed. He wiped his mouth with his flannel sleeve and returned the flask to his pocket. Then he made himself busy, restacking kindling.

Clara continued to watch him; all the while something was churning inside her, something that didn't feel good. She glanced around the room. Everything looked the same. She loved this little kitchen with its drop-leaf table and chairs that Daddy built. Mommy sewed the curtains with the roses on them and even made a matching cover for the daybed.

Daddy had built that, too, that and the pine rocking chair in the corner by the wood box.

Tears pooled in Clara's eyes as she stared at the empty rocker. She missed the creak of its constant to and fro, and the click of steel knitting needles that flew like magic through Mommy's fingers whenever she sat there. Mommy had always made enough socks and caps and mittens to stave off the bite of winter. But this year? Mommy cast on only the one grey sock and couldn't seem to remember how to turn the heel; she kept dropping stitches, muttering, unraveling, casting on again. Two whole hours she did this, until there was nothing but a tangled mess of yarn on the floor. When Daddy tried to pick it up, Mommy jabbed his hand with a knitting needle. He clutched the injured hand with his good one and stepped back to the daybed where he plopped himself down, mouth hanging open. Mommy hissed at him like water spitting from a boiling kettle and popping across a red-hot stove. Then she pushed off the arms of the rocker to stand and shuffled her way into the hall. She stopped at the front door of the house, opened it like she was going somewhere, but then closed it again. She made her way to the parlour on the other side of the hall, the room she had been sleeping in since Jimmy died. She used to spend her days in the kitchen; now she never left the parlour. Except for yesterday.

Yesterday, Mommy was on the landwash. Clara would never have believed it but she saw it with her own two eyes. Mommy running, hair flying, body bared—not a stitch of clothes on her. It was Mrs. Dulcie Mullins who chased Mommy down. Clara had just turned away and scurried to the house.

Now, as Clara tried to push the images of Mommy out of her head, she couldn't shake the feeling that trouble was coming. She dragged her sleeve across her eyes and looked to her darning. Before she had completed a single stitch, trouble arrived.

The front door flew open into the hallway and footsteps scuffed across the threshold. When the door closed again, Father Aloysius Mahony was standing on the woven doormat, announcing himself.

Clara dropped her darning needle. She stared, unblinking, at this short, thin man with curly blond hair and ice-blue eyes, this little man who marched right to the middle of the kitchen, filling up the room like he owned it.

Daddy strode across the kitchen, hand extended. "Welcome, Father." He shook hands with the priest and glared at Clara. "The priest, Clara. The priest."

Clara sprang to her feet. "Hello, Father."

"Hello, Clara." The priest stood feet apart, hands clasped behind his back.

Clara felt heat rise in her face. She rummaged her brain for words but none appeared so she just stared at the priest, lips clamped together.

Daddy shook his head. "Young 'uns today. Nary click nor clue." He pulled out a chair. Have a seat, Father. Can we storm the kettle for you? The stove's good and hot."

"No, thank you, Alphonse. You know why I'm here." Father Mahony folded his arms and focused his attention on Clara. "Your mother is sick," he said, "her body worn to rags by hard work. She's got the consumption and has to go to the sanatorium in St. John's."

Clara opened her mouth, then closed it again. She had nearly sauced him, the brazen girl. The priest was the next thing to God and she couldn't call him a liar. But he must think she was stupid. She was only ten, but she knew the truth: it was Jimmy's death, not the consumption, that broke Kathleen Kerrigan. Clara had prayed for help to come, but she hadn't prayed for Mommy to go. Now, with the priest standing here in front of her, she knew that Mommy was leaving and she could do nothing to stop it. Even her daddy couldn't fix this.

Father Mahony didn't stay long. He said he would be back the next morning to help escort Mommy to St. John's and was kind enough to bless the house before he left. Clara was sure the house was grateful. When the door closed behind the priest, Clara looked to her father. He did not meet her eyes, just slinked through the back door, silver flask in hand.

CHAPTER 6

———————

1920 - 1921

THE PAINFUL KNOT THAT HAD lodged in Clara's gut at the loss of Kevin hardened to a coal lump when Mommy left. It was weeks before she could peek through the door of the parlour where Mommy had slept; her first attempt had churned her, setting off rolling waves of fear. What in the name of all that's holy would become of her if Daddy disappeared too? Already the priest had showed himself again, this time with Mrs. Mullins in tow, offering to take Clara off Daddy's hands.

Clara had been in her bedroom at the time, pillaging the ragbag; Mrs. Fan, her ragdoll with the mismatched button eyes, was sorely in need of a new dress. Clara was holding a bit of a flour bag next to the doll, thinking that would do the trick, when she heard Daddy bellowing: "The only thing the likes of ye will ever be gettin' around here is a cup of tea, and a bare-legged one at that." The front door slammed. The whole house shuddered. Mrs. Fan toppled from Clara's hands and Clara barreled to the kitchen, stopping at the door, wide-eyed, watching Daddy pace the floor.

Face blazing, he threw his hands in the air. "Wantin' to take you away, they were." He moved close, put his hands on her shoulders, and gazed right into her eyes. "You're not going no place," he said, exhaling a whiskey stench that caused her to crimp her nose. A faraway look slid over him and, in a whisper, he added, "You're the eyes and face of your mother." He ran a hand down her cheek. Clara's innards shivered. Then, without warning, he jumped back and strode out of the house.

Clara blinked and scratched her head. Had she done something wrong? She pondered it for a minute but then shrugged it away. The important thing was that she was staying here, in the salt box house, with her daddy. No one, not Mrs. Mullins, not even Father Mahony, was going to haul her off like dried cod to the merchant store. Clara's insides lit up; her happiness spread to her toes and she danced a little jig. She would make Daddy's eyes twinkle again. Whatever he wanted, whatever would keep the dregs of her family together, she would do. She twirled around and around the cozy kitchen, coming to a complete halt when she spotted Daddy's silver flask near the wood box. Before she had a chance to grab it, Daddy reappeared.

"What in Gawd's name are ye at?" he said as he reclaimed the flask and marched out again.

Clara's joy fizzled and she dropped like an anchor onto the daybed. For seconds, she sat, stunned; then she crossed herself and muttered prayers to Saint Jude, the patron saint of hopeless cases. Maybe he could help her deal with the devil whiskey.

The next morning, Clara found Daddy in the shed, slouched over a saw horse, his salt and pepper cap askew. She lifted his arm and draped it over her shoulder. Grunting and groaning, she managed to get him upright. He was barely able to navigate, but when he turned to her, his eyes widened and he broke into song: *I'll take you home again, Kathleen.*

"Mommy's not here, Daddy. It's me, Clara," she said, staggering under the bulk of him. Somehow she got him into the kitchen and onto the daybed. As she was putting a quilt over him, she glanced through the kitchen window and caught sight Mrs. Mullins puffing her way up the path, a cast iron pot in her hands. *Sweet Mother of Jesus, God forgive me for swearing.* Clara shot through the door to head off the woman. Yes, Mrs. Mullins had a kind heart but she also had a prate hole the size of the Atlantic.

"Mrs. Dulcie Mullins! A grand morning, isn't it? Is that salt beef and cabbage I smells in that pot? It's weighing on you for sure. Let me have at it!" Clara swooped and pounced like a scavenger gull; she strode away, pot in hand, leaving Mrs. Mullins standing there, arms dangling like stockings on a clothesline. When Clara got herself into the kitchen, she looked through the window again and saw Mrs. Mullins huffing back the way she came. Clara blew out a sigh and planted the pot of food on the corner of the stove. That was it then, the way of things. She'd work to keep people from finding out about her daddy's drinking. Or at the very least, she'd tell herself they didn't know.

In the days that followed, she found that lying to herself meant keeping to herself. After she did her chores—scrubbing the kitchen, feeding the chickens, spreading seaweed in her vegetable garden—she strolled the landwash alone, only Mrs. Fan to keep her company. Often, other children were there, lunging in and out of the waves, skipping stones, shrieking, laughing. Clara held back, hugging Mrs. Fan.

Clara's life was all about work: cleaning the house and getting milking done before school; filling the lamps and getting the supper on the table after school. Every evening she put her father's flask beside his plate and, every evening, he tilted his head and sucked in the whiskey, all the while grumbling. "A hard life, fishin' fer the merchants with their bloody truck system. All they gives us for our catch is a bit of line or an anchor or hard tack. Never enough fish to pay for the goods I needs. Not a fisherman on this godforsaken island who isn't up to his arse in debt."

Clara took to standing tall, hands on hips. "We can farm. I'm strong, Daddy, and I can chop wood and grow vegetables. Mrs. Mullins will help me lay in food and make preserves for the winter. I can tend the cow and the chickens. There's the berry picking, too. You knows you're partial to a bit partridgeberry jam." She'd waggle a finger at him every time she mentioned jam. "No need for us to end up on a dry diet of salt fish and hard tack."

Daddy grunted. "Maybe I should just do like them lazy-arse han-gashores, give up on the idea of working for a living."

"It's the working that will keep us living. You knows that as well as I do."

"I suppose you're right, child. I suppose you're right." He stared at her, through her. "There's no mould on you now, is there?"

"So they tells me," said Clara who was eyeing his flask, planning to seize and hide it next morning. Only for the morning, though. Long enough to get the sober, but groggy, Alphonse off to fish the shore in the spring, summer, and fall. Things were good as long as he brought in the catch; Clara could make fish and mend nets as well as she could card yarn and knit mitts.

With more and more responsibility falling her way, Clara stopped going to the little school house. She worked at home, on the home, on the land, on the wharf. Taking care of Daddy. Daddy started smiling again, but never stopped drinking. He was good to her though. Never got in an uproar. Except once. And it was all her fault, what happened at Mass that Sunday.

Clara could have ignored that rowdy boy who was sitting on the far side of their pew, that rowdy boy who had winked at her. But she didn't. Instead, she smiled, relishing the tingling sensation that crept across her neck and face. She propped one foot on the upturned kneeler just so he could see it. She even teased her skirt up past her shin and leaned in, us-ing her hands to iron out a pretend wrinkle in her black stocking. From the corner of her eye, she saw the boy watching, grinning. She didn't see the priest walking onto the altar, but she jumped to her feet when she heard the start of Mass. "*Intro ibo ad altari dei...*" She got caught up in the service then and forgot about the whole thing until she got home where, the second they were inside the door, Daddy hauled off and slapped her.

Clara dropped like a stone.

Daddy leaned over her. "Don't let me ever be seeing you do the likes of that again. Showing your leg to that good-for-nothing arsehole.

Nowhere but...." He raised his hand again. She cowered. He recoiled and stormed out of the house.

Clara crawled to the kitchen daybed, pulled herself onto it, and curled up in a ball. What had she gone and done? Bad enough her mother was forced to leave; now her father was forced to hit. Even Kevin had walked away, leaving her alone. Did he go because of something she said? Whatever could she do to make things right? One thing for sure: she would never look at that rowdy boy again or any other boy, for that matter. Daddy was all she had left. She needed her daddy. As long as she had Daddy, she would be a good girl.

It took a couple of days for Daddy's fingerprints to fade from her face; then things went back to normal in the salt box house. Daddy never again spoke about that Sunday.

He didn't talk about Mommy either. Not a word. Sometimes, Clara ended her weekly session in the confession box by probing Father Mahony for news. His answers were always the same: light a candle, say a prayer. Clara would sigh and plod to the altar that housed an army of candles, each one in its own red glass, all the glasses in rows on black wrought-iron tiers. Week after week, she would ignite a wall of light and stare at it until her eyes blurred with streaks and stars. Then she would walk weary miles under the Stations of the Cross. Surely all this was enough for God to bring her news. But no news came. Clara tried sending letters to Mommy at the Hospital on Waterford Road in St. John's, but she never got a reply.

Time melted away like ice candles dripping from the roof. When a letter finally did come for her, it was not from Mommy. It was from someone named Mavis.

Dear Clara,

My name is Mavis Kerrigan and I am your brother's wife. Kevin is off on a banker schooner now, sailing back and forth from Boston; he's a hard-working man and the sea life suits him. There's no end to the things he does on sea and land for this family. He was not much for schooling,

I understands, so he don't write, but he reads a lot thanks to yer mother. He talks about you so I thought that being family and all, I would let you know that we have been married these three years. Our baby, Jimmy..."

Clara dropped the letter. Kevin, her big brother, was all grown up, a man now, a man who had named his little boy Jimmy.

KEVIN

CHAPTER 7

1921

A TWO-MASTED SCHOONER SLICED THROUGH silver sea, heading from Massachusetts to Newfoundland on a bait run. Aboard was Kevin who had made many trips out and back, a deckhand on this very banker. This trip, however, was one way only. He was not returning to Boston. Kevin had clenched his jaw around that decision. Nothing to do with distaste for the fishing life. Everything to do with love of his home life. He would erase all distance between himself and Newfoundland.

Kevin had sampled a different kind of living in the United States. When he left home at sixteen, he stole money to book passage from St. John's harbour to Boston where he got a job as an ironworker, putting beams into buildings that scraped their way into clouds. Kevin had no misgivings about heights and could climb with the speed of a powder monkey, but those steel beams had nothing on a schooner's mast. Nary a bit of sway. As for concrete, it was colder than pack ice. Harder, too. And the people in Boston? Best kind, most of them, just too many, that's all. Swarming like flies. In the city, he couldn't hear his ears for the ruckus. On the sea, it was silent, save for the thump of wind on sail, slap of wave on hull. Sure, the gulls swarmed and screeched when the boat was heavy with fish, but that was a different kind of noise. Music to Kevin's ears.

No gulls this morning; the breeze was slight but the staysail and jib dragged it in and the boat slipped along effortlessly. Kevin was coiling rope on deck, paying little heed to the coastline. When he did look up, his island home came into view and thoughts of his little sister, Clara, stabbed at him. He did not flinch. His father, should have, would have seen to Clara. That was the job of a man: to take care of his own.

Something punctured his hand. He dropped the rope. He held his arms out, palms toward him, and stared at his life mapped out in wide, white scars. Old man hands he had, and him only twenty-one. A line of red trickled across one palm. Kevin shrugged. Another lodged fish hook that, like every slip of a knife or hatchet, would forge a welt. He ripped out the hook and stuck his hand alongside, into ocean spray. As the sting hit, memory erupted again: Clara. He shook it off; he would not, could not, go back to Argentia, to the Avalon Peninsula. No, his home was across Placentia Bay, on the Burin now, with Mavis and the young ones.

Kevin's heart quickened as images of his wife, Mavis, and his children, Jimmy and Marie, ran loose in his head. Yes, definitely his last trip out of Boston; he'd made a good living on this schooner, nothing to be sneezed at. Times were hard, but the pull of home was harder. What was it the old timers said? All a man needed was a punt, a pig, and a potato patch and he could make his way. Was he foolish as a capelin, siding up with that thinking? Maybe, but he needed to be near home. Kevin couldn't recall where he was, what he was doing on the day that his baby brother died. All he knew was he had stumbled into the kitchen and there was Jimmy, still and blue in his mother's arms. He'd been too late to help Jimmy. What if something befell Mavis and the young ones in his absence? Kevin shuddered and went back to work.

When the schooner dropped its bow and stern lines in St. John's, Kevin took his leave. He boarded a coastal boat which skirted coves and inlets for many days before it docked in Burin. From there he started hoofing it: three or more miles from harbour to home.

It was early morning and the sun was sucking up rays—sundogs—from the water. Not a good sign, weather wise; could be some wind and rain coming in. Still it was a decent time of year, late spring: robins warbling from meadows spattered with clover, gulls wailing from wharves strewn with cod. He could picture the headlands later in the year: plump with the reds and yellows of partridgeberries and cranberries and bake-apples. Maybe he'd traipse the sponge of the bogs, berry picking, family in tow. A nice thought. Unlikely though. He'd barely have time to get his land legs in the summer; he'd be bobbing in the dory, jigging cod. Didn't matter. Knowing Mavis, the cellar would be crammed with jam for the winter anyway.

Kevin came upon the Catholic Church that was perched on a cliff at the water's edge. A miracle it was standing, the people said. Storms gusted in and out, still the church hung there, held up by what? The will of God? Maybe he should dart in, light a candle, grateful to be home from the sea. He tossed the idea around, then plodded past, making do with a bowed head and an abrupt sign of the cross. He was getting nigh onto home when he heard a familiar, raspy voice.

"Kev, b'y! How's she goin'?"

Kevin looked up and grinned. "Tom! How's yourself and the missus?"

"Finest kind, b'y. Finest kind."

Kevin had skipped the church, but, for Tom Murphy, he stopped. He clomped across the rocky road, releasing clouds of brown dust that danced and disappeared in the breeze.

Tom was in his own meadow, nearer the side of the road than to his house on the rise, shaping the keel of an upturned dory. No better man than Tom at the boat-building despite his affliction. It still touched Kevin's soul to see Tom's stumps of fingers. Only a thumb on his right hand, a couple of digits on the left. The result of a vicious sea that capsized his schooner. Tom and his mates had spent hours being battered by freezing water. When rescuers dragged Tom out, his body was frozen, stiff as a plank. Took days to thaw him out proper like. No finer man around than Tom Murphy.

"Where are them three brothers of yours?" said Kevin. "Think they'd be helping you with this here dory."

"Now you knows as well as I do that even if they gave her all she could suffer, I'd be finishing the work meself." Tom raised the plane and puffed at the blade; flecks of sawdust bounced onto on his scruff of beard. He set the tool down on the keel and pulled out a tobacco pouch. "Got time for a smoke, Kev?"

Kevin nodded. He watched, wide-eyed, as Tom rolled two cigarettes between what remained of his fingers. "Got it in my head that I'm not going back to Boston," said Kevin.

"Can't be blaming ya for that."

"Suppose I can make me living fishing inshore?"

Tom passed him a cigarette and stuck one in his own mouth. He worried his shirt pocket for matches. Cigarettes lit, he puffed out a smoke ring. "For a time, b'y. For a time. You're well able for it. You can always jump on a merchant schooner, if it needs be. There's the sealing, too."

Kev sucked on his cigarette, exhaling in a sigh. He picked grains of tobacco from his lower lip and flicked them into the breeze.

Tom leaned across the keel. "Not what you wants to hear, now is it, b'y? Truth of it is, living and working, working and living: same thing. You goes where the work is." He dragged on his cigarette and nodded. "Yep. Don't have to scrape me noggin much over that one. Working and living. One and the same, when you got a family to feed." Another drag on the cigarette. "Mavis was by here the other day having a cuffer with the missus. Them two can sure talk. You knows she'll be right glad at the sight of ya."

"Yes, b'y. Better be gettin' on home." Kevin killed his smoke, doffed his cap, and went on his way, mulling things over as he trudged along. Tom Murphy had a good twenty years on Kevin, an old dog for the hard road, he was. But Kevin didn't want wisdom, not yet. Would things come to no good end if he just hugged the shore?

As his home came into view, he picked up his pace. He stopped again, right in front of the house. It sat on a slight rise, a full two stories, a red door dead centre, multi-paned windows on each side, up and down. Behind it was the sea; no more than fifty feet from house to shore. The steep saddle roof dropped halfway down the back where there was only one story and one window. When the ocean gales slammed the rear of the house, struggle as they might, they could not find entry. Even rain falling in reeves, hammered in by wind, did no damage; it just washed over the angled roof and drained down the hill into the sea, keeping base and floorboards dry as a bone. Snow could drop and drift, banks of eight or ten feet, but there was no pile up on his roof. No fear of cave ins. Kevin nodded, proud of his skills; built the same house as his father, the same way his father built it, right down to putting in a second door at the side, not at the back, again to make it harder for the ocean wind to snake its way in.

Kevin let out a sigh. It was work that created this home, and work that would keep it. He'd have to allow Tom was right. He'd have to go where the work was. But for now, he was home.

The wind picked up, setting sheets on a clothesline to flapping. Obviously laundry day, but where was Mavis? As if in response, she appeared, skirting around to the front of the house, laundry basket on her hip. She dropped the basket under an empty clothesline. Kevin smiled. Mavis looked for all the world like a streel as the wind slashed at her clothes and hair. She stuck a clothes peg into her mouth and poked wayward strands of hair behind her ears. A fine waste of time, for as soon as she pegged a sheet onto the line, her hair was slapping her face again.

Kevin was instantly taken back to the first time he saw her, the first hello from her. The wind was teasing her then, too, whipping colour into her round cheeks. It wasn't laundry she was at that day; she was hauling lunch to her boss, the man in charge of that Boston high rise Kevin was working on. She had bumped into Kevin with her basket and he had turned. Her 'sorry' was from her heart and her voice was from his home, a distinctive Irish lilt. Mavis had smiled her hello, her eyes had twinkled, and he was done for. Completely in love with this stout little woman, around his age, he had figured, although he was never much for sorting people's ages. He couldn't see much of her hair that day as it was imprisoned under a maid's cap, but a few brown wisps stuck out, framing her face. He remembered reaching a hand out, poking a hair in for her. How brazen was he at all? He had instantly withdrawn his hand, figuring she'd turn heel and run. And he wouldn't have faulted her for that, not one bit. But no. She stood her ground, almost as if she sensed his embarrassment. Then she had swatted his arm, a playful gesture and smiled. No finer smile to be found.

As Mavis turned to shake out a stubborn lump of laundry, she caught sight of Kevin, and let out a squeal. The bunched up sheet was tossed aside as she came running. Kevin scooped her in.

"It's some good to have you home, b'y," she said.

———◆———

1921

WITH THE CHILDREN SETTLED THAT night, Kevin and Mavis sat at the kitchen table, the oil lamp aglow between them. "I won't be underfoot for long," he began.

"Underfoot?" Mavis chuckled. "And you as welcome as the angels in heaven."

Kevin smiled, lit with contentment. He would do whatever it took to preserve this feeling, to take care of his family. The way of it was to work for it. "I got to stake my ground inshore," he said. "There's more work than I can fit hands with: jig the cod, pile 'em to the gunwales, row 'em back, prong 'em to the stage, cut, head, split, wash and brine 'em. Then I'll be back out again. Dawn to dusk I'll be at it." He straightened in his chair.

Her smile could have covered the whole island, east to west. "Grumbling words, some might say, but I can see the light in your eyes. You can count on me to spread, dry, and tally the catch. It'll all get done in the long run."

Kevin patted her arm, letting his hand rest there a minute.

She pulled away and pointed a finger at him. "But you'll have to be dealing with Artemius Nolan at the merchant store." Mavis shook her head slowly. "He won't be giving you much for your labours."

"I'll get a fair price. Artemius is not bad as merchants go."

"Not bad? Merchants are all tarred with the same brush. That Artemius got more lip than a coal bucket, always going on about the strangest notions."

"He's been around the world and then some." Kevin shrugged. "Maybe his notions are not so strange in other places."

"You been everywhere; don't hear you spinning stories."

"No doubt I been as far as ever a puffin flew. But I go to sea for a living; men like Artemius go to see the world."

"True enough. But still, he's a merchant. Rogues, the lot of them. Might be easier if you went back on the Boston bankers."

"Better than building high rises. But Boston is not for me."

Mavis clapped a hand to her chest. "Surely be to goodness you don't be sorry you went to Boston in the first place."

Kevin smiled. "You knows better than that."

"And you didn't mind moving here to the Burin, Kev?" she asked, her voice halting, soft. "My aunt was sorely in need of help then, God rest her soul." She made the sign of the cross.

Kevin leaned in and took her hand. "Perish those dark thoughts, woman. I'm home. Happy a man as the ocean will allow." He released her hand and sat back. "I'll be off in the dory, harvesting that very ocean, the once."

"Not too soon, you won't," Mavis said. The dory didn't paint itself while you were away. One of the Murphy brothers offered to have at it, but I waved him off. Knew you'd be home in jig time. And, truth be told, I wants ya around for a few days yet." She angled her head toward the door. "Paint's in the shed where ya left it."

Kevin was up and about at first light the next morning. He examined the house. The inside was snug, but outside? A few clapboards winked at a nudge from the wind, the roof threatened to leak at the next drop of rain, and the chimney was stopped with soot, a blaze in the offing. Kevin nodded: nail, tar, sweep. As soon as he had the supplies, he would make quick work of those jobs. One thing he did stop to fix: the horseshoe over the front door. What good was a good luck symbol that was turned upside down?

He headed from the house toward the shore making a mental note to level out the ruts in the path so Mavis wouldn't trip. Once on the wharf, he stamped and scuffed across the planks; they swayed with the tide, but didn't give, nary a crack in them. He removed the tarp from the upturned dory; the gunwale sported a rift, the seams screamed at him. Well, that was that: he'd be hammering and caulking before slapping on the yellow and green. He ran his hand along the keel, scraped off a few chips of paint, and gave the boat a loving pat. They'd be working buddies again soon enough.

He strode from the wharf to the shed, the outbuilding where he kept all his provisions, tools, workbench, even carcasses over the winter. The door resisted, creaking, as he shoved it in. Sunshine flooded the cramped space. His footfall awakened cranky floorboards and set comfortable dust in motion. Kevin clomped around, investigating every shelf and bucket and jar. Mavis was right—plenty of paint. But other supplies were needed; the tar bucket was particularly wanting. There was nothing else to do here; it was time to pay the merchant a visit.

The bell above the store door jangled as Kevin entered. Nolan was standing beside the cash register, shoulders hunched, poring over an accounts ledger. His long face was haggard-looking, as always. Artemius was the skinniest human Kevin had ever laid eyes on, so thin you could almost see the sins on the man's soul. Long-limbed, gangly, too. His dark hair was plastered back with some stuff, Kevin didn't know what. Artemius must have heard the bell, but he didn't look up. Kevin didn't expect him to.

Kevin hovered; he hated owing and he hated asking. *Get on with it, b'y. The first sip of broth is always the hottest.* He stuttered into motion, stood at the counter. It was usually the merchant who had the first word. "Good morning to you, Artemius," said Kevin, crossing his arms.

Artemius peered over his eyeglasses. "Back from Boston, I see," he said, his voice sharp like the edge of a hatchet. He raised his head, pulled his shoulders back. "Boston bankers not to your liking?" He cackled, long and shrill, then turned back to his ledger.

Bile erupted in Kevin's gut and surged upward. He opened his mouth, ready to spew, then seamed his lips again. *Don't let your tongue cut your throat, b'y.* He scanned the well-stocked store. He would clamp teeth on tongue, get the things he needed, then leave. Could he jig enough cod to settle the debt he was about to incur? "Decided to fish inshore," he said.

"What are you looking for today?" said Artemius.

"Low on supplies. Work to do around the house. Then I have to get meself into the dory."

"Pick up what you need. I'll be keeping my accounts book handy."

"Hoping to settle my account come the fall, after a good summer of cod jigging. Who'll be the culler this season, Artemius?"

"Jacob. Finest kind, he is, finest kind. He'll grade your catch and give you a fair price. Mind you, hard to know now what that price is. Depends on the market. Changes with the wind and the tide, it does."

"Just tryin' to make sure I get my fair share, Artemius. Won't do to have me owing come fall. Have to support the missus and the children over the winter."

"Well, if the sea behaves herself, you'll do alright. You might even be able to get goods for Christmas."

"No odds about Christmas, not yet. Just want to stay home, off the bankers."

"Done a lot of travelling myself. Home is best, though."

Did Artemius mean "home" in Newfoundland, or "home" in England? The talk was that Artemius had two homes. Kevin let out another sigh. It was important to stay on good terms with Artemius. There's favour in hell if you make friends with the devil.

Kevin handpicked his supplies and stacked them on the edge of the counter. He glanced occasionally at Artemius whose hooked nose was still buried in his ledger. No doubt the man was king around here. Was he a rogue as Mavis suspected? Kevin had his doubts; he had once seen Artemius extend credit to someone who could never, ever repay. Artemius was a higher up, that's all. The way of things. Merchants were masters; fishermen were servants.

Before Kevin knew it, spring slid by, summer too. When the evenings started closing in, he settled his account with Artemius. Now that he was beholden to no one, Kevin's pride poured; for a time, he was every bit as good as his master. He had credit left over and could lay in supplies—molasses, flour, pork, and salt beef—for the winter.

In November, he made his way into the woods and chopped trees, enough to heat his home. He even piled up extra logs to haul to both church and rectory. Wouldn't do to let the priest get a chill now, would it?

In December, with dory upended and storeroom stocked, Kevin settled in, determined to make the best of being indoors for the winter. Daily, while the young ones were at school or asleep, while Mavis scraped porridge or scoured pots, he thumbed through a three-day-old newspaper. Then he spread the paper on one side of the table and dumped his project—whatever happened to need doing—on top of it. Whether he was tying flies, knitting nets, or polishing boots, Kevin felt comfort in fixing, his body listing, drawn by the lilt of Mavis' voice as she sang through her chores.

One odd morning, the air around him was hushed. He shifted in his chair. He was in the process of making boots, stretching leather over last, tapping nails into soles. The job required precision so he kept at it. Still, the stillness dogged him. Why wasn't Mavis singing? When the chair beside him clawed the floor, he ventured a glance. Mavis was perched on the edge of the chair, clutching an old sewing box, a sheen of purpose in her eyes. What was she on about? He put down his hammer. "Out with it," he said.

"I been writing to your sister for a few months now," said Mavis. She placed the box on her lap.

Clara? Kevin's spark of interest was doused by an icy chill. It crossed his mind that he should add some wood to the fire.

Mavis opened the sewing box and emptied its visible contents onto the table: reels of thread, a packet of needles, and a travel sewing kit. One spool of thread rolled off the table, bouncing and bumping to rest at a crack in a floorboard. Ignoring it, Mavis lifted the top level of the box to reveal another compartment which housed a bundle of letters tied in black ribbon.

"You've been keeping letters?" Feeling like he had to do something, not knowing what, Kevin got to his feet. He headed for the stove, shoved in another log, and then paced the floor. Out of the corner of his eye, he watched Mavis push the jettisoned sewing notions aside. She removed the letters from the sewing box. She didn't say anything as she untied the ribbon and fanned the letters onto the table. She leaned back in her chair.

Kevin, adrift in the middle of the kitchen, couldn't stop shivering. He glanced toward the porch. Surely there must be something that needed doing in the shed. He looked back at Mavis. Time stretched. He didn't move.

Mavis selected one letter and removed it from its envelope. The air sparked with the crispness of paper unfolding, the crackle of wood burning. Mavis held the letter open, poised, ready to read. Her fingers trembled. The paper rustled. She waited. After a few seconds, she patted his chair, a gentle nudge. Then she looked up, meeting his gaze.

It was the light in her eyes that ignited warmth in Kevin. He took a deep breath; ease filtered in. What would he ever do without Mavis? A dark premonition passed through him. He jerked forward, away from it, toward his wife. When he was beside her, he came to a standstill again. He couldn't free himself from the sensation that the world was some-how shifting. With his heart pounding, Kevin scooped up the runaway thread and reclaimed his chair.

Mavis moved the letter slowly toward him. He toyed with the spool of thread as he looked at the paper. The black lines on the page brought to mind the curls and holes in Mavis' knitted doilies: Kevin couldn't read handwriting. He did fine with printed words, but had left school long before he was allowed at pen and inkwell.

"I'll read it to you," said Mavis.

Kevin melted into her offer. A kind woman, Mavis. She would never comment on his lack of schooling. "So long as you reads news about Clara, about my father. Skip over the parts about Kathleen Kerrigan."

Mavis looked at him, her eyes searching. "But why--"

The torment of memories that Kevin had tried long and hard to bury now crept up to the rim of his thoughts. He felt his jaw tighten. How could he ever reveal the evil that was Kathleen Kerrigan to a saint of a woman like Mavis? What kind of mother would...? He dropped the · thread and gripped the sides of his chair. "Sometimes you got to leave well enough alone."

"All right then. I'll only tell you the things that won't upset you none. Good enough?"

"And when you writes back, you'll tell her we're all fine?"

"And that's as true as the Gospel," Mavis said.

"As true as the Gospel," echoed Kevin, shunning his fears and focusing on her words. Mavis was right. The ocean had been kind this year. The fish had been plentiful, darn near eating the rocks. He released his grip on the chair and glanced upward, a nod of gratitude to the heavens. It wasn't so foolish after all, his decision to hug the shore. He could forget the past and just focus on the now.

Losing his dory was the last thing on his mind.

CHAPTER 9

1922 - 1925

FEW FISHERMEN COULD BOAST THAT they had gone three seasons without sending so much as a jigger to the deep. Kevin didn't dare boast; Mavis wouldn't allow for it. "Pride goeth before a fall," she said, so he kept his gob shut. Still, he made no attempt to banish the puffed-up feeling that lived in his chest. Yes, for the past three years the sea had bent to his will, offering everything, taking nothing. He was grateful but proud, too. He had earned his victory.

In the spring of 1925, at the merchant store, he breathed easy as he bartered for supplies. He had no doubt that, come fall, he would again emerge debt free.

On the first morning out, the sun was with him. He adjusted his cap against the rays, not that they bothered him much. Sun, rain, and sleet were all the same to him. Wind was different; it was wind that he bowed to. Any fisherman with half a head on his shoulders would wait out, not head into, a gale. Fog could be trouble too, but it was manageable if it wasn't too thick. Had to be wary, that's all.

This spring, like every other, Kevin slipped with ease into the rhythm of the work: lowering the jigger, jerking the line, sensing the strike, reeling the cod in hand over hand. Steady and patient, he was. Every now and then he'd pause and check the sky, making sure Mother Nature was alongside. On this day, there wasn't a single cloud, except for the cloud of gulls screeching for a helping. Kevin tossed them an occasional morsel, but there was no end to their wanting. Ingrates, the lot of them. But they were part and parcel of everything. He let them scream and got on with the job.

It was a successful day, as was almost every spring day that followed. An occasional pitch of wind, mists in May, rain in June. Nothing untoward. It was late summer when the bottom fell out, and even that day started out right.

It was windless. Cloudless, too. A short fin maco had clamped onto a chunk of squid on the jigger and Kevin was grappling to release it. Small but feisty, the shark sank its teeth into Kevin's sweater sleeve. Kevin freed the intruder, tossed it back where it belonged, and examined the sweater cuff. He frowned. Mavis would be none too happy with that gaping hole, those dangling threads. He shook his head and glanced up.

A bank of fog was rolling in, thick, murky, just yards from his boat, moving fast. The moan of a foghorn cut the air, sending vibrations to his core. Maybe he had been too busy to notice the fog, but the horn? Where was his mind at all? How far offshore was he anyway? A sharp turn of his head and he took it all in: he was closing in on the jagged rock that fortified the shoreline. He yanked at the killick only to fall back, holding a chewed piece of rope. What the hell had happened to that anchor? The shark must have-- No odds about the shark. In a lick and a lap, he'd either be out of this mess, or into the drink. He grabbed for the oars which clattered as he set them in the oarlocks and tightened the tholepins. He leaned back and stopped, oars in mid-air, as a long, steady swishing sound reached his ears, a sound with which he was entirely too familiar. Jesus sufferin' Christ. How close was that damn schooner?

In seconds, the schooner's bow pierced the fog and it was upon him, scraping, grinding, crushing. The dory jack-knifed, the bow and stern rising slowly to greet each other, the thwart with Kevin dropping low. He let out a gasp as the shock of icy water slapped him. He jumped aside, anything to get out of harm's way. The tattered cuff of his sweater hooked on a tholepin and pulled him back; he grabbed at his belt for his knife. Not there. How stupid was he at all to tie the knife to the oar-lock? He flailed his arms but could not get at that knife. His boots were filling up, dragging him down. One thing he didn't want was to owe the merchant for boots. Christ Almighty! How stunned are ya, b'y? Better debt than dead. He reached again as he was going under, missed the knife, but kept his eyes on it. The sheathed knife, still tied to the sinking boat, was rising in the water, taunting, teasing. He pushed forward and grabbed again. He latched onto the sheath, released the knife, and slashed a swathe out of his sweater. Arms free, he pulled off the boots, and burst for the surface. He choked in a lifesaving breath just as the dory, his constant companion, breathed in its last. With a groan, the dory, with bait, tackle, oars, everything, joined his killick in the deep.

Kevin, still gasping, let out a rhyme of curse words even he didn't know he knew. But even as he was thrashing in icy water, he wasn't blaming the sea. Served him right. Him and his pride.

By the time the schooner owned its blunder and retrieved the oarsman, Kevin was beyond exhausted, almost cold enough to be anointed. But he was alive.

Before he was safely ashore, the depth of his negligence hit him. The summer was nearing an end and he could catch no fish in the fall. An empty stage, an empty stomach. He would have no supplies for winter. Yes, he could rebuild. No doubt about that. Like his father, Kevin Kerrigan could hammer a nail the same with the right hand as with the left. A new dory was no problem. But there'd be no time to launch it this season, no way to make up the loss.

His heart sank. In the fall, he'd be going to Boston, working a banker, or building high rises. With Mavis in a family way again, he had no choice. He could depend on neighbours to help his family stack wood for the winter, but he could not depend on them for everything. He'd be gone a long time; wouldn't come back until late spring, after he worked as a batsman with the sealing party.

Every mistake has a price. The fog was coming. He should have seen it.

CLARA

CHAPTER 10

———◆———

1925

CLARA TRAIPSED FROM WOOD PILE to house, arms loaded, sweat beading from her brow. She stopped for a breather. It was a summer day, too fine, too calm, with the gulls flying in from the sea. A weather breeder, to be sure. That's what her father would call it. It didn't seem possible though, that a day like this could turn on you.

The slam of a door turned her attention to the house. She watched as her father stomped toward her, thumbs hooked into his suspenders. "Yer mother is coming home this week," he said and brushed past, nudging her with his elbow.

Clara's arms went slack. "Ouch!" She jumped back as a chunk of wood landed on her boot. For a few seconds, she stood there, blinking. Then she collected the dropped splits and lugged them into the house. She plopped down at the kitchen table, still, silent, searching her soul. After eight long years, her mother was coming home. What kind of a daughter was she that this did not make her happy? Why was there such a sour taste in her mouth? Try as she might, Clara couldn't find a glimmer of joy. Just Clara and Daddy. That's the way it had been; that's the way she liked it. What would happen to her now?

On the day that her mother was to return, Clara cleaned every inch of the house and it gleamed. Then she planted herself on the daybed, biding her time until her father returned from the train station, her

mother in tow. She clutched her stomach which was skittering something terrible. Was she going to be sick? Again?

Earlier, her father had caught her outside, in the vegetable garden,
vomiting on the cabbages, and had dragged her into the house. "What
in the name of God ails you?"

"It's the nerves in me stomach."

For a few seconds he had gawked at her, his brow creased. Then he
took a step back. "Yer mother's coming today. Get a hold on yerself."

Clara had nodded, wiping her hand across her mouth. Then she
had retched again, spattering the freshly-scrubbed floor with the scant
contents of her stomach.

Her father abruptly turned his back. "I'm poisoned with this," he
muttered as he clomped to the door, through the door. Sniffling, she
waited. As was his way, he returned with final words. "Clean it up."

She had cleaned it up. Following that, she managed to suppress the
urge to spew. Then she had claimed her spot on the daybed and there
she sat while morning slipped into afternoon.

When the rumble of the carriage wheels reached Clara's ears, she refused to move. Not an inch, the stubborn girl. Her mother had left without
so much as a goodbye. Why should Clara be the one to do the greeting?

At the sound of the door, Clara sat up straight and crossed her arms.
She looked up as her mother toddled in, just inches ahead of her husband. Clara's resolve instantly vanished. "Mommy?" The word shot from
her mouth like a bird released from a cage.

"Mommy" took one look at Clara and fainted dead away.

Clara turned to her father who shooed her out of the kitchen and hurried to help his wife. And, instantly, grim truth struck. From then on, her
father's attention would be all-consumed: Kathleen this. Kathleen that.

Clara had lost her father.

In the days that followed, Clara struggled to keep her bitterness contained. She barged through her chores, shaking a fist as she pushed a
dust mop past the parlour where her mother slept. She served food to

Kathleen, rattling things around on the tray, baring her teeth in a smile, making her voice sing with unfelt sweetness.

One day, Clara was in the front hallway, dust rag in hand, when Kathleen's reedy voice sang out, calling her daughter. Clara froze, crossing her arms and waiting, hoping Kathleen would simply drift off to sleep. But no, the sound continued like needy bleats from a spring lamb.

"Cla-a-a-ra. Cla-a-a-ra."

A sudden wave of longing washed over Clara. She held her breath as she opened the door and leaned in. "You called me, Mommy?" She tossed the dust rag to the floor behind her, smoothed her apron, and stepped into the room, head and hope high.

"That's far enough." Kathleen held up one hand, palm facing Clara. "Go to the church," she said, her voice wavering. "Confession is good for the soul."

Clara blinked. "But what am I supposed to confess?"

Kathleen Kerrigan narrowed her eyes, let out a long sigh, and turned to face the wall.

Clara's mind raced, searching. "But what am I...?" She let the question hang there and retreated, pulling the door shut. For a few seconds she stood, her heart pounding in her ears. Then she retrieved her dust rag and launched into a cleaning frenzy, attacking banister and spindles and newel posts. At the top of the stairs, she paused, knowing. She had been tripping over herself to help her father, but had sulked and sneered over helping her mother. There it was then, the rights of it. Some gall she had, sinning against the fourth commandment. *Honor thy father AND thy mother.* Couldn't get much clearer than that. She scurried down the stairs.

At the Holy Rosary Church, Clara pushed through the door which clattered shut behind her creating a deep rumbling echo. She dipped her fingers into the pool of stagnant holy water, puzzling over the green mark that circled the inside of the font. The water dripped from her fingers. *Plop, plop.* Another echo. A person couldn't whisper a prayer in here without it being heard throughout the building.

Clara tiptoed into the nave and sat in a pew near the confessional. Not a soul around. It was Saturday, wasn't it? There were always confessions on Saturday. She squirmed. The pew was as hard as stone, polished to a sheen. She ran her hand over the smooth wood. Not a speck of dust in this place. How on earth did the women around here manage to clean everything, especially all those statues, the Stations of the Cross, and the main altar? Clara looked up at the huge bone-white altar with all its curls and spirals. She stared at the statue to the right of the altar, the Virgin Mary, the best mother of all. She let out a long, low sigh. Jesus would have been kind to his mother, she was sure of that. It was while she was staring at the Virgin's blue veil that Clara realized she had forgotten something. Women weren't allowed to be bareheaded in church. Quickly, she pulled a scarf from her pocket and tied it over her hair. Another sin. Seemed she was full of sins these days. Not that it mattered when there was no one here to witness it, and no one to hear her confession.

She was about to leave when she heard a distinct sound coming from the blackness of the confessional. The clearing of a throat. Someone was here after all. Father Mahony. Clara didn't hesitate. She went straight into the confessional and launched into "Bless me, Father, for I have sinned."

After confession, Clara slid back into her pew. Father Mahony had let her off easy: a few *Our Fathers*, *Hail Marys*, *Glory Bes* and a promise to be kind to her mother. Kneeling, she dutifully recited her penance. Then she lingered. A rainbow of light streamed into the church, brushing the pews, fanning the floor near the base of a pillar. Clara followed the light from tile floor to tall window: a stained-glass image of the Blessed Virgin Mary. Even Jesus had a mother. Had Mary always had that glow around her? Had she ever been a source of night to her Son like Kathleen Kerrigan was to Clara?

Ever since her mother had come home, Clara's world was as dark as the confession box she had just left. When Clara's mother first left, Clara had missed her. She had missed Kevin, too. But now? Things were fine the way they were, just herself and Daddy. What right did Kathleen Kerrigan have anyway, pushing her daughter toward confession today? It was Kathleen, not Clara, who had taken off, leaving her family to fend for themselves. Some nerve the woman had. Showing up again. Stealing Daddy away. Clara took a few deep breaths in an attempt to calm herself. Surely be to goodness she was sinning against the fourth commandment here, thinking such hateful thoughts about her own mother. In that case, she deserved to be here, didn't she, on her knees, saying penance? But she wasn't the least bit sorry; if anything, she was fired right to the eyes. Father Mahony said she should be grateful for her life, rise above it all, not be moping about and causing problems for her father. She would if she could. How many *Our Fathers* and how many *Hail Marys* would it take to rise above it all? The rosary beads rattled as she shoved them into her pocket. A whole rosary said. Did she feel any better? No. Her heart and soul were the colour of Alphonse Kerrigan's boot polish, no doubt about that.

Closing her eyes, she remembered the many times her father had used that black polish, wrapping a ragged piece of a flannel sheet around two fingers, dipping into the cake of polish, retrieving a black clump, and making tiny circles on the toe of his boot. Periodically, he would stop and look up, his eyes misty, his face sagging. His lips would part and a melody would pour, a wavering Irish lilt: *I'll Take You Home Again, Kathleen*. Every time, without exception, the singing cut her, deep. She would rush to him and…

Clara sucked in a breath and could have sworn that she smelled the polish. She shuddered and opened her eyes, wide. Fingers trembling, she fumbled in her pocket for the beads and started another rosary, muttering the prayers aloud, anything to keep dark thoughts at bay. When she got near the end, she slowed her pace; she was in no hurry to go home. Home, where her Dad would be wanting his supper, where she would have to peel potatoes to go with that salt beef she'd been soaking all day, where she would have to help with her mother. Clara's jaw throbbed from being clamped shut. Where was the fairness in all of this? Was there a God in heaven? If there was, He better show her some kind of sign, anything to get the evil out of her head. Right now, all she wanted to do was make her parents pay. Vengeance was supposed to be God's, wasn't it? Somehow in between her rampant thoughts, she managed to complete the rosary. Still in no hurry, she remained on her knees. It was so quiet here. Was there no one else about, just her and the priest? The confessional door whined open, clicked shut, answering her question. Father Mahony was done for the day.

She stood to leave. As she turned, she came to a standstill. Who was that, next to Father Mahony? A man, an older man, maybe her father's age. A man with blond hair. He was tall, taller than her dad, taller than her brother Kevin. Odd that he was wearing a suit. Suits were for Sundays and weddings and funerals. Not for weekdays. Here it was, a Friday, and this man was done up to the nines.

The stranger glanced at her. He turned away. But he quickly looked back, his eyes wide. He smiled. His eyes glinted. Blue. Bright blue. Why did those eyes look familiar? Clara felt her cheeks flush; the warmth spread, flooding her whole body.

Father Mahony hadn't noticed her so she sneaked behind a pillar, perking an ear as the two men conversed in whispers, their voices a series of overlapping echoes. Try as she might, she couldn't make out a word. It was the slap of shoe leather on tile that told her they were leaving. She followed them, scurrying down the aisle, to the foyer, through the door, to the outside. Blinded by the sun's glare, she raised a hand to her eyes. Thank God and all the Saints, they were still there. She exhaled, loud and fast, startling herself. She hadn't even realized that she had been holding her breath. The blue-eyed stranger looked at her again. This time, so did the priest.

"Clara," Father Mahony said, "you should be running on home now. Your parents will be needing you."

"Yes, Father." But then Clara made a display of pulling her head back and straightening her shoulders. She wasn't going anywhere.

The priest cleared his throat. "I hear your mother is doing better, poor Kathleen, God bless her. Did you light a candle for her today?"

"Yes, Father." The lie just fell off Clara's tongue and she let it sit there, on the church's wooden steps, in the sunshine of a June day. She could feel her cheeks warm from the lie, or maybe from the sun. She wasn't sure. Only knew that she'd be back in confession next week. No end to the penance for Clara Kerrigan.

"Ah, there's a good girl. You'd best be on your way now."

"Yes, Father." How stunned was she that she'd say the same thing three times? She pivoted and, in the process, cast a glance at Father Mahony's visitor. Clara was short for her age, "not fully grown," as her father always said. She was all of sixteen and only five feet tall. Her father must have been right because her sideways glance landed on the visitor's chest. She had to tilt her head back to see his eyes. Even bluer up close. She didn't know why her heart was trying to hammer its way out of her chest. She pulled off her scarf and stood there, staring.

Father Mahony cleared his throat again. "On your way now, Clara," he said, his voice taking on a no-nonsense tone. "Your dad is waiting for you, I'm sure."

"Yes, Father." Clara had no choice but to obey, even if she was taking her sweet time about it. Father Mahony was next to God, after all. She took a long, slow breath and dragged her eyes away from the tall fair-haired man. She trudged away, around the corner of the church. There she stood, glued to the wall, peeking out. Father Mahony had his back to her but the stranger could see her. He winked. She pulled her head in, breathless, and stuffed her scarf against her mouth to keep a giggle from escaping. Heaven forbid the noise waft on the wind to the ear of Father Mahony. Oh, the trouble she'd be in then. She poked her head out a second time. Father Mahony was looking at the ground. The stranger winked again. Again she pulled her head back. A child's game this, but Clara didn't care. What was she to do now? She couldn't leave. If she left, she might never see this man again. If she stayed, she'd surely be found out by someone darting in for a late Friday confession. But if sinners were going to show up, they'd be here by now, wouldn't they? Most people went to confession on Saturday, didn't they? She closed her eyes and pictured the face of the visitor, the high cheek bones and the steel blue eyes. Could her heart beat any faster?

A tap on her shoulder. She jumped. A voice in her ear: "I'm Patrick."

She opened her eyes and was looking into his face, for real this time. "Patrick," she repeated, loving the way her lips curled around the name. The softness of the P, the click of the K.

"Yes, Patrick," he said. "Happy to meet you, Clara."

A few months later, Clara was on a coastal boat, travelling across the bay to the Burin Peninsula to spend the winter with her brother's family.

KATHLEEN

———◆———

CHAPTER 11

IT IS SPECTRAL AND SILENT, the sea.

Today, the North Atlantic is a silver ghost under carpet of fog, slipping an arm into a small cove on the Burin Peninsula and hovering there. Waiting, perhaps, for an influx of March wind to roil it into breakers which taunt rocks and pylons. It hugs the landwash, eyeing the hued houses and inebriated stages and salt-coated flakes that stipple the shoreline. Breathing in, breathing out, caressing the land in sibilant whispers.

Fifty feet from shore, Kevin's salt box house is perched. An exact duplicate of the house his father had built in Argentia. White clapboard. Forest green shutters. Nary ribbon of paint nor chink of putty gone astray.

The door whines open.

The ocean inhales.

A young woman now, my Clara emerges, clutching her protruding belly. She wobbles down the path, her full-length, black woolen skirt swinging with her gait, and hobbles over beach rocks to the landwash, where she stands, brown eyes vacant.

The ocean exhales, fingering high-buttoned black boots. Clara raises her skirt with one hand and steps back, just out of reach. She clasps her shawl under her chin. Her gaze remains steadfast. Fog on sea. No horizon.

Gulls swoop and dive as they shriek their usual whys upon high. My Clara cringes. Does the avian cacophony gnaw at nerves already frayed by malaise of shame-filled days? Side-to-side she sways, murmuring "there, there" and humming "rock-a-bye." When her speech and melody dissolve to sighs, she lowers her eyes to the ripples pulsing the shore and tunes her breathing to their rhythm. Inhale, exhale. Does the smell of brine—the scent of home—offer a rivulet of contentment? Releasing her grip on her shawl, Clara slides her free hand across her swollen belly. Her hand recoils, a reaction to the exuberance of her unborn.

Tears flood my daughter's eyes.

Her sadness flows through me.

Clara is seventeen, banished. Soon she will return from exile, hollow. Her shoulders sag and tears cascade. She drags a corner of her shawl across her tear-stained face. The sea leans in and plants a kiss on the toe of her boot. She steps back, sniffles, and uses both arms to cradle her belly. It will be just hours before her child is plucked from her body like cod jigged from the sea. Her shoulders sink lower. Is guilt pressing her down? Does she wonder if she will rot in sin for the rest of her days?

Thunder rumbles in the distance. The sea shifts its mood, spitting ankle-biters. A gust of wind billows Clara's skirt, lifts her shawl, and steals it away. She thrusts her hand after it and then doubles over as a gush of liquid streams down her legs and a stiletto of pain slashes her back.

I ache, knowing that panic riots within her, that her heart is racing, her head spinning. She gulps in one giant breath, holds it for an instant, and discharges it in a raspy moan that escalates to a gull-like scream. Breathless, she tries to unfold, but the knife strikes again and her knees buckle. She sinks slowly, a foundered ship, slipping down, down until her brow thuds on a stone.

I watch, helpless, as the ocean slips in, surrounds, slides out. Clara's body stiffens with the shock of cold and then lurches, retching and convulsing. Sweat sluicing from every pore, she tilts her head toward the house. "Dear God and all the saints, send someone out to help me." Her prayer is a throaty whisper, swallowed by whip of wave and wind. Is her child destined to be born into the arms of the sea? Lost forever?

Wretched, I sigh. The child will be lost, at least to Clara, for Church and culture dictate that she give this child away. What was it I once told her? *It's the saddest thing in the world to lose your child.* How can she get past what I could not? How did I, as mother, allow the loss of one to obliterate the needs of all?

My heart bleeds for my girl.

CLARA

———◆———

1926

CLARA BLINKED REPEATEDLY AT THE blurred image of the house. Couldn't someone open that godforsaken door? Why in the name of all that's holy had her brother, Kevin, moulded his life around a mirror image of the salt box house they grew up in? She closed her eyes.

An image of the Holy Rosary Church reared up. The confessional, the black booth of the contrite. Shadows of bodies entwined, a sliver of light under the door, the jutting of a metal grate in her back as she was hoisted onto the tiny shelf reserved for hands folded in prayer. Herself and Patrick. A man nigh onto father's age. A man she had just met. A come-from-away. But from where? Had he just scudded to shore on wind and wave? Where had he disappeared to? What was it about him that compelled her to strip the good from her soul? Had there been any good left in her soul to begin with?

Waves whispered in and out, rocking her gently. A skiff slapped against a nearby pier. A fog horn wailed at inshore boats. Danger. Danger. She heard it, the warning. Yes, yes, she heard everything but could move nothing. It was only when the pain ripped through her again that her body jerked. She opened her eyes and gasped. Still splayed on rocky shore, the icy sea sliding around her, her baby pressing against her, pushing to get out. Still alone. Her fear swelled. With her last ounce of strength, she sucked in a breath, opened her mouth and released a clarion shriek. Through bleary, grateful eyes, she saw her sister-in-law,

Mavis, clutching her own ripe abdomen as she waddled down the path from the house.

In seconds, Mavis was upon her, beside her. "Dear Father in heaven. Where's your head at, child, coming down here by your lonesome with your time almost come?" Mavis sank to her knees and crossed herself. "Thank the Lord that the midwife is here or I'd never be getting back on me own feet, never mind getting you to yours. Were you trying to drop your child into the sea?"

Clara reached a trembling hand to Mavis. "I-I-I'm scared." Her teeth chattered and she couldn't stop them.

"Sweet heart of Jesus. Yer lips are blue." Mavis screamed for the midwife, lifted Clara's shoulders, and hugged her close. "Help is coming. That ocean will be claiming no young 'uns today."

"Thank you," whispered Clara and slipped into darkness.

Later, while Clara was sweating and grunting, her privates slowly ripping apart, the midwife, whose angular body was as sharp as the knife she used to slit Clara's, took great pains to inform her that God was punishing her for her sins. "You brought all this on yourself, missy," she said. "It's likely that the good Lord won't send you no more young' uns. Serve you right, it would."

Clara flopped back onto a pillow, her body sliding in perspiration and slime. "Dear God! I can't do this no more!"

"Oh, you have no choice in the matter. Once you're in a family way, the baby's coming whether you likes it or not. Should have thought of consequences before you sinned against the Church." The midwife's voice was cold and hard, like the stubborn spring ice on Miller's Pond just over the path.

"You knows nothing about me--" Screams replaced Clara's words as spasms struck again and she was commanded to push. She obeyed, focusing all her rage upon the midwife. The Church owned that woman, like it did the lot of them, like it had disowned Clara.

"And how lucky are you that you got Mavis here. Her belly more swollen than your own." The midwife yammered on while Clara was besieged with pain. "The poor thing. Lumbering over the road to the knitting circle telling us all she's having twins. Are we all stunned or what? And me, sitting there in the lot of them, just waiting for me services to be called on. Sure and she deserves better than this."

"My mother and father sent me here--"

"Sure and what else would they be after doing? You and your shameful behaviour. Thank the Good Lord and all the saints your poor brother is off with the sealing party. By the time Kevin gets back, both the babies will be born and Mavis will serve him up some flip-per pie and show him his twins. Men are an ignorant bunch and the women around here won't be putting light to nothing. That knitting circle is tighter than a beginner's crack at knit-and-purl. And as for you, you better be prepared to be keeping your mouth shut for the rest of your days, missy."

Clara had heard enough, but that didn't stop the midwife's jaw from flapping. All Clara wanted was to be done with pain. To move on. 'You're wishing your time away,' her mother used to say. Clara couldn't wish this time away soon enough.

But Clara's mother was right. All too soon, the pain was done. Emptiness took over. A dark vacuum where warmth and love and pulse had resided. The midwife whisked the baby away. Clara's baby, Kate. Named for Clara's mother, Kathleen. Just whisked her away. In the dis-tance, the newborn cried and Clara's milk seeped. But Kate was hidden in the bedroom of Mavis, latched onto Mavis' breast.

Clara stayed at the perfectly built home of Mavis and Kevin and wore a path from it to the shoreline until March slid into mid-April. Then, she was released from exile. She headed home to Argentia, to her mother and father, Kathleen and Alphonse Kerrigan. Seventeen, shrunken, and shamed. Never again to see her child. Never to speak of her child. Maybe never again to know the weight of child. Home, where surely whispers of condemnation would trail her like her shadow. Home to the mirror image of Kevin's salt box house.

CHAPTER 13

CLARA GLANCED AT HER STONE-FACED father who had come to the wharf to meet her. She looked past him, searching. Clara lowered her head and allowed her shoulders and heart to follow. Her whole body was sinking, piece by piece, like a line of buoys dragged to the deep. Sinful girl. Had she really expected to see her mother?

Swallowing her shame, Clara lumbered down the gangplank. She angled an eye at her father and caught him looking at her belly. He nodded curtly. Her face flamed. She dropped her eyes and trailed him to the horse and wagon.

The ride to the house was silent, save for the clop of hoofs, stutter of wheels, and swish of waves. She stared at ocean spray spiraling from a cleft in the rocks. Was it spitting contempt at her? Nerves rubbed raw, she closed her eyes.

How was she going to live with this? Would anyone, would her mother, understand? From a corner of her soul, Clara dredged truth: her own loss did not hold a candle to her mother's. There was no coming back for Mommy's little Jimmy. But Kate? Hope fluttered in Clara's chest but, having nothing to cling to, slipped away. She latched onto the memory of herself as a little girl, sitting on a tree stump, waiting for Mommy to explain things. Mommy had always had a way with the stories, but that part of Kathleen Kerrigan was gone, as gone as little Jimmy.

Clara opened her eyes just as they rolled past a meadow, green now, dotted with yellow dandelions, lambs frolicking near their mothers.

Buds spiked on groves of lilac trees which would soon be awash with flowers and perfume. She sucked in a deep breath, seeking solace in the smells of home, the mixture of clover and salt air. None came.

As soon as the wagon came to a halt, Clara scrambled out, tore into the house, and headed for her tiny room on the second floor. She pulled down the rolled blind, closed the tatted curtains, and collapsed onto the bed. There she stayed, stroking the quilt that she had stitched at the knee of her mother, watching its rose pattern disappear with the daylight.

Once, only once, did her father knock on her door. He did not speak. He did not enter. Clara heard the stairs creak upon his retreat. She drifted to sleep, still clad in travelling skirt and coat. Her dreams tumbled: a little girl cowering under a daybed covering her ears, a young woman hovering on landwash cradling her belly.

The next morning, Clara awakened to drum of rain and odor of porridge. She reached to rub her eyes and discovered a face dripping with tears. A riptide of grief tore through her and she recoiled into a ball. She stayed that way, shuddering, until she heard the murmur of voices in the kitchen. Visitors? God, she hoped not. Clara raised herself to an elbow. She spotted a tray on the floor, just inside her door: breakfast. No way had her father made that porridge.

She pushed herself off the bed and cringed as a painful spasm hit her gut. God was still punishing her; she deserved it, she supposed. Slowly she made her way from bed to tray. She picked up the tray, put it on her dresser and opened the door, just a crack. From the kitchen came the voice of Dulcie Mullins. Clara rolled her eyes. Of course, Dulcie was making a dart in. Who else would it be? Clara could picture the chubby woman, curls and hairpins sticking out, offering her help.

"Lots more where that came from, Alphonse," Dulcie was saying. "I'd be happy to oblige with whatever you needs while Clara is recuperating from the consumption. 'Tis a blessing she made it home. Kathleen getting better, too, is she?"

Clara cringed. Consumption? Her heart accelerated and she shut the door without waiting for Alphonse Kerrigan's response. She sucked in a breath and held it, knowing that if she let it out, a scream as sharp as her father's splitting knife would accompany it. Everyone in the community knew her father to be an honest, God-fearing, hard-working man. Clara clamped her lips together and snorted her breath out. A sob escaped. She sniffed in again, hoping that she had not been heard. She pasted her ear to the door. No sound of approaching footsteps, only mutter of voices. She closed her eyes. Breathe. That's all she had to do. Just breathe.

Clara clung to the doorknob long enough to gather her senses, long enough for the steam to disappear from the porridge, long enough to be sure that Mrs. Dulcie Mullins was well on her way home. Then, tray in hand, she sneaked down the stairs, and tiptoed past her mother's room. She continued to the kitchen and sat at the table. She picked up her spoon and ate, never raising her head.

Her father hauled out a chair across from her and dropped down, sighing heavily. "One day off from the fishing I can do. But I has to lay in fish and get the catch to the merchant. Tomorrow, I'll be heading out in the dory. I'll be needing your help to keep the house going. With your mother sitting in a darkened room..."

Clara flinched.

Her father continued. "You'll have to help with the fishing. Splitting and salting the cod at the stagehouse. Spreading them on the flakes to dry. You can do the tally, too. Not for a few days, mind you, but after that..." His voice fell away, and the background hammer of rain on the kitchen window took over. The pane rattled in its casing.

Clara glanced at the daybed in the corner, the very one she had hidden under on the day that Jimmy was buried. She tightened her fingers around her spoon.

Her father stood and walked to the window. "Have to put them storm windows back up if that wind doesn't die down. Took them down first sign of spring. The b'ys said I was foolish. Should have listened. But, here it is, almost May...."

Clara raised her head and watched as he pulled out his pocket knife and poked at the side of the window, dislodging a few grains of putty. There was something different about him. What was it? He was just standing there, straight and tall, no tilt to him. Her eyes widened. Holy Mother of God! He was sober. Alphonse Kerrigan. Stone cold sober.

He angled toward her and shook his head. "Got to shim the window to keep 'er from rattling." Off he went to the porch where she heard him shuffle into boots and coat and clomp his way out to the shed.

Clara scraped her spoon across the bottom of her porridge bowl, revealing the rose pattern that her mother once loved. Wild roses, like the ones on her bedspread, like the live ones that sprang up, outside the kitchen window. No nurturing, no encouragement of any kind; they just blossomed, year after year. How did flowers grow like that? She raised her spoon; the milky remains of porridge covered the roses, buried the roses. She glanced toward the parlour, her mother's room. Longing filled her.

A foghorn sounded in the distance, its groan aching through her core. The outside door squeaked open. She didn't look up. He father's voice boomed through the kitchen. "Just so we're clear here. Not a word is to cross your lips about where you been and what you been at." He stormed back the way he came, leaving the door clattering in his wake.

Clara's father said nothing more about the subject. After that day, he rarely said two words to her. Clara plodded through her days, no heed to wind and wave, sun and rain, day and night. She tended to her mother's needs, dressing her as she would a porcelain doll, feeding her with a spoon. Her mother gazed into the dim room with glassy eyes, no sign of life other than the rise and fall of chest beneath thin, flannel sheet.

Clara's life stretched before her, an aimless expanse: an empty sea.

It was a few months before her father informed her that he had found her a husband.

CHAPTER 14

A SOUND LIKE AN OUTBOARD motor pulled Clara from her sleep. She blinked. Had she been dreaming? She was awake now, no doubt, but the sound kept on. Too loud to be a punt slipping up to the wharf. Yes, the spluttering noise was real and was coming from outside, not from the wharf, but from beneath her bedroom window. She jolted into a seated position. Not a boat. It was a motor car. And there was only one in the whole place. The saints preserve us! Father Mahony was here. Her father had called in the priest. Was her mother dying?

Heart racing, Clara rolled off the bed and crawled to the window. Keeping her head low, she unlatched the window, pushed it up, and shoved her Mass book into the opening. Only she had shoved too hard and the book almost went sailing through. She snapped her fingers over the end of the ribbon bookmark and yanked it. The book fell to the floor; the window slammed shut. She shrank back, panting. Had she been heard? She raised her hands to the sill and pulled herself up. Father Aloysius Mahony was there, in front of the house, perched like a statue in the seat of his Ford. The engine was still spitting and stammering; it would take a whole host of slammed windows to be heard over that. She took a deep breath, crossed herself, and with quick, sure movements raised the window and lodged the book properly. She dropped to the floor just as the motor ceased its rumbling.

"Thank you for coming," she heard her father say. She pictured him opening the door of the motorcar and helping the priest out.

"Does she know I'm here?" the priest asked.

"No, Father," was the response.

"And what about Kathleen, then? Does she know I've come to see Clara?"

Dear God. The priest was there for her, not her mother. Clara scrambled to her feet and scurried to the door. Soundlessly, she turned the knob. She crept to the head of the stairs and cocked an ear to the kitchen. She waited, picturing her father and the priest in conversation as they walked into the house. Maybe she should have listened at the window a while longer. Darn that priest anyway. Always had his nose in other people's business. Even way back before little Jimmy was born. Always showing up. At school, she would be settled in to doing her Arithmetic and the priest would show up to give a times-tables drill. Like he was in charge of everything. Everybody listened to him, faces pale with fear. Maybe it was hell they were afraid of. Hell was big with the Church. She herself probably had a reserved seat in hell. Unless she made it to confession. A wave of heat came over her. Did the priest know about Kate?

The front door creaked. Feet shuffled. Voices mumbled. Heavy footsteps thumped across the floor.

"Can I offer you something, Father? A mug of tea?"

A chair clawed the floor and the handle of the kettle squeaked. Footsteps approached. Clara drew back, plastered to the wall like wallpaper. "Clara," her father called, "Father Mahony is here. Come downstairs and be making the good priest some tea."

Clara slid down the wall to her haunches; she sucked in a breath and held it. Maybe, if she didn't respond, her father would just let her be.

"Clara," her father called again.

So much for holding her breath. Knowing she had to make herself visible, Clara clambered to her feet, gripped the banister, and padded down the stairs. Head low, she slinked into the kitchen. "Good morning, Father," she said.

"Good morning, Clara. Feeling better, are you? You don't have to bother with the tea if it's too much trouble for you."

"Nonsense." Alphonse's fist met the table with a thud. "She's a good one for making the tea. There's bread, too, if you wants. Dulcie Mullins brought it over, hot out of the oven this morning. Smells good enough to make a man forget his troubles."

"That won't be necessary," said Father Mahony in a soothing voice.

Clara raised her head. Maybe she had an ally after all. "Dad wanted *me* to make the bread," she said as she picked up the teapot from the table. "Has the pot been warmed?"

"Not yet. The kettle is still boiling." Alphonse pointed to a chair. "Sit down for a minute and talk to the priest."

Clara obliged.

"I guess you are glad to be back home, Clara."

Clara felt a tightness in her chest. She bit her lip and nodded.

"It's hard being sick and being away. But you went to your brother's home, didn't you? Tell me, how is Kevin doing?"

"I-I don't really know," she said. "Kevin was away. On a schooner and on the sealing boats, he was. I only saw Mavis, his wife."

"You have nephews and nieces there, don't you?"

She nodded again. "Three." Then she shook her head. "I mean five. Yes, there are five." She stared at her fingernails. "Mavis had twins while I was there." She raised her head.

Father Mahony lifted his eyebrows. "Well," he said, after a moment's hesitation, "it must have been wonderful that you were there to help."

Clara's heart was pounding like it was going to leap out of her chest. What kind of useless girl was she that she couldn't even count! The shriek of the kettle saved her from screaming. She jumped into movement, spinning her anger into the making the tea, to serving the men. Wasn't that what women were supposed to do anyway? Should she kiss their boots while she was at it?

Clara couldn't stop her hands from shaking as she poured the tea. Father Mahony sat in silence, waiting for her to complete the job. When the cups were steaming, the milk served, the sugar offered, she sat again and folded her hands as if she were in the confessional. She clamped her fingers tight and took a deep, silent breath.

Father Mahony cleared his throat. "Clara, I want you to know that you can come to me if you have any problems you wish to discuss."

Clara swallowed. Her face, neck, and ears burned with the rawness of it all. She searched for words. None came.

"What I mean is, I know it's hard to get back on your feet after an illness and that you have your chores here, but if you want to get out a bit more, you can help Mrs. Sallivan at the Rectory or at the church."

Clara chuffed out a long sigh. He wasn't asking about the baby. "Thank you, Father. I'll do that."

The topic of conversation changed to the weather and the fishery. Shame, like a shroud, fell around Clara. Was that the way it was going to be the rest of her life? Sitting silent, guilt pouring out of her pores. Why did men never get blamed for anything? She glanced at the priest's face. Crinkles around his eyes. Bright blue eyes. Pretty close to her father's age, wasn't he? Surely he must have committed some sin at some time. Did it matter? Neither her father nor Father Mahony would ever know shame. What would it be like to live like a man? Or, in Father Mahony's case, a God?

Clara glanced toward the hallway. Certain they wouldn't notice her leaving, she slipped out of her chair and padded her way out of the kitchen and back up the stairs. She stopped at the top of the steps to eavesdrop again.

"It's no picnic, Father, a man trying to raise a daughter on his own. She's a hard case, that one. The bottom fell out when Kathleen went away."

"Your poor Kathleen has been through a rough time."

"Yes, well you would know all about that now, wouldn't you, Father? It was you who helped get her into the Mental."

Clara cringed. They had noticed her empty chair after all. If they hadn't, her father would have kept the lie alive, would have said that

Kathleen Kerrigan was at the Sanatorium. He never would have come out with the word "Mental."

"Now, Alphonse, you know yourself was the only thing left for us to do. She needed help. No knowing what harm she would have done to herself."

"Guess you're right there, Father. She not doing herself no harm now; the truth of it is that she does nothing at all." There was a pause before Alphonse spoke again. "But it's not Kathleen I'm worried about today. Herself there (Clara pictured her father's bony finger pointing at the chair in which she had been sitting), she got into a bad way before and I'm afraid it could happen again."

"I doubt that, Alphonse. Clara is much sadder and, I'm sure, wiser than she was the last time I saw her."

"Still, I wants to be on the safe side. She's seventeen now and I wants her out of the house. There's lots of good men looking for a wife. Have you met that British fella, Robert? He sails in and out of the community all the time."

Clara clutched the front of her dress. Good men? Looking for a wife? Had her father lost his mind? Was he going to give her away? Her whole body stiffened.

"Robert Caulins, you mean? Yes. I've met him. Now, Alphonse, you know that Robert Caulins doesn't use that schooner the way God intended, don't you?"

"Yes, of course I do, Father, but these are hard times. A man has got to make a living. And I can get rid of worries about herself, as long as I gets her married off. A load off my mind, to be sure."

"I understand. And I'm sure the good Lord would, too. But what about Kathleen?"

"Whatever I say here goes for me and the missus, Father Mahony."

Another pause. A slight tapping. Was the priest tapping his fingers on the table? Was he going to agree with this? "Well then, as for Clara, a child must do as the father bids."

Clara slid down the wall to the floor. Her father had gotten the priest's approval. They were handing her off to a stranger. She heard the chairs shift. She heard the back door creak and bang. Footsteps approached the stairs. "Clara." She jumped at Father Mahony's voice. She should have run for her room when she had the chance. Too late. There he was, at the foot of the stairs, staring up at her. She slid to the top step and sat there, head down.

"Yes, Father." She slowly looked at him.

He raised his hand and beckoned her.

Clara used the banister to pull herself to her feet. Never taking her eyes off Father Mahony, she made her way down the stairs. When she reached the third step from the bottom, she stopped. She didn't know where she came up with the gall to do it, but she stood there, eye to eye, with Father Aloysius Mahony.

"Your father is waiting outside. You know he can't resist having a look at my motorcar." His half-hearted chuckle slid into a sigh. "I just wanted to have a word, to let you know that you can come to the presbytery to talk if you need. You are not alone. Your poor mother would want you to seek help."

Clara nodded.

"That's all then."

Dismissed, Clara turned, crept up the stairs, and went back to her room. To the window in her room. She watched as her father opened the door of the motorcar, as the priest drove away. She cast a glance to the sky. The rain was steady, not threatening, not yet. But dark clouds were forming. Soon a heavy carpet of them would roll across land and sea. Today her father would remove rows of cod that were drying on flakes. He would gather and stack and move the fish from the flakes into the stage before the wind and the sea reclaimed their lifeless bodies. Tomorrow, he would gather her up and toss her into the hands of a stranger.

CHAPTER 15

———◆———

ON THE DAY AFTER FATHER Mahony's visit, when morning light had cut the sky, when Clara was certain her father had vacated the salt box in favour of the landwash, she crept downstairs, clinging to the brown-painted banister like a toddler. Step. Feet together. Move hands. Step. Feet together. She hesitated at the bottom of the stairs, then slinked toward the kitchen, and stopped dead, hand on the door jamb, breath catching at the sight of her father parked at the table, staring at the half-empty whiskey bottle in front of him. She closed her eyes and, like magic, the scene turned to darkness. She harboured a wish that she could make herself disappear as easily. Her escape attempt was a slow but sure pivot, like a dory under skilled oars.

"Stop."

Caught. Clara froze.

"Get your arse in here, missy."

Heart pounding, stomach churning, she obeyed. She came to a halt three feet in front of him.

"What are ya afeard of? For Gawd's sake, child, pitch." Alphonse pointed to a wooden chair already angled toward her like an unwanted invitation. She slipped into it and cast her eyes to a jagged hole in the flowered oilcloth table cover. A blood-red petal ripped from a rose, hanging to the blossom by a sliver. Clara reached a hand out and fiddled with the stray jut of red oilcloth, letting its serrated edge slide along her finger.

Alphonse swatted her arm away. "Don't be making things worse than they is."

Clara fisted her hand and brought it to her lap. She pinched her lips together.

"I'm done with the whiskey."

Clara snapped her head toward him. For the first time since she returned from exile, their gazes met. His black eyes glowed hard for an instant, but then he blinked, and something soft, like sadness, flickered. Clara shifted in her chair.

"You're the face and eyes of your mother." Alphonse whispered, sliding one hand across the table.

Clara flinched.

He retreated, looked away. "Done too much drinking after your mother... Things got out of hand."

She waited. The perpetual sound of ticking clock and muted whoosh of wave to shore.

He sucked in a breath. When he spoke again, the softness was gone from his voice. "Can't be taking the risk of you blighting the family name a second time, missy."

Clara let her spine slide into a curve. She opened her mouth and then clamped it shut, gritting her teeth, biting back what the midwife said, that God would likely send her no more children anyway. No proper conversation for father and daughter, this. She tensed her legs and shoved her hands under her thighs, pressing her fingers into the unforgiving pine chair.

Alphonse folded his arms and leaned back hard, making the chair spindles creak. "It's time for you to be getting a husband."

Clara's jaw slackened. She blinked repeatedly.

"Lots of men looking for a missus. Come to shore just for that purpose, they do, and I got you a good one. You're going to marry him and there'll be no ands, buts, or maybes about it."

"Married? A stranger?" Clara glanced across the hall, toward her mother's room, then back again.

"Don't be looking for your mother now at all. She wants you out of the house worse than I do. The deed is done. He'll be showing up here tomorrow afternoon." Alphonse stared at Clara for an instant. A quick nod. He was done talking.

The cry of a single gull jabbed a hole in the silence, ripping along it like a filleting knife. An isolated life, that of a bird. Apart from the world.

Alphonse grabbed the whiskey bottle and jumped to his feet, thrusting back his chair which crashed to the floor, rattled in protest, then gave in to its fate. He let it be. He unscrewed the cap on the bottle and the familiar, acrid smell filled the room. He looked at the bottle with parched eyes. Clara felt her skin tightening. But he didn't drink, just shook his head and marched to the outside door. She listened: door creaking on its hinges, liquid glugging from the bottle, glass smashing against jagged rock.

"Good enough then," he said as he blasted back into the kitchen. For a few seconds he stood there, dark eyes darting all around the room. What would he do next? Clara held her breath. He stormed back toward the porch. She watched: feet cramming into boots, arms shoving into sleeves, hand grappling with doorknob. He thundered to the out-of-doors and reached back to haul the door to, leaving it shivering in its casing.

Clara let her breath out, long and slow. Remaining fixed in her chair, she let her eyes jounce around the room as she trawled her rampant thoughts for options. When she heard her mother's bedroom door closing, the *clack* of it hitting the kitchen like a gunshot, Clara's mind ceased its rambling. A deep sigh seeped out. She could dredge for fixes 'til the cows came home; wouldn't make no never mind. She planted her hands on her thighs and pushed against them to stand. She unrolled her body and plodded to the other side of the table. "Good enough then," she said as she righted her father's chair. It offered no resistance as she slid it home.

The next morning, Clara was on all fours, scrub brush in hand, leaning in, muscles straining as she scoured ingrained boot marks and stubborn berry spills from the kitchen floor. Cleansing and purging. Wishing it was as easy to soap the sins from her soul. She laughed out loud. No removing those stains. Black as the bottom of her father's tarring bucket.

"How delightful. Laughter amid life's labours."

Clara tilted her head enough to see the toes of shiny leather shoes and the cuffs of pinstriped wool pants. She released the scrub brush into the bucket. *Plop.* Water sloshed over the side, creating tiny puddles, scattering soapy bubbles. She straightened her back and wiped her hands on her apron. So, he was here, just like her father had promised. What was she, cattle? Heart pounding, she pushed herself to her feet.

At her full height, hands slammed on her hips, she parted her lips, ready to lash out but, when she met his gaze, she stopped. His eyes, grey, twinkling like the sea in the sun, spoke kindness to her. An easy smile played at the corners of his mouth. When he removed his hat, a shock of wavy brown hair bounced out. "Where are my manners?" he said. "I am Robert Alistair Caulins. And I believe you must be Clara." He extended his hand.

Clara curtsied, like she was taught to do as a child, proper behaviour for greeting a priest, or meeting your elders, and then stood politely, hands clasped in front of her. His smile spread across his face and the corners of his eyes crinkled like fine lines carved in stone by sea. But there was nothing hard about this face. Was he around the same age as her father?

At the thought of her father, resentment curled, a fleeting pinch. How dare he, how dare her mother just hand her off like this; she would not love this man. But did she have to love him to marry him?

She tilted her head. Such a charming voice he had, British and all. She'd always liked wavy hair. He was still standing there, a few feet away, waiting, nonthreatening.

The visitor cleared his throat and raised an eyebrow. Maybe this was his gentle way of reminding her that his hand was still extended. She grinned, sheepish, and reached out. What perfectly rounded, clean fingernails he had. Had this man ever seen a day's work? Her hand met his and the answer came in the feel of bumps and calluses. Not the hands of a man of leisure. Nonetheless, a gentle man. A gentleman.

CHAPTER 16

———◆———

IN AUGUST, ABOUT FIVE MONTHS after Clara gave birth, her father marched her down the aisle. Clara clamped her hand on his arm, lowered her head and plodded, feet leaden. At the altar, she did not, could not, release her clutch. Alphonse Kerrigan pried her fingers off, one at a time. Then, without as much as a sideways glance at her, he slid from the altar toward the front pew. Trembling, she watched. When he sat, she looked from him to the empty space in the pew beside him, the one reserved for her mother. The space would remain empty. Kathleen Kerrigan was anchored to her darkened room like a root vegetable to deep soil.

Clara summoned all her stubbornness, refusing to cry. With blurred gaze, she looked around the church, at the congregation, the lot of them gawking at her. Surely they all knew, didn't they? Shame flared in her cheeks. Was her gut still thick from baby weight? Fatigue oozed from every pore. If she just let go, just plain fell, maybe the floor would have the good sense to devour her. Clara swayed, contemplating. It was a sliver of a thought that saved her, the only clear thought she could muster: people were supposed to stare at the bride, weren't they? She straightened, almost smiling at her silliness, but her thoughts took off again, correcting her, torturing her. The timing of this wedding alone was enough to draw eyes to her. No one got married in the summer; summer was for fishing. Weddings took place in winter, when men were off the boats and hunkered down with their families. A summer wedding was evidence of a secret, usually one stashed under an apron.

A sudden memory arose, that of the baby, growing, moving inside her. Clara's heart jumped from patter to pound. A few seconds ago, she could barely unclench her fingers, could hardly manage to stand, let alone walk. Now, at the slightest pinprick, she could, would, sprint down that aisle, through those doors, into the sea air, toward the wharf... and then what?

As if on cue, Alphonse Kerrigan cleared his throat, a long, low rumble. Clara's whirlwind of thoughts stopped. She looked into his glaring eyes for a second. Abruptly, she turned to face the altar. Robert was standing there, beside her, but she did not afford him a glance. What was he, a good man, doing with the likes of her anyway? She had led him to believe she was a pure girl. Maybe she should have splayed her soul to him, to everyone.

Many times, she had prayed over it. Standing on the Argentia shore, with rosary beads looped like a cat's cradle over her fingers, she had cried, mourned, pleaded. "If only God would forgive me...." she would whisper, repeatedly, in steady rhythm, like waves pulsing the shore. But then the wind would rise and her heart would flood and the raw truth would erupt, a rogue wave: "If only God would give me back my child...." The sea sucked in her pleas and spewed them back. Shushing her. No forgiveness. No giving back.

Clara shook her head. Her netted veil rustled against her satin dress. A white dress, for purity and promise. One of her eyes started twitching; there was nothing she could do to stop it. There was nothing for any of this but to let it all happen. Her mind raced again, down a completely different path. Yes, she believed that the British gentleman beside her had a kind heart, but what if he--.

It was the voice of the Father Mahony, his steady litany of Latin that interceded. Clara looked at him with gratitude. Father Mahony was as good as men came, a man of God. She had never confessed her shame to him but surely Alphonse Kerrigan must have let secrets fall. She could picture her father, on his knees in the confession box, spilling the tale of the wayward daughter who had sinned with a stranger.

Then again, maybe her father had said nothing; maybe Father Mahony had simply guessed her situation. Hadn't she herself almost bumped into him as she was boarding the coastal boat in September of last year, at the onset of her trip to the Burin Peninsula, to Mavis? Father Mahony had caught her eye and raised a finger to his lips. Was he telling her then to keep the secret? She had nodded and slid past him in silence.

Now, she lifted her head and looked into his eyes. His return gaze contained only kindness. Maybe Father Mahony knew nothing. Why else would she be allowed to be married on the altar? That wasn't the usual fate of sinful girls. They got married in the vestry, a tiny room at the side of the church. No banns announced. No joy allowed. Surely Father Mahony wouldn't shatter the laws of the Church, certainly not for the likes of her. Priests couldn't do that, break the rules. Popes could. They were the infallible ones. Not priests. Maybe Father Mahony knew nothing at all about Clara's sins, about Clara's daughter, Kate.

When the wedding Mass was done, one whole hour of Latin intonation and response, Clara turned, took the arm of her husband, Robert Alistair Caulins and prepared to walk down the aisle. All eyes were upon her again and, now that she was a legitimate woman, she smiled and met their gazes, one at a time. A brazen attempt to rise above it all. It almost felt right, too, until she spotted a lone figure near the back of the church. He was clutching his cap and leaning on a pillar, under one of the Stations of the Cross. Her smile evaporated.

When had her father abandoned his pew? He was not watching her; he had his eyes low, his fingers clenched over the brim of his salt and pepper cap which he rotated slowly. Clara felt her legs weaken.

Alphonse Kerrigan peeled his weight from the pillar and slipped through the exit.

Clara clutched her husband's arm and hobbled down the aisle.

CHAPTER 17

IN THE VESTIBULE OF THE church, the newlyweds paused to accept well wishes. After that, they boarded their carriage.

It was Clara's choice, that of going to her parents' home after the ceremony. A quick dart in, that's all it was going to be. Not to claim her belongings. Everything had already been moved to a brand new house, just a mile away. But Clara had a purpose in mind: maybe, just maybe, she could persuade her mother to attend the wedding reception. The likelihood was faint, but Clara's hope was stubborn.

In front of her parents' house, Robert stepped down from the carriage and helped Clara out. He made a move to follow her inside.

Clara raised a hand, palm out. "Please, I have to do this myself."

Robert nodded. He took up a standing position beside the carriage.

Lifting the hem of her wedding dress, Clara stepped through the open door and into the kitchen. Alphonse sat at the table, flask in front of him. He sniffed as she strode past him.

At the parlour door, Clara paused, anxiety tearing at her innards. Slowly fisting her fingers, she tapped. No response. A twist of the knob, a shove at the door, and she was inside, crimping her nose at the onslaught of stale air. In a couple of steps, she confronted the window, flinging curtains, prying sash. Sunlight and sea air leapt in, pushing at the gloom and musk. Clara turned and blinked at the dust motes that danced in the ray of the sun. Clara followed their path to the bed.

Kathleen Kerrigan was lying still, facing the wall.

Clara leaned in. "I am married now, Mommy," she whispered. "See? I'm still wearing my wedding dress. I made it myself, from yours." She stepped back, twirled and swished. And waited.

Kathleen Kerrigan turned her head. Her eyes were wide, expressionless at first. Then a streak of sadness appeared and tears sprang, filling her eyes to the brim. Emitting a halting sob, she turned away.

Clara's heart sank. "Mommy?" she said.

There was no answer.

Shoulders drooping, Clara returned to the window. She stared through it, at the waiting Robert. She looked down at her fingers and toyed with the thin gold band that now owned her. Foolish, she was. Why had she come back to this house? There was nothing, no one, here for her anymore.

Clara closed the window and drew the curtains, overlapping them. There was no welcome for sunlight here. She slumped to, and through, the door. As she was about to shut it behind her--

"Cla-a-a-ra." The same bleating voice Clara had heard a long time ago.

"Mommy?" Clara swung around, her heart leaping.

"I had no choice." A feeble effort, followed by a sigh.

"What do you mean?" Clara rushed to the bed.

"I had no choice. At least, it's all over now."

For a second time, Clara leaned in. She reached for her mother's hand.

With a flick of a wrist, Kathleen Kerrigan waved her away.

Clara recoiled. And waited.

In seconds, gentle snores filled the space. Had her mother really drifted to sleep? Blinking back tears, Clara hovered, hoping that Mommy would open her eyes. She counted: four breaths, five, six...eight...ten...

Clara tiptoed from the room.

In the kitchen, she came to a halt in front of Alphonse. "What about Mommy? Who's going to take care of her?" she asked. "I can't do right by her if I'm not here every day."

Alphonse rose from his chair and folded his arms. "You got some face on ya, showing up around here after all you done. Dulcie Mullins will see to yer mother. Too hard on my Kathleen, seeing the likes of you day in, day out." He cleared his throat, and spat a wad of phlegm into the kindling box. "My Kathleen will come out of that dark room now, with you out of the way."

Clara had the sickening sensation that her heart was plunging. A black memory emerged, that of him slapping her, of her dropping like a stone. Enough. She sprinted from the house.

"They don't want me," she said to Robert, the depth of the words crushing her chest. "Neither one of them. They don't want me at all." She looked back at the house, at Alphonse who was now standing on the stoop. Automatically, she lifted her hand in a wave. He brushed his hands together as if wiping off dirt.

"It will be fine, Clara." Robert patted her head, like a kind grown-up comforting a crying child. "Just give it a little time. You can come back. Although I don't understand--"

Clara cringed.

Robert said no more. He offered her his hand.

Clara accepted it, grateful for the support as she boarded the carriage. She glanced at her husband as he took up the reins. Maybe he was right: she could go back. Their new house was just a mile from her parents'. A short distance. Still, she knew her father had exiled her. And this time, it was permanent.

What pained her more was the fact that her mother had rejected her. Again.

CHAPTER 18

———◆———

INSIDE THE NEW HOUSE WHICH was heavy with the odor of pine and paint, Clara looked at Robert Alistair Caulins, her husband, with curious eyes. She barely knew this man. She had an inkling about his age, but she had never asked. Why on earth had he chosen her? What was a travelled, older man doing here and why did he want an eighteen-year-old bride?

She watched, intrigued, as he sorted his belongings, among them several books. An educated man, Robert, if this collection was any indication. "Do you want me to put them on the shelves?" she asked, pointing at the pair of matching bookcases with glass doors. Beautiful bookcases—a deep, reddish colour. It warmed Clara's heart just to look at them. Mahogany, Robert had said. Shipped all the way from England.

"I can manage that, but to do feel free to read any you choose."

Clara picked up *The Scarlet Letter* and riffled its pages. "What's this one about?"

"Hawthorne's *magnum opus*. That is a story of a young woman who commits adultery and is forced to wear a red letter 'A' on her dress as punishment."

"A red letter?" said Clara.

"Well, yes, you see, she had a child out of wedlock. Things did not end well for her, I'm afraid."

Clara dropped the book. Its title glared up at her.

Robert laughed. "I guess it is a bit shocking, that story. It won't hurt you; go ahead, pick it up. Look it over. If Hawthorne is not to your liking, then maybe you'd prefer Dickens or Hardy."

Using only her thumb and forefinger, Clara retrieved *The Scarlet Letter* and held it away from her body, as one might a dead rat. She deposited the offending book on top of a bookcase and then wiped her hands on her apron. While gathering her senses, she stared at the spines of other books: *Richard the Third* by William Shakespeare, *Oliver Twist* by Charles Dickens, *Middlemarch* by George Eliot. So many titles—bright, gold lettering on warm, brown leather. When her eyes started to blur, she shifted her attention to the recordings: Mozart, Beethoven, Bach. The names she had heard before, but the titles? Foreign languages, the lot. She didn't, *couldn't*, read any of them...yet. She would learn.

A wave of gratitude engulfed her. Teary-eyed, Clara placed the flat of her hand on her over her heart. What had she done to deserve these wonderful things? How had Robert come by them? And how had this educated, well-groomed man drifted into her life? "Where did you come from?" The words popped out, unbidden.

There was a pause, just a bubble. "I was in Canada before I came here," Robert said in a monotone. He instantly turned to the phonograph. "Now, this you have to wind up." He eased a round, black disk from its paper sleeve and placed it on top of the machine.

Just like that, Clara's question was brushed away, the slide from one topic to another as smooth as a wave slipping over the landwash. Intrigued by the workings of the phonograph, Clara did not ask again. But as the music of Mozart flowed through the parlour, a memory, that of a conversation with her father, rippled her mind. According to Alphonse, Robert had arrived in Argentia on his very own schooner.

"So he's a fisherman, Dad?" Clara had asked.

"Enough with you and your questions," Alphonse snorted. "You don't need to be knowing that. The man has money falling out of his pockets and ye'll never want for anything, not like the most of the people on this island who have neither meal nor malt to their name. Better than you deserve." He stormed away then. Clara did not pursue him.

A few weeks ago, when Robert first handed Clara a wad of folding money—her household allowance—she trembled. At that point, she didn't care about the source of Robert's riches; she was just giddy with the lightness of "having." As the daughter and granddaughter of fisher folk, she had seen very little money. Most of her meager belongings were received in trade for cod. She had even learned to barter her sewing and knitting, skills acquired at the knee of Dulcie Mullins, for flour and molasses.

Clara instantly decided to plot a path for each dollar. Some of them would, of course, go to the Church. People always had to put God first; at least, that's what Father Mahoney said. Clara always donated when Father Mahony knocked on the door looking for dues; however, she pocketed far more than she gave. What God and Father Mahoney didn't know wouldn't hurt them.

Now, as a new bride with a well-to-do husband, in a new house with books and shelves and the music of Mozart, Clara smiled, contented. Her life had taken a fine turn and she would drink it all in: the music and the books and the money, especially the money. She looked at her husband. "I like Mozart," she said, pointing at the recording as it spun round and round.

"It's pronounced Mozart; the "z" in German sounds like "ts" in English," Robert said in a matter-of-fact way.

Clara nodded, grateful. "Mozart, it is," she said.

CHAPTER 19

———◆———

EVERY FEW WEEKS, ROBERT CAULINS took to the seas, returning with the boat weighted to the gunwales, or so he always told Clara. Lies, she knew. Yes, Robert's boots were stained with sea salt, but never with the glitter of fish scales, the sinew of entrails. His sweaters smelled only of fresh sea air, nary a sniff of cod. Were women assumed to be stupid? Certainly, they were supposed to accept whatever men did without question. 'The way of things,' as her sister-in-law, Mavis, had said to her in a recent letter. For a while, mostly due to having money, Clara was content with "the way of things." Eventually, she wanted the why.

What puzzled Clara most about her husband's activities was the rarity of trips: why would he, any fisherman, be obsessed with sailing on moonless nights? Didn't a ribbon of moonlight on black water dispel some of the danger of life on the sea?

One clear day, when she knew the schooner would be pulling in, she walked to the wharf.

Born and raised here, in Argentia, a fishing community, Clara had met many fish-laden vessels, maybe not full-sized schooners, but certainly dories. She, like most of the men, women and children in the community, had unloaded, split, gutted, cleaned, and salted no end to the codfish. Salted codfish were everywhere, drying on flakes, gardens, clotheslines.

Clara knew that Robert's schooner would slide right in, alongside the wharf. Argentia was blessed with a deep water harbor. Not like other communities where the ships anchored offshore and skiffs and dories were lowered to bring in cargo. She grinned as she strutted along. It would be easy to get a good look, maybe even to get aboard.

Rocking back on her heels, she waited as Robert's schooner, the *Elizabeth J*, breached the horizon and slipped into the harbour. Clara expected the sound of the arrival to match that of the bustle on the wharf, but the mooring was mum, save for the clunk of ropes on pier. If Robert had wanted to slide in, unnoticed, he had achieved his aim.

Clara crept closer until she was just feet away, in full view of everything. Robert's vessel was as sleek as on the day it left. The decks were clear; the nets were rolled, unused. The holds were open: no silver sight, no acrid smell, no flopping sound. So, what was in those bait barrels that the crew was hauling from the hold? And what about the wooden crates and burlap sacks? The only smells that wafted to her from the schooner were those of sawdust and straw. She was so intent on seeing everything that she didn't see a crew member approach. "Yer in the way here, Missus," said a gruff voice. "Best be moving along."

She complied, not too happy about being brushed away like a cobweb. Her lip curled. The likes of him. Didn't he know who she was? She didn't know his name but she would find out. Probably the only one of Robert's crew with bushy, red hair and freckles to boot. Eventually, she'd give him a piece of her mind Clara didn't want Robert to see her so she retreated to the far end of the wharf, feeling like a proper spy. There was offloading, but no catch of any kind. Unless she counted the crates, most of which were hefted onto wagons and carted off. Neighbours and strangers greeted her husband on shore, sliding something into his hand and grabbing at boxes that rested beside him. She overheard Robert give instructions to one of his crew. "Two crates to Father Mahony. No compensation. Just drop it off at the presbytery. Use the back door. The housekeeper will take it in. The rest goes to Silver Cliff."

With that, Clara knew. Nobody went to Silver Cliff—the abandoned silver mine—anymore. Nobody except rumrunners. Her husband was one of the many who had traded cod for cargo. A rumrunner. She sniffed, just once, an expression of amusement, not of judgement. Robert, this quiet, educated, articulate man, a law breaker. Supplying the community, even the priest. Like her father had said, money was falling out of Robert's pockets. The priest would never report the criminal activity, not a chance. Father Mahony was no stranger to a drop of drink. And surely the Church was getting its share of the profits.

A feeling of smugness flooded through Clara and she liked it. She had often thought of herself as a needy, poor girl taken in by a sympathetic, rich man. Maybe her marital match was not so uneven after all. Robert Caulins and Clara Kerrigan: sinners, the both of them. She let the sensation of comfort sink deep. Yes. Definitely sinners.

Up to this point, Clara had scoured pots and darned socks, a good housewife. Suddenly, she wanted to be better. What did that mean? Her one shortcoming sank in like a haunting. The job of a wife was to bring forth children. The well-meaning women of the community were at her all the time: "Got to get yerself a few young ones, there now, Clara. Got to have at least seven children if ya wants yer automatic in to heaven." Did that mean that Clara's mother would never make to heaven? She was left with only two children after the death of Jimmy.

Clara crept away from the wharf and headed for home, determined to be a dutiful wife. She would participate in the act, even appear to want it. The thought stabbed at her. No, she could not appear to enjoy it; that was sinful in itself. With new hope, she tolerated Robert. As often as he bid her come to him. Yet, her womb remained as barren as overworked soil. God's punishment? She didn't know. All she knew was that, despite repeated seeding, she bore no fruit. All around her, watchful eyes pierced. No little ones, Clara? The good Lord blesses the woman with little ones. Clara heard it so often that she despaired over it. What was a woman's body if not a vessel for her man's seed? Despite the fact that Robert made no reference to having chosen a barren woman, hunger gnawed at her like a termite.

Often, her thoughts drifted across the water to Kate. Her daughter who knew of her, but only as aunt. Kate was being raised as a twin to

Kevin and Mavis' son who was born the day after she was. They looked enough alike, the letters from Mavis said. No one knew. Not even Kevin. Clara would never, could never tell. Best for her. Best for the child not to carry the mark of bastard through her life. With the secret held in, little Kate could be baptized. The proper thing, Clara knew but always held out hope that someday Kate would return to her. She prayed for it, devoutly, intensely, daily. In the Church, in her house, on the ocean shore. Asking, begging God to intervene on her behalf. Kate. Give her back her Kate. Days slid to weeks, to months. For years, she prayed.

Three years and eight months after Kate's birth, God answered.

KATHLEEN

———◆———

CHAPTER 20

IT SHIFTS, AND SURGES, THE sea.

The North Atlantic is a leviathan, seemingly boundless, surprisingly bound by wind and moon. The wind taunts, the moon tugs, the tide complies. Can it be that even giants have masters? A chuckle of amusement—mine—flits on the breeze. Nature's so-called 'masters' of the sea cannot contain a force which is beyond their ken.

A 'tidal' wave is independent of wind and moon; it starts deep beneath the seafloor where layers of gases, compressed and building for years, scream and claw for release. The floor ruptures. The earth rattles. The sea reacts, sucking self from shore, scraping fingers on floor, pulling back, back, into a giant, roiling wall of foam. The seabed is splayed naked, a banquet table for seabirds which hop along, scooping up witless prey. When the sea can retreat no farther it pauses, then plunges, forward, from the bottom, at monumental speed, slowing as it reaches shore, building a back wall so high that it becomes a murderous mountain of emerald marble. Rushing, heaving, burying all in its path....

NOVEMBER 18, 1929

It is an unseasonably warm, autumn day on the coast of the Burin Peninsula, the sun beaming off the rocks. A few clouds sketch the sky, poked along by a playful wind. The ocean ripples, almost smiling as it gurgles to landwash.

A flurry of wings brushes past, bidding me turn. I oblige, observe, as a flock of gulls soars from sea to shore; they perch, one by one, along the roof line of a salt box house, Kevin's home, that sits, innocent, unaware, fifty feet from shore.

A thud of a door. My son's wife, Mavis, stands in front of the root cellar. She grunts as she hefts a puncheon laden with carrots, potatoes, and cabbage, up a trio of steps. On level ground, she pauses, resting her burden on her ballooning stomach. Another mouth to feed soon. The way of things for her, in this time, in this life.

Mavis planks the puncheon onto the ground and stretches, rubbing her lower back. She stares at her little home and smiles, her eyes shimmering with tears. She drags a corner of her apron across her face and glances through the open shed door where a depleted woodpile is revealed.

Ah, yes. Kevin is away, refurbishing the supply. This I know, yet on every visitation, I experience hope. The shadow world is full of gruelling hope.

Mavis bends and grasps the rope handles of the barrel tub. She heads for the house and enters through the side door. Lumbering into the pantry, she drops the puncheon on a table, grabs a knife and a potato, and sets in. Once the vegetables are stripped, she washes and chops and carts them to the stove. With a well-practiced hand, she drops all but the cabbage into a steaming, bubbling cauldron, pungent with the odor of salt beef. She pokes at the fire then heads for the side door. "Jimmy," she yells in the direction of the shed, "ye better be haulin' in some firewood."

Ten-year-old Jimmy appears, grabs some splits stored beside the house, and charges up the steps. "The chickens are fed, Mom. I'll take care of the stove. You just rest for a bit." He hurries to unlatch the stove door.

Mavis chuckles. "Me, rest? Sure the only rest I'll be getting is when the good Lord takes me."

A cold shiver snakes through me into the bones of the salt box house. Its response is a slight sound, a cracking of knuckles. Unheard, perhaps disguised by pop and spit of firewood.

Mavis pats Jimmy's shoulder. "Make your father proud, you would. Just feed the fire enough to keep the stove good and hot. Where's Marie?"

Marie's voice floats from the second floor. "I'm with the twins, Mom. Need me for anything?"

How many times have I heard this dialogue? Hundreds? Thousands? So many that I utter eight-year-old Marie's words in concert with her. Every syllable is etched, indelible, on my soul. Sadness pours through me. The desire to flee presents itself, but I am sinner, doomed observer. A phantom, sighing.

Mavis grabs a damp rag and wipes the oilcloth cover on the table. "Just take care of Joey and Kate for a bit," she calls to Marie, then counts seven plates and lays them on the table.

"There's only six of us, Mom," says Jimmy. "Dad's off chopping, remember?"

Mavis re-counts. "Where's my head at today?" She returns a plate to the cupboard and counts out the correct number of knives and forks.

"I wishes Dad was home," says Jimmy, as he stokes the fire.

"Yer father's away 'cause the woodpile is wanting. He was in a hobble for days about the leaving." Mavis pauses from the laying of the table and stares vacantly through the window. "Strange, that: he's usually more for the work than the worry." She shrugs. "Finally, he says 'things don't get done by turning them over in your mind' and off he goes."

"Maybe I can go with him next time?" Jimmy slams the stove door, turns, and pulls himself to his full height.

"Oh." Mavis locks her eyes with his. "Yer father wants you to be the man of the house when he's away. You understands that." Her voice is soft, reassuring.

Jimmy slumps, nodding.

Mavis sighs. "Good. Now, where's the rest of the young 'uns?"

In seconds, footsteps pound the stairs; the twins barrel into the kitchen followed by Marie who is balancing the baby, Johnny, on one hip.

For a few seconds, I experience that thing called joy. The sight of all my grandchildren is a splinter of light, an absolution of sorts, cruel in its brevity.

"Yer a fine lot; makes my heart sing to look at ye," says Mavis, articulating what I cannot.

"I'm hungry," whines three-year-old Joseph.

"Me, too," echoes his twin, Kate.

"I'll get ye a bicky to hold ye over 'til supper," says Mavis.

"I'll do it." Jimmy rushes into the pantry.

"Fill a bucket with water while you're at it."

The response comes: a belch of the pump, a gush of water. In seconds, Jimmy is back, biscuits in one hand, bucket in the other.

"Meant for ya to leave the bucket in the pantry, son. I'll be needing it to clean the dishes."

Jimmy grins; his face reddens. He places the bucket on the floor while he doles out biscuits. While the twins are chomping, he veers back, ready to grab the bucket. He hesitates, staring. The water is trembling, forming concentric rings. "Mom..." He looks at Mavis, question marks in his eyes.

The vibration is a slight movement at first but it swiftly intensifies to a violent shudder, tearing through the core of the salt box house. Mavis latches onto the back of a chair with both hands. Knives and forks shimmy across the table. "Mom! Mom!" Arms flailing, the children grab for her skirt. She drops to the floor, pulling them all down with her. The cupboard doors rattle and fly open. Dishes dance to the edges of shelves and toss themselves to shattered ends on the floor.

The family huddles, trembling, in the pool of water that has spluttered from the bucket. "Our Father, who art in heaven," Mavis starts, as her children scream and sob. Mavis clutches her brood and raises her voice. "Our Father, who art in heaven, hallowed be Thy name..." One whole *Our Father* slips into two, followed by five *Hail Marys*, and one *Glory Be to the Father.*

Then, "Sssssh," she says, barely a whisper.

The children are still bawling.

"Sssssh, will ye?" Not a whisper, but a yell. The result is immediate silence. "Now I can listen proper-like," she tells them. They hover. Somewhere in the distance, a dog howls. A long, fearful cry. When it stops, Mavis sucks in a breath and makes the sign of the cross. She pauses, then sighs. "Thank the Lord. It's all over. Whatever it was, it's all over."

With children still clinging to her, she edges to the front door. Standing on the stoop, her arms encircling them, she peers out. A cluster of people hovers in the meadow next to Murphy's Pond, just yards up the road. "Jimmy," she says, "you and Marie take care of the young ones while I finds out what's going on." She scurries then, as much as she can on stubby legs weighted by burden of child. Panting, she comes alongside the crowd, at the centre of which is the store merchant, Artemius Nolan. She hitches in a breath, perks up her ears.

"Could be a tidal wave this very evening," says Artemius. Giggles roll through the crowd.

"Ah, go on with ya, b'y. Yer talking off the top of yer head," says a bystander.

"What are ye all sayin'?" asks Mavis. "What's goin' on? I got the youngsters to think of, scared out of their britches, waitin' on the porch."

"Artemius here thinks we're going to have a tidal wave." More snickers.

Artemius throws his hands skyward. "Ye can all laugh if you wants, but mark my words," he says. "Earthquakes bring tidal waves. If I was ye, I'd be getting to higher ground. The missus is standing at the gate of my place on the hill, rosary beads in hand, ready to greet the lot of ye." He turns away and climbs, voices peppering the air behind him.

"Don't be worrying the people with nonsense, Artemius."

"Came out of the womb at a slant, you did."

Mavis pauses, looks at the landwash, at the people around her.

Despite repeated viewings, despite knowing the outcome, I am enmeshed. *Listen to Artemius, Mavis. He has travelled the world. He knows of such things.*

Mavis blinks, deciding. She sees others trudge toward their homes. She shrugs and follows suit.

Slouching, bereft, I trail along behind her.

At the door step, she smiles. "Nothing going on," she says. "Nothing at all, but won't we have some story to tell your father when he gets back?" She takes the baby from Marie's arms and enters the house. "Jimmy, Marie, be careful you don't cut yourself picking up them broken dishes." She deposits Johnny in his crib near the stove, and straightens the misaligned forks and knives on the table. The children, wide-eyed, do as told. When supper is ready, they sit in their usual places. They pick at their food and look at each other.

When supper ends, the dishes are removed, but no child moves. Kate yawns. Her head droops. Mavis lifts her and carries her upstairs to bed, then returns. She beams at the sight of Marie practicing her handwriting, at Jimmy, sitting beside Joseph, reading him a story.

Jimmy turns a page, pauses, looks up. "Mom, shouldn't we..." he starts, but Mavis waves away the concern registered on his face. Jimmy's dark eyes do not falter, a blank stare.

Mavis turns and picks up her mending. She ambles to the rocking chair and makes herself comfortable. She breathes an audible sigh.

The kerosene lamp on the center of the table flickers. "I can't see to do my lessons," says Marie, licking her stump of a pencil. "The teacher says...." She raises her head as a muffled roar begins.

Jimmy stands. Timidly, he approaches the door. He twists the knob, tugs it, peers out. "The ocean's leaving," he says.

Mavis stops rocking. "What's that you say, Jimmy?"

"The ocean's gone. The boats are all atilt, just lying there. The gulls are picking food off the seabed. We have to...."

Jimmy turns toward his mother, his eyes wide.

It is always my hope at this point that the ocean will be merciful to the salt box house, somehow pass it by. But it never complies.

The roar grows until it thunders. "Mommy!" screams Joseph. He bolts from his chair, knocking it over. His mother reaches one arm toward him. The house screeches and moans as it is ripped from its foundation. Mavis and her little ones are tumbling, swirling in a mass of frigid water.

Yes, I had hoped it temporary, this penance. I had hoped it lessened by repetition and time. I had hoped it would fade into the dark as this scene does once the kerosene lamp on the table stops flickering. But I am still here, watching green, marbled waves explode, listening to roar and growl and scream, as all that was loved by my son is ripped away in a thirty-foot wall of foam.

KEVIN

CHAPTER 21

NOVEMBER 18, 1929

KEVIN WAS IN THE WOODS, miles from home. A few days ago, he had rowed away from the rocks of Burin, beached the dory, and hiked inshore. The plan was to chop trees, lop branches, and pile logs, enough wood to keep his family warm through the long nag of winter. He'd leave the lot of it there until the bay was thick with ice. Then he'd return with horse and sled to cart it all home.

Kevin paused from chopping and wiped the sweat from his brow. He leaned on his axe as he scanned the November sky. Hard to take in that the winter would be upon them soon, not on a day like this when the sun was darn near splintering the rocks. Be willing to bet that the sea was a flat calm today: easy day on the water. Didn't miss being in the dory, though. The woods lacked lull of waves, shriek of gulls, and tang of salt, but they had their own magic: chatter of sparrows, rustle of branches, smell of pine. Heaven, it was.

He remembered a recent visit to the merchant store, when the shop was overrun with offshore fishermen, fresh in from the big city ports, dragging the world and its problems with them. Why was it that people always looked for reasons to get themselves in a hobble? Raspy-throated voices had popped up all over the place, all worrying about the same thing:

'People losing all their money and jumping off them tall New York buildings. Can you imagine the likes of that?'

'The whole world's going broke, b'y.'
'They'll be talking about the Market Crash of '29 for years to come.'
'It's going to be the death of the lot of us.'

Kevin would hear tell of none of it. "Don't know what you're all up in arms about," he spluttered. "We all had good fishing this year. Last year, too, if I remembers right. Crops are right fine. The larders are full, b'ys. Newfoundland don't got to worry about the world's money problems. Long as we got the sea and the land, we can make our way." He stormed out, the guffaws of seamen echoing in his wake.

Fools the lot of them. Not going to let that rowdy bunch get in the way of things. Everything was in its place at home: house, barn, wharf, stages. Yep. Life was the finest kind. This year, he'd even managed to make enough fishing inshore; no slaving on the merchant bankers like he did two or three years ago after the ocean swallowed his dory. Maybe, come spring this year, he'd have to take to the ice for the sealing. But for now? No point in bidding the devil good morrow 'til you meet him. Time to focus on the task at hand.

As Kevin was raising the axe for the thousandth time, a host of finches burst from ground to trees, perching on open branches, screeching something fierce. He dropped his axe and clapped his hands over his ears. A tremor needled into in his feet and exploded to a roar that belched up through his body. Balance thrown, he fell to his knees. Smotherin' Jeesez! What in all that's holy was going on? There was nothing for it but to wait.

After a few seconds, his body stilled itself. Kevin jumped to his feet and grabbed his axe, gripped it like a weapon, ready to pounce. He pivoted, examining every tree and branch. Nothing. Even the birds had stilled their cackling. He looked straight up through the treetops and glimpsed hints of sky: blue, a few wisps of cloud. He cocked his head, listening. A gurgling sound in the distance: that was the stream had passed earlier. He breathed out a long sigh and scratched his chin. What the hell had happened? An earthquake? He shook his head. Come in out of the wet, b'y. No such thing on this island. He shrugged. Trees must have toppled over someplace handy. That was it. It took a few minutes of convincing, but he settled on that. Trees dying, falling, that's what it was. He shored up his stance, and got on with the job at hand.

For the rest of the day, he chopped. Then he settled in for the night. But sleep did not come. Something ailed him, couldn't tell what, but fear had a grip on his chest.

At first light, he headed home, his heart quickening with every step. Had to get back to Mavis and the little ones. Maybe he had left too much responsibility on Jimmy's shoulders, asking him to take care of everything. The boy was only ten. Still, when he himself was that age, he was helping his own father in that way. Kevin smiled as his mind replayed times when he worked side by side with his father and took care of his little sister, Clara. Then, when he was fifteen, his brother Jimmy came. And left. And nothing was the same. No, nothing was ever the same. The thought caused his heart to slam against his ribs; he picked up his pace.

Kevin hadn't wanted to leave home at all a few days ago. It always wrenched his gut to pry himself away, but this time he had stalled the leaving: he had built a railing on the cellar steps, shored up the storm door, and oiled every hinge he could find. He figured he'd need new sawhorses in a couple of weeks, so he built those, too. When he couldn't find anything else to hamper him, he set out.

So focused on speed was he now that he slipped on a patch of ice and almost lost his footing. "Watch where you're going, b'y," he said, and forced himself to examine every step. A steady pace now, almost to the shore. It was the smell that hit him first, brine mixed with what? He didn't know, something sour, out of place. He looked up, expecting a limitless span of sea. The water was there, yes. But it was strewn with wreckage: chunks of stages and wharves and barns and houses and boats. Kevin stared, mind blank, all power to move lost.

CHAPTER 22

———◆———

HOW LONG KEVIN STOOD THERE, he didn't know. Movement came gradually, first a blinking, then rubbing of eyes. He turned his head from side-to-side. Just days ago, he had beached his dory in this very spot. The boat was nowhere in sight but that made no never mind. What kind of fool would try to row through such a backlog of rubbish anyway? The only way home was to walk around the shore. Seconds after he came to that conclusion, he stuttered into motion. Home. Had to get home.

But when Kevin arrived, there was no home. There was nothing but a few residents gathered on a hill, staring. All the stages, wharves, flakes, the salted cod, the dories, the skiffs were gone. Sucked up and spat out again. Matchsticks, the lot of them. Everything destroyed. Everything twinkling with glitter, compliments of Mother Nature who had dropped the temperature below freezing overnight. Kevin searched the crowd, his heart floundering. Where were Mavis, Jimmy, Marie, Joseph, Kate, Johnny?

Tom Murphy sidled up to him and put his stump of a hand on Kevin's shoulder. "A tidal wave, Kev. They're all gone, b'y. All except for the little one, Kate. The missus is taking care of her...." Kevin turned to Tom whose eyes emitted stark truth. He listed then, like a ship with no ballast. Silent, overcome, he dropped to his knees. Out of the corner of his eye, he caught a glimpse of his salt box house. What in God's name was it doing sitting at the edge of Miller's Pond, a few hundred yards from where it was supposed to be?

For days, Kevin wandered, glassy-eyed, seeing and hearing everything, responding to nothing. He watched his friends and neighbours use pulleys and chains to drag his house from Miller's Pond and put it back on its foundation. He strolled up to the sagging front porch and sat, like he was waiting for his wife and children to walk up the steps. Just sat. For a long time. Two whole days, they told him later.

It was on the third day that the parish priest came and sat beside him. "My son, you're in shock, yes, but you have to think of Kate now. She's a miracle child, your Kate." Kevin felt a hand thump his back. "She's *your* miracle child, Kevin," continued the priest. "God must have spared her for a reason. I know it's a terrible thing you're going through, but you have to take care of your little girl. Do you hear me at all, son?"

Kevin heard every word from the priest but couldn't form a single word of his own.

"The Lord wants you to go on, Kevin, or else He wouldn't be leaving you with such a miracle. You have to take care of yourself so you can take care of her. She needs her father."

Kevin's jaw was clamped. He sat frozen in position, unable to move even his head.

The priest sighed. "I'm sorry, son, but you leave me no choice." There was a swish of cassock and rattle of beads as he rose to his feet. "Okay, Tom, get yer brothers. He's all yours."

Kevin registered the trudging of feet and felt vise-like grips on his wrists and ankles. He offered no resistance to being carried along like a gutted pig; he did not question the destination. He felt his body rise and heard the voice of Tom Murphy. "Let 'im go, b'ys." Without a word, the Murphys dropped Kevin into the water trough located on high, unscathed ground, outside Tom's home. The thin pane of ice that formed during the chilly November night shattered with the force of impact. Knives of cold shot through Kevin's body. He screamed in agony. And once he started screaming, he couldn't stop.

Kevin knew they were all watching, listening, doing what they must. The Murphy brothers' seemingly cruel act had a desired effect. The pain was emotional, not physical; Kevin's screams were like those of a tortured body but it was his soul that was shrieking.

Eventually, the four men pulled Kevin out of the trough and wrapped him in a coarse blanket. His screams turned into howls that were gradually reduced to sobs. It was only when the sobs became whimpers that the brothers brought him inside, into Tom's house. Another vat of water waited for him there, this time a warm bath in a puncheon beside the wood stove. Tom's missus had pots of boiled water at the ready and kept pouring them, one after the other, into the barrel tub, all the while scolding her husband and his brothers.

"Can't believe ye'd be leaving the poor man to wilt on his front porch for so long. Waiting for the priest. As if that would have made any difference to a man who just lost his family. No, it's not a priest he be needing now. A clean bed and a good bit of grub. And a warm drink. Tom, you best be making him a hot toddy."

There was no movement.

"Don't you look at me like you don't got no rum hidden around here someplace," she continued. "Sure as I'm standing here, one of the four of ye be having a flask in your pocket."

There was shuffling and rattling and clinking followed by the pungent smell of alcohol.

"Four men. Four flasks. Now that's more like it," Tom's missus said. "Well, what are ye waiting for? The kettle is boiled and the sugar is in the cupboard. You make the drink, Tom, and the rest of ye can sit yourselves down and have a bite to eat. There's bread and molasses on the table and you're welcome to it, but be darn well sure ye save the best of it for this poor unfortunate."

Kevin ate the bread; he drank the toddy. Two toddies. After that, he lost more time, during which he slept on the daybed in the Murphy's kitchen. When he woke up, he remembered four words: "'She needs her father.'" The priest's words. They hovered in a thick fog. No meaning. Kevin recited the phrase over and over, like a Hail Mary in a rosary, until its significance dawned: he had to take care of Kate. Once Kevin grasped the concept, he clung to it like barnacle to hull. But what to do? How to do it?

When Tom Murphy's wife put Kate onto Kevin's lap, he hugged his little girl, inhaled, and choked back a sob. The very essence of Kate conjured up a picture of his family—all of them, in the kitchen. His wife's face beaming, his children's eyes gleaming in the glow of the oil lamp. The memories nudged him into a slight rocking motion. Kate slept soundly in his arms.

A chair scraped the floor as Tom Murphy pulled up beside the pair. "You can only imagine me surprise when I found her, Kev." His voice was a whisper. "She was on the second floor, in the bedroom. That's what saved her. The ocean swept in like a broom and took the house out. Mavis and the others didn't have a prayer. Artemius tried to warn everyone..." He stopped. "The priest is right. Your Kate is a miracle, she is. A miracle." Tom dragged a shirt sleeve across his gnarled face. "The house going out to sea and coming back. I don't know how..." His voice faded away.

Kevin pulled Kate closer and buried his face in her hair. If he could just go back a few days in time. All he ever wanted in life was to take care of his own, to keep them safe. His little salt box house was as snug as could be. Had he been there, would he have saved them? Would he have had the good sense to pull them away from shore? Would he have listened to Artemius?

Maybe. Maybe not.

Never in a million years would he have called the ocean Judas. Never would he have worried about it turning on them. The likelihood was that, had he been home, his body would have been found with the rest. Now, he was here, and he had Kate. Kevin heaved a sigh just as Kate raised her head.

"I want my mommy," she said and stuck her thumb in her mouth.

"So do I," he whispered, "but your mommy is in heaven." As he rocked her gently, the tears that fell from his eyes mingled with the ones already streaming down her face.

It was days before the telegraph poles were repaired, before the world was informed of the disaster. When ships came, bringing relief, they carried things the people of the Burin Peninsula had never seen: apples, oranges, rolled oats, brown flour. The caring of strangers and the kindness of neighbors were all blurred to Kevin, all a part of a nightmare from which there was no relief.

After five wakes all rolled into one, five funerals all rolled into one, Kevin decided to take his little girl and move back to the home of his childhood: Argentia. Sure enough he'd had concerns about his mother and he'd had scuffles with his father. But a great deal of time had passed, dimming memories. And now, a great shock had come, deleting others. He and Kate would be welcome in Argentia. Clara would help, as much as he would allow. He just needed time to scrounge out a living—fishing and farming and hunting. They'd be fine. The Lord wouldn't dare give him more trouble—he'd already had more than his share.

"Are you hearing me, Lord?" he said, eyes raised to heaven. "Do I be needing to say it again after this? They say that God helps those that help themselves. Well, with Tom and his missus here as witness, I'm saying that I'll be doing my part—helping myself. You spared my little girl, so I'll be taking care of her, but don't you be sending me no more trouble. A man can only stand so much in one lifetime, Lord. Yes, a man can only stand so much and I'm just about done in. So here's the bargain: I'll do my bit and you give me no trouble. Do you hear me, Lord?" Relief swept through him, a clear message: God had heard and agreed. To seal the deal, Kevin made the sign of the cross.

"When bad things happen, Katie girl," he said, "you got to pick yourself up and start over. And that's just what we're doing."

They left on the first available boat.

CLARA

CHAPTER 23

———◆———

1929

CLARA HAD JUST SHOOED AWAY a stray sheep that had been chomping on a pair of long johns flapping from her clothesline. No great damage done. The victimized underwear would be right as rain with only a few pricks from her sewing needle, but she'd have to keep a scattered eye out. Darn sheep would eat anything they could get their mouths around. Now where had she left her laundry basket?

As she was searching, the wind picked up and lashed at her hair. She raked her fingers from brow to nape. A useless endeavour, for as soon as she let go, her long brown curls veiled her face again. Sometimes it seemed like the wind blew nonstop for months on end. She whipped a scarf from her apron pocket, and battled the gale as she tied her mop down. Still no sign of the laundry basket but she did catch sight of Dulcie Mullins who was panting her way up the path.

"Great day on clothes," Clara sang out. She wrinkled her brow when Dulcie did not respond. Odd, that. Odder still was the fact that the little teapot woman was not smiling. In fact, her round face sagged with worry.

"It's a sad thing I got to be telling you, me ducky, a sad thing," said Dulcie. Then, she just stood there.

"Bad news don't get better with the keeping. Out with it. What's ailin' you at all?"

Dulcie shook her head. "There's been a tidal wave on the Burin. The way I hears it, people are lucky if they got out with their lives. Kevin's fine, I hear tell, but he lost the most of his family. All but one child. A daughter, they're saying down at the merchant store. He'll be bringing her here now, I suppose, the poor young'un."

Clara's first response was a single thought: Kate. Her next was to grab the clothesline for support. It gave way and she collapsed with it. As she lay there, with Mrs. Mullins fussing over her and the wind flinging her skirts into her face, it occurred to her that she'd have to wash all those long johns and sheets again. Backbreaking work, scrubbing against the rigid accordion wall of the washboard, its legs submerged in the grey water of the galvanized tub, her hands wrinkling before their time. But she'd have to do lots of cleaning anyway, especially if Kevin was coming home and bringing a little girl. But which little girl?

After Clara digested the news of the tragedy, her limbs dragged with the weight of it. She told herself she must be a caring person. Why else would she be so consumed with grief? Her soul balked every time she asked herself that question. *Liar, liar, liar.* What sluiced through her was not grief at all; it was hope which rushed forth in a wave, filling her heart, then slid out again, erasing her soul. She hoped that the Lord had saved her Kate. She hoped that the Lord had answered her prayers. She hoped the Lord would silence wagging tongues that pitied "poor, barren Clara."

Yes, Kevin was coming home, to Argentia, and was bringing with him one child. Not his wife, not his other four children. The Lord took them weeks ago when the earth shook, hurling a giant wave to their shores. "God rest their souls," Clara said repeatedly to anyone and everyone, punctuating the words and pushing down her guilt by making the sign of the cross. Kevin was bringing only one child. A daughter. That much Clara knew. But which daughter? Marie, the older girl? Or Kate? Her Kate? Clara prayed until hope flooded her pores. When the telegram finally came, the one saying that Kevin was indeed coming home, that Kate was coming with him, Clara prayed again, gratitude springing from her soul. God had saved Kate and God was sending Kate back to her.

After three-and-a-half empty years, Clara would be the mother she was meant to be.

CHAPTER 24

———◆———

1929 - 1930

IN ARGENTIA, JUST DAYS AFTER the news of the tragedy had arrived, winter barged in. A dump of snow came down, a dull thud, hushing the world. The fisherman folded to the season's will: they tarped schooners and skiffs, repaired nets and traps, chopped wood into splits.

For Clara, winter meant waiting; it would be March before Kevin returned to Argentia. She filled her time as did all women of the community, with the swish of carding, clack of spinning, click of knitting. Everyone, everything hunkered down while the north side winds piled snow high against the windows and lifted it in powdered waves from the rooftops.

The season of Advent approached with its ritual weekly candle-lighting in preparation for the birthday of Jesus. This year, Clara saw it as her own special preparation, for the arrival of her daughter. An interminable wait. Through the four candles of Advent, to the swell of Midnight Mass, to first toll of New Year, through the drawn-out January when the wind swooped down, whipped trees, drove snow, stung noses, burnt lungs. By February, she was beside herself with anticipation. Within the community, the long stifle of winter brought cabin fever which occasionally exploded in a scuff and a scoff: a kitchen party, where an accordion squawked an Irish lilt, where floor boards vibrated from the dancing, where stew pots bubbled on a Waterloo stove.

Still the waiting.

Finally, March showed up, in like a lion. Mother Nature gradually smiled, warming things up a bit, but she frowned again around St.
Patrick's Day, unleashing another storm, the annual Sheila's Brush. It
was the end of the month before the weather settled into lamb. Clara
was in a dither of nerves: the coastal boat was due to arrive from Burin
at the end of the month.

When the big day came, Clara arrived at the wharf two hours early.
Waiting and waiting. Still waiting when the clock ticked past the ap-
pointed time. Where was that boat?

Her father, Alphonse Kerrigan, crept up beside her. Too close. So
strong his will, a black cloud, that she took a step away from him. He
moved closer. "Don't be telling things outside the house," he muttered.

Clara swallowed. She sidestepped again. To heck with him. No, to
hell with him. Kate was *her* child. She would have *her* child. What would
Kathleen Kerrigan have done if she had had the opportunity to get her
little Jimmy back? Ever on her mind and close to Clara's heart was the
story her mother had told about her ancestors who first seeded these
shores. So many women losing their children to illness and the sea. How
had they gone on?

Alphonse moved closer to deliver another mutter. "Can't be leaving you to your own devices." Clara felt that stab in her soul. Her own
devices. That was what her mother used to say. She dismissed the words
now, wouldn't let them override her excitement which was bubbling over
the sides of her. Again, she moved away. She leaned into the wind until
she was standing on the balls of her feet. She began bouncing up and
down, up and down.

A cheer went up from the waiting crowd as the boat was sighted entering the harbour. Clara craned her neck and switched her bouncing
to rocking, side to side, waiting. She caught herself humming. What was
it? A lullaby? Yes. The very rock-a-bye she had hummed on the day she

stood on shore in Burin, the day she gave birth to Kate. The crowd grew as the boat sidled its way into the dock.

Time dragged on. Passengers dragged off.

Clara searched until she spotted a tiny girl, her arms wrapped around the neck of a man. Kate. It had to be Kate. It *was* Kate. Clara felt her heart pound, slamming its way out of her ribcage. Her breathing was fast and shallow. Would her knees hold up? They would have to. There was no one she could latch onto. Certainly not her father.

Clara lurched into motion and threaded her way to the front, to the gangway. God had sent back her child. God was merciful. God had forgiven her sins. Clara, eyes riveted to the little girl, almost slammed into the man who was carrying her. An automatic "excuse me" spit out as she looked into the man's face. The sight of him shocked her into stillness. Dear Lord! Was this her brother? Had he shrunk? His face was pale, hollow. All skin and grief. He showed no acknowledgement of Clara, just hovered like Marley's ghost from that Dickens' book. Kevin was clinging to the child, Clara's child, Clara's Kate, like a drowning man to slab of driftwood. His eyes were empty. Glass orbs.

"Hello, son." Alphonse was there now, uttering a greeting.

Kevin did not acknowledge it.

Clara returned her gaze to the little girl with the plaited brown hair who raised her head from Kevin's shoulder and blinked.

Alphonse leaned toward Clara's ear. "She's the face and eyes..." he breathed. Clara twitched, pulled away. She stepped closer to Kevin. Smiling, she opened her arms to Kate, slowly, tentatively, a mother reaching for the gift that had been denied her so long ago.

But the little girl instantly recoiled, poisoning Clara's hope. "I want my mommy," she said.

The waves rolled onto shore, the gulls screamed overhead, the air was pungent with salt. And Clara's little girl buried her face deep into the overcoat of the shell of a man who carried her.

Clara dropped her arms. She took a deep breath, almost forgetting for a moment, almost whispering her soul's disappointment. But then, her whole body jerked, the result of an elbow ramming her ribs. A reminder from Alphonse.

Clara let out her breath and took another.

"I'm your Aunt Clara," she said.

CHAPTER 25

———◆———

1930

"No point in lollygagging," said Alphonse as he shuffled from one foot to the other. "Don't s'pose there's bags to be carried. You be helping your brother, missy, and I'll see the lot of ye at the carriage." Then he was gone, a quick motion, like a dark cloud ousted by a gust of wind.

Some of the tension in Clara's body slid away with him, freeing her to dwell on this moment: she wanted to hold in her heart forever the memory of the first time she laid eyes on her little girl. But, as she stared at the tiny waif in her brother's arms, an urge to wail writhed its way into her throat. She swallowed it back and turned her attention to the decks of the coastal boat, now devoid of passengers. Alphonse was right about one thing: not a suitcase in sight. Anywhere. She blinked. Had Kevin and Kate traveled all this way with just the clothes on their backs? Dear God!

Clara pulled the flat of her hand across her sweaty brow. All this time, ever since the news of the tragedy had pricked her ears, she had been thinking of no one but herself. Never a thought for Kevin and his troubles. Her face burned with the shame of it. What kind of sister was she at all? Rotten as dirt, that's what. Was she even fit to be prayed for? She fisted her right hand and brought it to her chest. *Mea culpa, mea culpa, mea maxima culpa.* She took a deep breath and let it slide out. Too late to be picking your miserable self apart, missy. Shelving the guilt, Clara stepped up, alongside her brother.

The instant she took Kevin's arm, all niggling thoughts of self dissolved to dust: Kevin was shaking; a trifling of a tremor, it was, but one that needled through his whole body. "It's time to go, Kev," she said, her voice hitching with emotion. She tugged him forward. Kevin, still cleaving to the child, stumbled into movement. Clara led him to the horse and carriage where Robert and Alphonse awaited.

In silence, they boarded. In silence, they rode. The clip-clop of horses' hooves. The ruts in the road. The bouncing and jiggling. At one point, Kate's tiny leg jostled Clara's hand, burning like a lightning strike. Clara closed her eyes and allowed the shock wave to course through her whole body. The carriage wheel jutted into another pot hole and the feeling jolted out. But she did not open her eyes until the carriage came to a halt, until Robert tugged at her arm.

She blinked and widened her gaze. "Why are we here? At my parents' house?"

"At your father's insistence, my love," replied Robert.

Bent on objecting, Clara cast a defiant glance at Alphonse Kerrigan. He glared, his jaw locked, determined. She hesitated. She'd defied that look once before and had wound up with the imprint of his hand upon her face. Maybe there would be no such consequence now, with the eyes of the family upon him, but she would not test him. She could bide her time. She looked away.

The family disembarked and filed, in funeral procession fashion, to the door of Alphonse Kerrigan's salt box house. First Clara, then Kevin with Kate, then Robert, Alphonse at the rear. Clara opened the storm door and then held it for all. She was about to close it behind Alphonse, but he grabbed it. "I'm going aback of the house, to tend to the horses." He fixed his eyes on hers, but spoke no more. Clara nodded. One curt nod. He let out a deep breath and left. She stared after him, saw him reaching into his pocket. Her heart fluttered. Was he drinking again? She closed her eyes to it and entered the house.

Clara shrugged off her coat, hung it on a hook, and stepped into the kitchen. There she stopped, mouth agape.

Not a thought had Clara given to the idea that her mother might be in the kitchen, her mother who had rarely left the parlour, who had said hardly a word for more than a decade. But there she was, Kathleen Kerrigan herself, seated at the table, hair disheveled, fingers toying with the tiny red bow on the neckline of her nightgown. A plaid flannel nightgown. The kind of cloth used for men's shirts. Was there a sale at the merchant store or what? And what the hell was she doing thinking about flannel shirts? Clara refocused, staring questioningly at Dulcie Mullins who was standing beside the table, biting her lip and wiping her hands on her apron.

Dulcie shrugged, eyes blank.

Clara started toward Kathleen. "Mommy?"

When Kathleen put her hand up, palm out, Clara came to a standstill.

Dulcie Mullins dipped into that stillness, grabbing her coat, excusing herself. "I'll just be heading back where I came from and leave ye to your own now, Kathleen." No one said a word to Dulcie as she threaded her way through the group to the door. "Supper's on the stove," she sang out. The door thudded behind her.

Silence visited then, the silence of a funeral where mourners are squelched by shock. Kevin holding onto the child, Clara gaping at her mother, Robert staring at the floor. A memory glimmered for Clara, that of being a child in this house, playing *Statues* with Kevin.

It was Kathleen Kerrigan who started things moving. She planked her hands on the table and pushed herself to her feet. Tottering toward Kevin, she stared first at him, then at the child in his arms. Kate obliged by lifting her head and staring sleepily back.

Kathleen jerked her shoulders, raised her head, and fisted her hands. "She's the spitting image of..." Kathleen said, and then snapped her head around to stare directly at Clara, through Clara. "It's a foolish woman who picks up her children before they fall down," she whispered.

Clara's mind raced. What was her mother on about? Was there a click of common sense to it?

"Maybe not so foolish after all," continued Kathleen. She cupped Clara's face in her hands. "If I could go back..." Abruptly, she pulled away. "No point in walking backwards. That's when the devil overtakes you. We'll be keeping our eyes on God and closing them to the demon."

Clara trembled with uncertainty. Was her mother on the verge? She remembered the time she had seen Kathleen Kerrigan running along the landwash, nary a stitch of clothes on her, with Dulcie Mullins waving a patchwork quilt as she chased after her. The next day, her mother was gone, carted off to the Mental in St. John's, courtesy of the priest. Could all that happen again? Clara glanced at the door. Maybe she should bar it off. Maybe she should charge through the door herself, hightail it after Dulcie. Maybe she would need Dulcie's help to get Kathleen back into her parlour bedroom. Maybe--

"And Kevin, my son." Kathleen's voice, ripe with caring, sliced a path through Clara's rampant thoughts. "My son, there was no help for this. You built a home. You built it safe. Sure and there's no finer carpenter than yourself. Unlikely, it was, that the ocean would show up at your door." She let out a long, low sigh. "Why is it, I wonder, that the unlikely prospers? It's only the good Lord Himself can answer that. But one thing I do know is that, as hard as you try, you can't save your family from all the demons. Sometimes you can face them down, but other times..." As her voice trailed off, she put one hand on Kevin's shoulder. "God bless you, you and your miracle child." She clicked her tongue. "What's the good Lord thinking at all, to take so many all at once? God rest their souls." When she lowered her head and made the sign of the cross, Clara and Robert followed suit.

"We'll all be sitting at the table this evening," said Kathleen, again breaking the stillness. "After we finish supper, Clara, you and your Robert will take Kevin and Kate to *your* home." Her voice had a commanding tone now, one that Clara had not heard before. "Surely be to goodness they can stay at *your* home for as long as they like. Isn't that right, Clara?"

Clara opened her mouth but couldn't make a sound.

"Have you been blown through by a fairy wind, child?" Kathleen's voice vibrated, as if anxiety ridden. "Kevin and little one will be going to your house. Are you after hearing me at all, Clara?"

Clara nodded. "They're welcome. As welcome as the angels in heaven." Now where had she heard that expression before? Oh yes, it was--.

"Mavis." Kevin inserted the answer before Clara could complete her thought. She looked at him, eyes wide. All waited, another game of *Statues*. He offered no more words.

Again, it was Kathleen who pushed them into the next moment. She placed one trembling hand over her heart and let out a loud sigh. "I'll be needing to set myself to rights," she said, as she vanished across the hall into the parlour. In less than a minute, she was back, fully dressed, hair netted. She pulled an apron from a hook near the stove, a bibbed apron with purple flowers. As soon as she had tied its strings, she set about laying the table.

Clara guided Kevin and Kate to the daybed and watched, blinking, as Kathleen Kerrigan, her very own mother, burst forth like a crocus through the hard, cold ground of winter. After fifteen years in a stupor, her mother was back. No warning at all. What in the name of God had just happened?

Clara jumped when the storm door slammed. Boots scuffed the floor. Alphonse Kerrigan appeared, filling the kitchen door frame. The sight of his wife brought him up short. "Sweet Heart of Jesus," he said, leaning against the door jamb.

Kathleen darted her eyes at him, then turned her back to him. "Like I was saying, we'll be keeping our eyes on God now." It was then that she went to Kevin and placed a gentle hand on the head of the little girl. "Clara will finish the laying of the table while I rock my grandchild."

Little Kate looked up. Without hesitation, she reached for her grandmother.

With a sigh, Kevin released her.

With a snort, Alphonse stormed out.

Clara and Robert stared blankly at each other.

Kathleen padded her way toward the rocking chair, her grandchild in her arms. In one flowing motion, she sat, swayed, and spoke, her voice muted in lullaby fashion. "Her name was Kate, just like you," she said.

Clara perked up an ear. A story? Time melted. She was a child again, spine tingling, waiting for Mommy's words.

"The table, Clara?" This prompt came from Robert. Clara nodded, and indicated for him to take her place on the daybed, beside Kevin.

As Clara took to the task, all of her senses awakened. Her mouth watered at the odour of pork roast, her face flamed from the blazing heat of the stove, her eyes filled at the sight of Kathleen and Kate in the rocking chair. Was that picture real? Imagine it: *her* mother, *her* child, sitting together. She dared not blink, afraid that the image would vanish.

Clara worked soundlessly, one eye on her mother, one ear to her mother. What story was Kathleen Kerrigan about to tell?

Kathleen drew Kate close and let out an audible sigh. "Yes, her name was Kate, just like you. A little girl, just like you. This Kate loved to eat bakeapples. Would you happen to know a little girl who loves bakeapples?" Kathleen paused and smiled down at her granddaughter.

"Me," Kate said, pointing her thumb at her chest.

Kathleen nodded and moved on. "Now that don't come as no surprise to me at all. Sure and it's a delightful thing when the spongy, green barrens are dotted with them cloudy, yellow berries. On berry picking days, this little Kate would fill her basket and pop berries into her mouth. Couldn't get enough of them. Makes your mouth water just to think of it, doesn't it?" Another pause, another smile.

Kate nodded and smiled back.

"One day, this Kate decided to go traipsing on the barrens all on her own, she did. Stubborn child. Many a time, her mother warned her against it. The wind alone was bad enough on the barrens; it would blow so hard that even the crows took to walking. But it was not only the wind you had to be wary of: it was the fairies too."

Kate Kerrigan stared up at her grandmother, wide-eyed. She blinked, once.

At this point, Clara plopped down onto the daybed, eyes fixed on the duo in the rocking chair. What kind of story was this? Should she interrupt? When Clara herself was little, Kathleen Kerrigan had diverted her from the dory by telling her a story about coffin ships. *Coffin* ships. Sweet Mother of Christ. Kathleen wasn't going to tell anything like that to poor little Kate, was she? Clara moved to the edge of the daybed, poised to jump.

"Mind you, they don't like to be called fairies," continued Kathleen. "They are the Little People. But you can call them fairies as long as they don't be hearing you doing it. Now everyone knows you shouldn't go to the barrens alone, certainly not without a bit of bread or a few coins in your pocket to keep the fairies away. But do you think this little girl listened to warnings from her mother?

"Of course she didn't," said Kathleen, answering her own question. "One fine summer's day, she was yearning for them yellow bubbles on the green barrens, so off she went, no bread crumbs, no coins, nary a thing."

Kate Kerrigan lifted her head from her grandmother's shoulder. "But if you turns your sweater inside out, the fairies won't bother you none." She stuck her thumb in her mouth and kept her eyes wide, focused on her Kathleen's face.

Clara let out a quiet sigh. Kate knew the folklore. Stories from her mother, perhaps. Maybe from her older sister, Marie. And here Clara was, in a tizzy for no good reason whatsoever. Still, she stayed alert.

"Now isn't that the truth?" Kathleen replied to Kate. "But on this particular day, this particular Kate was not wearing a sweater. And, sure enough she came upon a clutch of fairies, each no more than a foot tall, all dressed in green save for their red hats which bounced as they danced a jig. Shaking in her boots, Kate was, as she tiptoed away. Thought she was getting away easy, but didn't she go and trip on a twig and land flat on her face? When she rolled over, she was right in the centre of a circle of fairies."

The story stopped then, interrupted by gurgling and spitting sounds. Kathleen looked up. Clara glanced at the cause of the commotion, the boiling pot of potatoes which was spewing starchy foam down its outsides. She leapt into action, grabbing woven potholders, slanting the pot's lid, halting the vexing hiss of water on hot stove. She slid the pot to the warming side of the stove and hurried back to her rigid position on the daybed. Had she missed anything? Holding her breath, she looked at her mother who was silent, staring into the face of her grandchild. Clara exhaled. And waited.

"As I was saying," Kathleen continued, "Kate lay on her back in the middle of a circle of fairies. She widened her eyes first, but then squeezed them tight, pretending she hadn't seen the fairies at all. A good thing too: fairies act up, if they got a mind to, when humans stare at them. So she stayed very still, not moving a muscle until she was certain the fairies were gone." Kathleen paused, fingering a lock of Kate's hair. "There you have it. Now, why do you think I'm telling you this story, Katie girl?"

Kate remained transfixed.

Clara remained riveted to the edge of the daybed. Maybe she should have intervened. How in God's name was Kate supposed to know the why of this story? Darn good question, that. Why in the name of God was her mother telling this strange yarn to this little girl?

"It's simple," said Kathleen. "Kate didn't have a breadcrumb or a penny in her pocket to protect her. She didn't have a sweater to turn inside out. And I guarantee you that those fairies knew she saw them. If the fairies had wanted her, they would have taken her."

Kate continued to suck her thumb, her face blank.

After a long sigh, Kathleen said, "I guess there's one more thing I should be telling. Yes, I am your grandmother, your nanny. But my name is Kathleen, just like you. When I was little, everyone called me Kate, just like you. Who do you think the little Kate in my story is?"

There was a popping noise as Kate withdrew her thumb from her mouth. She grabbed onto the bib of Kathleen's apron, fisting her fingers over a spray of embroidered purple flowers. Not for a flutter of a moment did her eyes leave her grandmother's face.

Kathleen's voice came again, gentle and true. "If the fairies had wanted me, they would have taken me. The fairies sent me back."

Silence returned, a bubble suspended in time. Clara glared at her mother, anger rising. Was Kathleen Kerrigan going to explain herself or what? Was she just going to leave poor little Kate dangling? Poor little Kate who--

"The ocean sent me back." Whispered words. From the mouth of Kate.

Clara's hand flew to her throat. Dear God in heaven. She swallowed a sob.

Kathleen Kerrigan merely nodded. "Yes, the ocean sent you back."

Kate reached up and hugged her grandmother.

"The ocean didn't want you now at all," said Kathleen. "You are safe. You are safe here. I'll see to that for the rest of my days." She planted a kiss on Kate's forehead and carried her to the table. "It's time for everyone to come to supper." For the first time since she began her story, Kathleen looked at the other people in the kitchen.

Clara jumped from the daybed and escorted Kevin to the table. Kate chose her own seat, between her father and her grandmother. There was no sign of Alphonse, so Clara ushered Robert to Alphonse's chair and then sat beside him.

Kathleen bowed her head. ""Bless us, O Lord, and these Thy gifts," she began. As Clara joined in, she shot a glance at Kate who was carefully dislodging something buried under her sweater. Prayer forgotten, Clara stared. When the object appeared, Kate placed it on her lap. Clara drew in a quick breath.

Her daughter had survived the tsunami. So had her daughter's doll, Mrs. Fan, Clara's very own Mrs. Fan which she had made as a child.

At the end of the blessing, Clara managed to exhale the appropriate "Amen."

The group ate in silence.

After supper, Kathleen lifted Kate from her chair and placed her on Kevin's lap. She raised Kevin's arms, one at a time, and wrapped them around the little girl. Then, she took to her rocking chair and took out her knitting needles. From her little corner of the room came comfortable old sounds: creaking, humming, clicking. Clara watched, listened, her eyes and heart filled to the brim.

Robert edged toward Clara. "I'll get the carriage," he said, patting her on the shoulder. "Will you meet me outside?"

Clara cast him a grateful glance which he absorbed with a smile. She reclaimed her coat and led Kevin outside. Shortly, Robert reappeared with the carriage; he was at the reins and there was no sign of Alphonse. Robert offered no explanation. Clara and Kevin climbed aboard, Kate still clinging to Kevin's shoulder, Kevin's body now jerking like a ripped sail in a storm.

Once home, Clara led Kevin to the door and then she spoke to Robert. "Leave the team here," she said. "I'll just get Kevin settled and I'll take the carriage back."

"I'll take care of the carriage," said Robert.

"Shouldn't I go back and check on my mother?"

Robert approached, lightly touching her shoulder. "I can do that, too, Clara." He sighed. "Look, I may not be fully aware of everything that's going on, but that does not matter. I am your husband. I will return the team and check on both of your parents. You need to help your brother now." He planted a kiss on her forehead.

Clara reached, touched his arm. "Thank you," she whispered.

A brisk nod and he was gone.

Clara headed into the kitchen where she found Kevin, sitting on the daybed, rocking Kate. Clara stared for a moment. "There's a spare room ready for you," she said. Kevin stood. Again, Clara led him, through the kitchen, up the stairs, to the small bedroom at the back of the house. He placed the child on the bed, covered her with a patchwork quilt, the one with the wild, red roses, the one Clara's mother had stitched. He stood and faced Clara, his shoulders slumped, his eyes glazed. Her heart aching for him, Clara took his hand and guided him back to the kitchen.

"Tell me, Kevin, just get it all out. Tell me everything," she said.

Mute, he sat on the daybed and stared into nothingness, a man devoid of soul. A sudden coldness jolted Clara. It had never occurred to her that men felt loss the same way women did. Men were supposed to be strong, weren't they? Rigid, unmoved, like oak trees or lighthouses. Even her husband, with all his British elegance, was that way, wasn't he? She pictured him standing on the deck of the *Elizabeth J*, as tall and straight as the vessel's mast. Nothing could bend him. Or so she thought. But now, as she focused on her brother, sitting in front of her, a shattered version of his former self, truth set in. Some storms could topple anything.

"Why don't you just lie down here, Kevin?" She slipped his overcoat from his sagging shoulders and slung it over a chair. She nudged him gently from seated to supine, hoisting his legs onto the daybed. She untangled knotted laces and removed muddied boots. A pillow for his head. A quilt for his body. Then Clara surveyed her brother, her childhood hero, whose eyes were wide, staring, vacant. Yes, some storms could topple anything. How selfish had she been indeed.

Clara stayed, a guardian angel of sorts, until Kevin's eyes drooped. When his breathing became deep and regular, she headed to the pantry, unconcerned that the noise of the pump might awaken her brother. Tragedy and exhaustion had taken their toll. He would sleep for hours.

CHAPTER 26

IN THE DAYS THAT FOLLOWED, Clara made herself indispensable to Kevin and Kate; she hovered around them, waiting for a cue, a sign that she could help. But she was a mere bystander, watching the two cling to each other, fused by time and tragedy. Daily, Kate keened for her mother, for her siblings. Daily, Kevin embraced his daughter, arms locked around her. He would allow no one else, even Clara, to get too close. Sometimes it seemed to Clara that Kevin was making special efforts to keep her at bay.

For the most part, Clara's guests were quiet. She adapted to the sound of their ghost-like footfalls on floorboards, to the fact that her life was a series of monologues. Never a response from Kevin or Kate. Alphonse stayed away entirely. As did Kathleen. It was two weeks before Kevin said anything.

Then, one day, "Clara?"

His voice startled her, a surprise echo from her past. She plopped the kettle onto the stove and swerved, hand over heart. She stilled herself, ready to listen.

"I need to set things right now that the little one is upstairs asleep." He let out a deep sigh. "God bless you for all you done for us, Clara but you knows as well as I that we have to be leaving here." He lowered his head and laced his fingers, pressing the tips into the backs of his hands until his knuckles turned white. "It's just that she's all I got left. I have to make a home for us, however I can. The Lord saved her for a reason. I want to have my own home for her come the fall."

Clara gulped back the urge to scream in protest. Edging toward him, she nervously wiped her hands on her apron. "Robert and I can help you with whatever you need, Kev," she said, breathless. "The men will help you build. You can always work on Robert's schooner--"

"No. No, I'll not be going off to sea and leaving my little one. I was gone when...." He waved his arm through the air, brushing the words away. Then he cleared his throat. "She's had enough loss. I'll take the help with the house; can't be raising money, or walls for that matter, by myself. I'll take some help with the child." Clara smiled but when Kevin shook his head her smile evaporated. "Not you. I know you means well, Clara, but you're only twenty-one and you got no young 'uns of your own." His glance changed to a glare and he looked away. "It's okay for now, having you tend to Kate, especially while we're under your roof, but as soon as we move, Dulcie Mullins will take over. Her young 'uns are grown and gone. She knows about the upbringing of a four year old. She'll do it for nothing, she said. Happy to feel useful, she is."

With her thoughts racing as she scrambled to understand, Clara dropped onto the daybed. She stared up at Kevin who was paying her no mind whatsoever. Just talking and talking.

"I'm not straying. I can earn a living with a little inshore fishing. I can plant vegetables, snare rabbits." His face took on a faraway look then, like he was lost in a memory. "Always had a brace or two of rabbits in my storeroom." He shook his head violently. "One thing I'm not doing is going on the open sea. The ocean is no friend of mine. It is a cruel witch who takes what she wants when she has a mind to." His voice grew louder, trembled. "My Mavis and Jimmy and Marie and Joseph and Johnny. What was I thinking at all, naming a poor child Jimmy after..." He stopped, shuddered. "Besides, I know how that husband of yours makes a living and I want no part of that. I'm not judging the man or nothing. That's between him and his God. And the ocean put the fear of

God into me. I am content to be a hangashore: whether the people sees me as lazy or not makes no never mind to me. Kate needs me. I have to provide for her." He looked at Clara, his eyes dark, blank pools. "What's the good of a man if he can't take care of his own?"

Clara nodded because that's all she could do. Kevin was leaving and he was taking Kate with him. No two ways about it. She bit hard on her tongue, and attempted to deny the evil inside her. All the want and need and anger were scratching at her innards, threatening to surface. *Dulcie Mullins*? Sure enough, she had cared for Clara a long time ago. But now? Tending to Kathleen *and* taking over Kate? Clara opened her mouth to spout some form of objection but Kevin was already standing, his back to her, his shoulders stooped. He slumped toward the stairs, muttering thanks.

Clara still sat, her mouth hanging open. Temptation swirled inside her, a violent sea pent upon finding its path to shore. She sucked in a deep breath and spit out whispered words. "I understand, Kevin, but the child is mine." But Kevin was already out of sight, floorboards on the second floor creaking under his weighted footsteps. She remembered the day he had first left home, the day she had spewed words that had eaten at her insides, the words about Jimmy's death. He hadn't heard her then, either. Did she really want him to hear her now? Maybe she should follow him. She stood, hesitated, took one step.

Just then the storm door on the porch squeaked open. She turned.

Her father entered the kitchen.

Clara's heart quickened.

With head low, clutching the familiar salt-and-pepper cap, shifting his hands around the edge of the cap like he was steering a schooner into port, Alphonse stepped to the middle of the room and planted his feet. He neither raised his head nor uttered her name. "I never knew much about your time on the Burin," he said, his voice barely above a murmur. "I never knew which little one was under your apron. But I knows now. And I come here to say that you can never tell him nothing.

Your brother's been hauled through a knothole. He can't be taking it. You got to be thinking of the girl, too."

Heat rushed to Clara's face. How in the name of all that was holy had he known what she had been contemplating? "The only one you're thinking of is yourself!" she sputtered.

Alphonse raised his head. "No selfish, brazen girl such as yerself should be holdin' so much power." He stepped closer, reached out one hand and grabbed her wrist. "You can't be blabbering this, missy. You got to be grown up, responsible. You got to do the right thing for Kevin and the little one."

"You mean for yourself, don't you?" Clara hissed. "Heaven forbid you should have the shame of a wayward daughter licking at your heels."

Alphonse stiffened. "No one would be blaming me if I give you a lacing for your impudence even though you're a married woman." He released her arm. "Be grateful that the whiskey don't claim me no more." He plopped his hat on top of his head.

Clara sniffed. "Something will always claim you; if not the whiskey, then the devil, or--."

It was Alphonse's raised right arm that stopped her from launching into a complete tirade. She gulped and put her hand to her chest. He formed his fingers into a fist and slowly lowered his hand to his side. "If it's Dulcie Mullins Kevin wants to be caring for the child, it's Dulcie Mullins he gets," he said through gritted teeth.

Clara felt a flush creep across her cheeks. Alphonse Kerrigan had heard her conversation with Kevin. Spying on her, he was. Standing outside, listening. Why hadn't she heard the wagon or the horses? Had Alphonse walked all the way here? It didn't make no never mind. Her eyes flitted, her mind raced. There was no where she could go, nothing she could say to escape this. She gripped the edge of the table. She recalled her exile to Burin; she was sinner, pariah, obeying her father. She had taken her child away, left her, let her be claimed by another woman. Obeying her father. She had always obeyed her father, hadn't she? Always.

"You hear me?"

Clara fell back into her chair. A resigned thud. "I hear you," she muttered.

Alphonse let out a long sigh. He retreated.

The door slammed shut, the clock ticked on, and for the second time in her life, Clara had agreed to relinquish her child to another woman's care. There was no choice. She had no choice. She could not chase Kevin. She could not tell. Not ever. Not ever. Not ever. The words ricocheted around her brain, each hit stabbing her, punishing her, inciting her with anger. *Never tell. Never tell.* Over and over. She stifled a sob, bolted from her chair and ran to the porch where she grabbed her coat and fisted her way into it. She couldn't tell Kevin, but she had to tell someone. She had to.

The church door seemed heavier than usual. Clara thrust it open and it responded with an elongated groan. She flinched. This visit should be silent, secret. She gripped the door before it could slam shut. She depressed the latch and eased the grainy oak monster back into its casing. She swallowed with relief when it responded without so much as a squeak. She nodded, turned, and took a full step forward. Her laced boot hit the floor like a hammer to metal. She froze, shoulders hunched, eyes shut, mind sputtering a *Hail Mary*. When she reached the Amen, she opened her eyes to the empty foyer. Safe. Undiscovered. On tiptoes, she made her way to the holy water font where she doused her fingers, blessed herself. She sniffed. Was this mission truly blessed? She continued in, toward the confessional at the back of the church. Genuflecting, she slid into a nearby pew. She lowered the kneeler, dropped onto it and let her thoughts fly. Could she do this? Should she do this? She had promised herself, promised her father, that she would not tell. She could not hurt her brother. Certainly not her daughter. But here? Confession, that was different now, wasn't it?

Father Mahony was supposed to listen, to forgive. He wasn't allowed to repeat his parishioners' sins. She clasped her hands over her galloping heart. It was only by a hair's breadth that she had managed to contain herself today. Had her father not shown up, she might have trailed her brother up those stairs. She might have let the words fly. She had to tell someone. God was the best choice, and the nearest thing to God around here was Father Mahony.

Determined to get it over with, Clara planted her hands on the pew in front of her and pushed herself to a standing position. She sidled out of the pew and headed toward the confessional. Her footsteps started strong, but courage dwindled rapidly; by the time she reached the door of the confessional, her knees were weak. She hesitated, hand on the doorknob. Maybe she shouldn't... *It's the saddest thing in the world, to lose your child.* Her mother's words, clear as a church bell on Christmas. If Clara was to get beyond this loss, this emptiness, the unfairness of it all, she had to at least confess her sin. Clara turned the handle, stepped into the darkness, closed the door and knelt, resting her folded hands on the narrow shelf provided. Instantly, the small door in front of her slid open and the only thing that divided her from the priest was rectangle of wire mesh. The aroma of coffee filtered through. Clara's nose twitched at this unfamiliar scent. Her mind settled for an instant on the image of a rum bottle and a tiny sensation of comfort gave her strength. Everybody, even Father Mahony, had secrets, now didn't they?

"Bless me, Father, for I have sinned."

"How long has it been since your last confession, child?"

"It has been two weeks, Father." A splinter from the wooden kneeler pricked her knee.

"Tell me your sins, child."

She opened her mouth but could not find the words. Her breath was coming in short gasps.

"Are you ill, child?"

"No, no. Not sick, Father. Just hard to..."

"Ah, I see. Just take your time. It's Clara, isn't it?"

Clara gripped the shelf to keep from crumbling to the floor. Her instinct was to run, but how useless was that? He'd said her name, hadn't he? Wouldn't do to have him show up at her house. Things never went well when the priest showed up. She dropped her jaw and emptied her soul. "The whole world is coming down on me, Father. I had a baby." A searing pain hit her throat and tears burned her eyes. "I had a child and her name is Kate." She sniffed. "Kevin thinks that she is his because when I was in the family way, my father sent me to the Burin and Mavis took me in and she was in the same way herself, and the babies were born one day apart and Kevin was on the seal hunt so he never knew nothing about it and, when he came back, Mavis told him they had twins and he believed her." Clara stopped and sucked in a deep breath. As she exhaled, a shaky laugh came out. She clapped her hand over her mouth. Why was she laughing? This was nothing to laugh at.

"Don't worry, Clara. The body has a strange way of showing relief sometimes. Just take another deep breath and let it out, long and slow."

Clara did as instructed. Her body felt lighter, like she had dropped a heavy load.

"Kate is here now, isn't she, Clara?"

"Yes, Father."

"And you want to raise her as your own?"

Clara bowed her head and whispered, "Yes, Father."

Father Mahony shifted in his chair. He tapped his finger on the shelf. Clara's heart floundered. Would he bestow upon her the gift that was hers in the first place?

Father Mahony took a deep breath. "But of course you know that you can never do that." His voice was crisp, clear as the shallows on a sunny day.

Clara raised her head. She must have misheard. "I know that I can't tell Kevin *now* because she is all he has." She swallowed, continued. "But, in a few weeks' time--"

"There are no buts. You can *never* tell him, child."

The words slapped her, silenced her. She was fading away. "Why not?" she whispered, all the while knowing, all the while denying.

"A sin is a sin, child. The Lord does not reward women who have children outside the precious bonds of marriage. The child had to be taken from you."

"But I--"

"Clara, you thought you left sin behind when you left the baby. But sin has followed you home. My child, you cannot act on your thoughts here. You cannot take that little girl from your brother. Hasn't he suffered enough? The loss of Kate would be the end of him. Can you see that you hold the power of life and death over him? You have to keep him safe now. Remember how he took care of you and your mother while your father was away in the Great War? A long time ago, I know, but it's your turn now."

Clara said nothing.

Father Mahony continued. "And what about the little girl? Kate? What about the life she would lead with the knowledge that she was born out of wedlock haunting her? There are no buts, Clara. I allowed you to be married in the church at the request of your father. And your poor mother, if she could have asked, would have wished the same. You have good parents who do not deserve the anguish of a wayward daughter. You must not ever tell Kevin, or Kate, about *your sin*. Never."

There was something about the way he stabbed at the words '*your sin*,' something that triggered the memory of the day she was here, in this very confessional, with a strange man named Patrick. Guilt roared up inside her. She was not fading anymore now. She was gone.

"For your penance you will say five *Our Fathers* and five *Hail Marys*. A small penance for a grave sin. However, the punishment of silence will be yours for the duration of your existence on earth. Be grateful at least for now that you have confessed your sin, the Good Lord can choose to accept you into his kingdom upon your death. God bless you."

Clara, the sinner, was silent.

"In nomine patris, et filii, et spiritu sancti."

The priest waited a second for her response which came automatically.

"Amen," she said. Instantly, the tiny door to the priest's wisdom slammed shut. Clara stayed in the confessional, on her knees, frozen in time, in darkness. After a few seconds, she rose to leave.

As she was turning, she heard the tiny door on the other side of the priest squeak open. Clara froze. Was the priest opening the door to someone else? How long had that person been there? Had someone overheard her as she emptied her soul to the priest? Clara had been so engrossed that she forgot to keep an ear cocked. The muttered words "Bless me father..." floated through the darkness. Whose voice was it? Panic fluttered. Had a piece of herself slid, unbidden, into the ears of someone she could not trust? She opened the door and scurried from the church, reciting her penance as she went. Five of this, five of that, and a lifetime of nothingness. Not the usual procedure, this praying on the run, but she had to get out without being seen by the other sinner in the confessional.

Once outside, when her heart slowed down a bit, it occurred to her that she had accepted, without question, the judgement and sentence of the priest. The Church owned her, just like it did all the rest of them. She wasn't different at all, like she used to think. Just another sheep in the flock.

She was yards away from the church when the rumble of its heavy door reached her ears. Curiosity overtook her and, like Lot's wife in the Bible, she looked back. A single glance revealed Dulcie Mullins, her neighbour, former caregiver, current enemy, standing in the doorway, staring at her. Clara was torn between contempt and fear. Fear proved the stronger of the two; it clutched Clara's heart, holding her still as Dulcie approached. Had Dulcie heard Clara's secret?

"It's a great day on clothes," said Dulcie, echoing what Clara had said on the day Dulcie had delivered the news of the tidal wave. "But still, even if the weather's tempting you, some things you hangs out in the wind, some things you doesn't." She patted Clara on the shoulder as she slid by.

As gratitude filtered through her body, Clara's eyes filled with tears. "Thank you." A mere whisper which fluttered away in the wind. Clara took a deep breath and wiped away the tears.

Clara watched as Dulcie Mullins chuffed along the road. A kindly woman that. Kevin's decision to choose Mrs. Mullins over Clara still burned. But didn't Dulcie just say she would keep her mouth shut? Maybe Clara could let her hurt feelings slide; maybe she could work with Mrs. Mullins in the raising of Kate. Clara inhaled, letting the sea air expand in her lungs, and exhaled long and slow. She continued to watch Dulcie who was nearing her own home. As Clara gazed, something niggled at her. Dulcie Mullins had never kept her mouth shut about anything; in fact, she talked all the time. Words sliding in and out of her like a tide to and from shore. Should she follow Dulcie? No, she would just watch. Clara swallowed her doubt when the little teapot of a woman toddled up the rocky path to her own house. She wasn't going anywhere. She wasn't telling anyone.

Clara's secret was safe. For now.

KEVIN

CHAPTER 27

1930

KEVIN POSITIONED A NAIL, RAISED his hammer. He paused, arm in mid-air. Was the job nearly done? Hard to grasp that, after only a few months in Argentia, he was about to drive the last nail into a new house. His house. Built with his own two hands. Not for lack of help, he reminded himself. The people here were the finest kind, offering help galore. Sometimes he accepted: a man could hardly raise a wall by himself. More often he spurned it: a man needed to build a life for himself.

This new house was a single story A-frame, far removed from the shape of his Burin salt box and far removed from the reach of the Argentia shoreline. The furniture was new, too. Hand built by him. Clara didn't see the sense in any of it. No need to be cutting and shaping pine, she had said, when her house had room enough and furniture enough for the lot of them. He had sniffed, sure that if Clara had her way, she would be parent to Kate and he would be visitor, no more than that. Kevin pressed his lips together. Sure enough, it was the way of things for a widowed man to give a girl child over to the care of her aunt. Even Mavis would have nodded on that, but Kevin would have none of it. Kate was all he had left. A man can't rip away the thread that binds the rift in his soul.

He swallowed the bile burning his throat and pulled his thoughts back to the house. Yep, the labour was pretty much his. As for land and lumber? Different thing entirely. That came from his rich brother-in-law, a man Kevin had met just months before, a man he rarely scraped shoulders with, despite living under his very roof.

Robert Caulins was a quiet man who walked easy, yet the sight of him rattled Kevin. A man like Robert, with an uppity British accent and a mountain of thick books, must be full of deep thoughts and big ideas. What would a simple man like Kevin have to say in the face of that? The threat of conversation was no concern at first; no one expected a word out of a Kevin after the Burin. When Kevin found his voice again, he used it to soothe Kate or placate Clara. But, at supper, in Robert's company, Kevin stayed silent, kept his head low, and, as soon as he was finished chewing, hightailed it to the shed.

It was Clara who put an end to the flinching and fleeing when she came out and said that Robert had no designs on flushing out Kevin's lack of schooling. Kevin gnawed on that for a bit, then nodded. Clara was right. If Robert Caulins had deep thoughts, he kept them to himself. It was the contents of his deep pockets that he passed along. Kevin wondered, almost asked once, if Clara knew that Robert's riches came from hauling cargo, not cod. In the end, he decided not to come over the subject. It really made no odds. His sister wanted for nothing money could offer, and now, neither did he.

Kevin didn't gnaw over accepting Robert's money. Sometimes a man has to sling pride into a back room and slam the door. He had to take help, for Kate. Every now and then, he wondered if he and Kate, money in hand, should have gone to another community entirely. But where? He could not have rebuilt on the Burin Peninsula. Had to escape the Burin. So he rebuilt in Argentia, the very place he had fled when he was just sixteen. Always running, it seemed. So why had he come back? Somewhere in his mind, he had a rosy picture of home. His childhood home. Argentia. Back before the trouble came.

Yes, he needed to be here, in Argentia, so he could tackle the beginning of things in hopes of making sense of later things. Maybe he could rekindle the glow he had felt as a little boy. There was a glow, wasn't there, in the days before there was a baby brother named Jimmy? And where was he on the day Jimmy died? Why wasn't he home? He sucked in a deep breath. Had to block thoughts of Jimmy before they dragged...

It was too late. Grief awakened inside him, its heaviness consuming his torso, overloading his limbs, melting his joints. Was he still gripping the hammer? He couldn't feel it. Yes, the nail was still in position, set against the wall, but it jiggled, blurred, and then clattered to the floor. The tremble in his fingers wormed its way up his arm, through his shoulder, until his whole body was shaking, intent on betraying him. Was there no mercy in heaven?

His knees buckled. He plummeted and curled into a ball. Sucking in a breath, trying to hold it. Failing. Sobs escaping, one after another after another until he was wailing. Maybe Clara was right. Maybe there was no point to all this building. His Mavis. His children. Gone. He tried to lift his head, but it was weighted like an anchor. Sinking. Sinking. Was he here or was he in the dory, tossing a killick, watching it drop, waiting for it to lodge on the bottom? He gritted his teeth to sever the wailing; still the sobs wheezed out. Maybe he should just stay, pressed to the floor, forget about getting up. Just let it all go. What the hell was he supposed to do now? Where was Mavis when he needed her?

'You're a good father to the young 'uns.' His body jerked. That was Mavis' voice in his ear, as clear as if she were right beside him. Instantly, the sobs stopped, the tremors vanished, the weight was lifted. He lay very still, breathing, listening. Was anyone about? Had anyone heard? There was no sound other than the thrum of his heart and the thrust of his breath. *'You're a good father to the young 'uns.'* Mavis' voice came again.

And, instantly, Kevin knew the point of it all: he still had a child. Kate. A man has to be a good father. A man has to take care of his own.

Slowly, Kevin made his way to his feet. He lifted his right arm, his eyes widening when he saw that his hand was still clamped around the hammer. He then bent low and, with sure fingers, retrieved the dropped nail. He positioned it, pounded it, a steady rhythm, and then gave it one last whack. Done.

Time to move on. Time to get Kate and move on.

Clara was not going to like this, not one little bit.

CLARA

CHAPTER 28

———◆———

BEFORE KEVIN AND KATE ARRIVED in Argentia, time was spread out for miles in front of Clara, unrolling like a massive map, one filled with unlimited possibility: someday, some time, she could and would step toward and embrace her daughter. Now however, that map unrolled just a bit at a time and could be snatched from beneath Clara's feet in an instant. She had to make the best of each tiny inch of time.

Clara did whatever she could think of to win favour with Kate, her Kate, a little girl clutching a little doll, a mirror image of herself as a child.

"Do you want to help me make bread?" Clara asked one day. When Kate did not respond, Clara mixed the bread by herself and set it aside to rise.

"I have a book of fairy tales. Would you like to read with me?" The pages of the Hans Christian Andersen book made a fluttering sound as Clara riffled through them. Kate did not look in the direction of the sound. When Clara placed the book on the daybed beside Kate, Kate ignored it.

"I could use some help with the cleaning." Clara cleared the cupboard and buffed the shelves with a flannel shirt turned dust rag. Kate didn't move.

After a time, Clara changed her methods. She stopped asking, cajoling. She took to leading Kate around by the hand as she went from chore to chore, inside and outside. When Clara picked partridgeberries or bakeapples, Kate trudged along behind her, holding her little basket.

One morning, Kate stood in the spongy barren and turned around slowly, eyes searching.

"What is it you're looking for?" Clara asked.

"Aunt Clara, do you suppose the fairies are here?"

A response? One that included her name? Clara's heart melted. "There'll be no fairies today, little one. They're not likely to show themselves to the two of us, now are they?"

Kate nodded and reclaimed her place behind Clara.

Clara hoped that Kate's response was the beginning of daily conversation but days passed without another word. Clara tried. She played dress up. She braided Kate's hair. She bent low on the bog with her, examining pitcher plants. She taught *Cat's Cradle* and *Statues* and *Hopscotch*. She read stories. And she made mistakes. Simple mistakes, like the time a ladybug landed on Clara's hand and she recited the Ladybug rhyme. *Ladybug, Ladybug, fly away home, your house is on fire and your children are gone.* Only when the words were out of Clara's mouth, when she realized their significance, did she pause and rethink. Why in the name of all that's holy would people write such things for children? Clara flicked her hand, launching the ladybug into the air. "There she goes, flying away home." That didn't help any and Clara felt her soul sink to her shoes. As she glanced down at Kate, the silent Kate, Clara caught sight of a small white stone beside a clump of jagged grass. Maybe-- "When I was little like you, I collected white stones and kept them in a jar on the kitchen window sill," she said.

From the pocket of her coat, Kate pulled a tiny white stone and held it up for Clara to see.

Clara reached for it.

Kate pulled it back.

"Can I hold it?" Clara asked.

Kate shook her head. She returned the stone to her pocket.

Clara felt suddenly, inexplicably weak. Had she missed an opportunity here? "Should we get a jar for you to collect pebbles?"

Kate patted her pocket. Then she spoke, but not to Clara. "The water took my jar, isn't that the truth of it, Mrs. Fan?" With a little help from Kate, Mrs. Fan nodded. "This one is my rememberer, isn't it? It was near my old house. I found it the day Daddy took me to the boat."

"Oh," said Clara, not knowing what else to say. The child was more like her than she could have imagined. She and Kate looked the same, loved the same doll, and even collected the same kind of pebbles. Yet Kate was adrift, in a dark, dark world. Clara was on the outside, powerless. Was there no way to reach her daughter?

It was in a moment of letting go that Clara bridged the gap. One day, of her own accord, Kate went outside. Concerned that she might wander, Clara watched at the kitchen window. When Kate climbed onto a sawhorse and stared at the sea, a statue, Clara sighed away from the window and into her chores. Periodically, she checked back. She was fluffing pillows, a final touch to bed-making, when a cry from Kate pierced the air. Clara sprinted down the stairs, her heart hammering. She was almost at the outside door when Kate burst through, tears streaming. In her hands, she held Mrs. Fan. "Aunt Clara, Aunt Clara." She hiccupped into sobs.

Clara stooped. "Whatever is it? What's wrong?" She examined Kate's face and hands. No blood. No visible injuries.

"Mrs. Fan. A nail on the sawhorse. Tore her dress." More sobs.

"Oh, I see," said Clara, relief flooding her. "Let me have a look."

Kate clutched the doll tighter.

"I won't hurt her. I promise."

Kate blinked. She released her grip and held the doll up for inspection.

Sure enough, Mrs. Fan had a rip in her dress through which stuffing dangled. "That won't do at all, now will it? I can fix it," whispered Clara. "*We* can fix it."

Kate's eyes widened.

"As soon as you stop your crying, we'll get the sewing box."

Kate stared at Clara for a few seconds. Halting her sobs, she released the doll into Clara's hand. After a short detour to grab the sewing box, Clara sat on the daybed. Kate stood in front of her.

As they picked through threads, Clara felt she was picking through strings of time. One day, long ago, she was searching for rags to sew a dress for Mrs. Fan. On that very day, the priest announced himself and tried to take Clara away from her home. In that instant, Clara Kerrigan hated Father Aloysius Mahoney. How could he even think of such a thing?

The memory made Clara's throat ache. What the hell was she doing, here, now, with Kate? Was she trying to get Kate to love her in the hope that the child would choose her over Kevin? Kate had already lost so much. Kevin, too. Unlike Alphonse Kerrigan, Kevin Kerrigan would always put the needs of his child ahead of his own.

Clara felt a sudden falling sensation. There was nothing left for her but to acknowledge the truth. Kate would leave. Nothing could stop it. She looked away so Kate couldn't see her face.

Kate tapped her on the shoulder.

Clara turned.

In her hand, Kate held a spool of thread. "Aunt Clara, maybe you need this?"

Clara accepted the thread. "Yes, we can use this to fix Mrs. Fan."

Kate shook her head. "First, we fix your heart."

"My heart?"

"You broke it." Kate's bright eyes bored through her.

Clara welled up. Kate knew. Kate knew exactly what she was feeling. Sadness should never be so recognizable, so familiar to a four-year-old child. In a moment of rawness, one that she had tried to conceal, she had bridged her way to Kate. Clara wanted to dwell, to vent. She didn't. Instead, she focused on Kate, whose face sagged with concern. "Oh, I'm not broken, little one," Clara said. "Mrs. Fan is the broken one. This thread is just perfect for Mrs. Fan."

Kate reached up, put her hands around Clara's neck, and pulled her into a hug.

As Clara wrapped her arms around her daughter, she felt crushed by the sheer weight of her love for Kate, so much love that she feared her heart would explode. Buried memories surfaced: the joy she felt when Kate danced in her belly, the pain when Kate was snatched away. Was it all going to happen again, love followed by loss? Kate slackened her grip. Reluctantly, Clara relinquished her hold, letting her arms fall to her sides.

With Kate was standing in front of her, waiting, Clara raised a limp arm and reached for a pin cushion. From it she extracted a needle. It took three attempts for her trembling hands to get the thread through the eye.

After Clara mended Mrs. Fan, Kate insisted on putting the doll to bed. "She needs time to get better," said Kate as she headed for the stairs.

Moments later, Kate returned to the kitchen. In place of the doll, she carried *Andersen's Fairy Tales*. Tingling with delight, Clara reached for the book. Smiling, Kate relinquished it. By the time Kevin came home, Clara and Kate were in the kitchen giggling over a story about an emperor parading in his underwear.

KEVIN

CHAPTER 29

———◆———

KEVIN TWISTED THE DOOR KNOB of Clara's house. A pitch of wind slammed into his back, shoving the door open, him through. His sod cap flew, bouncing off the porch wall before landing on the floor. Kevin wrestled the door closed, retrieved his cap, and slapped it on a hook. While tamping down his hair, he perked an ear toward the kitchen. They were there, Clara and Kate. He heard only Clara's voice, nattering, pausing, nattering again. No surprise there. Kate spoke few words these days, and those were mostly for his ears. There was sadness in that, but deep down, satisfaction, too. The very thought of sharing Kate with anyone, including Clara, especially Clara, made him scowl. He didn't ponder the sense of it. Just the way it was, that's all.

He started toward the kitchen, stumbling when he heard a giggle. Kate was laughing? With Clara? He put his hand on the door jamb to steady himself. Jesus Christ! Was he after lingering too long in this house? It was time to have at the situation before it was too late. Before Clara took over.

Kevin gritted his teeth and marched forward, coming to a dead halt at the sight of his daughter, the miracle of his daughter. Mission forgotten, he whispered Kate's name. She turned, beaming, raced to him and flung herself into his arms. He drew her close and waited, hoping that this time, she wouldn't ask.

She pulled back and stared into his eyes. "Did you go handy to the ocean today, Daddy?"

Should have figured. She always asked. "No. No ocean." The usual reply.

She kept her eyes on his, as if searching for the truth of it. After a few seconds, she echoed his words. "No ocean."

"I built you a new house," he said.

"A house?"

Kevin nodded.

"A *new* house?"

"Yes, a *new* house."

Kate tilted her head. "What about old houses?"

Kevin blinked. "Old houses?"

His little girl pulled away from him, out of his reach. Kevin let his arms go limp. He watched curiously as Kate looked all around the room, taking in every nook and corner before letting her gaze drift to the floor. Then she locked her eyes with his.

"Do houses get lonesome, Daddy?"

Kevin opened his mouth but no words made it through whatever was catching in his throat. It was Clara who let out a sound, a slight gasp, jolting him into the realization that she was still in the room. He raised a hand, palm out, toward her. Silence fell, interrupted only by baffles of wind that screamed through the chimney, clattering the flue. A storm was brewing; his new house would be tested soon enough.

"We left our old house all by itself," Kate went on. "It was beat up and soggy and we just left it there. Do you think it's lonesome?"

Kevin welled up. He reached out, pulling his little girl close, lifting her into his arms. Over Kate's shoulder, he saw Clara standing with one hand over her heart, the other touching her lips. He glared. Clara retreated to a corner.

"People get lonesome, not houses," Kevin said and then swayed, rocking his little girl gently. He took a deep breath. "It's time to forget about old houses. It's time to see our new house." He put her down. "Most of your things are already there, but you'd better get that doll of yours."

Kate nodded and headed for the stairs.

"She never goes anywhere without that doll," Kevin said to Clara.

Clara nodded. "It's a great comfort."

"She's been clutching that doll ever since Mavis made it for her when she was a baby."

Clara parted her lips to speak then closed them again. They both listened as Kate's feet pounded the stairs.

Kevin counted the steps that Kate took. When she was out of ear-shot, he said, "Mrs. Mullins will be mothering Kate from now on, Clara." He folded his arms.

Clara's face went blank. "D-d-don't you think that...."

"Think what?" Kevin stiffened his stance.

Clara gulped. "The little one's been through a lot." She lurched from the corner and paced the floor, daybed to stove and back again. "The little one's been through a lot."

"You're repeating yourself." Kevin lowered his head. "Maybe you means well. I don't know. She's all I got." He swallowed and shoved his hands into his pockets. "It was in the church, you know. The wake, I mean. Imagine the likes of that. No room for it anywhere else. All five of them at once. I left them to bring in wood and they died. Then I left their bodies on the Burin to come to Argentia. Kate is all I got and I'm not leaving her here." He looked up.

Clara stopped pacing and turned, her face ashen. "Don't you think that she'd be better--"

"Not when you got designs on wanting her for yourself. She's my daughter, in case you forgot." How cruel was he at all, saying such things to a barren woman?

Just then Kate bounced into the room, clutching Mrs. Fan. "We're ready," she announced.

Kevin smiled at her and scooped her up again. "What's that you were saying, Clara?" He glared at her out of the corner of his eye.

Clara clenched her hands in front of her apron. "Nothing," she said. "Nothing at all."

"Good-bye, Aunt Clara," said Kate, waving her pudgy hand. She held up the doll. "Say good-bye to Aunt Clara, Mrs. Fan."

CLARA

CHAPTER 30

———

AFTER KEVIN LEFT WITH KATE in his arms, Clara dropped into a chair, her heart pounding in her chest. Mrs. Dulcie Mullins would be mother to Clara. *Mother*! Yes, she'd admitted to herself that it was coming but that didn't take away the pain. The injustice of it slammed her, a gasp burst from her, and she fell to her knees. She sucked in a long, deep breath, the pain roiling inside her. It exploded in a ghoulish howl, launching her body forward like a violent wave crashing to shore. She lay there, arms spread wide, soul wracked by sobs. She lay there, plastered to floor like kelp to beach rocks. She lay there as morning filed by, its passing marked by banshee wind and lashing rain.

It was late afternoon when the wind died, when the rage inside her abated. She pushed herself to a seated position, her throat raw, her body all in. How was she ever going to live with this? How could she handle being so close to Kate, but never close enough? Shivering, she glanced at the stove which was black and cold, its silver paws rigid, commanding: tend to me. She scrambled to her feet, stumbled toward the kindling box, and lifted the bottom of her apron to create a cradle for wood. As she bent to gather, she stopped, eyes locked on the wooden crate that housed the kindling.

That very crate had traveled from the French island of St. Pierre via Robert's schooner. Before it had held wood, it had embraced rum, or whiskey, or whatever the spirit of the day was. A wooden box, reincarnated into a box for wood. A new life, a new use, all because of Robert and his schooner.

Clara let out a long sigh. Would that she had the wherewithal to start a new life. She grabbed a few twigs from the box. Yes, a new life. A chance to get away from things, that's what she needed.

The kindling tumbled from her hand. She blinked repeatedly. Could she go on the schooner? Her tongue, seemingly of its own accord, clicked in disapproval. Did she have a block of common sense at all? A woman? On a schooner? Rum running? She mulled it over, let the apron fall, and put her hands on her hips. A slow smile stretched across her face. Well, why not? There was nothing for her here other than the rage rotting her innards. What if she turned that anger outward? Her daughter and her brother would take the brunt of it and Clara wanted none of that.

But could she be so full of herself as to rise above the lot of women? Women were supposed to wait onshore, not follow their men to sea. More important, if she sailed away, could she leave this yearning for her daughter behind? Would it stalk her? A wave of dizziness hit Clara; she dropped to the floor, hands gripping the edge of the crate. She inhaled and exhaled as images of little Kate, clutching Mrs. Fan, the very doll Clara had made as a child, the very doll she had given to Mavis for Kate, taunted her. She formed a fist with her right hand and pounded her chest. "She's my baby. Mine. I want my little girl." She clamped her hand over her mouth. With a furtive glance, she looked around. No one here. No one heard. Still, she remained, hand over mouth. *Dear God in heaven.* She had to get away from here. But how in the name of all that was holy would she convince Robert?

On a regular basis, Robert sailed to the French island of St. Pierre, the centre of the liquor trade. There he loaded the schooner, and then headed to...? What was it they called it? Rum Road? Rum Row? Somewhere on the coast of the United States. They also smuggled booze to the city of St. John's and to Newfoundland outports. All under dark of night. The excitement of it sent a shiver through her. What would her father, never mind her father, what would the Church, meaning Father Mahony, have to say about her being involved in this activity?

The Church had already condemned her, a woman who had had a child outside of wedlock. That very same Church condoned rumrunners, men who made money outside the law. Clara smirked. Well, if she was going to hell anyway, she might as well do double duty. A nervous giggle slid from her. Could a woman stick her nose into the rum-running business? Clara's heart did a frenetic jig as she played with the idea. What if she got arrested? Not likely, at least not here in Newfoundland. The government did not have the money to police rumrunners. The long and short of it, as her father would say, was that men like her husband owned every doorknob in the courthouse. *Men.* Not women. The laws were made for men, by men. Women were chattel and baby-makers. Clara sniffed. She was nobody's property and she'd likely be making no more babies. She tilted her head to the side as she thought about Robert. Was he bothered about not having children?

"Not all it's cracked up to be, this parenting business," he had said, like he had had experience in the matter.

Clara had watched in wonder as this childless man had pulled little Kate to his knee and told her stories. He had spent an hour one day teaching Kate to snap her fingers and had grinned when the little girl's eyes popped wide at the slightest indication of success. Strange, that. Like he had been raising children for years. Where did a man get such skills? Handed down, she figured. Maybe that's the way his childhood was in England. She didn't know. What odds? If she couldn't give him a child, maybe she could partner him in business. Rum running. That's what she would do. She pulled in her grin and pursed her lips. First things first. She had to convince Robert.

CHAPTER 31

—◆—

ROBERT LOOKED UP FROM HIS reading and stared at Clara, wide-eyed. "Are you afflicted, my dear?" He placed his open novel on the kitchen table. A draught swept through the house, causing the pages to flutter. Robert shook his head. "Lost my place," he muttered. He located the correct page, inserted a bookmark, and returned his attention to Clara. "Maybe I'm losing my hearing as well. Would you please repeat yourself?"

"I said that it's high time I went on the schooner."

Robert's eyes twinkled. "I've always admired your spirited ways, Clara, but the schooner is decidedly no place for a woman."

Resentment smacked Clara's gut. When she was little, she had promised her mother she would stay out of the dory. That promise melted away just months later when her mother took to spending her days in a darkened parlour. It would be a cold day in hell before anyone could stop her from boarding a boat. "I intend to go on the schooner." She folded her arms and glared at him.

Robert let out a haughty laugh. He picked up his meerschaum pipe from its nearby stand and tamped down the tobacco. "You are rather amusing, my dear."

"I'm dead serious." Clara did not alter her stance.

Robert looked up at her and raised his eyebrows. "Indeed you do appear to be *dead serious*, but you could be just plain dead. I reiterate: the sea is not for women. Rum running is a dangerous business."

"I can manage it."

"I'll hear no more of it."

Clara stood rigid, hands at her sides. She clenched and unclenched her fists, then folded her arms again. "You'll not only hear more of it, you'll tell me all about it. And you will be taking me with you."

Robert returned his pipe to its stand. With a sigh, he rose from his chair and ambled toward her. He brushed his fingers down her face until they rested under her chin. She raised her head. His eyes, meeting hers, glistened with kindness. "What's this all about, Clara?"

Clara shivered. She inhaled slowly. Somehow the combination of his gentle touch and tobacco aroma played havoc with her determination. Tears leaked into her eyes. "I just..." She got not further because her voice dissolved into a whimper.

Robert reached for her shoulders and pulled her close. She let her tears flow into the soft fibres of his linen shirt.

"It's the little one, isn't it?" he said. "Kevin has taken Kate and, for the time being, has taken you out of the picture." He ran a hand through her hair then held her at arms' length. "Maybe that isn't the norm in this community, for a widowed man to keep a girl child, but Kevin has been through the bowels of hell. His daughter is all he has left. You have to let him be, Clara."

Clara nodded, sniffling.

"And now I'm taking off, too. That's it, isn't it?" Robert sighed. "What about your father, Clara? Does he need help with Kathleen?"

Clara shook her head firmly. "No. No. He doesn't want me in his sight. He thinks Kathleen is better off without..."

"I see and, believe it or not, I understand." Robert bit his lower lip. "You're feeling isolated." His eyes glazed over. "I had been away from England for a long time when I came here," he said in a low voice, a longing voice.

Curiosity piqued, Clara stopped sniffling; she had always wanted to hear more about Robert's life in England. But now? Not a chance. Now she saw an opening and she jumped in. "Then you met me and you weren't so lonely," she said. "Imagine how great it would be if we were at sea together."

Robert cleared his throat and stepped back, looking for all the world like he had avoided a near disaster. He wiped his mouth with his shirt sleeve and ran his fingers through his hair.

Clara tilted her head to one side. This was not like him. He was usually calm, not a flutter about him.

"Well if that is what you want, I won't try to stop you." His voice was as ruffled as his hair.

Clara frowned slightly, uncertain. "Are you saying yes?"

Robert returned to his chair. "Yes," he said and raised his head to reveal a charming smile.

Clara clapped her hands together, ran to him, and planted a kiss on the top of his head. "Thank you. Thank you. Thank you." She immediately bolted, heading to the vegetable garden. The cabbages didn't need tending but she feared lingering in the kitchen. Given enough time, Robert could experience a change of heart. Heaven forbid.

KEVIN

CHAPTER 32

———◆———

KEVIN HADN'T DIMMED CLARA'S DOORWAY in weeks. In fact, he hadn't set eyes on her at all, not even a glimpse. Probably just as well. The likelihood was that, had he seen her coming, he would have made himself scarce. But today? Couldn't escape her. There she was, at Sunday Mass, sitting a few pews in front of him and Kate. He sniffed. Well, he couldn't very well take to his heels, but he'd be giving her a wide berth after the service, that was for sure. He nodded. Decision made. Would have left it at that if Clara hadn't taken that very second to turn and wave. He hedged over responding but not little Kate; she shot her hand into the air and waved back.

A stab of remorse hit Kevin: had he been too harsh, taking Kate from her aunt? He had given his little girl a new house, a new life, a new caregiver—Mrs. Dulcie Mullins. Did he want Clara elbowing her way in? Kevin eyed Clara curiously; she was still looking, smiling a pleasant smile. Had he misunderstood? A single line can have two hooks. Had she been trying to help when he thought she was trying to take over?

After another tiny wave in Kate's direction, Clara turned to face the altar. Kevin stared at the back of his sister's head and pondered. Should he relent, just a little?

When Mass was ended, Kevin and Kate waited in the aisle for Clara. The trio exited the church together. "Nice to see you," Kevin said when they stepped outside, even though he was looking anywhere but at her.

"You, too," said Clara. "How's the little miss?" she asked Kate who smiled and clung to her daddy.

Kevin put his arm around Kate. "She's the finest kind," he said. "We're going visiting this morning, aren't we, Katie girl?"

Kate nodded, never raising her head.

Kevin patted Kate's shoulder. Maybe little Kate wasn't ready to look directly at people; maybe he needed to show her how. He raised his head, taking in an up close view of his sister. "You're looking good," he said. The statement was out of him before he knew it and he was struck by the stark truth of the words. His little sister, rosy-cheeked and bright-eyed? How had that happened? He combed through tangled memories but could not recall one in which she looked so content. It did his heart good, seeing her like this. He mirrored her smile.

"I'm the finest kind, just like Kate," said Clara, her voice bubbling.

"We're going to make a dart in at Nanny's and Poppy's." Kevin shifted from one foot to the other. "Do you want to come along?"

Clara shook her head. "Have to be getting home. Dinner's already on the cook. Have a great visit." She hurried toward a motorcar, driven by Robert.

"Will you look at that, Katie girl? Your aunt in a motorcar."

"Uncle Robert took me for a ride one day," said Kate.

"Oh." Kevin squirmed as he took in the woebegone look in the child's eyes. "Did you like living at Aunt Clara's?" he asked.

Kate shrugged. "Mommy makes better dough balls."

Kevin's heart lurched. His knees weakened. Get a handle on this, b'y. He could not let tiny triggers carve a giant hole. It was Kate's wide brown eyes, staring up into his, searching his, that kept him from sinking deeper. He tensed his muscles and took a deep breath. "Nobody, not even Mrs. Dulcie, can cook like your mommy," he said. He reached for her, picked her up. It took effort to lighten the tone of his voice, but he managed it. "It's time to visit Nanny and Poppy."

The visit was becoming a weekly routine. It was what families did, wasn't it? Landed on each other's doorsteps on Sundays? For Kevin, this was a way to build a family around Kate, to make things normal for her. Himself too, if he was to be telling the truth of it.

Today, as soon as they arrived, Kathleen Kerrigan emerged from the parlour, smiling, and took up her place in the rocking chair. At a sideways glance from her, Alphonse strode toward the exit.

Kevin raised an eyebrow. Alphonse often left the house soon after their arrival. What was that about? Was it Kathleen that made him take to the out-of-doors? Kevin shrugged it off. He'd probably be going outside himself, keeping his father company, but he couldn't, wouldn't leave his little girl alone with Kathleen Kerrigan.

Kathleen had been smitten with the child from the get go. Any fool could see that. A proper nanny she was, filling the child's head with folktales, fairy tales, and nursery rhymes. Little Kate, who rarely spoke to anyone but Kevin, was bright-eyed around her grandmother. At home, Kate even pretended to be like Nanny: knitting, spinning, praying the rosary. The sight of her baby fingers stumbling their way around a string of plump rosary beads always made Kevin smile. She often mixed up the words of the *Our Father* or the *Hail Mary*, but he didn't correct her. He left the praying to Kathleen. Kevin couldn't bring himself to pray much anymore.

Most Sundays, during the visit, Kevin was silent, watching and listening. Some days, like this one, ghostly memories flared. Images of his brother Jimmy, the baby boy with the bright blue eyes. The baby boy with the bright blue body. At least that's how he looked the last time Kevin saw him, in this very kitchen, beside this very stove, in Kathleen Kerrigan's arms. Those same arms now held and rocked his sleeping child. A peaceful sight. A calming sight. How could this same woman have ended the life of her own child? No reason or rhyme to it at all.

Without warning, a bolt of fear seized him, sending his heart racing. A familiar feeling, this. Always abrupt. Always brought him up short. What in the love of God had given rise to it this time? He didn't have to dig far. It was Jimmy, that's what. Why was he always getting himself upset over Jimmy's death? Kevin gripped the back of a chair and closed his eyes to darken unwanted images. But try as he might, he couldn't purge the ghosts. Nor could he expel the question that had haunted him his whole life: *How could Kathleen Kerrigan have taken the life of her own child?* A sharp pain in his chest erupted into a quiver that needled its way into his arms. In seconds, the quiver escalated to shaking. This was his cue: time to run. He refused. Steady as she goes, b'y, he reminded himself, a calming attempt that didn't take.

In two steps, Kevin crossed the kitchen floor.

When he reached for his child, Kathleen readily released the sleeping Kate and then looked up at him, her eyes beaming with love for the little one. In that instant, the question that preyed upon Kevin tumbled from his lips. "How could you?" he whispered.

Kathleen's eyes glazed over, uncomprehending. "What in heaven's name are you on about?"

Kevin shook his head and strode from the house.

Outside, he spotted Alphonse who was setting a stripped tree trunk onto a log sawhorse. As Kevin drew closer, he glanced down at Kate whose head was buried in his shoulder. Still asleep. Hugging her tight, he paused to watch his father at work.

Alphonse planted his left hand onto the trunk to brace it. With his right, he leaned into the buck saw, pushing and pulling, giving her for all she was worth. The veins on his neck were blue and thick and ugly, like entrails from a freshly-gutted cod. Something about the distortion of the image, the noise of the saw, the billowing of sawdust, grated on Kevin. He swallowed the urge to spit. When he found his voice, he muttered a few words to his father. "Can't be leaving the little one here. Never knows what will happen."

A two-foot chunk of wood clunked from sawhorse to ground. Alphonse paused. "What's that you say, son?"

"Nothing," muttered Kevin. "Nothing of consequence."

Alphonse tapped the flat of the saw onto a leg of the sawhorse; flecks of dust flew from the teeth of the blade. "That little Kate, she's the face and eyes of her mother," he said, absent-mindedly.

Kevin frowned. "Her grandmother, you mean," he said. "She don't look much like my Mavis; come to think of it, you never met my Mavis."

"Yes, b'y, her grandmother. That's what I meant to say. Her grandmother. My Kathleen."

Kevin blinked, then nodded. A slip of the tongue, that's all it was. "Doing better now, *your* Kathleen, Dad?"

"Best kind, b'y, best kind."

"Can ye manage without Dulcie Mullins coming round here every day? I'd like to see more of her at my house. She's doing a fine job with Kate."

Alphonse nodded. "No need for Dulcie showing her face around here no more. Best kind, Kathleen is. Back to full throttle, chopping wood, manning oars, hauling anchor." He shook his head. "A fine piece of work, my Kathleen." He toyed with the blade of the buck saw, bending it, releasing it, watching it quiver. "You know, son, we can help tend the little one for you in the off season. I can take a dart in myself, any time. Not much doing for fishermen in the winter time."

"Thanks, Dad. Will keep that in mind. But I'll be hunkered down in the winter meself. Only doing inshore fishing. Home every night. Not going on the bankers. It's me who'll be helping you this year, with your sawing and hauling, I mean."

"We'll give the little one a Christmas, that's for sure."

Kevin's heart plunged. Christmas? He was just trying to make it through today.

CLARA

CHAPTER 33

———◆———

CLARA WAS HUMMING AS SHE laid the table; delighted with herself, she was, that she had put the dinner on the cook before leaving the house. The risk of burnt roast gave her a truthful excuse for avoiding a Sunday visit. Imagine it: trying to sit in her mother's kitchen, stone-faced, gaping at Kevin and Kate. Her hurt was still raw; she didn't think she had it in her to veil it. Besides, she had other plans.

When she and Robert had finished the midday meal, when the only remaining evidence of pot roast was lingering odour and larder leftovers, Clara's husband retired to the parlour, pipe in hand, and Clara headed to the bedroom, plans in mind. First, she'd rifle through all her belongings. What should she be wearing for her life at sea, with rumrunners? She had no idea. Needing to vent the excitement that fluttered in her chest, she paced the floor, back and forth, back and forth, all the while picturing herself strolling the deck of the *Elizabeth J.* So deep in thought was she that a tap at the door made her jump. She swung around. "Door's open," she called.

Robert leaned into the room. "You sound mighty chipper today, my love."

"Indeed I am." Clara grinned.

"You have a visitor."

Clara glanced at the clock on the mantelpiece. "Who would be making a dart in now?"

"Isn't it customary for visitors to show up on Sunday? In the afternoon?"

"Around here anyone can dart in, anytime. It's just that I had plans, that's all."

"I suppose I could excuse you, say that you are indisposed, but I think you'll want to accept this visitor."

Clara tilted her head. "Well, are you going to be telling me who it is?"

"It's your mother," Robert said, his face blank.

Clara took a step back. "Are you pulling the wool over my eyes?"

"Have you ever known me to do that?"

"Dear God in heaven! My mother's downstairs."

"Well, religious experts seem convinced of the fact that God is in heaven so I do believe I can accurately reply in the affirmative on both counts."

Clara leaned on the bed post to balance herself.

"I offered Kathleen a seat in the parlour," said Robert, "but she informed me in no uncertain terms that she has had enough of darkened parlours. She insisted on waiting in the kitchen."

"Understandable, that." Clara nodded, as she unraveled herself from the bedpost. At the mirror, she tucked in a stray tendril of hair. "Did you offer her some tea?"

"I'm not a barbarian, dear. The kettle is on as we speak." He stepped aside to allow room for her to pass. "May I be of further assistance?"

"Yes. I mean, no, I don't think so." Clara slid past him. She stopped and looked directly at him. "I think I need to handle this myself."

"I shall be delighted to make myself scarce." Robert performed a swooping bow. Then he grabbed a book from the nightstand and slipped into the spare room across the hall. The door closed silently behind him.

Clara breathed deeply as she aimed for the head of the stairs. Fearing that a slow pace would result in leaving off altogether, she charged down the steps and through the kitchen door without a single pause. Kathleen was standing over the table, adding hot water to the teapot. "Let me do that for you..." Clara meant to add "Mom" but the word clutched in her throat. She tried again. "Mom?" She hadn't meant it to come out as a question but there it was, nonetheless.

"It would be a sad day when I couldn't make a cup of tea for myself." Kathleen Kerrigan let out a giggle, as if amused by her own words. In a few short steps, she was standing in front of Clara.

For the first time in a long time, Clara stood eye to eye with her mother. It was like looking at herself really: the same, soft brown eyes she had just seen in her bedroom mirror; the same body frame, all willow and wire; the same dark hair, silken, falling in ringlets to shoulders. How old was her mother now? Forty-five, maybe. Would Clara's skin be like this—pearls and cream—when she turned forty-five?

Wanting to cling to the moment, to make a memory, Clara reached up a hand. As she slid her fingers down the side of her mother's face, she watched Kathleen's moment of lightness slip away. In its place was a long sigh.

"I guess there have been many sad days in my life," said Kathleen. She took Clara's hand and searched Clara's face, looking for... looking for what? Clara didn't know.

"It breaks my heart that I let them be your sad days, too," said Kathleen, eyes filled with regret.

Was this an apology? Clara blinked back tears. How long had she waited for this? And now she was completely baffled by it, whatever it was. Clara said nothing as her mother, her very own mother, led her to the kitchen table, as her very own mother did the serving. A complete reversal of things: Clara watching, Kathleen pouring. Was Clara dreaming? It took a few minutes before she could speak and when she did, the words came out in a whisper. "What are you doing here? Why have you come? After all this time, why have you come?"

Kathleen's eyes clouded over. "For you. For Kevin."

Clara's curiosity fled as fear-filled images, images of raging ocean flashed through her mind. Dear God in heaven. Was there another tragedy? Heart pounding, she spluttered, "What about Kevin? Is he hurt? Is Kate hurt?"

"No, no, no." Kathleen brushed her hand through the air. "It's not like that at all." She bit her lip.

"Well, what then?"

Kathleen took a deep breath. "Kevin..." She stopped. The only sound was a long, slow hiss as she let her breath fall away. She offered no more words.

"You made it to my door, through my door. Whatever it is, you might as well tell it as think it."

Nodding, Kathleen parted her lips. This time there was no hesitation. "Kevin doesn't want me near the little one. Why is that?"

Clara's response was a deep sigh. A sigh of relief. No one was hurt. Kevin and Kate were safe. She sat, silent, giving her body time to calm its churning. "Where did you come up with that? Sure and he visits you every Sunday, with Kate in tow. Told me so himself."

"True enough, he does. But he won't leave that child alone with me for five minutes. Always looking over my shoulder. Not an angel, but a sentry, he is."

Clara took a sip of tea. Too hot. It burned the tip of her tongue. She placed the cup back on the saucer. The cup rattled. Milky tea sloshed, dripped, pooled. Clara leaned back, folding her arms. How much should she be saying here? "Can't blame him for standing guard after what happened on the Burin."

"Yes, yes, I see that. But I don't understand why he won't let me near Kate. Only sixteen, he was, when he left home. I never understood why he was in a sulk when he took wing. And now, all these years later, we're still in the same ice. I'm the child's grandmother. I have a right to know the why of things."

"Why are you having at me with the likes of this? Can't you be asking him?"

"He glares. Short of 'how could you,' he says nothing."

"Maybe I don't know nothing."

"Maybe you know everything. When you were little, you chased him everywhere, drank in every word that fell from his mouth. It was

196

all I could do to keep you from climbing into the dory behind him, remember?"

"If Kevin wants you to know things, he should tell you himself."

"Oh, for Pete's sake."

"Not for Pete or anybody else."

Kathleen reached across the table and took Clara's hand. In a whisper, she said, "For all our sakes, then."

Clara raised her eyebrows. She waited.

Kathleen released Clara's hand. She picked up her tea cup. She swirled its contents and stared at the few floating leaves. What could she possibly be looking for in there?

Clara's agitation grew. "Well? Have you got words to explain yourself or what?"

Kathleen set her cup down. "The little one needs her family. And I need her. Maybe I can do it right, this time." She pulled a handkerchief from her pocket and dabbed at her eyes.

Clara's throat ached so much that she had difficulty swallowing. Would it help things if she spilled what she knew? The temptation overwhelmed her. Maybe she should pray on it before she-- "Kevin thinks you killed Jimmy," she blurted.

Kathleen gasped. "Why in the name of all that's holy would he think such a terrible thing?" She made the sign of the cross, twice.

Clara let out a long sigh. What had just come over her? So much for praying on it. "He saw you, with Jimmy. There was water in the tub beside the stove. You were pulling the baby, a blue baby, from the water."

Kathleen fell back in her chair. "Dear God. I was just cleaning the poor little thing, preparing him to meet his Maker. Beside myself with the shock of it all, I was. Never gave a thought to looking around, to seeing where you and Kevin were at. You weren't there, were you?"

Clara shook her head. "I was heading for the house but Kevin shuffled me away. I wouldn't have known anything about it at all except that I heard him and Daddy fighting in the shed. Kevin was beat up the next day, and many times after that. He left home a few months later."

"I'll have to put him to rights about this."

"Indeed you will."

"Imagine him thinking such a thing all these years. No wonder he ran off."

"No wonder at all, but maybe you should wait, give him some time before you give him the truth. Kevin is not very trusting since the ocean turned on him. Let the truth of things fall in his lap."

Kathleen did not look convinced. "I'll have to ponder it."

A new anxiety flitted through Clara. "Dear God in heaven. You won't tell him, will you?" She leaned forward and whispered, "You won't tell him that Kate is--"

"Stop right there, Clara. No need to go on. Never. I will never tell him that. He's had enough trouble for one lifetime."

Clara nodded with relief. "I want you to know that I'll be causing you no grief."

Kathleen placed the flat of her hand over her heart. "You're a good daughter, Clara. What have I done to deserve you? As for the strength of you, it boggles the mind. I'll have you know that what you're planning comes as no surprise to me."

Clara raised her eyebrows. "What I'm planning?"

"Robert tells me you'll be sailing on the *Elizabeth J.*"

"You don't think it's a shocking thing for a woman to do?"

"Women won't stay in the kitchen forever, Clara. I know it's hard in this day and age, but sometimes we have to take charge of things." She leaned in. "And I know you're doing this to help your brother. And yourself." She rose to leave.

Clara walked with her to the door. She put her hand on her mother's arm, held it there, looked straight into her mother's eyes. "Why did Jimmy die?" she asked. "I mean, what killed him?"

If Kathleen was perturbed by the question, she didn't show it. Not a feather out of her. After a long pause, she said, "It was the diphtheria, girl, the diphtheria what killed him." She held up one hand, palm forward, and Clara knew she was done talking. Sure enough, seconds later, without another word, Kathleen left.

Clara considered going after her mother, maybe offering Kathleen a ride home. She dismissed that idea. If Kathleen Kerrigan had it in her to find her way here, she could darn well manage to find her way back.

Clara returned to the table. She picked up her tea cup and put it to her lips to it. Cold as harbour ice. She set the cup down but didn't move. She wasn't ready to move, not yet. She was torn up in her mind about something, but she didn't know what. After a few minutes, when she couldn't lay claim to an answer, she rose from the table.

As she rinsed the cups, she reviewed the conversation with her mother. Nothing untoward there. Clara shrugged. She lumbered up the stairs to the bedroom. Robert entered behind her.

"Well?" He stood, waiting.

"I have no idea where to begin."

"At the beginning, one would assume."

Clara frowned. She shook her head. "I think I just better get back to my packing."

Robert nodded. "As you wish, my dear." He slid back into the guest room.

Gratitude, a tingling sensation, filtered through Clara. She didn't want Robert knowing all her secrets. Maybe not ever. Certainly not now. The only thing that concerned her now was preparation: she had to get ready for life at sea.

A glimpse at the line of flowery dresses hanging in her clothes cupboard led her to roll her eyes. Not much use for dresses aboard a schooner. Trousers, that's what she needed. She looked at her husband's clothes and smiled.

It was time to thread the Singer.

KATHLEEN

CHAPTER 34

———◆———

It empowers and enslaves, the sea.

The North Atlantic in this time is a Promised Land, teeming with cod, proffering dreams of wealth galore. This, then, is the place where fishermen throng; they trawl and haul, slit and prong, toiling through days, striving for dreams. But, whether they work on banking schooners or inshore dories, the fishermen's dreams all come to naught. It is the merchant, only the merchant, who benefits from the wealth of the sea.

It is the merchant who advances food and supplies to fishermen in spring. It is the merchant who sets the price for the catch. It is the merchant who buys the catch in autumn, deducting the cost of supplies. Profit, if any, is paid to fishermen *in kind*—goods such as molasses, pork, flour, salt beef. No money changes hands in this, the truck system, inherited from England. When the value of the catch is lower than the cost of supplies, the fishermen fall into debt. Every year the debt deepens.

The result is a crust of well-to-do merchants and a core of poverty-stricken fishermen. Some fishermen claw their way from deep want by switching their harvest from cod to cargo.

These are the rumrunners.

1931

On this day, when the breeze is scented with clover and salt, my daughter, Clara, is about to join these rumrunners. She, too, is escaping cavernous want for she is fleeing a life of constant hunger for a child she cannot claim.

I watch as Clara prances through meadow to harbour. Laughing, she brushes her fingertips through daisies which peep over tall grasses. Clusters of onlookers chortle at the very sight of her, a young woman in sod cap and men's trousers. I feel a sense of wonder at this child of mine, who ignores taunts, defies convention. Something akin to pride rears in me, something to which I clearly have no claim. Wasn't it I who abandoned her? Wasn't it she who flourished, unguided? A transparent image slides past me, one of roses, the wild red roses that for years adorned the front yard beneath my kitchen window, surviving and thriving, completely left to their own devices.

As Clara steps onto the splintered, misshapen planks of the harbour wharf, she slows to a stroll. She pinches her nose and weaves through a steady stream of handcarts and wheelbarrows. There are no floral aromas here, only the malodour of fish guts, the fetor of raw sewage. Her eyes water, then widen at the sight of a sleek, ebony rat perched on a reel of trawl line. She recoils, knocking into a wheelbarrow, upending it, sending its cargo of salt cascading. As a rhyme of swear words spews from a disgruntled seaman, Clara slinks into the crowd, drawing her cap low. She watches from the sidelines as her unintended victim, pudding-faced Salty Joe Sallivan, grabs a nearby shovel and reloads. All around him, men are shifting and hauling and rolling bait barrels which clunk their way along the wharf. Grunts and groans ricochet from dock to hull as cargo is hoisted and heaved.

Clara catches sight of a black skirt swishing past clomping sea boots, its hem dragging along the wharf. She scowls as she raises her eyes from salt-stained hem to flour-bag apron, to the moon-faced Dulcie Mullins. Dulcie, her stubby arms wrapped around three biscuit tins, comes to a halt at the salt scene.

"What in the name of heaven are ya at, Joe?" Dulcie asks. "Fine mess you got here."

"Some rowdy arse slammed into me and took off. He better be long gone. He'll be getting a clout if I sees him again." Joe pauses and looks around.

Heart thumping, Clara ducks behind a bait barrel piled high with mackerel. She swats at a swarm of flies as she peeks around the middle stave of the barrel.

Dulcie smiles and offers Joe a biscuit tin. "Tea buns," she says. "Made them meself. Lots of currants in 'em."

Joe grins. "As good as gold, you are."

"Won't take long to shovel up the salt, Joe. Season's almost done, b'y. Last haul before fall, I suppose."

"Hope it's a good one. Getting paid in kind."

In kind. The phrase hangs. *In kind*: in goods, not cash.

Dulcie and Salty Joe stand, silent, nodding, as Clara hides, motionless, waiting.

"How's yer young fella doing, Joe?" Dulcie asks.

"Not good at all now, not good at all. Too poor for medicine. Maybe after this catch."

Dulcie nods. "The diphtheria, is it? Hard life when the merchant decides which of your children gets medicine, and schooling too, fer that matter."

"Hard life indeed. It's no wonder there's rumrunners." He points to a low boat at the end of the harbour. "Maybe Robert Caulins and his crowd has the right idea."

"The good Lord wouldn't fault you none if you joined up with them."

Joe grins. "Maybe the Lord has a forgivin' nature, but the missus? That's a different thing altogether." He loads the last of the salt, stabs the shovel into the centre of it, and grasps the handles of the wheelbarrow. "Have a look in on her while I'm gone, will ya, Dulcie?"

"That I will, b'y. That I will." Dulcie puts a biscuit tin on the salt pile beside the shovel and he shoves off. She waits until he is out of sight; then she marches directly to the bait barrel where Clara is hiding.

"Here you are, missy. Been looking all over. Brought these tea buns for you and Robert. That's his boat over there, isn't it? The *Elizabeth J*?"

Clara straightens, spitting away a fly that lands on her lip. She drags a flannel shirt sleeve across her face and then crosses her arms.

"Ya always were a bit stubborn. Look at the sight of ya," says Dulcie, shaking her head. She smiles. "Truth be told, child, I don't mind what yer wearing, or what you're at. I just cares about you and your mother. And Kate."

Clara glares at her. "Don't you dare be saying nothing to Kevin about Kate."

Dulcie steps closer and whispers. "What I told you before is the God's honest truth. Some things you hangs out on the line; some things you doesn't. You're the one that wants to do the telling, not me. And if I can't tell nobody about the little one, then neither can you. Kevin asked me to look after her and I guarantees you I'll do a good job of it. I did the finest kind with you, didn't I?" She reaches up and gives the brim of Clara's hat a tug, then three tugs, just like she used to do when Clara had pigtails.

Clara's only response is a sneer.

Dulcie shakes her head and saunters away, carrying her biscuit tins with her.

When activity on the wharf abates, Clara abandons her hiding place. She heads toward the boat at the end of the harbour, the one that slinks lower than any other. Her eyes are bright, her shoulders high, as she tramps up the gangway. A brave soul, my daughter smiles at the first deck hand she meets but he walks past her as if she were invisible. Her demeanor sags a little, but this is a temporary discouragement. All the crew will come to know and cherish my Clara.

The crewmen here are come-from-aways, the lot of them: Robert Alistair Caulins chooses them in Nova Scotia and St. Pierre. On my first telling of this story, I wondered the whys of that, but like everything else, it becomes clear in time.

As I watch Clara now, it amuses me to think that, when she was little, I hedged over letting her in the dory. Then, my greatest fear—the loss of a child—materialized, and I left her to her own devices. It was Kevin who tended her; there was no one else looking out for her in those days. Maybe it was not such a bad thing, Kevin teaching her the ways of the sea. Isn't it logical that all who live beside the sea learn these things? I myself, as a child, spent much time in a dory: rowing or baiting or huddling in the bow while I knit mitts for my father. It is gratitude I feel for Kevin then; because of him Clara knows about waves and tide and the danger of dark clouds.

No such danger on this day as the *Elizabeth J* sets sail. A single fluffy cloud floats over the horizon, teased along by offshore winds, multiplying until an entire flock of cotton clumps, brilliant white, dots the sky. They cross the sun, creating a shadow here, a shadow there, but there's no ill effect on the weather.

This is not the usual, run-of-the-mill schooner, this vessel of Robert's. In fact, it is not the schooner that Robert sailed just months before. This boat is new, built in Lunenburg; it is long and sits low, so low that it is called a banana boat.

The sleek vessel cuts a smooth path through willing water. Nary bump nor stutter. Robert Caulins grins at my Clara. "Enjoying yourself, are you? Well, we're not out of the harbour yet. You may want to retreat below."

Clara laughs and waves a dismissive arm at him. When they round the point into open water and she grips the gunwale in order to remain upright. The schooner dips into a chasm. The look of confidence on her face slides away. Up and down, up and down, each crest of wave seeming higher than the last.

I wonder at this point if Clara, realizing that the schooner is nothing like an inshore dory, regrets what she has gotten herself into. She's a bold woman, but if she is experiencing difficulty on a clear day, what will she do when the sea turns dark and brooding?

Clara glances at Robert standing in the bow, arms folded. He turns to her and laughs, loud and long.

I catch the first sounds of laughter, but the rest dissolves in a blast of wind. With the next rise of the boat, Clara pitches herself toward the wheelhouse. She sidles along the gunwale, hand over hand, until she is inside. She drops and puts her head into her hands.

"Here you go." Robert's voice, still tinged with laughter, is followed by a scraping noise; a bucket slides along the floor as the boat dips. Clara clutches at it and locks it in place between her feet. The boat rises and falls again. Clara lurches and spews.

"The sea is no place for a woman," he says, standing over her.

Clara retches again.

"I'll take the wheel," Robert says to the brawny, red-headed first mate who takes his leave without a word. After a few clicks of his tongue, Robert repeats, "The sea is no place for a woman, Clara."

Does he think that she did not hear his condescending words the first time? He expects her to fail; she is here to learn a lesson, one that will make her choose stay on shore. In her little house. A good little woman.

It amuses me, his naiveté, for I know that my Clara will endure.

Clara stands, picks up the bucket, stumbles from wheelhouse to starboard and heaves the porridge-laden vomit into the wake. On the next dip of the boat, she catches the spray and swishes the bucket. Then she returns the bucket to the wheelhouse, where she stays, eyeing her husband.

The cook shows up, tea kettle in hand. Wordless, he pours two cups and leaves. Clara sidles up to Robert and picks up her tea.

"So why the *Elizabeth J*?" she asks.

Robert does not respond.

The schooner dips, the tea sloshes, and a hot wave washes over Clara's hand. She flinches.

"Stick your hand in that." Robert points at a nearby pitcher of water.

Clara obeys without question. Her relieved sigh is instantaneous.

"That's much better, isn't it?" he says.

She nods, pulling her hand from the pitcher, examining it.

He reaches for her, draws her close, and mutters in her ear. "Wouldn't you rather be at home, carding and spinning?"

When Clara scowls, he pulls back abruptly, setting her adrift. She remains close, gripping a nearby ledge for support.

"Why did you christen this vessel the *Elizabeth J*?" she asks again.

If I could, I would scream the answer. There are disadvantages to knowing a whole story, to the pain associated with the knowing, to the impotence of non-interference.

"My mother's name," says Robert the rumrunner.

My sigh is unheard in the wind.

Rumrunners are good men, as men go, experienced seamen who want to feed their families. Clara is joining them in order to protect her family, her child, her brother, from her own selfish yearning. Maybe I have no right to pride with regard to my Clara. Admiration then. Clara is stronger than I.

Robert Caulins is not representative of all rumrunners. My admiration for Clara is accompanied by disdain for him.

His mother's name. Indeed.

CLARA

CHAPTER 35

1931

"MY MOTHER'S NAME," SAID ROBERT.

"Oh." Clara raised an eyebrow. Was this the time to tunnel into his past? What if he revealed something she was ill-equipped to handle? What would she be after doing then? Here she was, on *his* boat: no way out, no way off.

With thoughts swirling and head throbbing, Clara grimaced. She was getting nowhere like this, her mind flitting about 'like a fart in a windstorm,' as her father might say. *Alphonse Kerrigan.* She flinched as a sharp pain lanced her side. It was quick—the torment—there one instant, gone the next. As it withdrew, she cut through indecision. Locking her eyes on Robert, she cleared her throat. "You never come over the subject of your family much. Are your parents still alive?"

No response.

Time yawned between them, a gaping hole. Clara fidgeted. Was he going to answer or what? Maybe she should just go out on deck, take in some air. Then again, maybe she should wait: God forbid she miss even a morsel of information.

Silence stretched. The vessel tipped slowly. By now she could have gone on deck and scrambled from bow to stern of the *Elizabeth J.*

Finally, Robert said, "They've long since passed."

"Oh." Clara continued to eye him, curiosity burning. What was behind the lengthy pause? She took a sip from the remains of her tea. "It's a hard thing, losing your family," she said.

He turned toward her, his brow knitted into a frown. "You still have your parents, Clara," he said, his voice clipped.

Clara's eyes widened. It was not often she could rile him. In fact, she wasn't sure she ever had. At least, not until now. Had she even tried? Before she could finger an instance, the vessel dipped and rose. A wave of stomach acid erupted and a string of new questions emerged: What was this fresh taste of vomit about? Was it swell of the sea? Maybe the sting of his tone?

Thirst banished, Clara put the teacup down. "Maybe, after a time, my father will forgive me for being the face and eyes of my mother," she said. She blinked. Where in the name of all that's holy had that come from? It wasn't only the words that stunned her; it was the bitterness that kept them company. She was willing to ponder it but the ocean wouldn't permit it. As the vessel plunged then reared again, Clara lost her balance. Thoughts and words were swept away as she struggled to regain her equilibrium. She grimaced. How long would she allow herself to be tossed at the whim of the sea?

A fleeting glimpse at Robert, at the smug look on his face, caused Clara's blood to surge from simmer to boil. How dare he enjoy her discomfort. Never mind being tossed by the sea: how long would she allow herself to be tossed at the whim of men? Men like Alphonse Kerrigan, Father Mahony, even Patrick— what was his last name anyway? Did it matter? Good for nothings—sleeveens—the lot of them. Well, maybe Robert Caulins was steering the schooner but he sure enough wasn't going to steer the conversation. "What about you?" she asked. "Have you no family left then?"

"Nary a one." Ease had returned to his voice and an easy smile accompanied it. "Wait," he said, pointing a finger. "Let me amend that: there's *only the* one, my beautiful wife and true love of my life." He nodded, his face serene with confidence.

Clara bit her lip, hard. He had thwarted her question and, in the process, squelched her anger. Should she dig deeper? Maybe she should just swallow her questions. What good would it do her to harp on Robert now anyway? It would be a long time—days, maybe weeks—from anchor to anchor. Lots of time to ask, or choose not to.

Switching her focus, she smiled. "You can cut a notch in a beam, no doubt about it," she said, her voice perched on playfulness.

Robert gave her a puzzled look.

"It means you are good with the compliments," she explained. "But are you sure you don't have a 'true love' in every port?"

Robert shook his head, a slow, deliberate motion. He let out a long sigh. "Clara, have you once gazed into that gilded mirror I gifted you?"

Clara blinked repeatedly. "What on earth are you on about?"

Before she knew what was happening, Robert reached an arm for her. He pulled her close, lifted her chin, and stared into her eyes.

Clara scrutinized his face which was granite, full of authority; he could make a person feel small if he had a mind to. But there was kindness in the crinkles around those sea-grey eyes, in the creases beside those upturned lips. Not the face of a criminal, this. She was tempted to twirl the lock of curly brown hair that fell across his brow. She held back.

Maybe his was not face of a criminal, but he *was* a criminal, nonetheless.

Robert brushed his fingertips down her cheek. "Long lashes, liquid eyes, full lips," he said. "You're beautiful, Clara. Why would I even glance at another woman?"

"Oh." The word was a mere squeak. A flurry of pleasure frolicked through her. Was she foolish to be enjoying this? Maybe. But she was no fool. Robert Alistair Caulins was trying to mould her. Brought her father back to mind.

Alphonse Kerrigan had a talent for that, moulding. He could strip a tree trunk and carve it into a kitchen chair. But he didn't limit himself to sticks of furniture. He shaped people, too. He had certainly moulded her, hadn't he? Clara had glommed onto the attention then, craving it, and she was doing the same now. Would her body ever stop whining for attention?

She offered her hand to Robert.

He held it.

"Are you going to tell me what I'm in for on this trip?" she asked, eyes riveted to his. "What's it like, really? What happens on Rum Road?"

Instantly, Robert snickered.

Clara blinked. Pure mockery, that laugh of his, but why? She lowered her head as heat flooded her face.

"It's not Rum *Road*," he said. "It's Rum *Row*, a place on the United States coast where ships wait offshore."

Clara pulled her hand from his. An abrupt movement. "You don't go ashore?" she asked, returning to her place beside the ledge. She wrapped her arms around herself, like a spider contracting. All the while, she watched him.

If Robert was bothered by her withdrawal, he did not show it. He returned his attention to the wheel. "We have to stay outside boundary lines."

Clara clenched her teeth. If he wasn't bothered, she wouldn't be either. "How far outside?" she asked in a controlled tone.

"It used to be three miles. Now it's twelve. As many as fifty schooners—a flotilla—all line up at one time, waiting. Small boats speed from shore, barter from schooner to schooner, seeking the best price. They pay us. We leave." He raised both hands and dropped them back to the wheel.

"Oh," said Clara. *They pay us. We leave.* So where did Captain Robert Caulins keep all the money? Under the pretense of adjusting her cap, she scanned the wheelhouse. What was that metal box for, the one with the giant keyhole? Must be a treasure box. Why else would it be strapped to the base of the ship's wheel?

Until this moment, it had never crossed Clara's mind that she could have, should have, her own money. Akin to blasphemy, this thought. Women never had money, that is, unless their husbands stooped to bestow it. But now it struck her, clear as daylight, the wrong of it all. For some reason unbeknownst to her, she was harbouring a gnawing distrust for this man, the criminal with the kind face. What difference did it make if Robert gave her money or not? She was a worker, a deckhand on this boat. She stared directly at her husband. "When do I get paid?"

Raising both his voice and his eyebrows, Robert asked, "You? Paid? Women don't get paid. What do you need with money? Don't I supply you with your every whim?"

Clara straightened her back. "If I'm a deckhand on this vessel, then I should be paid, just like all the rest of them." She planted her hands on her hips.

This time Robert's laugh was an outright guffaw.

Clara bristled. "This is no joke," she said.

Her words silenced Robert, but not the flock of gulls which took that instant to fly overhead, screeching their ridicule.

A new wave of amusement rolled through Robert's eyes.

Clara absorbed the joke, even itched to giggle. But she maintained her stance, her jaw set.

Eventually, Robert sighed. "I'll give you half of what the men earn."

Clara pursed her lips. Half? Should she argue this? What was it her mother had said? *Women won't stay in the kitchen forever.* Maybe Kathleen Kerrigan was right. Maybe, at some point, women would work with men, make money like men. But that would be done in a lot of little steps, wouldn't it? And what was it that Robert had just said? Something about small boats, *bartering*?

Clara shook her head. "Not half. Three-quarters." She offered her hand to shake on the deal.

Robert widened his eyes. He bit his lower lip and slowly drew his teeth over it. With a decisive nod, he extended his hand. "You drive a hard bargain," he said.

Satisfied, Clara took a deep breath. She didn't linger in the glow of the win. She never lingered. Good things get stripped away if you look too long, or love too much. "Now, tell me about the tires on the sides of the *Elizabeth J*," she said. "What are they for? Damage prevention?"

"There is no end to your questions today."

"I'm a hired deckhand. Shouldn't I know these things?"

Robert nodded. "The tires muffle sound. The last thing we want is to draw the attention of the Coast Guard cutters."

"Coast Guard cutters?" asked Clara, pretending ignorance. Truth be told, she knew that the Coast Guard cutters were patrol boats, that rum running had risks: being caught, being arrested, being shot. It came as a surprise to her now that, despite the danger, her innards were not churning. Yes, the vessel was still rising and falling, its beams groaning, but Clara was standing steady. Getting her sea legs, the old salts might call it. Getting a handle on her life, she would call it. In this moment, as she listened to Robert's yarns about cutters and schooners, she felt prepared to tackle both the peril and profit of life at sea.

She was breathing easy for the first time in a while.

KEVIN

CHAPTER 36

———————

AT THE MERCHANT STORE, ON a mission for roofing nails and blackstrap molasses, Kevin gave a morning nod to a group of men hovered around the pot-bellied stove. A usual gathering place, the stove. Great, if the talk was centered on fur, fin, or feather. Kevin was all for news that would help him earn a living. But that bunch? Come day, go day, God send Sunday. Gossiped like old biddy hens, they did. Be a cold day in hell before he'd join them.

There was no sign of the merchant when Kevin sauntered up to the counter. Probably in the storeroom at the back. Kevin pulled off his cap and obeyed the sign: *Ring bell for service*. He scanned the overcrowded shelves aback of the counter. There they were, the nails he needed, scads of them, in a brown paper bag with the top folded down. He nodded and leaned in for the wait. Tidbits of conversation floated his way:

"Imagine going off to sea with the likes of that bunch. Scalawags, the lot of them."

"Don't be talking like that now, b'y. Ye won't be calling them scala- wags when they shows up with yer rum in a couple of weeks."

Kevin grinned, dismissing an itch to voice his agreement. He was no stranger to the occasional bit of drink. Hard to come by, if it weren't for the rumrunners.

"Now b'y, ya knows I don't mean nothing by that," the first voice graveled on. "I likes me drop of rum as much as the next fellow. It's the woman I'm talking about. Out there on the schooner. No place for a woman."

A woman on a schooner? Kevin couldn't help it; he was eavesdropping now.

"If anybody can handle herself with a bunch of scoundrels--"

"Kevin, b'y! How you gettin' on?" The merchant's wife emerged from the storeroom, her frog-like face smudged with dirt. "What a state things are in back there today." She brushed her calloused hands together. "What can I be doing for you this morning?"

Kevin paused. Given a few more seconds, the gossip mongers would be sure to name the woman who was brazen enough to show her face on a schooner. He tilted his head in their direction.

"As I was saying, if anybody can handle herself with a bunch of scoundrels, it's Clara Caulins."

Kevin turned sharply, dropping his salt-and-pepper cap, instantly stooping to retrieve it. When he came to his taps, the chatter had stopped and the eyes of the lot were upon him, waiting.

"Ssh," someone whispered.

Kevin gulped. Clara? A rumrunner? Fearful that his heated face betray his shock, he glared into the core of the group. "Ye fellows waiting around for your dole cheques to arrive, I suppose?" With that, he turned and stormed out. He was halfway home when it occurred to him that he had not purchased the molasses he had promised his daughter. Made no never mind. Dulcie Mullins would bring some over on request. As for the nails, that loose strip of tarpaper on the roof could flap in the wind for another day or so. Wouldn't do no harm.

What was all this nonsense about Clara? He clenched his jaw and changed direction, heading for Clara's house. He opened the back door and tromped inside. For a few seconds, he stood in the kitchen. A waste of time: the place was empty, silent. Could Clara possibly be at sea with Robert? He shuddered. Should he just forget about it all and go home? No. In the back of his mind, Clara was still his baby sister. He had to get to the truth, and that meant one more stop.

When Kevin arrived at his parents' home, Alphonse was outside, spreading codfish on flakes.

"Dad," he plunged, "the lazy arses down at the store are saying that Clara is off with Robert, on the schooner with the rumrunners. For the love of God, that can't be the truth. She got more sense than that, don't she?"

Alphonse looked up. "Good morning to you too, son." He went back to his chore.

"Dad, for heaven's sake..."

"Clara is a strong woman. She'll be fine."

"Sweet Heart of Jesus. You're telling me this is true?"

"Don't be taking the name of the Lord in vain, son." Alphonse moved to the next section of the flakes and began flipping cod. "The thing about this chore is that you have to remember to dry both sides of the fish," he said.

Kevin threw his arms in the air. "What on earth are you telling me that for? Like I don't know it already. What about Clara? Is she rum running? Did you even try to stop her?"

Alphonse straightened his back and stared at Kevin. "You got to look at both sides of things, son. Clara's not happy staying home. She got nothing to occupy her time, no young ones of her own. Even the women need to feel useful."

"Useful?" Kevin rubbed the back of his neck. Was that why Clara had doted on Kate? To feel useful? He slumped like he'd been hit in the gut. What had he gone and done? "Do you think she took off because I asked Mrs. Mullins to take care of Kate?"

"And what did you do that for?"

"I just thought that... that..."

"That maybe Clara and the little one were getting too close?"

Kevin gulped. "How did you know?"

"A man loses almost everything, he can get mighty possessive over what he's got left."

Kevin grimaced as a flush crept across his face. Shoving his hands into his pockets, he lowered his head. He kicked at a small stone which clanged against the metal stay of a nearby bucket, then plunked back to the ground.

Alphonse pulled a handkerchief from his pocket and mopped his brow. "Did Clara ever flap on about taking Kate away from you?"

"No. Not a word."

"You sure about that?"

Kevin raised his head. "One hundred percent."

"Then maybe you shouldn't be showing your teeth when you got nothing to bite about." A slow smile spread across Alphonse's face. "She's a good girl, our Clara." He pursed his lips together and began whistling.

Kevin perked an ear to the lilt. It was familiar but he couldn't quite name it. "Maybe I was too hard on Clara," he said.

The whistling stopped dead.

"She shouldn't be on a schooner," continued Kevin. "No place for a woman, that."

Alphonse puffed out a mouthful of air. "Yep, I allow it's bad luck, a woman on a vessel. Worse than whistling in the wheelhouse. A wind breeder, it is."

"It's not about the luck, it's about the safety. You knows as well as I do that the U.S. Coast Guard don't take kindly to rumrunners."

"Go on with ya, b'y. She'll be fine." Alphonse let out a grunt. "As if the Coast Guard could catch *that* vessel." He waved a codfish in Kevin's direction. "The *Elizabeth J* got airplane engines, for Christ's sake." He dropped the cod, picked up the next one, and flipped it. "Them b'ys can even conjure up a smokescreen: they just rubs oil on the smokestack and stokes the engines." He clicked his tongue. "You have to allow he's a smart one, that Robert Caulins."

Kevin wasn't convinced. "What if they falls prey to the Newfoundland constabulary?"

"Newfoundland?" Alphonse's mouth twitched with amusement. "Sure Newfoundland don't have no money to police rumrunners. Even if they did, they wouldn't go after them. Like I told Clara, the Roberts of this world owns every knob on every door in every godforsaken court-house on this island."

Kevin sighed. "Maybe you're right." He took a deep breath. "Still, I think Clara would be better off at home. Maybe I should just let her take care of Kate."

Alphonse's nostrils flared. "Like hell you will!"

Kevin recoiled, jaw open like a baited trap. What was going on here? Didn't his father just say women shouldn't be on vessels?

With eyes pointed like daggers, Alphonse scowled at Kevin. Then he gulped and looked away. Tugging at the collar of his buttoned flannel shirt, he said, "Is you catching flies, son?" A low snigger slid out of him.

Instantly, Kevin clamped his lips tight. What was Alphonse on about? Why would he be set against Clara caring for Kate? There was a back-door here, no doubt. Was it worth the effort to barge through it? Kevin tilted his head, waiting.

Alphonse drew his tongue slowly across his upper lip. He cleared his throat, hawking up phlegm, spitting it to the ground. "Maybe you should just let things be. Like I said, Clara can take care of herself. You take care of *your*self and your daughter. You got to cut your losses and move on, son. Cut your losses and forgive yourself your sins. It's the only way to survive." He paused for a few seconds and stared at the ocean. "The only way," he said again.

Kevin folded his arms. What sins was Alphonse talking about? Kevin had nary click nor clue. But he knew about trying to forgive himself. Darn near impossible, that was. He should have been there when-- "Maybe you're right, Dad," he said, interrupting his own thoughts before they spiraled. "Maybe you're right." Kevin let out a deep breath. "I got some time. You want help with that?" Without waiting for an answer, he began flipping codfish. "I'm sure the blowhards down at the store are chewing the fat over me this very minute. I was so beside myself when I heard them gossiping about Clara that I accused them of standing around, waiting for their dole cheques to come in."

Alphonse chuckled. "Nothing stings like the truth. Lazy arse sons of bitches, the lot of them."

"Maybe you're right." Kevin said again, not talking about the gossipers. His mind had gone back to Clara. What was it that carped at him? Something was shrouded here, no doubt. He shot a side glance at his father. What if Alphonse *was* operating from a backdoor? No point in probing. The man would say nothing.

Alphonse Kerrigan was a different man since his drinking days when he had lashed his tongue, thrashed his belt, bashed his fists, leaving Kevin bruised and swollen. But now? He raised neither voice nor hand. A man of peace. For now. Because of that, for now, Kevin would close his mind and mouth to backdoors and what ifs. He would help his father, he would farm, he would build. He would live in Argentia. He would bide his time and rebuild his life. Easier said than done. Some mornings it was all he could do just to stumble from bedroom to kitchen.

He moved to the side of the flake opposite his father. One eye on Alphonse, the other on the task in front of him, he continued turning the fish, one at a time. *Flip, flip, flip.*

One fish at a time. One day at a time. The best he could do.

CLARA

CHAPTER 37

———◆———

As the *Elizabeth J* scudded across the sparkling waters of Placentia Bay, Clara's insides jangled with excitement. So much so that she often forced herself to stifle a bubble of laughter or swallow a shout of glee. There was no point in appearing foolish: Robert's crew already steered clear of her like a ship did a reef. Clara could not fault them: it was common knowledge that having a woman on board was bad luck. She often shook her head over the whole situation. Did she have some gall or what? Next thing she'd be serving Sunday Mass with the altar boys.

Despite Clara's brazenness, anxiety sometimes leached from her pores. It was the newness and the strangeness of everything that did it, caused her heart to race or her chest to tighten. She harnessed her nerves by focusing on the steadiness of the boat's captain, her husband. Clara found comfort in the sight of his face—bronzed and lined from sun, wind, and sea, and the strength of his stance—straight and tall like lighthouse, pine, or mast. Surefooted, soft-spoken, Robert never cast a sidelong glance at either her or the crew.

As for the crew themselves? Right off, Clara captured their loyalty to Robert. Their responses to him were "aye, this" and "aye that," never a locking of horns, not even a second guess. A strong man, a respected man, this husband of hers. Still, Clara cautioned herself to keep a wary eye. She didn't know much about Robert but even if there were no secrets *about* him, bad things could happen *to* him.

Clara's naive notion that men were unbreakable was squelched when she saw the effects of the tsunami on her brother. What life storm could stagger Robert? What would cause him to collapse? And would become of her in the aftermath?

Never far from her mind was the aftermath of the 1927 August gale which sank a local schooner, the *Annie Healy*, and claimed its crew. So many struggling widows, faces gaunt, stomachs growling. The images haunted, simultaneously unnerving and reassuring Clara. She had done the right thing in demanding payment for her time on the sea: money wasn't just a novelty for women, it was a necessity. If Robert fell victim, she could, and *would*, survive on her own.

After a few sunrises at sea, the crew began to make eye contact with Clara in passing; some even doffed their caps and nodded a "Morning, Missus."

"I'm starting to think your crew is the finest kind," Clara said to Robert one morning as they stood on deck, watching the foamy white wake of the vessel stream into wide ribbons behind them. "The first mate actually asked me how I was getting on."

The beginning of a smile tipped the corners of Robert's mouth. "This vessel has been polished like a yacht in honor of your presence, my dear."

Clara let out a delighted gasp which was instantly snatched away by the wind. "You mean it wasn't always like this?"

"Not hardly," he said, turning to her, his smile spreading to encompass his whole face. "I'll have you know that the men have taken to daily ablutions on your account. It's hard to fathom, but the lot of them are insistent on wearing clean clothes as well. As for the aforementioned first mate, Niall, his tangle of red hair now has regular encounters with a hairbrush. And just this morning, the wireless operator, Sparky, took a straight razor to his scruff of beard. Have you noticed that Patrick is actually wearing an apron?"

Clara laughed outright. She had taken a special liking to the round-as-a-barrel cook, whose skill with a skillet was unmatched. There was nothing like his breakfast servings of toutins—fried bread dough—and the obligatory cup of tea. "A grand cook, he is. But I'll have you know that he prefers to be called Paddy."

Robert tilted his head. "Strange, that. He never mentioned it."

"Maybe he hoped I'd do the mentioning. I only called him Patrick the one time and he would have none of it. 'Patrick was the name of the good saint who chased the snakes out of Ireland,' he said. 'Nothing saintly about me now at all.' He insisted on being called Paddy."

"One can't argue with that rationale. Paddy it is, then," said Robert.

Clara was secretly pleased. She did not want to hear the name "Patrick," not at all. She had banished the memory of another man named Patrick, stuck it into the attic of her mind. It returned now, pricking her with shame. The black box. The confessional. And Clara, at sixteen. It would not do to have the name "Patrick" needle her daily. Clara pushed the memory down hard like she always did when something troubled her. Yes, Paddy was better. No shadows there.

"It appears that we have company," said Robert, pointing starboard. Clara turned. A pod of seals, heads popped above wrinkled water, was staring at them. Robert wrapped an arm around Clara and the two stared steadily back. The seals then swam toward the stern where they frolicked in the wake of the vessel.

Robert laughed. "First they grab our attention; then they start performing."

Lightness filled Clara, triggering a smile. "A playful lot."

As the vessel sped on, its steady rise and fall was barely perceptible to Clara. Was it a part of her already? Beaming, she turned her attention from the seals to the sun which winked in and out of fluffy clouds. As warmth filled her body and spray misted her face, she placed a hand over her heart. Worth it, it was, the effort to get here. Would it all be like this? She pulled away from Robert, creating enough daylight between them to offer a mock salute. "So, Captain, where exactly do we go from here?"

"The island of St. Pierre, located in Newfoundland waters. Interestingly enough, it is owned by France."

Clara nodded. "St. Pierre and Miquelon, both."

"Correct. And France has no Prohibition. It's the United States that birthed Prohibition. Canada and Newfoundland followed suit. You can get liquor legally in Newfoundland, but only by medical prescription. All three places depend on rumrunners."

"St. Pierre must be flooded with money."

"Notoriously so. Gangs of rumrunners warehouse their liquor in St. Pierre."

"Lots of warehouses?"

"Row upon row. And not a single tree on the island."

Clara chewed on that for a moment. She frowned. "How do they build warehouses? Where on earth do they get the lumber?"

"From wooden crates, the very same crates used to ship liquor."

"Ah." Clara nodded. "No surprise there. Give a Newfoundlander a ball of yarn and he'll knit you a dory."

Robert grinned. "Well said. Anyway, the rumrunners took over. The St. Pierre fishermen stopped loading codfish and started loading cargo. Stevedores, they're called."

"Stevedores," echoed Clara, casting her glance toward the stern. With no warning at all, the pod of seals ducked and fled. She flinched. "Oh dear," she said, gazing further out to sea. "There's a huge shadow on the surface of the water."

"Whale?"

Clara nodded. "I know that all creatures must eat but…" She shuddered. "I hope those seals are fast swimmers." As the words fell from her lips, a seal whirled through the air, obviously hurled by the monstrous predator. Clara cringed and turned away. Did one always have to be on guard? Was that the way of things, darkness showing up when you least expected it?

Eager for a change of focus, she turned toward Robert and launched a spate of questions. "Where do we go when we leave St. Pierre? St. John's? Can we go to the shops there? What about money? When do deckhands get paid?" Breathless, she paused. Before he could respond, she leaped in with another question. "Are we going to Rum Row, too?"

"St. John's, yes. Rum Row, no."

"The shops? Payday?"

"Patience, my dear." Robert reached for her, encircled her wrist with his hand. "Yes, we will visit the shops." With his free hand, he patted her enclosed one. "You won't be paid on this, your maiden voyage. But, after this, you will be paid in port, just like all the men."

Clara withdrew, shaking off the shackle of his fingers. She crossed her arms. "Do men get paid on their *maiden* voyage?"

"Yes, of course, but--"

"I'll be waiting for my pay along with them."

Roberts didn't object. "Good enough. But I won't have you worrying about the shops. I have money for the shops."

Clara nodded in agreement, a brisk nod. Only a fool would argue with that one.

Robert let out a long, low breath. "Is that it then?"

That was pretty much it, but Clara sensed defeat in his lengthy sigh. A knock of opportunity, that. She walked through the door. "How was it you got into rum running?"

Robert tipped his head to one side. After a few seconds he cleared his throat.

"The idea of exploring has always struck a chord with me."

Exploring? Not money? Clara raised her eyebrows.

"Human beings are inquisitive by nature," continued Robert. "Men will always explore, often in pursuit of glory, God, or gold."

Ah, there it was: gold. "So, you did it for money," Clara said, matter-of-factly. Inwardly, she balked. Had she really said that out loud?

Robert chuckled. "You certainly bypassed the first two at a jaunt."

"Easy choice. You're a quiet man, never looking for praise. And I don't see you beating a path to the door of the church."

"Well done. You are right, of course. But... I am not Catholic, you know."

"The saints preserve us!" She removed her hat and clutched it tight. The wind whipped her hair over her eyes, blocking her vision, but not mental images of Alphonse Kerrigan. "Does my father know that?" she asked, raking her fingers through her unruly mop. "When he asked you to marry me, did you tell him?"

"We never spoke of it, Clara," said Robert. "But the religion of my birth, the Church of England, is similar to Catholicism. I am familiar with the routine of the Mass. And as for the Latin? I have studied flora and fauna; they all have Latin names, did you know that?"

"I've seen your entire load of books." Clara bundled her hair and clamped her cap over it. "Shelf upon shelf of books. I'll have you know that I've read many of them, too." She pointed a finger at him. "Are you still a member of the Church of England? Or am I married to an atheist?"

"Which is worse? Atheist or criminal?"

"I imagine it's six of one and a half-dozen of the other."

Robert laughed again. "You know what? I may just be grateful to have you along on this trip, my lovely. It gets lonely, travelling all the time. And I must say that you are delightfully amusing."

"So you made yourself a good choice then, marrying the likes of me?"

"I'd have to say I did. Yes."

Clara was about to respond in kind. But then it struck her.

No one had ever given her a choice, about any of it.

CHAPTER 38

———◆———

WHEN CLARA, DRESSED AS A sailor, hair stuffed under a salt-and-pepper cap, brim pulled over her eyes, stepped onto the pier in St. Pierre, she was swept into a sea of pushing and shoving, hustle and bustle. This wharf, which staggered underfoot with phantom ocean swell, was much busier than the one they had left back home. Some of the echoes were the same: the rattle of cartwheels on wharf planks, the grunts and groans of men as they hoisted cargo. Something that was distinctly different to Clara was the odour, or lack of it. There were no cod here, no cod fishermen, and no fetid, festering smell. The only fishing here was bottle fishing, just as Robert had said. Robert had also told Clara to keep quiet, to do nothing that would identify her as a woman. "This is a man's world," he had said, and Clara had nodded.

Clara traipsed behind her husband for the full length of the pier. Once, only once, did she raise her cap to steal a glance. Vessel after vessel lined the pier, all in varying stages of loading and unloading. To the right were warehouses, a line of them as far as the eye could see. When she locked gaze with a sailor who had paused to wipe his brow, his eyes widened. She dropped her head and pulled her cap lower. Now she watched only Robert's feet, plod, plod, plod. When he stopped at a door, she bumped into him and had to step back. The twist of a handle. The creak of the door opening. The jingle of a bell. The aroma of fresh-baked bread wafted up Clara's nose; her mouth watered. Good heavens, she was gut-foundered.

As soon as they were through the door, Robert took her by the arm and pointed to wooden tables in the far corner. "Go over there." Clara and crew trudged to them. She chose a chair facing the wall and, stifling her temptation to look around, just stared at the red and white checkered tablecloth. On the middle of the table were two candles, tall, white candles stuck into the tops of wine bottles which were spackled with drips of wax. Chairs beside her scraped as two crew members joined her: the wireless operator, Sparky, and the first mate, Niall. She heard her husband place an order of sorts but the words got lost in the clangor of pots, the clomp of boots, the crowing of men.

Clara glanced at Niall out of the corner of her eye. A slow smile was spreading across this first mate's face which was now almost as red as his hair. Even his freckles seemed to dance. What on earth was he on about? Was he grinning at her? No. His eyes were focused on, twinkling at, someone behind her, someone who was creating a clashing and clanking racket. Clara ignored her first instinct: to swing around. A whoosh of breath slid past her ear. Clara inhaled, sucking in a smell of stale tobacco. Her failed attempt at smothering a cough was covered by an interruption from a cackling female voice.

"Niall, me ducky, mon ami. I knew ye couldn't stay away from me fer long."

"Take a load off there, Missus." Niall, still grinning, pointed to the empty chair reserved for Robert.

"Sure I can't be doing that now, can I? I'm wearing me Sunday best."

Clara cast a sideways glance at the visitor who lifted her full length skirt. Clara's eyes widened. Underneath the skirt was a petticoat with deep pockets, each containing a bottle of golden liquid. Whiskey?

The visitor snarked out a laugh and dropped her skirt. "Nice to see you, Nially b'y, but 'tis business only I'm after. I'm sure there's someone in the lives of the likes of ye who could use a skirt like this. Are ye buying, b'ys?"

Clara kept her head low, hoping neither of the crew would look to her. Sparky kicked her lightly in the shin and a shiver of anxiety ran through her. Niall focused on the saleslady. He turned down her offer, after which she guffawed and clinked her way to the door.

"What on earth?" Clara whispered.

It was Sparky who leaned in. "Skirts like that come in handy for moving small amounts of booze in dry areas, mostly Nova Scotia."

Clara was still puzzled.

Niall laughed. "Coppers can't search women; it's illegal."

"Oh, I see." Clara was tickled. A whole new world, this. She turned her attention to the noise in the room. Especially interesting were the voices of the men at the next table. There was an accent she had not heard before, a loud, open voice that dragged out the words like each syllable was important. Not like Newfoundlanders with their high-paced mutter. Not like Robert with his upper class clarity.

No longer able to contain herself, she turned her head. There were four portly men at the table. Clara easily identified the one in charge: the other three hung on his every word. The leader had a jagged scar down the left side of his face. His hat was white. Was that a fedora? Unusual, a white fedora. A black, bushy eyebrow jutted beneath the hat and a stout, unlit cigar protruded from his teeth. As Clara leaned forward, intending to ask her companions about that man, Sparky spit a whisper in her direction. "Shhh. Capone."

Clara jerked upright, eyes wide. Capone? Al Capone? Robert had spun tales of St. Pierre. Chicago's Al Capone had made his wealth in bootlegging and the bulk of his business was based here, in St. Pierre. Had Capone ever visited St. Pierre? Robert had never said. Was Al Capone sitting so close that she could hear him? She trembled and glanced at Sparky again, whose face was split wide in a grin. Clara flinched. Did she have a block of common sense at all falling for Sparky's idea of a joke? That Sparky should've kept his beard; it covered up the ugly pock marks on his face. Her snide opinions catapulted from the front of her mind to the tip of her tongue, but she swallowed them. Yes, she was wound as tight as the spring of a timepiece, but she had promised Robert she would not draw attention to herself. She clenched her teeth and forced a smile.

Robert joined them then, dropping heavily into the seat across from her. On his heels was a waitress who plopped a pitcher of wine on the table, none of which splattered out. She scurried away without a word and returned a short time later with a wooden plank containing the longest loaf of bread that Clara had ever seen. The waitress whisked a knife from her waistband and stabbed it, upright, into the middle of the loaf. "Stew will be up in a minute, b'ys," she said and swerved back toward the kitchen.

"Where's the butter now, ducky?" Sparky called after her. The question hovered, unanswered, due to a noisy interruption from the next table where all occupants stood, grinding their chairs along the floorboards, and clumping their way out of the cafe.

"Did any of you notice who that was?" asked Robert as he spread butter onto a chunk of bread.

Sparky laughed. "I told the little woman here that it was Capone. Scared the heck out of her I did."

"No need to be scared," replied Robert calmly, "but that was Al Capone. And his body guards, the Torrio brothers."

Dear God in heaven. Despite Robert's words of reassurance, Clara shivered in her seat. She sucked in a breath. Thank the Lord they were safe. One glance at Sparky and she smiled a quiet smile, reveling in the blush that sprang to his pebbled face. That would teach him not to tease her. She turned her attention to the waitress who had scurried to the vacant table and was now rattling dishes onto a tray.

Was this place real? If she pinched herself would it all disappear? Was she really disguised as a sailor, working as a rumrunner? Had she really been sitting next to Al Capone? Feeling braver than she had in a long time, Clara straightened her back and widened her glance. When the waitress had cleared Capone's table, Clara's line of vision was no longer obscured. She could see past that table, to the next. There was only one man seated there and he was looking straight at her.

Instantly, all the good went out of her.

Robert must have noticed she was out of sorts because he reached out and discreetly patted her hand. "Not to worry. Capone was here for business just like all the rest of us. No harm will come your way."

Clara nodded, head down, eyes raised and locked. It was not Capone that she was concerned about. It was the man seated at the table behind Capone's. A man she hadn't seen in years. Someone she thought she would never see again. Someone she had often wondered if she could even recognize. Well, there was no need to wonder anymore, was there? There he was, his blue eyes skewering her, the man she'd had only ever met the one time. In a black box, the confessional, when she was sixteen years old. Patrick.

The glint in his eye told her that her disguise was useless; she might as well have been splayed naked. Heat rose through her body and flushed her face. There was a blur of movement as he stood. Would he dare approach? Sweet Heart of Jesus. He was heading straight at her.

Patrick circled her table and stood behind her, his right hand on the top of her chair. "Good to see you again, Mr. Caulins."

Dear God. Patrick knew her husband. Clara trembled. How was it that he knew her husband?

Robert nodded at him. "Good day to you, Mr. McMurty."

McMurty? His name was McMurty? Clara threaded her fingers together, pressing and locking them firmly. She kept her head low, her ears perked. Would Robert invite Mr. McMurty to sit with them?

But Robert offered nothing further, not even an introduction. Neither Niall nor Sparky acknowledged the visitor.

"Will I be seeing you in St. John's in a few days?" asked Patrick McMurty.

Robert cleared his throat. "In all likelihood, yes."

"Good enough then. I'll be taking my leave."

The air rippled around Clara. Patrick was turning, about to walk away. Clara's heart was shrinking. She longed to protest, to shout "no." The urge was stymied by a slight feeling, a fluttering, on the back of her shirt. Holy Mother of God. Had he just run his fingers across her back? A sharp current, like lightning, tore through her body. The floorboards shook with retreating steps, sending vibrations to her very core. As the door clicked shut behind Patrick, realization clicked in her mind: the question about St. John's was meant for her. Patrick wanted to see *her*.

The crew nattered on, still pent-up about Capone. Clara said nothing. The stew showed up. The crew scoffed it down. When a voice prodded her to eat, Clara merely poked at the dumplings on her plate. Her hunger had vanished.

Never could she have imagined it, Al Capone serving as a smokescreen for the shame that had leapt up inside her. Her stomach clenched. What a liar she was, lying even to herself. For what she had felt, what she was still feeling, was anything but shame. What was it then? She pressed her lips together. Whatever it was, it was hers and it was secret and it swirled inside her, filling her with such delight that it was all she could do to keep from grinning.

After eating, after trips to the outhouse, the group wound its way back to the vessel. There Robert met a ghoulish little man with a garish scar on his face. Clara trembled at the sight of him. What was it with criminals and scars? The man led to them to a warehouse. When they arrived, stevedores loaded a wagon which was then driven back to the vessel and a second transfer of crates began. The crew, four in number, including Clara, formed a chain from the gunwale to the hold and tossed the crates along. The crates were heavy, each containing a dozen bottles of rum. Clara was second-last in the chain and soon developed a rhythm, being careful not to take the full weight of the crate, letting it dip and rise like the flow of the waves. The last man in the chain stacked the crate and turned back to her, awaiting the next. On board, they transferred the bottles from crates to burlap bags packed with straw. "To cover up the clink of the bottles," Niall whispered to her. All crates were left on shore.

When Clara crawled into her bunk that night, she was wrung out like a used dishrag. But, as exhausted as she was, sleep did not come. Patrick had popped up, dredging up her past, stirring up her thoughts until they swirled like sand in a whirlpool. Here she was, away from home, on a cramped boat: her attempt at forgetting, at fleeing her past. Was there no escaping her sins? Not hardly. The very beginnings of Kate were glaring at her. Clara squirmed as her mind went round and round with images of her first encounter with Patrick. But, try as she might, she could not ward them off. Were they really so unwelcome? Maybe not. Maybe she should let the images play. With a sigh, she conceded.

The stranger, Patrick, had followed Clara to the side of the church that day. When he held out a hand to her, she accepted it. The touch of his fingers instantly dispelled the darkness that had covered her for so long. Was this the sign she had demanded of God?

"Are you going to hide here forever or are you going to come with me?"

Clara blinked at him. "Where's Father Mahony?"

"Gone back to the Presbytery. You coming?"

"Where?"

"In there." He pointed to the front door of the church.

God and all the saints were shaking their fingers at her to be sure. Clara shut them out. For the first time in a long time, she felt something other than anger and sadness. Her heart was light, like a feather, and her head was as giddy as a spinning top.

"I'll go ahead and meet you inside." He turned and left her there.

Clara hesitated. Then she lurched into movement, aiming for the door of the church, but, at the last minute, bypassing it. Instead of going inside, she walked around outside, doing one complete circle of the exterior, rosary pulled from her pocket, head lowered as she counted off the beads. She started with the *Our Fathers* and *Hail Marys* but abruptly stopped. It wasn't praying she was focusing on now; all she could think about were his eyes and his lips and the touch of his fingers. And, truth be told, she was thinking that maybe the Lord didn't get all the vengeance after all. Clara sniffed. This would teach her father for ignoring her.

She marched up the steps of the church and pushed open the door. Inside, she automatically dipped her hand into the holy water and blessed herself. The sound of her shoes echoed. There was no sign of the tall, handsome stranger named Patrick. Where was he? She stepped into the nave of the church. Still she saw no one. Had he just been teasing her? Anxiety crept in. She was a silly girl, thinking that a man who was tall and blue-eyed and handsome, a man her father's age, would be interested in the likes of her. She walked down the aisle and was halfway to the altar when she heard a door open behind her. She turned. He was standing in the doorway of the confessional, beckoning. Clara paused, looked around, and walked toward him, drawn toward him. Closer and closer. Larger and larger he loomed in front of her. She was almost there. Almost. He leaned in and his breath slid across her face. His lips brushed hers.

Just then, the exterior door to the church opened, closed, the slam rumbling to the rafters. Patrick pushed her away and retreated into the confessional. She reacted quickly, stepping into a nearby pew, pulling the kneeler down and assuming the position of the penitent. Head low. Hands folded. Her ears perked up at the sound of familiar footsteps.

Father Mahony stopped beside her and whispered, "Clara! You're back. What on earth are you doing here?"

"I had to come back, Father. You see, when you asked me if I had lit a candle for my mom, I lied. I'm so sorry, Father. I never gave a thought to lighting a candle today and I felt like such a bad daughter that I had to lie. Then I figured I should come back and say a few prayers and right the situation."

Father Mahony patted her head. "You're a good girl, Clara. Your mom would be proud. I'll just get my hat and leave you to your prayers."

She cringed. His hat? Was he going into the confessional? Would he see Patrick? She pressed her fingers so firmly together that her knuckles turned white. The sound of footsteps. The twist of the knob on the confessional door. She cowered, waiting for a shout of surprise. There was none. Just the closing of the door and the footsteps of the priest, retreating. She stayed on her knees, too scared to move until she heard the closing of the exterior door. Then, two strong arms slid around her from behind, pulling her to her feet. Patrick turned her around and leaned her over the back of the pew. Again their lips met, this time long and slow. He backed away and she stepped out of the pew and toward him.

"Not yet," he said.

Puzzled, she paused.

"First, light that candle."

Clara nodded. She hurried to the front of the church and fumbled with the candles and the matches. The first match flamed, then died before she got it to the candle, leaving nothing but a thin puff of smoke. The second and the third did no better. Anxious, she glanced behind her. He was still there, leaning on a pillar, waiting. The fourth match did it. Candle lit, she scurried down the aisle to the stranger with the blue eyes. Patrick opened the door to the confessional, the priest's cubicle in the confessional, and they squeezed in.

Two sinners. Together.

As Clara finished replaying the details of her first meeting with Patrick, she smiled. Lulled by the rocking motion of the vessel, she drifted into sleep, one final thought on her mind:

How long would it take the *Elizabeth J* to get to St. John's?

KATHLEEN

CHAPTER 39

———◆———

IT CROUCHES AND BILLOWS, THE sea.

The North Atlantic is slithering shadow at cusp of night, pitching and heaving its way toward St. John's harbour. Eager, perhaps, to reach the beacon which flickers from shore. Nearer and nearer it creeps until the Fort Amherst light sweeps across its path making its black waters glisten like star sapphire. Into, then through, the harbour's only entrance— The Narrows—until it is flanked by craggy hills silhouetted on indigo sky. Sheltered here, the sea stops undulating.

On this night, moonless and windless, the *Elizabeth J* glides along like gloved hand on polished oak. No rise or fall, no list or sway. Only a murmur of engine as the vessel passes Chain Rock—the narrowest and shallowest point of this channel—heading for temporary berth.

My Clara is poised in the wheelhouse, silent, at the elbow of her husband as he manoeuvres into port. Darkness veils visible signs of excitement, but her emotions are palpable: a slight shiver, a hitched breath, a galloping heart. All of these sensations ripple the air around me, through me. Clara is experiencing not only a secret slide into harbour, but also a virgin visit to a city.

The city of St. John's rambles and scrambles up a rugged, steep hill, and is the oldest city on the North American continent. Dreary and dingy and mostly of wood, it is, at this time, a squalid town. The setting is beautiful—shining sea and pine-clad hills; the innards are grisly—shabby homes and trash-filled streets. Mirroring these extremes is a class system of wealthy politicians and destitute citizens. Even justice seems divided amongst men: one law for the rich, another for the poor. As for women? Drudges and child bearers, the lot of them. A small city, this, yet hundreds of young girls are on the street, tossed, after bearing children for boys from wealthy families, boys who continue their secondary education, paid for by their parents, while the mothers of their children and the children themselves feed from garbage.

Clara is not yet privy to these harsh realities of the city of St. John's. Already, however, her senses are reeling. The vessel has sailed from the aroma of salt air into the stench of seal fat and cod liver oil, the lifeblood of Newfoundland, the mainstay in this harbour. This is the place where laden sealing vessels anchor after journeys across harrowing floes, where weighted fishing schooners moor after voyages in churning seas. This is where cargo ships from around the globe bring product, where passenger ships from across the pond bring visitors who are eager to explore this, one of Britain's earliest colonies.

Clara blasts air through her nostrils, certainly an attempt to rid them of rank odour. After a slight cough, she leans into her husband. "Are you sure we should be here? What about the Newfoundland Constabulary? What about pirates?"

Ah, there it is: my Clara's anxiety, audible, her quivering voice confirming messages already relayed by her shivering body.

Robert stifles a laugh. "No need for concern," he whispers. "Precautions have been taken."

"But what if--"

"Sssh!"

Clara slips into silence.

The outlines of many boats are visible now, all obediently crammed along wharves in the bowl of the harbour. Other than an occasional groan of strained wood, they emit no sound. Clara stays at Robert's side as he guides the wheel. A mere shadow, he is, tall and straight. He utters not another word, just focuses on the task at hand.

I focus on him.

How long has he been my daughter's husband? Four years, I believe. A nebulous concept in the forever, time. Irrelevant to me, perhaps, but not to my story, nor to my Clara. Yes, it has been four years since Alphonse, at my insistence, swept her from our home.

I had no choice but to send Clara away. I have come to regret what I sent her to: Robert Alistair Caulins.

Clara knows little of this husband of hers, other than that he is from England, moneyed, and educated. Clara is learning of the power of money and will use that to her benefit. For now it is his education that she has glommed onto. Robert's learned ways have been an influx of light in the life of my Clara who loved school, who left school.

A *mea culpa*—mine—floats in the night. Powerless now, I let it drift.

Clara was an avid reader as a young child, but books were scarce. Now, Robert lavishes her with books, even reads to her at times. For this I am grateful. As a result of time spent with this man and his music and his books which sit in his precious, mahogany bookcases in their ornate, Victorian home, my daughter, the very same daughter now clad as a deckhand, will eventually assume the attire and demeanor of a lady.

Clara's current reading choice is a novel about an adulterous affair. Do I approve of this? It matters little in the afterlife. Would I have approved had I known at the time? Certainly not. No mother can condone what the Church forbids. Would Clara have flinched at my disapproval? At God's disapproval? I think not. The brazen young woman does not even bother to conceal the titles: such a simple thing it is to fold discarded pages of *The Evening Telegram* over book covers. Why doesn't she protect their covers in this way, as she did her school books? In this, just as in rum running, she defies convention, pretending she doesn't care. An illusion, that, for in her heart, Clara Kerrigan Caulins cares deeply. Else why would she read about women who were forced to relinquish illegitimate children? Staring into mirrors, she is.

Unlike Clara, I have no strength for these reflections. The air constricts around me, thwarting my urge to flee. Unable to confront images of Clara's sad past, I change my focus: her future.

If I could prod my way into Clara's mind, I would tweak her desire to learn about Robert, his parents, siblings, especially about his ease with children. I know not why I ponder these things, for I have no influence here either. A useless lot, ghosts.

Robert guides his schooner to the far end of the harbour and heads into dock. Just as the boat nudges the pier, one of his crew tosses a rope. It is caught on shore by a lumpish figure who appears from nowhere and who makes quick work of knotting the rope, mooring the boat. Robert hops to shore, Clara on his heels. He stops short and she slams into him. He turns. Grabbing her shoulders, he swings her about and shoves her back toward the vessel. "Below deck until we're done," he whispers.

Clara has experience with menace; she obeys without question. Once aboard the vessel, she pauses and peers over her shoulder. Robert accepts an envelope from the stranger. Immediately, the unloading begins.

Below deck, Clara peeks through a porthole, straining in vain to see all activity on the wharf. Perhaps she hopes to catch a glimpse of the dock but soon it will disappear from view, appearing to sink as weighted crates leave the vessel.

When the work is done, the workers slink into the night. Silence drops. For a while, there is no sound but swish of water. No crates clanking. No boards creaking. Even the gulls have conceded to the dark.

Clara, still biding her time below, wrings her hands. She paces, shoulders stooped. She plops onto her bunk, jumps up, and paces again.

Robert appears, his entry announced only by squeak of cabin door.

Clara jumps. "You scared me half to death--"

He shushes her. He grabs her hand.

Clara picks up a small suitcase as they exit the cabin door. Together they climb to the deck. She sucks in a breath, and coughs as the full stench of the fetid air stings her nose and throat. Robert pulls her along to the starboard gunwale. He hops onto the dock and turns, arms stretched, waiting for her. First, she tosses the suitcase. Then she puts one foot on the gunwale, hefts herself up and jumps, landing in his arms. He lets out a tiny chortle and she looks up, into his eyes. Pupils wide, they stare at each other.

Does she see what I do in his eyes? There is amusement, yes, but also, want. He will approach her tonight and for many nights to come. My Clara is tolerant, does her wifely duty. Perhaps she hopes for another opportunity, another Kate to enter her life.

Sadness infiltrates. I let out a long sigh.

Robert and Clara amble from the dock toward Water Street, to a dilapidated rooming house. The minute Robert pushes through the paint-chipped door, the smell of fish and brewis wafts out. Clara's stomach growls, a long rumble that expands into a belch. She claps her hand over her mouth.

"Good evening to you, Mrs. McIlvoy," Robert says to the buxom, pie-faced woman who meets them at the foot of the stairs, lantern in hand.

Mrs. McIlvoy raises the lantern, revealing a pinched expression. "A fine time to be looking for a room. Sure and it's nigh onto nine o'clock in the evening."

Robert tilts his head. He waits.

"Humph!" Mrs. McIlvoy removes a key from her apron pocket and leads them upstairs. She unlocks a bedroom door and waves an arm for them to enter the room. An oil lamp, already glowing, sits atop of a chest of drawers. The iron-framed bed which is jammed against the far wall is covered with a turned-down patchwork quilt. The room is warm, the fireplace alight.

"I knew you'd be expecting me," says Robert, smiling.

Mrs. McIlvoy passes him the room key. "I suppose you'll be wanting a meal too," she says, blinking up at him as she fiddles with her hair, a dark mop of ringlets.

"If it's not too much trouble."

Mrs. McIlvoy casts a wary glance at Clara before she trudges off.

As soon as she's gone, Robert turns to Clara. "We must be quick. Else she might change her mind."

"I doubt that. Right taken with you, she is." Regardless, Clara wastes no time in pulling the chamber pot from under the bed. Before she drops her trousers, she crosses her arms and stares at her husband.

Robert opens his mouth, maybe to offer a protest, but none comes. He merely throws his hands in the air and turns his back to her.

Clara scrambles out of her trousers and plops onto the chamber pot, sighing as her bladder splashes its release. Once finished, she jumps up and pulls up her trousers. Nose crinkling, she covers the chamber pot, returns it to its place, and brushes her hands together. She looks around the room and then nods as she heads toward the chest of drawers.

Sitting there, beside the oil lamp, is a bowl and pitcher. Clara pours water and picks up a piece of tar soap. After she scrubs and rinses her hands, she giggles.

"What's so funny?" Robert is beside her now, taking his turn with the soap, dipping his hands into the water.

Clara shrugs, holding up one hand to show her nails which are caked with dirt and grime. "I was thinking about my dirty nails, about how bad they look. As if it makes any difference when I'm dressed like a man to begin with."

Robert smiles. "After we eat, I'll help you out of those sailor clothes. In the meantime, keep hands in your pockets. No one will notice your grimy nails."

Clara pushes a few stray hairs under her cap as they exit the bedroom. As soon as they have navigated the stairs, she fists both hands into her pockets. In her husband's footsteps, she treads across wooden floorboards to the dining room, where there is only one table, a clothed rectangle with straight-backed chairs, beside a tall fireplace, gone cold. Robert drops into a seat the near end of the table; Clara sits opposite.

This room is well lit: two oil lamps at the center of the table, two wall sconces flanking an oak sideboard. Scorched patches above the sconces obliterate the yellow floral pattern in the tattered wallpaper. Centered above the sideboard are two framed pictures, one of the Sacred Heart, the other of King George V.

Clanging sounds, the meeting of pots and pans, smash the silence. Clara and Robert abruptly turn toward the door at the far end of the dining room. When footsteps are heard, Clara lowers her head.

Mrs. McIlvoy clomps in, drops laden plates onto the table, and lets out a snort. "Imagine the likes of people, showing up at me door and expecting full meals, in the night time, no less." She swings about and tromps out of the dining room.

Robert grins.

Clara opens her mouth, as if about to comment, but Robert puts one finger to his lips. She nods. They dig in, eating swiftly. When the plates have been licked clean, Robert grabs her hand and they scurry toward the stairs.

Back in their room, Clara and Robert convulse into laughter. Then my Clara looks up, into Robert's lust-filled eyes. Does she see beyond the lust, to the streak of secrecy? Of course she does but, at this point, she cannot, or chooses not to, decipher its meaning. Someday, she will read those eyes. Someday she will know all his secrets. He leads her to the bed where she splays her body, ready for yet another seedless bout of grunting and groaning.

I hover in the dark, biding my time, until his heavy sigh signals the end of his want.

"How long will we stay in St. John's?" Clara asks, as they lie side by side under a down-filled quilt.

Robert's breathing is sliding from shallow to deep. "A couple of days," he mutters.

"Won't it be something to see it all in the daylight?"

"Not as grand as you might think."

"But I can visit shops and eating establishments," says Clara, propping herself up on an elbow and staring wide-eyed into the fire. "Were those really cobblestones on Water Street? It was too dark to tell."

Robert does not respond, but Clara is not deterred. "Can we attend a movie house? Perhaps a theater?"

"Maybe not," Robert mutters. "But you can buy a dress tomorrow."

"Why don't I just buy the cloth? I'm pretty handy with the Singer. I can make many dresses when we get home."

"Buy, not make. Tomorrow. Shoes, too."

Clara leaned in and whispered in his ear. "What's the rush?"

"Meeting the magistrate and his wife tomorrow evening."

"What? Now you tell me? I could have brought something to wear."

"You have an evening gown in Argentia? I think not."

"You think right. What on earth would I be wanting with an evening gown? Where are you planning on taking me?"

"Fancy dinner at the Newfoundland Hotel. Now get some sleep." With that, Robert yawns and rolls onto his side, his back to her.

"Sleep? How can I sleep now? I'm beside myself. If I weren't trapped between you and the wall, I'd jump up and dance a jig. You have to tell me more."

No sound comes from Robert's side of the bed. Just slow, steady breathing.

Clara shakes him. "Robert..."

He doesn't move.

"I might as well try to wake the dead."

Would that she could. I sigh, unheard.

It is a long time before Clara's excitement wanes but eventually her body drifts into much-needed sleep. I am witness to the steady rise and fall of chest beneath a down quilt. I wish her joy in her dreams of her first visit to a city. Reality will assault her soon enough, likely when she's tripping over ragged urchins whose filthy hands grope, or traipsing past the old courthouse whose hanged ghosts lurk.

I remain, watching, until the last fireplace ember ceases to glow.

CLARA

CHAPTER 40

WAS THIS WHAT PRISON WAS like? Clara was blocked in bed by an angular husband on one side and a warped wall on the other. She squeezed her eyes shut. Where was her exhaustion? A short time ago, she was all in, so tired she could have slept on a clothesline. But now her whole body tingled. How was she supposed to sleep with pictures of bright lights and linen tablecloths romping through her head? Imagine it, the likes of her prancing around among the higher-ups.

It was a good thing Robert had said she could buy a dress for the occasion; she couldn't show up looking like a Friday fish at a Saturday market. Were there really such things as ready-made, fancy dresses? Everyone Clara had ever known—her mother, Mrs. Mullins, even the merchant's wife—had threaded a needle when a dress was needed. Clara herself had only bought bolts of cloth, not finished products. And what about shoes? Her black boots were dusty, cracked, and salt-caked from tromping in dirt and on wharves. Even those were handmade, years before, by her father, from tanned leather he had bought at the merchant store. Definitely not suitable for the dining room at the Newfoundland Hotel.

The whole world of the higher-ups would be staring down their noses at her for sure. An ignorant girl from around the bay. She gritted her teeth. What odds did it make where you came from? Yes, the lot from home would look frumpy in town, but they were a capable bunch, all pretty handy with their fingers. It wasn't only clothes and boots they conjured up. They could make anything: mats, cakes, masts,

257

flakes. Even houses and ships were built by hand. Were she any kind of a person at all, she would strut into this gala, bragging about her people and her past. What was it that made her want to belong to the higher-ups anyway? Whatever it was, she knew she would bury her background. She would follow Robert's lead, even imitate his accent. How disloyal was she?

Half the night, Clara just lay there, fidgeting. Normally she would read in order to relax. Not now, though. Even if she could get past her locked-in position to access her book, the firelight would not allow for seeing fine lines. Clara let her thoughts fly and tuned her ear to the crackle of the fire. That sound, in combination with the steady rise and fall of Robert's breathing, calmed her. She felt herself drift.

When she opened her eyes, it was daylight. She was facing a bumpy, chinked wall, an unfamiliar wall. She blinked. Where was she anyway? Her loud yawn was accompanied by the moan of a foghorn and the rumble of motor cars. Reality struck. St. John's, that's where she was. She rolled over, anxious to begin her day.

Robert's side of the bed was empty. Where was he? She tossed off the quilt and instantly shivered. The room was ice, the fireplace black. The second she put her bare feet on the floor, she felt the need for the chamber pot. She pulled the pot from under the bed and removed its lid. She scrunched up her nose. Someone, perhaps even herself, should have taken pains to empty the pot the night before. She raised her nightgown and squatted. Footsteps in the hall made her rush to finish the job. She had barely put the lid on the pot and returned it to its place when Robert entered the room.

"Good morning, sleepyhead. Weren't you the one who wanted to go shopping this morning?" He grinned at her.

Clara grinned back. "I'll meet you downstairs in ten minutes." She shuffled the protesting Robert out of the room and tore open her tiny suitcase. A dress. She had one dress with her. Not stylish, dull brown in colour, plain in design, but a dress. After weeks in men's clothes she wanted to wear a dress and a sweater. No handbag, though. She was going to take one along, but Robert had scoffed at the idea. Well, she would just purchase one, that's all there was to it.

As ready as she could be, Clara hurried downstairs toward the front door. As she passed the open dining room, she caught a glimpse of Robert, seated at the same place they had been last night. "Breakfast first," he called.

Breakfast? Disappointment hit her like a hammer. Shoulders slumped, Clara walked across the dining room and joined Robert. She picked up her napkin and waited. It was not long before the owner of the boarding house, Mrs. McIlvoy, scurried toward them, smiling. Certainly a different Mrs. McIlvoy than Clara had seen the night before.

"Good morning, Mrs. McIlvoy," said Robert. He waved a hand toward Clara. "This is my wife."

Mrs. McIlvoy's eyes widened. "Jesus God." She clapped her hand over her mouth and looked around. There was no one else in the room. Mrs. McIlvoy let out a sigh and leaned in to Clara. "God forgive me for taking the name of Him and his Son," she whispered, "but it's just that I could have sworn you were a boy."

"Pleased to meet you," said Clara stiffly, not knowing what else to say. She glanced at Robert who was grinning widely. Her insides warmed. In the absence of rumrunners, there was no need for ruse. She looked straight at Mrs. McIlvoy. "I'm Clara," she said.

Mrs. McIlvoy wiped her hands on her apron. "Let's start over again, why don't we? Good morning to the two of ye." She brushed a ringlet out of her flushed face; it fell back. She ignored it. "Will ye be wanting tea or coffee this morning?"

"Coffee for my husband. Tea for me," said Clara as she straightened in her chair. For the first time in weeks, she was free to express herself. She burst into conversation. "What can you tell me about the shops, Mrs. McIlvoy? Where is the best place for me to get a fancy dress, ready-made?"

"Ready-made, dearie? Are you sure you wants ready-made? There's a fine dressmaker just over the road."

"I'll be attending a supper at the Newfoundland Hotel this evening." Clara felt full of herself, and delighted about it. "I've no time for a dressmaker."

"Well, then, if that's the case, after you've had a good breakfast, you just head right over to the Bowring store on Water Street. Finer merchandise you never seen. Comes straight from London. I hear tell all the grand ones from the hotel and Rawlings Cross gets their dresses and shoes and handbags right there. Mind you, I said, I hear tell... can't be saying myself because I have no money for such things. Hard enough to keep the wolf from the door what with me lot in life." She planked her hands on her hips. "Yes, sure and I lost me husband, I did. Died on the ice, God rest his soul." She made the sign of the cross. "Can't be bringing meself to make flipper pie ever since the day..."

The mention of flipper pie took Clara right out of the conversation and right back to the day Kate was born. What was it that the midwife had said? Something about Kevin returning from his time on a sealing vessel? Something about Mavis feeding him flipper pie and telling him he had twins?

Mrs. McIlvoy dragged on. "...it was a terrible thing, losing so many men--"

"Yes, I'm sure it was. We'll be having eggs and toast this morning," Robert said.

Mrs. McIlvoy blushed. "I do go on so. Yer breakfast will be coming up right away, dearie. Right away." She hurried off.

"Do you know where the Bowring store is?" Clara asked as soon as their host had vanished into the kitchen.

"I've been there."

"What's it like? What did you buy? Why did you go?"

"You'll see it soon enough." Robert picked up newspaper that had been placed on the table. He unfolded it. A flick of his wrist and the paper formed a wall between them. The conversation was over.

Later, Clara walked along Water Street at her husband's side, double stepping to keep up with his stride. It had rained earlier in the morning, but the skies were clearing now, showing patches of blue amid puffs of cloud. There was still fog off the coast, its presence announced by the persistent moan of the foghorn. A doleful sound, but it could not suppress her excitement which peaked the second they left the boarding house. What did put a crimp in things came not from the sky but from the street, in the form of dirty, barefoot children in ragged clothes, their hands out. Clara looked into the eyes of a few, but couldn't fathom the emptiness she saw there. Innards squirming, she slowed her pace, intending to toss pennies from her pocket, but Robert grabbed her arm, pulling her along and even stepping over urchins perched on boxes.

The noise and traffic beside them was constant. The horses and carriages were of no great concern to her; she was accustomed to that. But the motorcars? A different thing entirely.

A memory ruffled her mind like wind on water, that of the first motorcar she had seen, a motorcar owned by Father Mahony. Oh, the upheaval it caused in the tiny community of Argentia, all the children tearing toward the dirt road to see the vehicle stutter past. And yes, Clara's husband had a motorcar now. Still, such things were rare in outport communities. But here, in St. John's, motorcars were commonplace. People swarmed the street, buzzing in and out among horse-drawn drays and motorized vehicles, paying no mind to one nor the other.

Clara pulled her eyes away from the bustle of life on the cobbled stones of Water Street and focused on the shop windows. Even those were not what she had expected: they were dirty and smudged and contained no evidence of what was inside.

Clara didn't even see the sign on the Bowring store. She heard the jangle of the shop bell and saw that Robert had just opened a door. He pulled her inside, closing the door behind her. She looked up at the brass bell as it jangled again. "You go that way," Robert pointed. "I'll be back in two hours."

"But where--"

"I'm going to the men's department. You're not attending a gala at Newfoundland Hotel alone now, are you?" He grinned. "And I would prefer not to linger among sewing notions and ladies' knickers." He veered right.

Clara nodded, a wasted sign of agreement, for he was already gone. She stood, staring after him, uncertainty flickering. Here she was, adrift in a city shop for the very first time. She tilted her head and curved her lips into a smile: imagine the fun she could have. Clara clapped one hand over her mouth to keep from squealing with delight. She squeezed her eyes shut as she turned toward "knickers and notions."

An aroma of lilacs wafted, causing her nose to crinkle. Perfume? Quite the change from the stench of the inner harbour. She opened her eyes and blinked.

A single ray of sunshine, laden with dust motes, had sneaked through some unsullied pane. It caressed her left shoulder and fanned across the surface of shelves which were piled high with fabric. Clara had never seen the like. So much cloth. Row upon row, bolt upon bolt, in a rainbow of colours. She let her eyes rove, taking in the brightness and the patterns. Oh, the sewing she could do. But not today. Today she wanted ready-made. Where were the dresses?

Clara edged her way down a narrow aisle between mounds of material, her eyes moving swiftly from left to right. The smell of perfume was gone now; in its place was tinge of dye and hint of must. Clara raised a hand and slid her palm across velvet, wool, silk. So plush, so coarse, so smooth.

"May I help you, Miss?"

Startled, Clara swerved toward the voice. Ahead of her stood a prim little woman in a long black dress, over which was a crisp white apron. Clara glanced at the name tag: *Mary.* A shop girl, no doubt, in black and white, dressed like a nun, but not a nun. Nuns didn't wear name tags. Clara raised an eyebrow. Mary. All nuns were Mary something-or-other, weren't they? She had heard stories about nuns: a strict bunch, all religion and rules and rosary beads. She squirmed, just a little. "Perhaps you can help me, Mary," she said, her eyes still darting all around.

"What is it you are looking for, Miss?" Mary stood in a circular opening that contained a table and chair and was backed by a curtained wall.

"Perhaps you can help me," Clara said again, over-pronouncing every syllable. How proud was she at all, trying to elevate her station in life just because she was in a city shop? "I'm seeking a dress to wear to supper, I mean dinner this evening."

Mary tilted her head.

"At the Newfoundland Hotel," Clara added in haste, hoping that she was providing the desired information.

Mary nodded briskly. "Yes, I see. You're not the first visitor inquiring about attire for the ball this evening, Miss. I can show you our collection of formal dresses."

British, Clara decided. The clerk was definitely British, like Robert. "Yes, that would be quite the thing, I believe," said Clara, straightening her posture.

"Here it is, Miss." Mary walked to the edge of the curtain and grabbed the curtain rod.

"Actually, it's Missus," Clara corrected. "My husband..." Her words fell away as Mary whipped open the curtain revealing a long row of shimmering gowns.

"Very well. Missus it is." Mary swung around to face Clara.

Clara stood there, staring at the dresses, her mouth agape. She danced her eyes along the wall, delighting in the array of colour and sparkle. Out the corner of her eye, she caught a glimpse of Mary who was displaying a knowing smile. Her pretense uncovered, Clara winced.

"Your first ball, is it, Missus?"

Nodding, Clara looked straight at Mary, whose eyes were soft with understanding. All the black-and-white stiffness of her shop girl uniform seemed to have evaporated.

"Well, then, you'll be needing my help with everything then, won't you? Shoes? Gloves? Undergarments as well?"

Clara clasped her hands in front of her. "Yes, please. Very much so."

Mary nodded. "Why don't you just have a seat, Missus, while I show you some of these gowns? Once we get an idea of what you like, I'll fix you up, good and proper, as the people say here."

Clara took a deep breath. "Thank you," she said as she walked to the armchair and sat.

Two hours later, Clara stood in front of a full-length mirror, clad in a loosely-fitting, black chiffon evening dress, while Mary buzzed around her like a bumblebee around a rose bloom.

"Quite fetching on you, this chiffon," said Mary. "Do you like the appliqué silhouette on the bodice?" She waved a hand toward the graphic design.

Clara nodded. She had never seen swirls like that before. Well, perhaps a few on flowered wallpaper but she wasn't about to own up to that. For the life of her, she couldn't fathom how someone could stitch curlicues onto chiffon: such a flimsy, sheer fabric.

"And your satin slip? Is it comfortable?" Mary lifted the lacy handkerchief hem of the gown.

"The best kind, b'y," said Clara, reverting to dialect before she could catch herself. She let out a nervous laugh. "I mean…" Done with trying to sound elegant, she threw her hands in the air. "Mary, I've never felt the likes of it in all my born days."

A short time later, Clara, packages clustered at her feet, bounced on her toes as she waited beside the shop counter for Robert. She didn't stop bobbing until cash register drawer slammed, its final *cha-ching* marking the swallowing of full payment. Grinning, she helped Robert gather up the stockpile and then darted through the door ahead of him. Clara was all strut and song on the walk back to the boarding house. Nothing could dampen her spirits today.

With speed and in silence, Clara scaled the stairs to their room in the boarding house. Thankfully, Robert followed suit. Heaven forbid they should snag the attention of the long-winded Mrs. McIlvoy. All Clara wanted was to concentrate on her new wardrobe: she ached to rip open all the packages, just to stare, stroke, sniff.

Once they'd closed their room door, Clara plunked her parcels onto the top of the bed. She grabbed one and, heart racing, picked at the tiny knot in the twine. Stubborn knot. Tied too tight, but she could loosen it if--

"Don't open anything," Robert said.

Clara turned, blinking.

"We are just here to gather our belongings. Then we will take a taxi to the Newfoundland Hotel."

"Excuse me?"

"You heard me right. This boarding house is a fine stopover but the hotel is a better place to prepare for an evening event. I'm sure we can manage to get a room with a view of the harbour. You'd like that, wouldn't you?"

More than satisfied, Clara nodded. That's all she seemed to be able to do today, nod and bob, like a buoy in the waves. She could barely fathom it: shopping in the city, staying at a grand hotel, and hiring a taxi? All new to Clara. All maiden voyages, just like her stint in the schooner.

Within a half hour, Clara and Robert were outside, awaiting the arrival of the taxi which Robert had summoned while at the Bowring store. Perched beside them, in a stack on the stoop of the boarding house, sat all of Clara's packages.

Robert offered his arm and she took it, looking up at him with indebted eyes. Maybe she had done the right thing by leaving home for a time. Here in St. John's, her mind was not crammed with thoughts of Kate. Here in St. John's, her mind was jammed with images of shopping and money and-- Clara immediately pulled her eyes away from Robert and glanced up and down the street. Hadn't Patrick said he would be in St. John's?

A sudden booming noise hurtled through her, banishing her thoughts. She uttered an indrawn gasp, dropped her new pocketbook, and clapped her hands over her ears. What in the name of all that was holy...?

Robert patted her shoulder. "Nothing to worry about, dear. That was the twelve o'clock gun, fired daily on Signal Hill."

"Scared me half out of my wits," said Clara as she pulled a handker-chief from her pocket and dabbed at the muddy smudge on her rescued pocketbook. "Why on earth do they make such a racket?"

"A tradition. Its original purpose, in a time when not everyone could afford these..." Robert held up his gold pocket watch, "...was to let the military know the hour. You'll see the gun—actually a can-non—tomorrow morning when we sail through The Narrows. Unless, of course, Signal Hill is obliterated by fog." He clicked open the lid on his pocket watch and nodded. "This watch keeps good time, as does our taxi driver apparently."

The taxi pulled up and the driver scurried to usher Clara in. While she waited for Robert who helped with the stowing of luggage and pack-ages, Clara ran her fingertips over the knobbed leather seat. Smooth, it was, like the surface of risen bread dough. A well-used vehicle, this, but spotless, too. Clara nodded her approval. As soon as Robert joined her, she sat stiffly, attempting to keep her lips pursed, an elegant lady riding in her carriage. But, try as she might, she could not stop smiling.

It was a perfect room, so perfect that Clara wondered if it were real at all. Not one room, actually, but a suite, consisting of a sitting room and a bedroom. Its considerable size and buff-coloured walls reminded Clara of the Holy Rosary Church back home. She didn't dwell on the memory. Within the hollows of that church, Clara had been a mouse, bowing, whispering, shivering under the scrutiny of Father, Son, and Holy Ghost. The Newfoundland Hotel had no altars. Therefore, no genuflecting. And, praise the Lord, no penance either.

Clara was again playing a waiting game for Robert who had gone via the lift to the lobby. Something about seeking the agenda for the evening. Clara had nodded, the obedient wife, as he left the room. The second he was gone she danced and twirled and set out to explore.

The overstuffed chesterfield in the sitting room was brocade, purplish-red, its nap pressed from wear. She plopped and bounced. Comfortable enough. From there she rushed toward the pale curtains and flung them wide. She tugged at the window, a wasted effort for it was painted shut. But its four panes were spotless and afforded her a view of both city and harbour.

Clara was certain the city view would hold no interest for her; she had seen enough of it that morning, on the streets, in the fog, in the filth. But her eyes widened as she peered down. So this was what the world looked like to pigeons, crows, and gulls. Chimney pots poked from weathered rooftops and black smoke puffed into blue sky. On the roof of one house, a piece of tar paper slapped, untended, and on the fronts of many houses, sprained doors sagged, neglected. So many flights of steps, wilting. So many painted signs, fading. Clara sighed. Whether looking from street or sky, it made no never mind: the city was still dreary. The one highlight was the sight of the people, so tiny, so busy, scurrying like ants.

Clara cast her eyes toward the harbour and smiled. Nothing dreary about the ocean. Now that the fog had receded, the waters rippled and sparkled from harbor to horizon. Vessels of all sizes—skiffs and schooners and cargo ships—were entering and exiting The Narrows.

Leaving the curtains wide, Clara continued her tour. She headed toward the bedroom and paused in the open doorway. The bed was a four poster, in husky oak, and there was a cloth-covered table at each side of it. Blue and white patterns twirled on the quilt, the curtains, even on shades of the lamps which switched on or off at the turn of a little knob. There were two chests of drawers, a clothes cupboard, and even a writing table.

The sound of a rattling doorknob reached her ears. Robert was back. Already? Clara hurried to the bed, dropped to her knees, and lifted the bed skirt. No sign of the chamber pot.

"What in heavens' name are you doing, woman? I can take you to the cathedral later if you wish to pray."

Clara grimaced. "I'm not praying. I'm looking for the chamber pot."

Robert took her by the arm, and led her to a door that she had not noticed. He swung it open. Inside was a small room containing a bathtub, a basin, and a bowl-shaped object, all shining white. On the wall above the bowl was a brown box with a dangling chain.

"You open the lid of this, the toilet..." He demonstrated, "...you do your business and, when you finish, you pull that chain." He pulled the chain above the toilet and Clara watched as the water in the bowl swirled and swirled and disappeared down the hole.

Anxious to experience this luxury she'd only heard about, Clara nudged Robert out of the little room and dropped her drawers. Where was the splash? The sound of urine meeting water was barely noticeable, not at all like in an outhouse. And the smell? Was there a smell? She stood. The colour was pale yellow, lighter than that in a chamber pot. She pulled the chain and stepped back, ready to watch the miracle again. She was not disappointed.

Back she went, through the bedroom, into the sitting room, where she found Robert tamping tobacco into his pipe. She flung her arms wide. "Life doesn't get any better than this." In seconds, she was at the window again, staring down, ready to watch the people. Where were all those tiny people speeding off to anyway? She caught sight of one man, leaning into a lamp post, his arms crossed. He raised his head and doffed his hat.

Clara let out a tiny gasp and then pressed her fingers against her lips. She glanced toward Robert.

Robert's face was hidden by the newspaper he held. Smoke curled from his pipe.

Clara turned back to the window, hand raised, ready to wave.

Too late. Patrick was gone.

KATHLEEN

CHAPTER 41

———————

IT SIGHS IN SYMPATHY, THE sea.

The North Atlantic is an imposter, whispering solace to those who have lost, to those who are lost. At the core of its caressing and shushing lies truth: the sea itself is a cemetery, proffering, on impulse or if impelled, entombment for all who venture near. The sadness it seeps is naught but reflection of content: the North Atlantic is a receptacle for a mother's tears.

I hover above the whitewashed cemetery gate which is slamming, repeating, at the whim of the wind. Its creaking and clutching masks the sobs of a woman who crouches beside a simple white cross that marks an overgrown grave, the final resting place of the baby, Jimmy Kerrigan. The mourner's pain wafts, piercing the entity that is me. I moan, a wasted lament.

Here I am again at the scene that depicts the dawn of my downfall. I can do naught but own it for I am—more accurately, *was*—at its core. It is my corporeal self I am observing here. My very own self, yet, upon every viewing, the feeling that I am voyeur, intruder, causes me to lurch like the gate in the wind.

He is coming.

The approaching footsteps are silent, yet the kneeling Kathleen senses them, knows their owner. She stifles her sobs, secures her scarf, and clasps her rosary beads in the palm of her hand.

"All the praying in the world won't bring him back now, Kathleen." Alphonse's voice is low, gravelly.

On every visit, his voice gives me pause. Does it contain menace? I think not. I think as I watch this that he hopes to offer her peace. I know as I watch this that she wishes he would leave her in peace. At this point, she is content to wallow, bound like a shadow to her grief.

Alphonse sidles up beside her. Crouching, he places his lips next to her ear. "I shot myself," he said.

Kathleen turns sharply, slamming her face into his. "What?" Her voice is fractured, disbelieving.

He rubs his jaw, the point of impact. "I shot myself. In the war." His sigh is long and steady, like the *whir* of fly line spinning from reel.

With a jolt, Kathleen is on her feet. She steps back, her hand at her throat. "What in God's name are you on about? Why would you ever do such a thing?"

"Sssh, not so loud," Alphonse says, looking all around.

In the distance, the weather is threatening: a thundercloud suspended over waiting sea. Near at hand, the wind has ceased: a lull hovering over impending truth.

Alphonse plants his hands on his thighs and pushes himself upright. "It was all young men, you see. Dying. Not men, boys really. Not much older than Kevin, they were. Dying all around me. I couldn't..."

"Couldn't what?"

Alphonse draws his sleeve across his lips and reaches into his back pocket. The silver flask emerges. He unscrews the cap. Kathleen clamps her hand on his arm, halting the movement of flask to lips.

"You couldn't what, Alphonse?"

Alphonse looks at her, eyes brimming. "Did you know that when young men are dying, it is not their God they wants?" He shakes his head slowly. "Not a word out of them about God or Church or the Lord Jesus Christ. All they ever cries out, every last one of them, is a single word: "Mommy.""

Kathleen sinks back, her hand falling away from Alphonse's arm. "Dear God," she whispers.

Alphonse takes a swig from his flask. "The most pathetic sound you'll ever hear. I couldn't listen no more. Not for another second. I shot myself so I could get the hell out. At first, I aimed the gun at my leg, I did, but I figured the higher-ups would know what I done. It's no easy task to shoot yourself in the neck, and survive, but I managed it. Turns out it didn't matter one way or the other. They figured me out. A man of low moral fibre, they called me. Put that on my permanent record, they did."

"I saw the papers but I had no idea--."

"That's why I did it, you see."

"But to shoot yourself--"

"No, not the shooting." He points at the grave. "Jimmy. I couldn't stand by and watch Jimmy, growing up, going off to war or off to sea, and dying that way. I kept hearing his voice, crying out for you. I couldn't let him go through that kind of pain, couldn't let *you* go through that kind of grief. Figured he should just die as a baby. Then we'd be done with it. They should all have died young, the lot of them, Kevin and Clara along with him. Then there'd be just the two of us, the way it was meant to be."

Kathleen stares at him, her face blank.

He slides the flask back into his pocket and reaches a hand to her. "It's time to go," he says. In a whisper, he adds, "I'll take you home again, Kathleen."

It is a strange thing, watching, feeling your younger self come to a realization. All this time, Kathleen has believed that the tragic death of Jimmy was the result of revenge. Her punishment for being raped. That it was his blue eyes that determined his fate.

But now she knows the truth, the unadorned truth. It was the war that did it. The Great War murdered the mind and soul of Alphonse Kerrigan. The colour of Jimmy's eyes had nothing to do with anything. Had Alphonse even figured out that the child wasn't his own? It didn't matter. None of it mattered. Jimmy had never had a chance.

As Kathleen focuses on the horror of this now, it occurs to her that there's no going back, no changing things.

The wind picks up. The clouds move in. Rain spits, then drizzles.

Resigned, Kathleen reaches for Alphonse's hand. The long sigh she lets out is one of relief: her remaining children, Kevin and Clara, are adults. Safe.

I slink along, a shadow in the mist, as Alphonse, true to his word, leads Kathleen home. He remains outside: there's wood to be chopped. She aims for the kitchen: there are lamps to be lit.

I am in her presence now, watching as she gathers three oil lamps and sets them on the kitchen table. Metal scrapes against glass as she dislodges stubborn chimneys.

The strike of a match. Kathleen guides lurching flame toward willing wick.

In the background, the fall of the axe. Alphonse chops in steady rhythm. *Thud. Thud. Thud. Thud.* But then? An uncharacteristic sound, that of axe meeting stone, perhaps metal. *Clink.*

Startled, Kathleen flinches. In slow motion, she turns her head toward the door. Her eyes widen. Her hand twitches, repeatedly, uncontrollably. The match tumbles. As a strand of smoke threads upward from snuffed flame, Kathleen gasps, sucking in a breath, holding it.

The air around me is heavy. I wait.

Her face pinched and ashen, Kathleen stares into nothingness. Her exhalation comes, long and slow, a piercing whine. "Holy Mother of God," she whispers, as she drops her head into her hands.

There it is. The realization is complete. Yes, Kevin and Clara are safe. But what about Kate?

CLARA

CHAPTER 42

CHANDELIERS. THAT'S WHAT FIRST GRABBED Clara's eye as she stood on the arm of Robert at the threshold the Newfoundland Hotel ballroom. The beauty, the sparkle, the blaze of chandeliers. She could barely fathom it. At home, right this minute, people were engaged in the ritual of lighting the oil lamps that would shepherd them through the night. Of course, there *was* electricity at home. Clara had electricity—in her kitchen, only in her kitchen, where one naked, glaring bulb dangled from the ceiling, a string attached to it for turning it on and off. No bulbs in the parlour. No bulbs in the bedroom. Certainly no chandeliers. But Clara was familiar with them anyway; she had seen the Eaton's catalogue.

"Are you prepared for this, my dear?" Robert's voice was calm, encouraging.

Aware of her racing heart, Clara raised a gloved hand, intending to fluff her curls. With hand in midair, she paused. It wouldn't do to dislodge a well-placed hairpin. She retracted the movement and took a deep breath. "As ready as I'll ever be."

Robert guided her toward the center of the room. "This is the largest ballroom in town," he whispered.

Beads of sweat formed under Clara's chiffon gown. Why hadn't he kept that gem to himself? Her throat was uncomfortably dry. What was she doing in a place like this anyway? She stood on the edge of a cluster of chattering people and examined her surroundings.

On the periphery of the room were circular tables draped in white linen. Surrounding each table were eight chairs and at the centre of each was a candelabrum. The crystal and silver place settings caught the light and batted it back, all glimmer and shine.

Classical music, light and cheerful, wafted through the air. Clara turned toward the semicircle of musicians at the front of the room. There were two fiddles, another bigger fiddle, and a fourth so big that the player had to hold it between his knees. Clara blinked. She was accustomed to leg-bouncing accordion players and toe-tapping fiddlers. What was this group—an orchestra? She turned her husband. "Certainly a strange looking fiddle," she whispered, indicating the largest one.

He smiled down at her. "That is a string quartet: two violins, a viola and the big one is a cello. Not an Irish folk tune to be had, or more correctly, *heard* here. The music is Mozart. Remember my recordings?"

Clara smiled. Of course. Mozart. "Does this particular music have a title?"

Lines of concentration appeared on Robert's brow. "Hmmm. I can't quite recall--"

"It's *Eine Kleine Nacht Music*." This answer from a low, breathy voice, right beside Clara's ear. A man's voice.

A chill, like the riffling of a book's pages, filtered down her spine.

"Thank you, Patrick. It's good to see you again." Robert extended a welcoming hand past Clara. "I'd like you to meet my wife. Clara, this is Patrick McMurty."

Clara spun around, eyes wide, smile fixed.

Robert was still talking. "Patrick and I have been doing business together since I first set foot on the island. Patrick, this is my Clara."

Clara looked up into ice-blue eyes that flashed like light caught in water. Strength siphoning from her body, she faltered. Would she plummet into a puddle of black chiffon? Instantly, she pushed that image down, hard. In the end, it was only her fingers that failed her: her clutch purse tumbled.

"Allow me." In a chivalrous swoop, Patrick retrieved the purse and placed it in her left hand. "Very pleased to meet you, Mrs. Caulins." He then claimed her right hand and raised it to his lips. All the while, his eyes swept her body.

Heat flooding her face, anxiety churning her stomach, Clara wilted into a curtsy. Did he recognize her?

Patrick released her hand. "As I was saying, the music you are hearing is *Eine Kleine Nacht Music,* in English, *A Little Night Music.* It's a well-known string quartet. Do you like Mozart?"

Clara had no words. She managed a weak nod.

"Then I am sure you will have an enjoyable evening. This lot is upper crust: the Mozart/Haydn/Vivaldi types. Let me know if you get bored and I'll try to persuade one of the violinists to hammer out a jig for you." Patrick winked and turned his attention to Robert. "I must make the social rounds. Please excuse me." After a curt bow, he ambled to a table on the left side of the room.

Clara studied him, following his every movement. "How did you two meet?" she asked Robert.

"Oh, just one of the business men. Maybe St. Pierre. Maybe at a gathering here."

"Was he ever in Argentia?"

"Possibly. Patrick does tend to travel. Has a way with the world, and the women."

"McMurty? His last name's McMurty?"

"Yes, it is. Clara, are you well? You look a little flushed."

"I'm fine," said Clara, instantly straightening her posture. "It's just the excitement of everything--"

"Good evening, Robert." The drawling voice belonged to a stout, squat man with a balding head and a walrus mustache.

"Lord Abernethy, what a pleasure it is to see you again. May I introduce you to my wife, Clara?"

Grateful for the distraction, Clara fixed her attention on the bulbous face of Lord Abernethy. How did he manage to keep that monocle in place?

"Charmed, my dear, charmed." The lord reached for her gloved hand and bent to kiss it.

Again, Clara curtsied in response. Then she waited as expected, silent as a statue, while the two men talked. During this bubble in time, she tuned out disconcerting thoughts. A black-frocked waitress approached, offering champagne. Clara nodded her thank you. She sipped as she reset her focus.

A hum of conversation filled the room. So many voices—girlish, grating, and gruff—rising and falling. At one point, the voices stopped altogether, like a choir getting ready to sing "Amen." But then a demure *teehee* filled the void and the chorus started up again.

Clara and Robert moved about, greeting lords and ladies from London and the financial elite of St. John's. After a while, Clara shrugged off both her collision with her past and her concern with her presence among the upper crust. Would she see Patrick again? Yes, if she had any choice in the matter. As for hobnobbing with the elite, she could, and would handle that as well. Right now she was a rumrunner, a woman in a man's world. It was not likely that the British class system could deter her. Yes, she was a simple girl from Placentia Bay, a girl whose father had practically sold her into this world. Her father who had made her promise that she would never reveal the secret of her sins. Her resentment churned, a silent declaration of war. Nobody was going to keep her down.

Head high, Clara took in every detail of the evening, right down to the placement of the knives and forks. At dinner, she inquired about each selection of music offered by the orchestra which, she chided herself, wasn't an orchestra, but a chamber group—a string quartet.

All through dinner, she kept an eye on the man called Patrick, the man who had taken her breath away a few years ago. Did he really not remember her? Had she just been a little fool? She squirmed, creating a swishing sound, that of satin slip brushing silk stockings. Lifting her napkin from her lap, she ran her hand over her chiffon dress. So smooth. Things were not at all smooth when it came to her feelings for Patrick. Had she really fallen for him that day in the confessional? Or had she just fallen into his arms to spite her father?

Clara fingered her throat as she stared across the ballroom at Patrick. She smiled with remembered pleasure: his lips pressing against hers, his fingers stroking her neckline, his hands sliding down her body.

Awash with heat, watching Patrick, she reached for her water glass.

In that second, Patrick turned toward her, his gaze resting on her face.

A flicker of a smile pulled at Clara's mouth. Of course, he remembered. She returned her glass to the table and, keeping her eyes on his, ran her finger around the rim.

Patrick's lips changed from a thin straight line to a knowing grin. Without warning, he turned away.

Clara cringed. There one instant, gone the next. Was this so unlike her first encounter with him? Feeling every bit the fool, she blinked. Her cheeks flamed. The banter at the table no longer held any interest. She lowered her head.

Moments later, Robert leaned in. "Are you feeling well?"

"I'm fine." Clara straightened in her chair.

"Do you mind if we leave the gala early?" asked Robert. "It appears there's a meeting this evening."

Clara was giddy with relief. "A meeting at night?" she asked, pretending disappointment.

"My apologies, but there are no proper schedules in my world. I may be gone for a couple of hours. Do you mind terribly, Clara?"

"Of course not," she replied, already standing. "I'm in a grand hotel, with a luxury room. I'll be fine."

Back in her own room and left to her own devices, Clara peeled herself out of her clothes, one precious piece at a time. She stroked and folded chiffon and satin and silk. When she was completely unwrapped, she snuggled into her dressing gown—another new purchase—and headed for the bathroom, intent upon the luxury of a hot bath.

A sharp rap at the door.

Clara turned. She cinched her robe and edged toward the door. Just as she got there, the knock sounded again. Heart racing, shoulder leaning into the door, she said "Who is it?"

"You know who it is."

Sucking in a breath, Clara clutched the door knob, twisted it, and pulled. She stepped back.

Patrick's movement toward her was quick, an air of ownership about it. Inside the room, door closed, he reached.

God give her strength. She put a hand out, palm facing him. "What are you doing here?"

He folded his arms. "You *want* me here."

Clara pursed her lips. He was too smug, the likes of him, with his chiseled face and deep eyes staring right at her, claiming her. But was he right? Two hours ago, she craved him so much that she had the sensation of being flooded with heat. What about now? Heart racing, body tingling, Clara blinked.

She withdrew her hand, letting it fall limply to her side.

Patrick reached again, this time pulling her in, pushing her robe, baring her shoulders. He lowered his head and brushed his lips down her neck.

Tingling, lightheaded, she spoke, her voice trembling. "My husband will be back--"

"No, he won't. I've seen to it that he will not return for hours." He released the sash of her dressing gown which swished to the floor, a puddle of satin.

Clara inhaled, filling her senses.

The next morning, Robert returned, looking tired and disheveled. "So sorry, darling. Business ran on longer than I thought. I can't fathom it—those men, reviewing details again and again. Don't they have wives to go home to?"

"No apologies needed," she said in a lighthearted voice, one that she had rehearsed earlier. "I had a wonderful sleep and a delicious breakfast."

Robert smiled. "You're a pretty amazing woman, Clara. You dazzled all those aristocrats last night. I must say I had my doubts about taking you along, but you are an asset in this world. I trust that St. John's is to your liking?"

"Indeed it is," grinned Clara. "Now you just get some rest; we're heading out today, aren't we?"

"Yes," Robert yawned, pulled off his boots and lay down.

Clara padded her way to the chesterfield. On the edge of an armrest, poised to tumble, sat a brocade pillow which Clara rescued and tossed aside. As she curled into the plumpness of the chesterfield, she smiled, contented. An asset, she was, according to Robert. That suited her just fine.

Maybe she could never acknowledge that Patrick had a daughter, that *she* and Patrick had a daughter, but she wanted Patrick, could see no end to wanting Patrick, and would take advantage of every opportunity to be with him. A fine thing, this rum-running business.

Picking up the copy of *Madame Bovary* that rested on the table beside the chesterfield, Clara smiled to herself. It was Robert who had given her this book, this story of the unfaithful Emma Bovary. She opened to her marked place but, unable to concentrate, kept re-reading the same passage. After a while, she closed the book and let her rampant thoughts overtake her. What was that melody? Clara nodded. Ah, yes—*A Little Night Music*. Mozart.

Clara stood at the window in the Newfoundland Hotel watching schooners and skiffs sail in and out. The foghorn sounded, a precursor to the film of grey that misted in. Gradually, the sun burned through, dispersing the fog, silencing the low, steady moan of the horn. It would be a good day on the water, the sky so blue, a flat calm.

Perhaps she should awaken Robert but she was content in her little world by the window with the memory of Patrick still warm in her loins.

She felt no loss at being without him now for she was convinced that their fates were aligned. Soul mates. They would always find each other.

Robert stirred, rolled over, and opened his eyes. "What time is it?" he croaked.

"Time for you to be getting up if we are going to get on that ocean today, Mr. Caulins."

"Mr. Caulins, is it? Why don't you come over here and I'll show you Mr. Caulins?" He tossed back the sheets.

Clara suppressed the urge to shiver. She hadn't meant to sound coy; it was a repercussion from last night's lovemaking. Must she now defer to her husband's wants? She was not ready to mix the two, the passion with Patrick and the tolerance with Robert. No, she wanted to swim in the warmth of her sins much longer. "No time for that now," she said, reverting to her more natural dialect, accent exaggerated. "Ye men are all foolish. Sure and look at the time. It's after eleven o'clock."

"Eleven?" Robert jumped out of bed, desires apparently forgotten. "Woman, how on earth could you have let me sleep so late? Get your things together. We have to leave right away. The crew will be waiting."

"I expect they'll be dancing on their last nerve by now."

"You certainly have that right. Well, are you going to move?"

Clara pointed to her suitcase. "Already packed." She threw her arms out. "And, in case you haven't noticed, already dressed."

Robert stood still for an instant, taking in her appearance. "I have to say that you looked better in your evening attire than you do in those deckhand clothes, but you are still a mighty fine woman." He stepped toward her.

She put a palm forward. "Time to go."

He nodded.

Clara crimped her nose as she and Robert stepped onto the harbour wharf. The stench was familiar, but not the sights, for the *Elizabeth J* had arrived under blanket of night. But now? Eyes wide and stinging, Clara surveyed open buckets of tar, black plumes of smoke, rusted hulls of ships, and steaming piles of horse manure. Every inch of the wharf was in use, the whole place bustling with activity, rattling with voices, English and foreign, all speaking fish, either buying or selling. As she and Robert threaded their way through the boisterous crowd, Clara cast a glance at the water. Even that was crowded, overflowing with broken barrels, oil streaks, vegetable peels, and human waste. Shuddering, Clara returned her focus to her footsteps, just managing to sidestep a fresh splatter of gull droppings.

When they boarded the *Elizabeth J*, the crew was on deck, waiting. Pretty much silent, the lot of them, but there were occasional mutterings. Were they all glaring at her? Blaming her for their captain being late? She would normally blush under such scrutiny, but the fact that Robert overslept was no fault of hers now, was it? Inwardly, she cringed, knowing that she was lying to herself. Regardless, she lowered her eyes, ignored the crew, and dismissed her guilt. She was becoming an old hand at digging holes, burying secrets, and covering them with layers of justification. Not her fault, the events that pricked her life. Not her fault that her mother got the "consumption" and had to be sent away, that her father took to the bottle and used his daughter to drown his grief, that her brother got in an uproar and moved to the Burin.

As for Patrick... She was a girl when she met him, only sixteen, desperate for attention. It was natural that she would fall into the arms of a lover like Patrick. She had no idea what was happening to her body when Kate started growing inside her, no idea until she saw the look in the eyes of her father who shipped her off to have her body ripped of evidence. Then, her father had buried his own shame by marrying his daughter off, to Robert Alistair Caulins.

Well, she would stay with Robert but she felt no compunction to be faithful. Why should she care about that? Why should she care what Robert's crew thought of her? Robert was not her choice, but her father's, her mother's too. Patrick *was* her choice. Perhaps the midwife was right: there would likely be no more concerns about Clara being in a family way. Even if the midwife was wrong, Clara would see to it that she had no worries. She may have refused Robert's advances this morning, but she would not continue to do so. If any more seed took root in her womb, the resulting offspring would have Robert's name.

The voyage home was uneventful. They swung around Cape Race and headed back to St. Pierre where they stopped for food and cargo. There were no other stops on this, Clara's maiden voyage. A heaviness fell over her when she discovered that they were not going to Rum Row. More disappointed when she discovered Robert's plan: he would never take her there.

"Not on any voyage, my darling," said Robert when they were back home.

"Why not?" asked Clara, following him to the parlour.

He turned to face her. "No place for a woman."

"That's what you said about letting me aboard the schooner in the first place." She sidled up to him and reached her arms around his neck.

Robert pushed her away. "I won't change my mind about Rum Row." He took up residence in his easy chair.

She slipped back, into the doorway, and watched as Robert pulled his tobacco pouch from his copper-lined humidor. As he opened the pouch, Clara inhaled the scent. Sweet. Comforting. She exhaled quickly and drew in another breath before the distinct aroma had time to blend with smells of cooking and cleaning and ocean. Robert retrieved his pipe from a nearby ashtray and knocked out the ashes. Two taps on the rim of the ashtray. Always two taps. Steady, deliberate. Never in a hurry, Robert. He slid his pipe into the pouch and filled it. Tamping the tobacco down, he ambled to the fireplace where he struck a long match, and stood there, puffing. A round red glow appeared in the bowl of the pipe. When he removed the pipe from his lips, he let out a long sigh, releasing a grey plume of smoke into the parlour. Without another word, he selected a book from his mahogany shelves and retraced his steps to his chair.

Clara relented, telling herself that she didn't really want to go to Rum Row anyway.

In the kitchen, Clara sat at the table in the stillness, swaying gently, side to side. When the muted hum of a lullaby pierced her senses, she ceased her movement. How long had she been away from home? Weeks. But not long enough apparently. Here she was, back home, humming like mother to child. Enough of that. She was Aunt Clara now.

It was time to visit Kevin and Kate.

KEVIN

CHAPTER 43

———◆———

CROUCHED IN HIS FRONT YARD, in the process of mending nets, Kevin Kerrigan jabbed his hand with the needle. Damn. He had to pay attention. What the hell was gnawing at him anyway? Most days he was in a fog, just doing what he had to. Muscle memory. On this day, there were holes in the fog, like his senses were waking up. He didn't want that. Had to keep it all shut down, for Christ's sake. Couldn't unleash that hell. He shook his head. Out of the corner of his eye, he saw Clara, strolling up the garden path. There it was. The source of the prickling. The cronies down at the merchant store had told him that Robert's schooner was back in the harbour. Didn't take Clara long to show up. What the hell was he going to say to her? He tensed up his muscles, went back to knitting nets.

"Kev?"

Maybe if he paid her no mind she would take to her heels.

"Kevin, aren't ya even going to say hello?"

Kevin was saved from response by his little girl, now five, who flew through the back door and bounced down the steps. "Aunt Clara!"

Kevin raised his head. His gut clenched when he saw Clara pick up Kate and spin her around. Laughter and giggles and sunshine all over his front yard. Was he going to put up with the likes of that? "Kate, did ya finish yer lessons?"

Kate didn't answer.

"Kate, are ya after hearing me or what?"

Kate turned, stilled, the smile gone from her face.

A glut of self-hatred whacked Kevin. He crammed it down. The feelings were piling up inside him, like a cord of stacked wood. Had to be careful. It would all come tumbling. He dropped his net and his needle, stood, and forced a grin. "Welcome home, sis."

"Thanks, Kev."

Kate's smile returned. "Daddy, can Aunt Clara stay for supper?" Her words were hesitant.

"You have to ask Mrs. Mullins."

Kate clapped her hands. "Be right back," she said to Clara. She raced toward the house.

"I'm sorry, Kevin," said Clara immediately.

What was this now? He tilted his head to one side.

"It was wrong of me to try to take over Kate's life. I just wanted to help—no, that's not true." She pinched her lower lip between her teeth.

Kevin pulled a rag from his overalls and wiped his fingers, one at a time, taking care to scrape the dirt from under his fingernails. Whatever she had to say, she could get it out on her own. He wouldn't turn a hair to help.

Clara cleared her throat. "The truth is... I wanted her for myself. It's a hard thing for a woman, having no young ones of your own. People say things. They don't mean to be hurtful, but they are. But I'm done with all that. I'm here if you need me but I won't try to take her away. Not ever." She moved closer. "She's your little girl, Kev."

Kevin's emotions lurched; he almost reached to embrace her. The craving to unleash, to share his pain was shoving him forward. Was he right before, that day after Mass, when he had the urge to let go of his distrust? Tears leaped into his eyes and thickness enveloped his throat. He let out a halting breath. Clara was not trying to take his child away. Clara was family, his sister, who had been so kind to him in his time of need. Maybe he ought to be doing his share to take care of her.

He stared at her, eyes brimming. What had possessed his parents, marrying their only daughter off to a criminal? Worse yet, what was she doing on the sea in a world where men ruled and cruelty prevailed? Should he attempt to haul her away from this rum-running business? If so, how? Kevin took a hesitant step toward Clara.

Just then the door of the house swung open. "Mrs. Mullins says to tell you she's right delighted," called Kate from the step.

Kevin swallowed and slid his sleeve across his face. He nodded. "See you inside," he managed.

Kate danced down the steps, grabbed her Aunt Clara's hand, and pulled her toward the house.

Kevin watched until the door closed behind them. Then he turned away, eyes cast upon the ocean. He fisted his hands at his sides. Two years it had been since the events on the Burin. Two years and he was still broken, body and soul. There was no end to the things he could repair—nets and rooftops and boats—but it wasn't likely he could ever mend himself. Kevin fell to his knees and grabbed the net and the needle.

The past was no place to be idling. It was the now, the work that kept him going. That and Kate. Clara too, if she'd allow it. How was he going to talk his sister out of a life of crime?

CHAPTER 44

———◆———

IN THE WAKE OF CLARA'S visit, a fog settled over Kevin's concern for her. For a while, he considered helping her, but when no sure method cropped up, he just let it sit. Given enough time, the fog would burn off. If an opportunity presented itself, he'd lock on.

Sure enough, one morning a couple of weeks later, as he was scraping the last bite of fried eggs from his breakfast plate, he glanced through the window and snagged a shadowed outline of a human being. Dressed like a man, but with the shape and gait of a woman. Jesus H. Christ. Clara. No doubt about it. What was she doing, traipsing along that muddy path before dawn? Where was she off to? No sign of her husband, but he was likely on Rum Row. Wasn't that where rumrunners headed on moonless nights? And why wasn't Clara with him?

A ripple of memory edged Kevin's mind, that of hauling six-year-old Clara from the lip of the sea. He squirmed in his chair. He had seen to her then. Should he follow her now? He perked an ear toward his daughter's bedroom. Folks around here wouldn't think twice about leaving their house while their little ones were asleep; they'd just flick droplets of holy water over the child and go on their way. But Kevin had left his family unprotected once before and--

A gruff knock. The storm door squeaked open, clattered shut.

Kevin looked up.

Minutes later, Kevin was slinking along behind Clara at a safe distance, keeping an eye on the dot of light that flickered from her lantern. About twenty minutes in, he knew full well that she was bound for the abandoned silver mine. What he couldn't figure was the why of it. He glanced at the sky which had already turned from black to indigo. The sun would rise before they arrived at Silver Cliff, for Christ's sake. Half an hour to go, at least. Had she timed it that way? What on earth would she be doing there anyway? The entrance to the place was pocked with scraps of twisted metal and chunks of rotting wood. Not safe for a woman. For anybody, for that matter. Surely that husband of hers would not allow her to tackle Silver Cliff alone.

Clara was a few feet inside the mine entrance, adjusting the flame in her oil lamp, when Kevin caught up with her. He grabbed her wrist.

She jumped, yanking her arm away. "What are you doing here?"

"More like, what the hell are you doing here? In this mine?"

Clara stepped back, in the process tripping over a jutting chunk of railway track. Balance lost, she flailed her arms.

Kevin reached, snatching both her and her lantern before they hit ground. He held her, then helped her to a boulder near the entrance where daylight could wink its way in. Kevin patted the boulder and stepped back, swinging the lantern at Clara. "For God's sake, pitch!"

Clara obliged.

Raising the lantern, Kevin shed light on his sister's face, a hard-set face, cold as the rock he had parked her on. "You're going to come to no good end, Clara. You got to stop this rum running."

She sniffed. "You can't tell me what to do, Kevin Kerrigan. I've got a mind of me own. If I want to go rum running that's exactly what I'm going to do."

Kevin paused, remembering Clara, at the age of eight, sitting in the dory, telling him she'd do what she pleased. Well, Clara was still doing what she pleased. Some things didn't change. But what was she in a huff about this time? Shrugging, he peered into the depths of the mine.

Silver Cliff was a maze of tunnels, darker than pitch. Clara's flimsy lantern wouldn't have much effect. The whole mine was soaking, slimy, slippery. Even from here Kevin could hear water trickling down walls, dripping into pools. A constant echo. He sighed. Perhaps he should take a different tack. "It's dangerous, sis," he said, his voice low, calm. "I got a right to be concerned about you."

"Nothing to be concerned about. I'm not going that far into the shaft."

"What are you after doing here anyway? Hiding cargo?"

Clara sniffed. "Do you see me lugging cargo?" She spread her arms wide.

Kevin attempted a half-hearted smile. "Good enough," he said. "I'll allow you that: no cargo. But you're up to something. What is it?"

"That's for me to know."

"Maybe that's for me to find out."

Clara leaned closer. "Never mind me and my doings. What about Kate? Who's looking after her while you're chasing after me?"

"My Kate is right as rain. She was sound asleep when I left."

"Surely be to goodness you didn't leave her on her own? Is Dulcie Mullins showing up before dawn now? Why didn't you ask Mom to take care of Kate?"

"Are you serious?"

"Yes, I most certainly am serious." Clara folded her arms.

Kevin put the lantern down beside Clara. Throwing his hands in the air, he clomped through the entrance into full daylight. There, he stopped. Straight ahead, a short distance away, was a grove of trees, pines, five of them, dwarfed, stunted by sea wind and sea salt. Five trees. A veil of memory scraped across his mind: five lives stopped by the sea. He shook his head to clear the images. Instantly, another one cropped up, that of his brother Jimmy, one child killed by--

He spun about and stomped back to Clara. "I can't be having Mom tend to Kate when it was her that killed Jimmy!" And there they were, the words that had gripped his throat for a lifetime.

Clara, her face blank, slowly rose from her stone seat. "You said that before, a long time ago. Remember?"

Kevin looked at her, blinking. No such memory emerged. He knitted his brow, searching. But the only memory that arose was one in which water was trickling, dripping. Steady sounds, like those weeping from the walls of the silver mine. He felt the touch of Clara's hand on his shoulder.

"Are you sure, Kevin?" Her voice was a whisper. "That's a hell of an accusation to make."

"Indeed I am." He dropped to his haunches and put his head into his hands. "Indeed I am," he said again. He swallowed a thickness in his throat. "I walked into the kitchen. She was pulling him from the old tub beside the stove. The water poured off. He was so tiny, so naked, so still. He was blue."

Clara sighed heavily. "I think you're wrong, Kev."

Kevin raised his head.

"Mom already asked me what was irking you. She wanted to know why you wouldn't let her near Kate."

"What did you tell her?" Kevin was on his feet now.

"Only that, when I was very small, I heard you tell Dad--"

"Tell Dad what? I never would have told Dad anything with you around."

"I was loitering and listening, outside the shed when the two of you were going at it. I heard you say that Mommy killed Jimmy."

"Sweet Heart of Jesus."

Clara put a hand on Kevin's arm. "I'm asking again. Are you sure?"

"I know what I saw." He nodded slowly.

"You got to give her a chance to explain."

"There's only one explanation for it."

Clara shook her head. "She told me she was just washing the body. She didn't kill him. Jimmy died from the diphtheria."

Kevin gnawed on the inside of his cheek. He hunched his shoulders, then let them fall, a slow, deliberate motion.

"You got to admit it's possible," said Clara.

Kevin took to movement, prowling back and forth in front of her.

"Mom was broken after Jimmy died," Clara continued. "Never in her right mind. Hardly a word out of her. And then she left." Clara let out a whimper.

The sound pierced Kevin. Abruptly, he turned. "I'm sorry, Clara," he said.

"You're sorry? What have you got to be sorry about?"

"I left *first*. I should never have left you alone. But I figured that you had Dad there to take care of you. A man has to take care of his own."

Clara sniffed. "Some caring he did."

There was an edge of desperation, of defeat in Clara's voice. Uneasiness crept into the bottom of Kevin's heart. "What do you mean?" he said.

Clara paused for a moment, a shadow of uncertainty on her face. "I, I mean, he…"

"He what?" Kevin watched her doubt fade into a blank stare. It would be a waste of time, repeating the question, but he did anyway. "He what?"

"Oh, nothing." Clara tossed her head. "You didn't leave Kate all by herself just to drag me away from Silver Cliff, did you?"

"Of course not. Dad made a dart in. He said I was as thick as a marsh bog, hobbling over a rum-running female like…" Kevin hedged. Clara didn't need to hear the rest of that. "Anyway, I up and informed him that if he didn't have the good sense to stop you, then I was going to do it myself."

"And where is he now?" she asked, her tone shrill, wary.

Kevin pointed a thumb toward home. "He was more than happy to keep an eye on Kate."

Clara jerked in a breath. "Jesus, Mary, and Joseph!" She broke into a fit of coughing. "Jesus, Mary, and Joseph!" she said again.

"What is it, Clara? What the hell is it?"

Clara stammered, struggling to get the words out. "Y-y-you can't do that."

"Do what?"

"Y-y-you can't let him take care of Kate."

Kevin sniffed. "We have talked about this. It's my decision." He was pushing words at her now. "Kate is *my* daughter. And Alphonse Kerrigan is her grandfather. If I want him to take care of her, if I want Dulcie Mullins to take care of her, so be it."

"You don't understand." She clutched the lapels of his coat, pulled him close. "How did you get here? Motorcar? Wagon?"

"Are you out of your mind, woman? Where would I get a motorcar? Not that it or a wagon would survive the ruts on that road. I hiked here, the same way you did."

"We have to go!" She released her grip.

"Clara!" Kevin blared, to no avail. She was on the move, kicking up mud and dust. He grabbed the lantern and followed.

KATHLEEN

CHAPTER 45

———◆———

IT PREPARES, AND PLUNGES, THE sea.

In the chasm before dawn on this, the deciding day, the North Atlantic is skulking shadow, motionless and soundless, all sway suspended. Why this cessation of ebb and flow, of rise and fall? Is the sea holding its breath? Is its stillness a sign of sanction? Maybe. And maybe all that lies at the base of its hush is hope. Maybe it hopes to refrain from extreme.

But how long will it linger?

In life, mired in hope, I remained idle. A grievous sin, my stalling. A sin that spiraled downward to another and another: the death of a baby, the departure of a son, the disposal of a daughter. Eventually, there was an elongated fall into nothingness where darkness was both haven and grave. With lives of offspring ravaged, I had no call to resurface. For an eternity, I lay, stagnant.

Now, weighted with wreckage, I sigh into the sea. Is there such a thing as ascent from the rubble of sin? My query floats. Adrift alongside it, I ponder: was the ocean waiting for me, for this particular day? Was it intentional, the ocean heaving Kate back to shore on the day of the tsunami?

When four-year-old Kate appeared at my door, I roared to life, a raging Lazarus, jolted by the child's single flaw: little Kate, like Clara, is the face and eyes of her mother. In a flick, I saw it. One look at Alphonse told me he saw it too.

Through flow of tide and turn of days I was vigilant, all the while hauling oars, chopping splits, butchering livestock. At Jimmy's grave on the day that Alphonse unlocked his soul, I flinched but did not falter. In the time that followed, I coaxed and coddled, keeping my husband close. Isn't that what one does with one's enemies?

As for Clara, my daughter, she is braver than I, stronger than I, a better mother than I. Clara is selfless, shielding her child—and her brother—from the agony of truth. Would that I had protected her the way she protects Kate.

The way that I would protect Kate on this day.

A rush of regret enters on a spit of wind: why had I lingered so long?

It is early morning. The sky is black, moonless. The stars blink, innocent, unaware.

On a ripple of air, I float across the threshold of my son's house.

Alphonse stumbles from the kitchen toward me, Kate in tow. He grabs a tiny sweater from a coat hook beside me and pulls it over the five-year-old's head. "A ride in the dory is just the thing, child," he says. "You don't be needing your father or your nanny to be telling you different. The ocean is a friend." Alphonse clutches Kate's wrist.

I swoop low, an attempt to thwart him.

He inhales, a sharp breath, and blasts air out, thrusting me backward. I hit the door, soundless, plastered to the grain like a layer of paint.

"Stop your whimpering, child," says Alfonse. "Never saw your Aunt Clara being afeard of the dory."

Kate fists her tiny hand through the sleeve of her sweater. "Daddy says it's not safe in the dory."

"Not safe." Alphonse sniffs. "No such thing. Your father was born and raised on the water. You're in for a grand time." He picks her up.

The scene appears ordinary now—a grandfather taking his little granddaughter on an outing. He reaches for the door.

I unpeel myself from it and slide with him through it.

Outside, in the darkness, Mother Nature is idle: no swish of waves, no whip of wind, no lash of rain. Only a wheezing breath from Alphonse and a sleepy yawn from Kate. All too hushed.

It is sudden, the panic that overtakes me. Like a stone released from a slingshot, I hurl through the air ricocheting off gravel path, wood pile, storm door—searching. *What if, what if, what if?* What if, this time, she *does not* show?

It is scripted, this anxiety. Part and parcel of everything, I know. Yet, every time feels like the first time. There's nothing for it but to wade through it.

She is here. This time, as every time, Kathleen, the corporeal Kathleen, is crouching beside the back door.

Instantly, I settle into the air beside her.

At this point, Kathleen has quelled questions, demolished doubts. She has bided her time, rebuilt her strength. Many times, she has headed out, in the dory with Alphonse, huddling for long hours in the bow, clicking away on her steel knitting needles. Sometimes she has lifted the long oar and sculled, steadying the boat while Alphonse jigged for cod. All the time, she has been watching, eyeing the rhythm of, deciding the fate of this man, this fisherman.

This fisherman's pace is unsteady now as he lumbers to the dock, Kate in his arms.

Kathleen trails along behind him. For a few splintering seconds, she pauses. Hands in her pockets, she shifts her head side to side.

Another wave of panic filters through me. *Don't waste time.* If I could, I would prod her onward. This, despite knowing she will go forward of her own accord.

Alfonse breaks into song: "I'll take you home again, Kathleen." His voice is gruff, low, like the rumbling of an offshore storm.

Kathleen perks an ear to the melody. She jerks forward. Catching up to him, she taps his side, creating a dull, knocking sound. Her knuckles have hit the silver flask in his pocket. "Alphonse?"

He turns. "Ah, *my* Kathleen." A husky voice, loving, intimate.

"Yes, *your* Kathleen." Her tone is practiced, liquid. She reaches for her granddaughter.

Without question or comment, he relinquishes the child.

Kathleen stares down at Kate whose features are indistinguishable in the dark. Has the little one fallen asleep?

Kate moans. The odor of her breath wafts.

Stone-faced, for shock must not show, steady-voiced, for words must not incite, Kathleen says, "What are ya thinking at all, Alphonse? You can't be giving the child whiskey." Closing her eyes, holding Kate tight, Kathleen spins about, heading back toward the house. Her steps are slow and steady at first. As she accelerates, a prayer falls from her lips.

Unheard, I join in: *Our Father, who art in heaven...*

The clomp of boots behind her, closing in.

She picks up her pace.

The point of a knife at her side, threatening.

Kathleen gasps. She stops all movement.

"You'll be getting into the dory now," he says.

Tightening her grip on Kate, the sleeping Kate, Kathleen scrambles down, into the boat, onto the bow seat, facing centre.

The lump of shadow that is Alfonse drops to the centre thwart, his back to Kathleen. A clattering comes from beneath that thwart as he discards the knife. He sets the oars and leans in. "We'll just have done with this. This one's too young to marry off. Won't it be some grand, just the two of us?"

Kathleen does not respond. She cringes, clutching her grandchild, her body rigid.

Specter and spectator, I slouch over the gunwale. Would that I could reassure her, field her dread. A recurring nightmare, this. Agonizingly slow, like wading through waist-deep water.

"This will be easy," says Alfonse. We'll just finish off what the ocean started back on the Burin. The child shouldn't be here in the first place. Nothing but trouble." His back to Kathleen, he rows and hums. His song. *The* song.

"A lovely lilt, Alphonse," says Kathleen. "Where are the words, b'y?"

Alphonse switches from croon to bellow, a drunken outpouring of slurred lyrics.

Kathleen slips Kate from her arms, gently, placing her down into the bow of the boat. She pauses, leans an ear to the child. Kate sleeps.

The oars slap and swish. The song stutters, then stops altogether. "Sweet Heart of Jesus, Mary, and Joseph," Alphonse says. "I forgot the words to me song. Where was I when the boat turned over?" He snorts out a laugh.

"Just start her over, b'y," says Kathleen.

He clicks his tongue. "A fine idea, that."

As his voice blares, Kathleen creeps, slowly, steadily forward. She reaches low, fumbling beneath the centre thwart until she locates the splitting knife. She grabs it. She drops it. True to form, it clatters. She recoils, freezes.

Alphonse takes no notice.

Shaking now, Kathleen reaches again, too fast, too hard.

Despite its flat bottom, its stable design, the dory sways.

"Easy there, woman," says Alfonse, steadying the boat.

Kathleen holds her position.

Alphonse falls into rhythm: *Lean, set, pull, release. Lean, set, pull, release.*

With a barely discernible nod, Kathleen keeps time. On the heels of the third cycle of oars, she stretches her fingers and touches the blade. A flick of her fingertips and the knife is in hand.

Alphonse does not break tempo.

On her haunches now, Kathleen waits out the next cadence. As Alphonse leans for the fifth time, she presses down on her knees, unrolling until she is upright. She locks her legs and coils both hands around the hilt of the knife.

He sets the oars, poised to pull.

Kathleen raises her arms. With the sinewy skill of a woman who has spent a lifetime at labor, with the unbridled rage of a mother who has spent an eternity in regret, she plunges the splitting knife into his back, through his heart.

There is a single gasp as Alphonse clutches his chest. He slumps.

Kathleen elbows him aside as she claims and secures the oars. She retracts the knife and shuffles him, limb by limb, to the gunwale, over the gunwale.

With a splash, he meets the ocean.

As light breaches the horizon, Kathleen stares at Alphonse, face down in the water. She makes the sign of the cross as she watches boots fill, bubbles pop, and bulk slip below the surface. When his body is gone from view, she swishes the blood-stained knife in a swell of grey. Without as much as a sigh, she mans the oars, and rows back the way they came.

I hover in the air beside her, revelling in the freedom of relief.

At the dock, Kathleen moors the dory, just long enough to lift Kate to safety and scramble out herself. Then she unties the dory and pushes it, giving it up to the tide.

The sea responds, stirring into motion.

Kathleen carries Kate up the path to Kevin's house. She undresses and washes the child and slides a nightgown over her head. Then she tucks her in and kisses her forehead.

Under cover of darkness, Kathleen Kerrigan went to sea. At break of dawn, she returned, to the home of her son. To the home of her grand-daughter, Kate.

As I am whisked away in a wisp of chimney smoke, the corporeal Kathleen is nestled inside an ill-fitting coat, Kevin's coat, which she plucked from a nearby hook. In the kitchen, she sits, waiting.

Lingering no more.

CLARA

CHAPTER 46

———◆———

MORNING WAS STILL ON THE climb when Clara, panting from exertion, thrust open the door to Kevin's home. She breezed through the porch and into the kitchen where she came to a full stop. There was her mother, perched in a chair by the east window, the sun brushing her shoulder, a blue scarf draping her head, an oversize coat shrouding her body. An image of the Madonna jumped into Clara's mind. The only thing missing was--

"Where's Kate?" Clara asked, heart pounding.

"And where the hell is Dad?" Kevin's voice blared behind her. Without waiting for a reply, he barreled toward Kate's room.

Kathleen loosened her scarf. "The little one's fine," she called after Kevin. She shook her head; her hair cascaded. "The little one's fine," she said again, a whispered voice, this time directed at Clara.

Clara stared, her eyes widening at the sight of telltale silver threads among her mother's dark curls. Dear God. It wouldn't be long before her own hair would be just the same. Clara swallowed hard. How vain was she at all? What had her mother just said? Kate was fine, but nothing about-- "Where *is* Dad?"

"Fishing." Kathleen didn't as much as blink. "Said he wanted to get out before first light."

Clara narrowed her eyes. "How did you know Dad was here?"

"Some things you just know."

"Did you follow him here?"

Hesitation glimmered on Kathleen's face. She opened her mouth but, upon Kevin's return to the kitchen, she pressed her lips tight.

"Kate is sound asleep." Kevin turned to Clara, his eyebrows raised. "Whatever were you on about? You had me in a hobble over leaving Kate with Dad."

Clara felt a rush of blood to her cheeks. Truth fluttered. "Well--"

"Well, Alphonse don't know much," said Kathleen in a controlled voice. "About caring for little ones, I mean. Isn't that right now, Clara?"

Clara blinked into her mother's hard-pinched expression. "Yes, that's it," she said, her voice wavering. She took a deep breath. "That's exactly it." Good. Her voice had evened out.

Kevin looked warily from Clara to Kathleen. Eventually, he let out a sigh. "Everything's fine, thank the good Lord." He glanced around. "Where did Dad go?"

"Fishing," said Clara, still eyeing her mother.

Kathleen shrugged. "Yes, fishing. I'll be heading home now," she said, rising from her chair, letting the oversize coat fall from her shoulders. "There's your coat now, Kevin."

"I'm going with you," said Clara, her curiosity peaked. Where was her mother's own coat? What kind of web was Kathleen caught up in?

Kevin stepped forward, hands raised, palms out. "Hold your horses, the both of ye." He faced his mother. "I have something that needs saying." He paused.

Clara tilted her head. A sideways glance showed Kathleen reclaiming her chair, folding her hands in her lap. Kevin was fidgeting, not a word out of him. A knot of tension formed in Clara's gut but she might as well ignore it, settle in. A waiting game, this.

Clara gazed into the single sunbeam that fanned the room. The second she did that, the light in the kitchen faded. Was the sun playing cat and mouse with a cloud? The rattle of the chimney flue drew her attention. Was that just a baffle of wind, or was there a gale brewing? The answer came in an escalating screech of gulls. No doubt they were traveling in from the sea, probably bringing a storm along with them.

"It's just that..." Kevin said, and then cast his eyes into every nook and cranny of the kitchen.

Clara pursed her lips. Did he think the words he needed were dangling from cobwebs? Should she jump in? Say something? No. A skilled man, her brother. Still this was hard for him, harder than the hobs of hell. Would Kathleen help him through? She looked at her mother.

As if on cue, Kathleen brushed a hand through the air. "Kevin, son, there's no need to--"

"There's every need," said Kevin. "At some point, a man's got to put things to rights. Clara tells me I was wrong about little Jimmy."

"I could never have harmed that child." Kathleen's voice was steel, all strength and truth.

"But I saw..." He edged closer to his mother.

Stepping back, Clara placed the flat of her hand over her heart. She eyed the door. Should she stay?

"Son, in life you can't see all you see, you can't hear all you hear." In a sure, steady motion, Kathleen rose to her feet.

Tears filled Clara's eyes. She didn't dare let them spill because, when she looked at her brother, his eyes were brimming, too. His moment. Their moment. Not hers. Mute as a mouse, she headed for the door.

"You stay put, Clara," said Kevin. This is for your ears, too."

Without comment, Clara retraced her steps. She aimed for the day-bed, almost sitting on top of Kate's ragdoll, Mrs. Fan, whose black button eyes were peeking from under a newspaper. Clara frowned. What was it doing here? She picked it up.

"When I saw Jimmy that day, the water pouring off him--" Kevin stopped. He slid his shirt sleeve across his face.

In a heartbeat, Kathleen was in front of him. She placed a trembling hand on his forearm. "I was preparing the baby for burial, son. That's all there was to it."

Kevin let out a sigh. "I thought it was another thing entirely. I was so torn up in my mind..." After a gulp and a nod, he continued. "Like I said, a man's got to put things to rights. Kate and me will be darting in, later today, if you'll have us. I can chop wood or tend livestock while you spends time with your granddaughter."

A strange sensation of calm settled over Clara as she watched mother and son embrace. No longer feeling like an intruder, she eased her way toward them. "I'll walk back with Mom, Kevin," she whispered. There was no response so she touched her mother lightly on the shoulder.

Kathleen turned toward her, eyes glimmering with tears.

Kevin stepped aside.

Clara passed the doll to him. "It was on the daybed."

Placing one arm across her mother's shoulder, Clara said, "I'll take you to your home..." She let the words trail away, but in her mind they repeated, the familiar melody spinning round and round. "I'll take you to your home, Kathleen," she whispered. Clara turned to her brother. "Are you good with that, Kevin?"

"Right as rain. I'll be here with the little one." He held up the doll. "Thanks, Clara. For this, for everything." He narrowed his eyes. "And you--"

"I'm fine," Clara said, severing the questions that lurked in his eyes. Heaven forbid he should ask about Alphonse Kerrigan or Silver Cliff.

Kevin shrugged. "Good enough then."

Clara let out a sigh. "Ready, Mom?"

In the porch, Kathleen picked up her coat which was folded, inside out, on the floor behind the door. They stepped outside, into a warm breeze.

A rare morning this, in Argentia. No fog at all. Just a short time ago, Clara was convinced that a storm was threatening. Strange, that it had not manifested itself. The ocean was streaming silver in response to the sun that skimmed its surface. Clara looped her arm into her mother's and they walked in rhythm with the waves that washed the shore.

When they reached their destination, Kathleen sat in her rocking chair. Clara took up a place on the daybed.

Floorboards creaked under the steady to and fro of the rocker. The pendulum on the hall clock counted the seconds, the minutes. With silence screaming at her, Clara limped into conversation. "Should I put on the kettle, Mom? Are you wanting some tea?"

"No tea."

Clara waited. Maybe there was no talk coming at all. How long had it been since she visited this house? Everything looked the same: the beige rollup blinds, faded rose-patterned curtains, the oilcloth table cover. Only one thing clashed with her memories—the puddle of yellow sawdust beside the kindling box. A broom was needed there, but everything else was in order, right down to the pile of grey woolen socks, threads dangling, awaiting darning.

As the stillness lengthened, Clara stared into the built-in cupboard with the glass doors. The grazed china cup with the red flowers was still there, front and centre. Her great-grandmother Clara's cup. How had it survived so long? She took a deep breath and let it out, long and slow. Yes, everything was the same. And somehow, everything seemed smaller than it was in the days of her childhood. A grownup now, Clara stood. She padded her way to the door.

"I'm going to be needing some help from you, Clara," said Kathleen, her voice shivering.

Clara froze. "What do you mean?" She slowly faced her mother.

"He's not coming back," said Kathleen, her mouth clamped, her eyes fixed.

A tremor slid through Clara. "What are you on about? Where is he?"

Kathleen raised the hem of her dress. Secured by her stocking, hilt revealed, was Alphonse Kerrigan's splitting knife. "I found a good use for this." Kathleen retrieved the knife, removed the rag that covered the blade, and released her grip. The knife hit the floor, rattling to rest near the silver paw of the Waterloo stove.

"What have you done?" Clara's voice was a mere squeak.

"I done what had to be done. Something I should have done years ago." She shook her head slowly side to side. "A changed man, he was, after the war. Not an ounce of sanity left in him."

"But what did he do? *Then*, I mean? When he came back from the war? What did he do *then*? It was much later when he..." Clara couldn't find the end of that sentence.

"The last thing any mother wants to hear is the words you're struggling to tell." Kathleen rummaged the pockets of her bibbed apron and plucked out a set of plump, black rosary beads. "Agony for the both of us, child, this is, but you got to spit them words out." Kissing the crucifix, blessing herself, she threaded the beads through her fingers.

A memory twigged for Clara. A game she had played once. Cat's Cradle. The innocence of her early life closed around her, filling her with a longing to return to it, to eclipse what came after.

"There's no going back," said Kathleen. "You might as well have out with it."

Clara sighed her way into a chair at the table. "I don't know if I can."

"There was no excuse for it."

Clara plunked her elbows on the table and dropped her head into her hands. "Sure I didn't know what I was doing. I was scared and lonely and needed attention--"

"Dear God, no one's blaming you, child."

Clara jumped to her feet and prowled the floor. "What you mean, no one's blaming me? I'm the one that allowed it. I encouraged it too, truth be told." She faced her mother full on. "I'm the sinner here." She pointed a thumb at her chest. "Me. No one else. Sometimes I even gave him whiskey and led him--"

"For the love of God, child." Kathleen jolted from her rocking chair. "It was not your fault, none of it!" She charged forward and grabbed Clara's arms.

Clara flinched, jabbed by both voice and crucifix.

Her mother's words came at her again, voice in full fury, eyes flashing with rage. "It was not your fault. It was mine. All my fault. Mine and mine alone."

A sudden coldness hit Clara at the core. "You knew." She choked back a sob. "Holy Mother of God, at the time, you *knew*."

Kathleen released her grip on Clara's arms. She fisted her right hand and brought it to her chest. "*Mea maxima culpa*," she whispered.

Clara dropped to her knees. "You knew and you did nothing to stop it?"

Lowering her head, Kathleen returned to her rocking chair. "It was too late." She pocketed her beads. "I knew the second I stepped back into this house that you were growing something under that apron of yours. I did the best I could--"

"What are you talking about?" Clara was on her feet again, arms flailing in front of her. "What do you mean, 'the second you stepped back into this house?' I wasn't carrying the child then."

"Of course you were. Why else do you think I fainted dead away? The shock of it. The shame of it. The guilt, dear God, the guilt. I left you alone with that man. I left you and look what happened."

Clara stumbled backward, tripping over her own feet, landing on the daybed. Could she ever have been that young? That stupid? Kate was fathered by Patrick, wasn't she? That day in the confessional? Why would her mother be saying such terrible things? Was it even possible for a man to plant a seed in his own daughter? She pictured Patrick's face, his stark blue eyes, his light alabaster skin, his blond hair. Sweet Mother of Christ! Kate Kerrigan had brown eyes, like her, like Kathleen, like Alphonse. She blinked in disbelief.

"I couldn't allow the child to be born in this house," Kathleen was saying. "Thank God for Mavis, the good Lord rest her soul. She opened her heart and sealed her lips. Kevin never knew." She glared at Clara. "He must never know."

Clara shook her head. "All this time, I spent--"

"All this time, you spent hoping, maybe even plotting to get the child back." Kathleen's fingernails drummed on one arm of the rocking chair, a steady patter, like crows' feet on the roof. Abruptly, she stopped. "I know how hard it is to lose a child, Clara Kerrigan. But you haven't *lost* Kate. She's still here. And she's a saviour to your brother."

Clara nodded, her head awash with sin and secrets. Imagine not even knowing who fathered her own child. A stab of humiliation hit her. She veered from it, spitting new questions at her mother. "What did he do? Dad? When he came back from the war? You said he did something, that you should have handled it then. What did he do?"

Just as Kathleen parted her lips, the storm door squeaked open. "Good morning," a cheerful voice called.

Clara jumped. Jesus H. Christ. The last person they needed, right here, right now was Dulcie Mullins. Where the hell was the knife? She followed the ray of morning sun to the splitting knife, glinting from the floor. Clara scooped up the knife, rewrapped it, and stashed it inside her coat.

Dulcie bubbled her way into the kitchen. "Just dropping off a loaf of bread on my way to Kevin's house. Fresh out of the oven, it is. My, but it's chilly here this morning. Clara, did you stoke the stove? Never you mind now. I've got time for tea. Just let me have at the kettle."

"That's very kind of you, Dulcie." Kathleen stood. "You see to the stove and I'll see Clara out." Kathleen's steps toward Clara were slow, a sense of quiet purpose in them.

Clara offered no resistance as Kathleen took her arm and led her into the porch. "Bye, Dulcie," Clara called.

"Bye, me darlin'," Dulcie said. "Ye might want to feed the chickens on the way. They were pecking at the dirt something fierce when I came."

"We'll do just that." Kathleen called, as she pulled Clara outside.

"What the--"

Kathleen put her finger to her lips and slammed the door, tight. She turned. "Alphonse killed Jimmy," she said, her voice flat.

A nervous laugh emerged from Clara's throat. It changed to an inward gasp when she saw the pained look in her mother's eyes.

"It's true," whispered Kathleen.

Clara winced as if her flesh had been nipped. "Why?" It was the only word she could manage.

Kathleen shook her head. "No time for all that now," she said. "You better take my coat." She pointed at the bundle under the steps. "I'll never get the blood out."

Clara widened her eyes. Why hadn't she noticed her mother putting that coat there? When had she done it? Did it matter? All Clara knew was that it couldn't be left there for someone else to find. "I'll burn it," Clara said. An easy decision, but one that triggered a fear-filled thought. What would happen when some lone fisherman found the corpse? "How far offshore did you dump the body?"

"Far enough. Tide took it out."

"And what of the dory?"

"Didn't moor it. I pushed it away from the dock."

Reassured, Clara nodded. "Just one more thing—why in the name of God did you keep the knife?"

Kathleen shrugged. "Would you have believed me if I hadn't?"

"Yes, I would," Clara said instantly. She paused then, struck by the raw truth of her own words. "I'll be on the *Elizabeth J* soon. The knife will never be found."

"God forgive me for saying it, but I hope they don't find him either."

In concert, they made the sign of the cross.

CHAPTER 47

———◆———

THERE WAS STILL NO SIGN of the missing Alphonse two days later when Clara set off on the *Elizabeth J.* However, the dory had been found, rocking itself in the waves three miles offshore. After that, there was the waiting, the wondering, the tongue clicking of men who knew the trials of life at sea. A dangerous life, that of the fisherman.

Upon Clara and Robert's return, as the *Elizabeth J* was gliding into dock, Clara caught sight of Father Mahony and Kevin on the pier. Certain that news had come, she shivered. A ghostly image hovering over her brother, an image of her father, confirmed it. Her heart pounded but she couldn't look away. What was it that those lips were mouthing? *"I'm sorry?"* Ghosts be damned. She blinked away the apparition and raised a hand to wave at the priest and her brother. They did not return the greeting. "I guess they don't see me," she said to Robert.

"Pretty misty out there," he said.

Clara took a deep breath, preparing. As soon as she and Robert descended the gangway, her brother and the priest approached.

When Clara's rested her eyes on her brother's face, she was anguished. The pall that engulfed Kevin was so palpable that it eclipsed both drum of waves and cry of birds. How tired could he get before he succumbed to the weight of the world? "What is it, Kevin?" she asked, her heart filled with dread.

"It's Dad, Clara."

"He's sick? The consumption?" Lies were needed here.

Kevin shook his head. He lowered his eyes to the cap clutched in his fingers. Clara placed her hands on his arms. "Look at me, please."

Without raising his head, Kevin said, "He's gone, Clara. Gone. Drowned off shore."

Clara let out a hysterical giggle which caused the eyes of all around her, including those of Kevin, to stare. She slapped a hand over her mouth, gulped, and cleared her throat. "I'm sorry. So hard to believe. How could Dad drown? He's been fishing inshore his whole life. Knows every rock, every shoal."

Father Mahony stepped forward. "There's no accounting for the mood of the sea, Clara. It rocks you into a state of trust and then steals your soul. A gale must've come up and sent waves crashing upon him." He mopped his brow with a handkerchief pulled from his pocket.

Clara leaned in. "Was he drinking, Father?"

Father Mahony hemmed and hawed.

Clara knew she had chosen the right approach. She wasn't about to let up. "Did he have his flask with him?"

The priest nodded. "He was a good man, if not for the booze. Could usually manage the fishing just fine. I guess the Lord had other plans for him, God rest his soul."

Clara felt her knees buckle. The ground was rising. Robert grabbed her, held her tight. Clara accepted his help: her reaction was one of relief, not grief, but no one else needed know that. "What about Mom? How is she?"

"As well as can be expected. This all happened just a few days ago," said Father Mahony. "We've waited for you. Usually three sunsets from death to burial. The funeral is tomorrow."

The next day, as Clara stared into the gilded mirror gifted to her by her husband, she scrutinized her mourning dress, her black hat. A memory grazed her mind, that of Robert asking if she ever took into account her own beauty. She sighed. Nothing beautiful about her today. The face looking back at her was withered: the lines on that brow did not belong to a twenty-two year old woman. Clara turned away. Her husband was waiting for her, her patient husband, who would never cue her to hurry.

The cue came, nonetheless, in the form of the church bell. It tolled once, a reminder to all that a service was pending in a half-hour's time. Alphonse Kerrigan's body had lain in the parlour of her father's house overnight. A closed casket wake, yesterday. Not the usual thing, but, apparently, the fish had "had at him." Not much left. The body had been loaded onto a carriage this morning, a carriage that now waited in front of Clara's house. The second it began to roll, the church bell would begin to toll, a single gong every few seconds: the death knell.

Clara plodded down the stairs to the kitchen. Robert sat at the table, hat in hand. Without a word, he stood, took her arm, and led her outside. Clara's eyes flooded when she saw the carriage. "My handkerchief," she said. "I forgot my handkerchief."

Robert withdrew a folded one from his pocket. "I have three," he whispered.

Clara nodded, accepting the offering with gratitude. For a second, she looked into the eyes of this man. Perhaps she was not kind enough to him, doubting his loyalty, hiding money. Did she really need to guard herself that much? Maybe not. Thoughts of Patrick brushed her mind. Where was *her* loyalty? Secrets and sins. There was no going back.

"It's okay, my dear. I'll help you through this."

With those simple words, a weight slipped from Clara's shoulders. She would allow him to bear it. Wasn't that what husbands were for? To carry the weight of the world as women carry the weight of the world's children?

The toll of the church bell was accompanied by the drone of the fog horn. Clara thought about her mother, her mother who would not attend this funeral. Sanctioned by the priest, her absence. Too hard on her, he said, after all the trouble that had clouded her life.

The funeral procession—one horse and carriage carrying Clara and Robert and her father's body, another horse and carriage driven by

Kevin with five-year-old Kate at his side, the pallbearers who traveled on foot—arrived at the church within twenty minutes. As Clara alit from her carriage, she saw Kevin helping Kate from his.

The little girl looked bewildered and Clara resisted the urge to run, to hold her, to hide her from this sad memory. Hadn't she experienced enough tragedy? As Kevin neared, Clara opened her mouth to say something, but caught sight of Kate's eyes and stopped. Kate was glad to see her. Clara melted. She bent down and hugged Kate, who wrapped her arms around Clara, warming Clara's heart. "Can Kate sit beside me?" Clara asked, knowing Kevin was a pallbearer.

After a nod from Kevin, Clara grasped Kate's hand. Into the church and down the aisle they went, past friends and neighbours, to the front pew. Clara stepped aside and ushered Kate in first. As she slid in beside her, she turned. The pallbearers were poised. The pump organ let out a wheeze. When Clara saw Mrs. Sallivan's hatchet face peering from the choir loft, she braced herself. Sure enough, the soprano screech came, attacking the opening strains of *Dies Irae*. *Day of Wrath* indeed. The dirge dragged along, as did the pallbearers. Clara took a deep breath after the final reedy words—*dona eis requiem*. Now that the casket was in place, the pallbearers took their seats. Kevin sat beside Clara and Father Mahony appeared on the altar.

Clara sat, at first listening to and then tuning out, the words of the priest. She stared at her mud-splattered shoes. That wasn't good, not in church. Delving into her pocket, she retrieved her handkerchief, but stopped herself from bending to wipe her shoes. Not right, that. Instead, clutching the handkerchief, she folded her hands in her lap and closed her eyes.

Father Mahony's voice flowed in such singsong fashion that she almost slipped into sleep. It was an abrupt cough from him that caused her to resurface. She pulled her rosary beads from her pocket and fingered them, shakily, one at a time, counting off the *Our Father*, the *Hail Mary*, the *Glory Be to the Father*. She did not raise her head again until it was time for the sacrament of Communion.

As she approached the altar, she prayed that God would forgive her for her part in all this. Was she pure enough in the sight of God to receive this sacrament on this day? This day which was in honor of her father? Her father who loved her, loved her so very much. Clara called a halt to these thoughts: they only served to detonate anger. She would accept this sacrament in honor of her mother who had suffered enough, who had saved Kate's life. Clara knelt at the altar just as Father Mahony approached with the chalice. As soon as he finished saying "*In nomine patris, et filii, et spiritu sancti,*" she blurted "Amen" and looked up. Father Mahony placed the communion wafer on her tongue. She lowered her head.

The rest of the service was a blur. She filed out behind the casket with Kate in tow.

The sky that had been light grey upon their entry to the church was now dark and rumbling. Clara and Kate stood on the steps of the church while the casket was returned to the carriage. As the church bell began its knell, as Clara led Kate to the carriage for the ride to the cemetery, Dulcie Mullins appeared.

"Clara, me darlin', sure and it's a hard cold day. The Good Lord is going to open up the heavens before long. The little one will be soaked. I'd be more than willing to take Kate to my house today."

Clara awaited resentment; none came. She was about to nod but the decision was not hers to make. She glanced at Kevin. He nodded.

"Yes, thank you, Mrs. Mullins," she said, letting go of Kate's hand. A tiny sting pierced her heart as the tiny fingers slipped away. Would she spend her whole life feeling this pain as she released Kate's hand? The answer fell like a stage curtain. She would be there, in the wings, but never centre stage in her daughter's life.

"Good-bye, Kate," she said.

"Bye, Aunt Clara," replied Kate with a smile. Without hesitation, the little girl hugged Mrs. Mullins.

"Aunt" Clara climbed into the carriage.

During the burial, the rains came. Tears poured down Clara's face, unchecked. Robert offered his arm for support and she leaned in.

When the casket was lowered and the first shovel of mud tossed, the reality of the situation slammed Clara. Alphonse Kerrigan was no more. Never to be in her life again. It surprised her, the wrinkle of sadness that emerged. Clara sniffed. She would get over it.

Interminable, this burial. Shovel after shovel of mud. Every cell in her body prodded her to run. Not possible, that. She'd have to wait until the bitter end. Then, and only then, could she go see her mother.

As the last layer of mud was placed, the fog horn moaned. Clara shivered inside her coat and, along with the other mourners, turned to leave.

Flanked by Kevin and Robert, Clara walked the muddy cemetery road. She and Robert boarded one carriage, Kevin the other. Clara looked back at the cemetery which was disappearing into the encroaching blanket of fog. Clara watched until she could see nothing but grey. Typical grey. Two hundred days of fog a year. A few days of sunshine. Mostly fog. She faced the front, and lowered her head as the carriage stuttered along the dirt road.

With a promise of picking her up later, Robert dropped Clara at her mother's house. Kathleen was, as Clara expected, in the rocking chair, knitting.

"Mom?" Clara's steps were hesitant.

Kathleen raised her head. She swept her eyes over Clara's mourning clothes.

Clara bit her lip. Perhaps she should have changed before coming here. But that would never do. Black was the way of things, on the day of, and long after, the burial.

Pointing a steel needle toward the daybed, Kathleen said, "Have a sit down, my love. You look all in." She shifted her knitting from one hand to the other.

Why was her mother still knitting grey socks? For Kevin, perhaps? Clara wasn't about to ask.

"Did I ever tell you the story about the potato famine?" Kathleen asked, the second Clara took a seat. "All those women, losing their families, sacrificing their children to the ocean in an attempt to create a new life." She shook her head. "The saddest thing in the world."

"Indeed," said Clara. Clearly, Kathleen didn't want to talk about Alphonse's funeral, but where was she heading here? Clara had no clue.

"You're a fine woman, Clara. A heart of gold."

"You're mighty fine yourself." Clara looked curiously at her mother. "It's remarkable, you know, your kindness to Kate, considering her beginnings."

Kathleen stopped the knitting and the rocking. She gave Clara a penetrating stare. "Her name was Clara--"

"I know, I know, Mom. Not today, please. The story of my great grandmother and the potato famine can wait for another time."

Kathleen seemed unperturbed. "Her name was Clara," she said again.

Clara drew in an exasperated breath.

Kathleen raised a hand, palm out. "Her name was Clara, and *she was you*."

Tears sprang to Clara's eyes. What was this?

"One fine day, when Clara was just a little girl, she sneaked into the dory and curled up in the bow. She almost drowned that day." Kathleen let out a long sigh. "I guess it was a sign of loses to come."

Clara blinked, uncomprehending.

"While Clara's brother struggled to save Clara," Kathleen continued, "Clara's mother was struggling to save herself. A strange man came, if you can imagine the likes of it, and darkened the doorway of the shed. Black as pitch it was, in the shed. She couldn't make out his face because the light was aback of him. But he was soaked to the skin and stank like seaweed. There wasn't a word out of him, at least not that she could ever recall. All she remembered was thinking: 'Did he come from the ocean? How had he found her? Why her? How was she going to be able to chop the wood afterwards?' Strange the things that hammer your mind when a man is pounding his way into your body." Kathleen shuddered. She released her grip on her knitting which tumbled, unchecked, to the floor.

Eyes stinging, heart racing, Clara could have dissolved at a nudge, but she pushed the urge down. "Was she completely alone?" she whispered. "Where was her husband?"

"The Great War. No conscription or nothing but off he went. A volunteer, part of the Newfoundland Regiment."

"But, if he was away, then…"

Kathleen nodded. "She birthed the stranger's child. After the Great War, her husband wouldn't look at that baby boy. Jimmy was his name, poor thing. Clara's mother never once uttered the story of the stranger in the shed because she somehow blamed herself." Staring at Clara, eyes tinged with sadness, Kathleen said, "It's always the fault of the women, isn't it, when the men goes wrong?" She shook her head. "Even though she never told him herself, she figured her husband knew Jimmy wasn't his. Any fool could see the child had eyes bluer than glacier ice. Sure he must have fathomed it: why else would he kill the child?" For a moment, Kathleen was as still as stone. "She should have ended that man then, shouldn't she?"

"But you, I mean *she*, did end him, eventually." Clara crept toward the rocking chair and crouched on the floor in front of it. "What made her do it? After all that time, what…" She placed a hand on her mother's forearm. "It was Kate, wasn't it?"

Kathleen stared into nothingness. "At first, she worried that little Kate would be the same as Clara in her husband's eyes. But she figured wrong. Not just about Kate, but about Jimmy too. Turns out her husband killed Jimmy to keep him from suffering as a grown-up. So many young men dying in war, he told her, crying for their mothers."

The words made no sense to Clara, but her mother's voice was wrapped around her now like water around a rock. She didn't move.

Kathleen continued. "Clara's mother went away for a long while after her Jimmy died. And her husband? His mind was so far gone that he thought little Clara and his wife were one and the same. 'The face and eyes,' he always said. As for Kate, in his mind, she was in the way. He wanted just the two of them: himself and his wife."

Kathleen fell silent.

Understanding seeped. Clara's whole body shivered. She had no words.

Kathleen nodded. "He gave the child whiskey, you see. Enough to make her sleep. Three sheets to the wind himself, he was, when he up and announced that he was giving her up to the sea."

The urge to crumble surged in Clara now. Tears flowing, she dropped her head onto her mother's lap.

Kathleen smoothed her hand over Clara's hair. "A wonderful child, the Clara of my story," she said. "An innocent child, dragged into a world of sins and lies. She suffered for it, didn't she?"

"Yes," said Clara, blubbering.

"The wonderful Clara had a child herself, another innocent, birthed through sins and lies. Little Kate suffered enough with the loss on the Burin. Do you think she should be suffering more?"

Clara's raised her head and blinked into her mother's face.

Kathleen stared back. "Not so remarkable, is it, that I am kind to Kate?"

"Not remarkable at all."

The repeated gong of hallway clock stretched across to them, twelve tones, overlapping dots of sound. As the last one faded, Clara stood and cleared her throat. "As long as I got breath in me, you will never know want," she said.

Eyes glowing, Kathleen nodded. With a long sigh, she reclaimed her knitting.

KATHLEEN

CHAPTER 48

IT CALMS AND CONTINUES, THE sea.

The North Atlantic is a lexicon of emotion, holding within its glossary the rolling black of shame, emerald foam of rage, cerulean blue of peace. Both moderate and maverick, it cherishes and nurtures, batter and buries, recovers and shines. At storm's end, with all manner of flotsam concealed, it is silver and serene. Poised. Waiting.

The breeze whispers through me on yet another sunny day. Again my daughter makes her way down the wharf to adventure, on the *Elizabeth J*. I wonder if she feels lonely, my Clara, craving the company of women on these voyages. I wonder if she is aware that she is breaking ground. Do other women see her as making strides? Likely not. The whispers in the wind are of poor pitiful Clara, no babes to speak of.

Despite the gossip *about* her, no one breathes a negative word *to* her. Why would they? In the beginning of her traipsing off to sea, she was the object of raised eyebrows. The novelty subsided. It might now be that the women approve. Rum running is clandestine, its participants, pariahs, but when liquor flows, especially in the off season, wives are content to have their fishermen's senses dulled: it alleviates the men's boredom and prevents them being underfoot. Perhaps then, at some point, these women will champion Clara.

When Robert sails to Rum Row, Clara remains home, just another wife in the community. Then, like all the wives of all the men who have ever gone to sea in schooners or skiffs, she clings to a thread. Waiting. Unlike other wives, some of whom have a dozen children, Clara waits alone. When a well-meaning neighbor offers the loan of a daughter—a Teresa or Mary or Anne Marie—to keep her company Clara smiles her refusal. Company holds no appeal.

Every day, she reads *The Evening Telegram* from start to finish. She pores through old school books, parsing every sentence. She studies maps and charts that Robert has left her. When time nags, she loses herself in a nineteenth century novel. The treadle on the Singer dances underfoot as she creates gowns for galas at the Newfoundland Hotel.

Does she concern herself with being caught in the rum-running business, this daughter of mine? Does she fear that money found in her home will be taken? Possibly, if frequent trips under shadow of night to the abandoned Silver Cliff are any indication. A long hike for a lone woman. Heavy-footed on the way there. Lighthearted on the way back.

As Clara strolls the pier on this day, there are the usual hoots and hollers from fishermen, creaks and groans from wharf boards, rattles and thumps of barrels and carts. Up ahead is Dulcie Mullins with her biscuit tins. Clara does not avoid her this time. She sallies right up and stares her in the face. There are question marks in my daughter's eyes. Dulcie's full moon face splits into a wide grin. "Some things you hangs out in the wind..." She offers Clara a tin of biscuits.

Clara smiles. "...and some things you doesn't." She accepts the gift. "Thank you, Dulcie, for everything." Clara moves on.

When she reaches the gangway, she meets Robert. Her husband, Robert. A tall British gentleman, a man of chosen words, a man whose carriage and demeanor speak authority, caring, integrity. A man who has named his vessel in honour of his own mother. The *Elizabeth J.*

I look from the name of the vessel to the man who named her. Who was it that traveled ancient Greece, lantern in hand, searching for an honest man? Diogenes, I believe. I think I would have settled for one could do no harm to my offspring, my seed. The worry of it haunts me, fills my afterlife. Almost amusing, that I am the ghost, yet I am the haunted. I stare across the water that served as temporary tomb for my husband.

I sneer at the man who is temporary husband for my daughter.

Would that all of our demons were asleep in the deep...

———————

Dear Reader,

Now that you've read **Of Sea and Seed**, *please take the time to visit Amazon.com or Goodreads and write a review.*

Don't miss out on updates about The Kerrigan Chronicles! *Sign up for my newsletter at www.anniedaylon.com. Receive a free short story, information about books and blogs, and, occasionally, fun facts about my beloved island of Newfoundland. And... send feedback! What do you think is, or should be, in store for the characters of* The Kerrigan Chronicles?

My best to you,

anniedaylon@shaw.ca
www.anniedaylon.com
@AnnieDaylon

QUESTIONS AND TOPICS FOR DISCUSSION

---

* In what ways is Daylon's Kathleen Kerrigan similar to Coleridge's Ancient Mariner?
* Daylon believes the setting of the novel is as vital as her characters, that the setting is another character. Do you agree?
* The very title, *Of Sea and Seed*, is a metaphor. How does Daylon apply the metaphor of the *sea* to Kathleen, of the *seed* to Kathleen's offspring?
* Daylon chose to write Kathleen as a ghost, not only to create a narrator/overseer for the story, but also to eliminate boundaries of language. How do the voices of Kathleen, Kevin, and Clara vary? Could you readily identify the three points of view? If not, what would you suggest to Daylon?
* Basic to the novel is the natural order of life, its flow from generation to generation. How important to the novel is Kathleen's statement, "It's the saddest thing in the world to lose your child?"
* The drastic action that Kathleen eventually takes is prophesied in the opening of the story. How does the author do this?
* Clara appears to be at the cutting edge of twentieth century social change. What propels her to be self-sufficient in a world where women are meant to be dependent?

- What was the misunderstanding that led Kevin to leave home? Why did he not come out and ask the question that would unlock whatever mystery or secret there was? Do you believe that secrets hold power?
- What was Alphonse's confession? Were you surprised to learn why he did what he did?
- Do you think that the voice of Kate, Kathleen's granddaughter, should, at some point, come into the mix? Why or why not?

———

Acknowledgements

———◆———

FIRST AND FOREMOST, THANK YOU to my father, Andrew Lannon, who sparked this particular writing journey when he told me a true story about a little girl who survived the 1929 Newfoundland tsunami. (My father, as I write this, is 93 years old and still tells me stories of war and rumrunners and shipwrecks and u-boats and spies.)

Thank you to my wonderful husband, David, for his unending love, support, and encouragement throughout all my creative endeavours. He is my rock.

Thank you to Thursday "Tea & Critique" partners, Fran Brown and Mary Keane, and to Tuesday critique partner, Michael Hiebert, for their invaluable input. Great writers, great friends, greatly appreciated.

Thank you to: Ron Young, founding editor of Newfoundland's *Downhome* Magazine; Paul Butler, author of *The Good Doctor;* Nellie Strowbridge author of *Ghost of the Southern Cross;* and Darrel Duke, author of *Thursday's Storm* for their generosity in taking time to read and endorse this novel.

Thank you to Brian Rodda at www.roddawrites.com for creating the inset map of the Avalon and Burin Peninsulas of Newfoundland.

Thank you to Ken Loomes, Heather Burles, Lois Peterson, Richard Lannon, and Lillian Day for reading/critiquing early chapters of this novel.

Thank you to the Writers' Alliance of Newfoundland and Labrador for advice and support. Through their manuscript evaluation program I worked with author/editor, Paul Butler, whose input proved invaluable.

Thank you to the Federation of British Columbia Writers www.bcwriters.ca for information and support, in particular to past president, Ben Nuttall-Smith, author of *Secrets Kept, Secrets Told,* for his ongoing encouragement.

Thank you to British Columbia's Chilliwack/Abbotsford bookstore **The Book Man** www.bookman.ca for its enthusiastic support of local authors.

Thank you to Kathy Meis and all at www.bublish.com for their ingenious book bubble system!

———

Also by Annie Daylon:

Castles in the Sand
Maggie of the Marshes
Passages: A Collection of Short Stories
The Many-Colored Invisible Hats of Brenda-Louise

BIBLIOGRAPHY

Andrieux, J. P. 2009. *Rumrunners.* St. John's, NL: Flanker Press.

Bond's Path and Southeast Come Home Year Committee. 2006. *An Armful of Memories.* Placentia, NL: Transcontinental.

Cashin, Peter. 2012. *My Fight for Newfoundland.* St. John's, NL: Flanker Press.

Collins, Gary. 2013. *The Gale of 1929.* St. John's, NL: Flanker Press.

Collins, Gerard. 2011. *Finton Moon.* St. John's, NL: Killick Press.

Duke, Darrell. 2013. *Thursday's Storm: The August Gale.* St. John's, NL: Flanker Press.

Duley, Margaret. 1941. *Highway to Valour.* New York: The MacMillan Company.

Fitzgerald, Jack. 2005. *Newfoundland Disasters.* St. John's, NL: Creative Publishers.

—. 1989. *Strange but True Newfoundland Stories.* St. John's, NL: Creative Publishers.

Freshwater Come Home Year Book Committee. 2002. *Freshwater Come Home Year.* Freshwater, NL: Robinson-Blackmore.

Hanrahan, Moira. 2006. *Tsunami: The Newfoundland Tidal Wave Disaster.* St. John's, NL: Flanker Press.

Houlihan, Eileen. 1992. *UPROOTED! The Argentia Story.* St. John's NL: Creative Publishers.

Johnston, Wayne. 1999. *The Colony of Unrequited Dreams.* Toronto, Ontario: Vintage Canada.

Lannon, Alice, and Mike McCarthy. 1991. *Fables, Fairies, & Folklore of Newfoundland.* St. John's, NL: Jesperson Press Ltd.

Neary, Peter. 1988. *Newfoundland in the North Atlantic World 1929-1949.* Kingston and Montreal: McGill -Queen's University Press.

Neary, Peter, ed. 1996. *White Tie and Decorations: Sir John and Lady Hope Simpson in Newfoundland, 1934-1936.* Toronto: University of Toronto Press.

Power, C. Olive, ed. 2012. *Bridging Places & People from Big Barasway to Ship Harbour.* Placentia: Placentia Intertown 2012 Come Home Year Book Committee.

Romkey, Bill, ed. 2009. *St. John's and the Battle of the Atlantic.* ST. John's, NL: Flanker Press.

Strowbridge, Nellie P. 2008. *The Newfoundland Tongue.* St. John's NL: Flanker Press.

1988. "The Placentia Area." *Decks Awash: The Placentia Area Volume 17, No. 3.* St. John's, NL: Memorial University of Newfoundland, May-June.

Young, Ron. 2006. *Dictionary of Newfoundland and Labrador.* St. John's NL: Downhome Publishing Inc.

—. 2005. *Downhome Memories.* St. John's, NL: Downhome Publishing Inc.

AUTHOR BIO

———

ANNIE DAYLON WAS BORN AND raised in Newfoundland. She studied music at Mount Allison University and education at both the University of Manitoba and the University of British Columbia (M.Ed.). After many years teaching, she delved into her passion for writing. Annie lives in the British Columbia Fraser Valley with her husband, David, and their dog, CoCo. You can find out more about Annie at www.anniedaylon.com.